ANNA JACOBS

Farewell to Lancashire

HODDER

First published in Great Britain in 2009 by Hodder & Stoughton
An Hachette UK company

First published in paperback in 2010

2

A CIP catalogue record for this title
is available from the British Library

ISBN 978 0 340 95406 5

Typeset in Plantin Light by
Ellipsis Books Limited, Glasgow

Printed and bound by
CPI Group (UK) Ltd, Croydon, CR0 4YY

Hodder & Stoughton policy is to use papers that are natural,
renewable and recyclable products and made from wood grown
in sustainable forests. The logging and manufacturing processes
are expected to conform to the environmental regulations
of the country of origin.

Hodder & Stoughton Ltd
338 Euston Road
London NW1 3BH

www.hodder.co.uk

In loving memory of my mother, Lucy Sheridan, who passed away in 2008. I hope she and Dad are dancing together 'up there' now that they're together again.

And with thanks to my wonderful sister, Carol, who cared for my mum devotedly when I couldn't.

With love to you both

Anna

PROLOGUE

1861 – Outham, Lancashire

On a cool Saturday afternoon in May, Edwin Blake lowered his newspaper and let it rest on his lap. He stared into space for a minute or two then looked across the room, his expression softening involuntarily at the sight of his four daughters. Eh, he was a lucky man to have been gifted with children such as these. No, not children now. His girls were all women grown and he didn't know whether to be sad or glad that none of them had married, that they still lived with him.

'Are you all right, Dad?' Cassandra asked.

He might have known she'd notice he was worried. As the eldest, she tried to look after them all, had done since she was fourteen and her mother died.

'I've been reading about this war in America.'

'It's good, isn't it, that they're trying to free the slaves?'

He nodded. 'Of course it is, only . . . if the North and South are busy fighting one another, what's going to happen about the cotton? Without slaves, who'll plant and harvest it?'

'They'll have to pay people to do it.'

'Where will they find the money for that? Wars cost a

lot of money, my lass. Look at what happened in the Crimea only a few years ago.'

There was silence, then he shared his worst fears. 'And even if they do still produce cotton, how will they get it across the sea to us here in Lancashire? When there's a war, they set up blockades, then ships can't get through.'

'We've been on short time before,' Xanthe said. 'We always manage.'

'Short time is one thing. I've been trying to puzzle it out and to my mind, no cotton reaching Lancashire would mean no work at all.'

There was silence and he could see them thinking about what he'd said. Well, he'd always encouraged his lasses to think for themselves. Just because they were ordinary working folk didn't mean they had to act like sheep and let other people shape their opinions.

'Surely the war won't last more than a few months?' soft-hearted Maia asked. 'It's brother fighting brother. I can't bear to think of that. Imagine if one of my sisters suddenly became an enemy.' Her eyes filled with tears at the mere thought.

'Brother's been fighting brother since the world began,' Edwin said. 'Look at Cain and Abel in the Bible. And your uncle Joseph hasn't spoken to me for over twenty years, didn't even come to your mother's funeral. He walks past me in the street now as if we're strangers, as if we didn't share a bed and play together when we were children. He said it was because I'd become a Methodist, but that seems a poor reason to me.'

'I think it's because of his wife,' Cassandra said with

a sigh. 'She looks at us as if she hates us. I used to be frightened to walk past her in the street when I was little.'

'I don't like the woman either, but she'd never *harm* you.'

'She looks as if she wants to.'

'She and Joseph never had children, that's why she resents you so much, I'm sure.'

'Well, that's not our fault, is it?'

He didn't say anything. It was an old pain, his brother shunning him. Every now and then he had to speak about it, purge the bitterness a little. His sister-in-law was a mean-spirited woman, who had never lifted a finger to help them while his wife was ill. He'd tried to forgive her, because that was what they were taught at chapel, but he wanted nothing to do with her. He wasn't usually fanciful, but something about her was – evil. It was the only word he could think of to describe her.

'You don't need anyone else when you've got us.' Pandora leaned forward to lay one hand on his gnarled fingers.

He looked down at her smooth young skin. His hand was worn by life and hard work, his knuckles painful and stiff in the mornings, thickened with age. At twenty-two she had hands that were soft and pretty, even though they were reddened from work. 'I shouldn't still have you, though, not living with me, any road. You ought to be wed by now, all of you, with homes and families of your own.'

She got up abruptly and went to stir the stew, not turning round till she had herself under control. Edwin was annoyed with himself for causing Pandora pain with his thoughtless words. She was the only one of his four who'd found herself a fellow, a decent, lively lad. She'd have been wed now if poor Bill hadn't died suddenly of pneumonia last year.

But whether the subject was painful or not, he couldn't help finishing what he had to say as his eyes settled on his eldest daughter. 'You're twenty-eight now, Cassandra. Don't leave it too late to find a fellow, my dear girl. To grow old without children would be very sad. You four are the joy of my life.'

'How can I marry? I could never find a man half as clever as you,' she said lightly.

He frowned as he looked at her. 'Is that what you think of first in a husband? Being clever?'

She nodded. 'That and being kind, like you. I couldn't live with a stupid or boring man. I tried once when Tom Dorring wanted to court me, because he was so kind. But it was no good. He talked of nothing but work and the neighbours.'

Edwin managed a smile, but it was yet another thing to worry him. His girls were all clever, but Cassandra had the quickest mind of them all. It was the one thing that had made him wish he was rich, to give them better chances to use their brains. He'd made sure they got as much schooling as he could afford, so that after they started work they could read well enough to continue their education on their own, as he had.

The whole family now borrowed books regularly from the public library to feed their minds. Eh, that library was a wonderful thing! He wished it'd been there when he was younger. It had opened in 1852, but the law said the ratepayers had to be polled and two-thirds had to be in favour before the money could be spent. It had been a near thing whether Outham would have one, but they'd got enough votes, thank goodness.

But perhaps, being girls, his lasses should have hidden their cleverness, just a little. Most men didn't want their womenfolk to be quicker thinkers than they were.

No, Cassandra was right to hold out for a man whose mind could match hers. He didn't want his girls chained to dull men, who hadn't a thought in their heads beyond where the next meal was coming from and whether their jobs were safe.

'The food's ready. Shall we eat now?' Pandora asked.

Edwin led the way to the table but after a few mouthfuls put down his knife and fork, bringing up the other subject which was weighing on his mind. 'I must stop taking Greek lessons.'

'But you love learning Greek!' Cassandra protested.

'I can puzzle on by myself for a while.'

'Why stop?'

'Because of this war. I think we should all start watching our pennies carefully, making every farthing do the work of two and saving as much as we can. Hard times are coming, harder than we've ever known.'

There. He'd said all that was on his mind now. He broke off a piece of bread, picked up his spoon and began to eat his stew slowly.

The girls were quiet after that, thinking over what he'd said, and he didn't try to force conversation. If bad times were coming, best they all faced that fact, thought about it, planned for it.

I

In early November Cassandra lost her job when the small mill where she worked closed down. She'd missed a few years' work while the other girls were young, running the house and caring for them all after her mother died, so was one of the first at her mill to be turned off. Her sisters had been working half-time for a while and their father was the only one in full-time work now.

To be without work at all made her feel deeply ashamed. 'I'll take over the housework and shopping, and you can be sure I'll make every penny count,' she told her sisters. 'It's no use me looking for other work. There's none to be had in the whole town.'

The following morning she kept a smile on her face as she saw everyone off, but when she was alone she couldn't hold back the tears, allowing herself a few moments' weakness. Then she wiped her eyes and decided to clean the house from top to bottom. She had some warm water left from breakfast but wouldn't waste coal on heating more. Water was free, so you could stay clean even if you couldn't afford to heat it.

Just as she'd filled the bucket, there was a tap on the back door and she opened it to see the little boy from two doors away.

'I'm hungry, missus,' Timmy said.

She fought a battle with herself and lost, giving him the crust of bread intended for her own dinner. He was a child born of disgrace and although the mother's husband had taken on her bastard child as well, everyone knew the poor lad was unloved and wasn't as well cared for as the other children.

Cassandra sighed as she closed the door on him. You could see Timmy's unhappiness graven deeply in his face. His three younger half-brothers were bigger and plumper than he was. How could anyone treat one child in the family so badly?

She went back to work, scrubbing the flagstones on the kitchen floor but stopping often to think. Her father had been right all those months ago. The war had indeed stopped most cotton shipments getting through and times were hard now in their small town. People said things would get worse before they got better, which was a terrifying thought.

Some families were already on relief from the Poorhouse Board, others were selling their furniture and spare clothing piece by piece, doing anything rather than accept charity. You lost your independence once you were on relief, because the Board's officers poked their noses into every corner of your house, making you sell nearly everything you owned before they'd give you any money.

She and her family were managing – thanks to their father's foresight. There was still money in the tin box in his wardrobe. But it was dwindling more quickly than it should, because Edwin couldn't help giving to neighbours with tiny children crying for lack of food. It was one thing to see adults clemming, but he couldn't bear to see children going hungry. And even though he only gave a few pence each time, that was emptying the pot more quickly.

And she'd just given what she'd meant to have for dinner to the neighbour's child. She'd go hungry today. But Timmy wouldn't, poor little thing.

When Edwin came home from work a few nights later, he felt sad and weary.

'The millowner told me this morning he has only enough cotton for three more months,' he said over tea, which was a meagre meal these days, mainly bread or potatoes with a little butter. 'And to last even that long, he must turn off more operatives.' He looked at the twins. 'You'll be losing your jobs from next week, Xanthe and Maia. Mr Darston's trying to keep one person from each family in work, as far as he can, and for us, that'll be me. He's a good man, doing his best to spread what work there is fairly.'

'What will people do if this war goes on and on, and there's no work at all?' Maia asked. 'Already some folk look half-starved. I feel guilty that we still have something to eat every day.'

'The Queen won't let Lancashire folk starve to death,' Edwin said stoutly. 'When she realises how bad it is, she'll tell the government to help us, I'm sure.' He had great faith in Her Majesty, who lived a good life with her husband and children and cared about her subjects.

Xanthe clutched her twin's hand. 'I don't ever want to

ask for relief. What if they force us to go into the poorhouse? I'd starve first. It makes me shiver even to walk past that place.'

Edwin could understand her feelings. The Vicar of the parish church, who was responsible for the management of the union poorhouse which served their own and the five neighbouring parishes, was a hard man, who treated the poor as if they'd committed a crime. Any charity offered under his auspices was grudging in the extreme.

The law said conditions inside had to be worse than anything outside, and while most poorhouses in the north refused to implement this rule strictly, the one in Outham kept to the letter of the law. The inmates were kept on a starvation diet while the Vicar went home to stuff his own belly till it looked as if it was going to burst out of his trousers. He also made sure they separated man from wife 'to prevent fornication', even the elderly who were beyond that sort of thing.

Edwin didn't regard this Vicar as a true man of God, which was why he'd become a Methodist in the first place.

'Going into that place will be the last resort for any of us, the very last,' he said gently. 'We can hold out for a good while yet. But if it's go into the workhouse or die, I hope you'll choose life, Xanthe love. I certainly would.'

Cassandra came to link her arm in his. 'I heard today that they're going to set up a soup kitchen in the parish church for those who've no work at all. It doesn't matter if you're a member of the congregation or not. It's to be held there three times a week, Mondays, Thursdays and

Saturdays. We can get a meal there on those days and that'll be a big help.'

Edwin wasn't sure whether it was a good thing to do this in the parish church. He'd been hoping the Minister of their own chapel, a more compassionate man, would organise something. But the Town Council in its wisdom had decided that all charity efforts were to be combined because help would go further that way. And since the parish church had the biggest hall by far, the soup kitchen was to be held there.

What was the world coming to when his lasses had to go out and eat the meagre bread of charity?

Maia still had two days' work a week, so on the first Monday the soup kitchen was open, the other three sisters went to get tickets for it. People waited patiently in the long queue outside the church hall, not saying much. It was shaming to depend on charity and they felt the humiliation keenly.

Cotton workers might be used to tightening their belts when there was a downturn in trade, but they weren't used to this almost total lack of work. Some had already left the town, seeking jobs in the woollen industry of nearby Yorkshire. Others had braved the south, where people spoke differently and the land was softer. It was said there was still work to be found there.

Those men who found it too hard to leave spent their days wandering round Outham like lost souls, not knowing how to fill their time. It was easier on the women, who at least had their homes to keep tidy, their children to care for.

When they got to the front of the queue, Cassandra and her sisters had to answer questions about their circumstances before they could be given anything.

The man from the committee, who was a member of the parish church, questioned them in a sharp, impatient voice, then said curtly, 'I hope you'll thank your Maker on your knees for this generosity.' He waved one hand in a dismissive gesture. 'Go to the next table for your meal tickets.'

There a lady asked yet again, 'Name?'

'Cassandra Blake.' She saw the lady write down Cass Blake. 'That's not my name.' Her father had always refused to have their names shortened, saying he'd chosen them because they were beautiful names, belonging to the Greek goddesses he'd read about in the books the Minister had lent him.

The lady stared at her in outrage then turned to the person sitting next to her. 'The impudence of this creature! She comes here to beg for food then corrects what I write.'

The Vicar came across. 'Is there a problem, my dear Mrs Greaves?'

'There certainly is. This young madam has actually dared to correct what I've written.'

'But you asked for my name, then wrote something else down,' Cassandra protested.

He bent over the long book in which the names were being inscribed. 'Cass Blake.'

'My name is Cassandra. I've never been called Cass in my life.'

'My dear young woman, you should be grateful that

this lady is generously giving her time to help you and not fuss about such unimportant details.' He looked down his nose at her. 'In any case, Cassandra is a most unsuitable name for a person of your station. I don't know where your parents got that from but I wouldn't have allowed them to christen you by such a name in *my* church. Now, take your tickets and move along quickly or I shall have you removed from the hall. The food is over there. One ticket for each day, remember.'

He spoke as if she hadn't the wit to understand that. She hesitated, feeling outraged. But she'd eaten virtually nothing for more than a day, having slipped most of her portion to her father and Maia the previous night, because they still had to go out to work and because he'd been looking so tired lately.

When she went across to where they were serving the soup, she found herself facing her uncle Joseph's wife on the other side of the table.

Without a flicker of acknowledgement, her aunt said, 'Give me your ticket and take a bowl!'

The next lady ladled some soup into the bowl and a third lady passed Cassandra a piece of stale bread and a battered old spoon. 'Here you are. Don't forget to take the bowl and spoon to the table over there when you've finished.'

Cassandra forced a 'Thank you,' then escaped to a trestle table as far away from her aunt's glare as possible. She set down her food with fingers that trembled, shaken by the encounter. Such hatred!

A short time later she was joined by Pandora, whose cheeks bore red patches and whose eyes were sparkling with anger. 'That woman put down my name as Dora. *Dora!* And the Vicar scolded me when I tried to correct her.'

Xanthe followed her, setting the bowl down and splashing soup on to the table. 'She put *me* down as Susan.'

A young man came across to join them. 'I heard what that woman said to you. I think it's shameful. Absolutely shameful. What right have they to change your names?'

Cassandra watched Pandora smile at him, saw how he blinked. Yet another male was entranced by her youngest sister, who didn't even seem to notice the effect she had on men. She was definitely the beauty of the family, with hair so dark it was almost blue-black and eyes of a vivid blue.

'Do you mind if I join you?' he asked. 'I'm on my own and I don't know anyone else here.'

'You're welcome to sit with us,' Cassandra said.

They began to eat. The bread was so stale and hard, they had to dunk it in the soup to soften it, which wasn't good manners and drew scornful looks from the Vicar as he passed. But you couldn't waste food.

The hall was soon full. The soup was unappetising, made mainly from cabbage, potatoes and bones, but no one left a drop.

'Poor thin stuff this is!' Pandora muttered. 'I could make better myself. And the bread is days old.'

'At least it's not mouldy. And it's free.' Xanthe sighed. 'I can see why Father stopped coming to this church, if that's how they treat you. Do they think poorer people have no feelings?'

When they went outside, they parted company from the young man and strolled home slowly. People used to walk briskly, Cassandra thought as she saw others sauntering along. Now there were so many long hours to fill, no one hurried.

She looked up to see only a few thin trails of smoke instead of a sky criss-crossed with thick plumes of dark smoke from mill chimneys. It looked wrong, as if this wasn't their town any more, only a ghost of Outham.

It wasn't till they were nearly home that Pandora said what they'd all been thinking, 'Our aunt looked as if she hated us, didn't she?'

'Yes. Don't tell father we saw her. It'll only upset him.'

Pandora was silent for the length of the street, then said thoughtfully, 'She always has such a strange look in her eyes.'

'Never mind her,' Xanthe said. 'I want to go and change my library books. At least we'll be able to do that any time we want now.'

'I think we're going to be very grateful for that library,' Cassandra said. 'At least reading costs us nothing.'

Joseph Blake closed his grocery store at nine o'clock that night as usual, saw his employees off the premises and locked up. He walked reluctantly up the stairs to the comfortable rooms where he and his wife had lived ever since her parents died. He'd eaten a meal with Isabel at six o'clock, seen what a foul mood she was in and claimed an urgent need to finish some accounts in the shop. There, as he supervised his employees and attended to the more important customers himself, he'd tried to work out what she could be so angry about this time.

She was often in a bad mood these days, it seemed. Their poor little maidservant was regularly reduced to tears, but Dot needed the work, because her family had no other source of income, so had to put up with it. If Joseph had tried to intervene, Isabel would have been even harder on the girl, so he bit his tongue and contented himself with slipping Dot the occasional treat from the shop, a broken biscuit or the untidy scraps of ham. He knew Isabel kept an eye on how much their maid ate and wasn't generous.

Perhaps his wife had seen his nieces while she was out. That always put her in a bad mood. They were fine-looking girls and the youngest one was truly beautiful. He was sorry he didn't know them, but Isabel had made it very clear before they married that if he wanted her, he had to sever all connection with his brother, and he'd given him his word, thinking he'd persuade her to change her mind later. But she never had. She came from high church stock and was proud of that, wanted no truck with those she called 'canting Methodists'.

Only it seemed to him that she was the one doing the canting, mouthing meaningless religious phrases and living in exactly the opposite way to what the Bible taught. She'd been extremely jealous of his brother Edwin's wife Catherine, who hadn't been exactly beautiful but whose smiling face and kindly ways made friends for her everywhere. Isabel had few friends and her plain face was made even plainer by her sour expression.

It might have been different if they'd been able to have

children. When they were first married, Isabel had carried one for seven months, seeming to soften and grow kinder with each month. But then she'd lost the baby, nearly dying herself in the process. She'd been too narrow and the birth had torn her inside, the doctor said. He'd added that she'd not be able to carry any more children to term so should avoid getting with child again.

She'd been ill for so long they'd moved in here with her parents, where her mother could look after her. And they'd not shared a bed from that day onwards. Which was a relief.

He'd soon learned to spend as much time as he could in the shop, had quickly understood why his father-in-law also did this. You could always find something to do there, checking the shelves, making sure the boy took out the deliveries promptly, seeing the salesmen from the various firms from whom they bought stock, or just sitting quietly after the shop closed, ostensibly checking the account books but in reality reading a newspaper or book.

When his parents-in-law died, he changed the shop's name to Blake's Emporium, which angered his wife but for once he'd stood up to her. He'd carried on running it in much the same way as before, however, because his father-in-law had been a good businessman.

Since the war in America things had changed. There was no need to order as much stock these days, because the Cotton Famine had affected people at every social level. The more affluent folk were unlikely to stop buying the basic necessities and wouldn't starve like their poorer neighbours, which meant he would continue to make a living. But nearly everyone in the town had had to cut back their expenses, so his profits had gone down.

No putting it off any longer. He made sure the flaring gas lights were all safely extinguished and climbed the stairs to their living quarters.

Isabel was sitting waiting for him in her armchair near the fire, back stiffly upright, mouth tightly pursed, hands clasped in her lap. 'How did business go today?'

'Takings are down, but we're still making a decent enough living.'

'You should dismiss the youngest lad to keep the profits up.'

'There are no other jobs in town and he's the sole support of his family, so I'll keep him on for as long as I'm able.'

'My father would have dismissed him long before this.'

'I'm not your father.'

She made an angry growling sound in her throat, but he didn't care because she had no power to change anything. The shop had been left to him not her, thank goodness, because Mr Horton hadn't believed women were able to understand business.

'I'll ring for our cocoa and biscuits,' she said abruptly.

It wasn't till they were sitting in front of the fire that she revealed the cause of her bad mood. 'I saw *those girls* today. Three of them, anyway, I don't know where the other one was. They came to the soup kitchen.' Her narrow chest heaved with indignation as she added, '*Like beggars!* I was so mortified I didn't know where to look. I didn't acknowledge them, of course.'

He was surprised. 'Are they that short of money? I'd have thought Edwin would still be earning something.'

'They must be out of work or they'd not have been given tickets. I dread to think what people will be saying behind our backs, knowing we have relatives seeking charity like that.'

'A lot of folk in the town need help now. It's not my nieces' fault there's no work for them.'

'Trust you to take their side. I'm sure those lazy young trollops don't want to work.'

He didn't argue, just sipped his cocoa and kept his expression calm as she went on and on. There was no doing anything but endure when Isabel got into this sort of mood, imagining insults where there were none and maligning his nieces, who were decent lasses.

He'd known she wouldn't be an easy wife, but he hadn't realised how bad living with her would be. He'd wanted the shop that came with her, the shop where he'd worked hard for ten years, so when it was clear that no other man was likely to marry her, he'd risked asking his employer's permission to court his thirty-year-old spinster daughter.

His brother Edwin had hungered for learning but Joseph had hungered for money and comfort. Most of all, for a shop of his own.

He'd thought having children would soften Isabel. Now he knew nothing would ever soften her. Her mind was so warped with spite and temper, he sometimes questioned her very sanity.

But he would keep his promise to her father: he would always look after her, however difficult she was, in return for being given the shop.

2

In late November the whole country was outraged by the Trent Incident, when a US Navy vessel from the Northern States stopped and boarded a Royal Mail steamer which had just started its voyage from Cuba to England. At gunpoint they removed two passengers, who were Confederate diplomats on a mission to London.

The nation erupted into rage, and even those hungering from lack of cotton forgot their woes for a time as they expressed their outrage. Britain wasn't at war with America, either North or South, but had declared its neutrality. The Americans had no *right* to do this! Many people clamoured for war to be declared on the North.

Edwin shook his head over this. 'War's a shameful way to settle a quarrel and I'm sure our dear Queen won't allow it.

'The Northern Captain was wrong, though,' Cassandra protested. 'He had no right to stop a British ship.'

'No right at all.' He smiled at her. He loved the way she understood what was happening in the world, though some folk said it wasn't women's business.

The Blake sisters, fretting over their lack of work, were more upset by the news their father brought home in early December about the local cotton industry. His employer had told him that twenty-nine mills in Lancashire had now stopped production and over a hundred others were on half-time.

'So many people out of work, so many going hungry,' said Maia. 'Why does no one set up proper relief schemes to help us, instead of these soup kitchens?'

'They're talking about setting up a work camp for men just outside town,' Edwin said. 'Breaking stones.'

'But that's work for convicts!' Pandora exclaimed.

'It's the Vicar's idea. He's a hard man, Saunders is, says people should be grateful for any work and at least the town can use the stones to mend the old roads and make new ones. They're going to pay the men a shilling a ton for the stones they break.'

There was silence, then Cassandra asked, 'How long will it take to break up a ton of stones?'

'A day, they tell me, perhaps a little less if a man is strong.'

'Six shillings a week isn't enough to feed a family properly!'

'No.'

'Well, I'd do anything to earn money again,' Xanthe said, 'even break stones. But they won't let women do that. *We* always have to depend on our menfolk.'

'And you've only got me,' Edwin said. 'I wish you'd married, my dear girls, at least one or two of you, so that you could have strong young men to depend on, not an old fellow like me.'

'I'll not marry till I meet a man I can love and admire,' Xanthe said, 'and who will recognise that I'm able to think just as well as him.'

'I sometimes wonder if there are men like that for women of our class,' Maia said sadly.

Cassandra was more concerned about the way her father had spoken of himself as 'old'. He'd talked like that a few times lately. Was he feeling his age?

And he was right. What would they do if anything happened to him, especially now?

December was a very mild month, which was a godsend for people unable to afford fuel to heat their homes. But the end of the month was heavy with sorrow for the whole nation, because on the 14th the Prince Consort died. Everyone prayed for their Queen in the various churches and chapels. They'd all experienced loss of a loved one, after all, and knew how painful it was.

But the newspapers said the Queen was inconsolable, her grief going beyond the normal measure.

'That poor lady bears a heavy burden as monarch,' Edwin said. 'She needed Prince Albert's support even more than other women need their husbands. And she lost her mother last March as well, so it's been a sad year for her. But at least she has her children to comfort her. Children are a wonderful consolation, a sign that life will continue.'

He looked round, smiling at his own lasses. 'I don't know what I'd have done without you after your mother died.' Then he turned to Cassandra and proved his eyesight was as sharp as ever. 'Take back that piece of potato you just slipped on to my plate. We'll share what there is. I don't want you going hungry for me.'

'You've looked so tired lately.' And had hardly touched his Greek books.

'I'm growing old. I'm sixty now, after all.'

She didn't say it but her uncle was two years older and yet he looked rosy and vigorous. Perhaps good food would make a difference to their father? Only she didn't know how to get it for him. 'You'd tell us if anything was wrong with you, wouldn't you?'

'I'm just tired, that's all, my dear lass. No need to worry about me. And Mr Darston says he'll keep me in work, at least half-time. He's a good man, my employer is.'

Since Sunday was fine, Reece Gregory walked the five miles into Outham from the farm where he'd found work and a place to sleep. The Dobsons, who were cousins of his, couldn't pay him much but they fed him decently, gave him a shilling or two when they were able, and in times like this, that was worth a lot. Better by far than going on relief.

He made his way to the churchyard, intending to sit on the stone bench near the grave of his wife and child. It had been two years now since they died and the sharpest grief had faded, but still he found it comforting to sit there with them from time to time. Heaven knew, he wasn't the only one to lose a wife in the aftermath of a difficult childbirth, or to have a child who only lived a few days.

This peaceful place was where he thought about his life, tried to make plans and having made them, abandoned them and made others. He'd been drifting for a while now, he knew that, must take himself in hand.

Today, to his disappointment, someone was already occupying the bench, a young woman with a book in her hand, though she seemed to be doing more staring into the distance and sighing than reading.

He took a step backwards, intending to find somewhere else to sit, but his feet made a crunching sound on the gravel and she looked round.

'I'm sorry. I didn't mean to disturb you,' he said.

The Town Hall clock began to chime the hour and she got to her feet. 'It's a good thing you did. It's time I went home.'

She dropped her book and he bent to pick it up, glancing at its title instinctively: *A Journey to Egypt*. It was a heavy tome for a young woman to read, but he'd have read anything he could lay his hands on. He'd always loved reading, but there were no books at the farm, except for the few he'd brought with him, and he'd read those till he nearly knew them by heart.

He smiled as he recognised the title. 'I've been a member of the library since it opened. I read this book a few years ago. It made me long to see Egypt.'

She smiled as she took it from him. 'Me, too. I've never been anywhere but Outham, and I don't suppose I ever shall. But if we can't travel, at least we can see these places through the eyes of those more fortunate than ourselves.'

It popped out before he could think what he was saying. 'Most women have no desire to travel.'

She put up her chin. 'Well, I'm not most women. I had the good fortune to be brought up by a father who taught his daughters to learn about the world. Have you read the same author's book about Greece?'

'No. And I doubt I shall. I'm working on my cousin's

farm now the mill's closed down and I can't get into town at any time the library is open. I just come in on Sundays sometimes to visit my wife's grave.'

'She must have died young.'

'Twenty-four. Childbirth.'

'I'm sorry for your loss.'

'It happened two years ago. The worst pain has faded now.' He smiled, finding her face very attractive, lit up as it was by intelligence.

She nodded and started to walk away, then turned round and came back. 'Look – I could get books out of the library for you, if you like, and give them to you on Sundays. I hate to think of anyone starved for something to read.'

He was surprised by her offer, which she'd made as one equal to another. 'Would you trust me to bring the books back?'

'You don't look like a villain. I'll need to know your name and address, though, for the librarian, and perhaps you could sign a piece of paper asking for me to borrow books in your name. Why don't you come to my house now and do that, then I can have a book ready for you next week.' She offered him her hand, as a man would have done. 'I'm Cassandra Blake.'

He took her hand and shook it. 'Reece Gregory. I think you must be related to Edwin Blake.'

'Yes, he's my father.'

That explained her open ways. Everyone knew that Blake had raised his daughters to read and think freely. There were those who said too freely, but thoughts should fly free, in Reece's opinion.

'I met your father at a lantern lecture, and once or twice at the library since. He's an interesting man to talk to.' He watched her smile light up her narrow face into near beauty.

'He's the best of fathers. He always makes me think about the world in ways I'd never have conceived on my own.'

'How are you managing?' No need to explain what he meant by that. It was a very common question these days.

She shrugged. 'Dad is still on half-time. My sisters and I go to the soup kitchen three days a week.'

At the house Reece renewed his acquaintance with Edwin, shocked at how the older man had aged in the last few months. He agreed to come there the following Sunday to pick up the book they chose for him then walked slowly back to the farm, enjoying the fine but chilly day, wishing he didn't have to live in another man's house and behave as if he was a young man again. He'd been a man in charge of his own affairs before this damned war in America.

He thought about Cassandra Blake several times that week. She was a strange young woman, not like any he'd met before, expressing her opinions as freely as a man – and having more sensible opinions than most of the men he knew, too. And she might not be beautiful, but her eyes sparkled with intelligence as she talked and he wanted to spend more time with her.

He tried not to think such thoughts. A man with no means of earning a living had no right to be attracted to a young woman.

*

In January 1862 Wigan set up a Relief Committee to deal with the results of the Cotton Famine, the first town in Lancashire to do this in a thorough way.

It took until late March for the Poorhouse Board to come round to the idea of doing the same thing in Outham, and even then, they discussed it for weeks before actually doing anything. They should have started long before, Cassandra thought angrily, not doled out tiny amounts of relief to individuals here and there, forgetting others who were too proud to ask for help. The two soup kitchens now running, one in the parish church, the other in the Roman Catholic church, weren't nearly enough. No one stayed strong and healthy on a few bowls of thin soup a week.

From now on, food was to be provided every day and there was to be a collection of clothes for children and babies, because even at times like this, new life still made its way regularly into the world. More men were to be set to work on breaking stones and it was to be better organised – which was desperately needed. The man in charge was a verger at the parish church, who didn't know anything about the task. The new foreman was more experienced – and kinder, too, it was whispered.

Sewing classes were to be set up for the women and girls and those who attended would be paid. Cassandra and her sisters waited impatiently for this to be organised. What did the Board think people would do in the meantime? Sell their possessions, that's what, she thought angrily. Some people had little left now except the clothes on their backs.

She was glad she'd never married because though it

hurt her to see how unhappy her sisters were, how much worse must it be to watch the suffering of children born of your own body? Or to see them die? The number of paupers' funerals was increasing steadily, and the ones with tiny coffins always brought tears to her eyes. As for little Timmy down the street, he was thinner than ever and she had nothing to spare for him.

With a sigh she slipped a little extra food on to her father's plate as she served their simple meal and contented herself with what was left, spreading it out on her own plate to look like more. But as she looked down at her hand she was struck suddenly by how thin it had become. Two meagre meals a day were not enough. She glanced furtively at her sisters. They were the same, far thinner than before, their clothes hanging on them, their skin pale and their hair dull.

How much longer was this war going to continue? Did the people fighting it know how badly Lancashire was affected? Did the rest of England know?

Livia Southerham was always happy to escape from her in-laws' house and go for a brisk walk on the moors with her new husband. She strode out beside Francis, glad the day was mild and she'd not been penned indoors with the other ladies of the family, who were far less vigorous than she was.

'Did you have another talk with your father this morning? Do you know yet how long we're going to be staying with your parents?' she asked as they paused for a breather on the tops, where the dry stone walls ended and the moors took over from the farms.

He put one arm round her shoulders and sighed. 'I've not yet managed to persuade Father to give his blessing for our move to Australia. I'm not asking him to give me a fortune, but we do need some money from him to set us up out there. He could easily afford to give me a share of my inheritance now, instead of leaving it to me when he dies.'

She didn't say that his father was being cautious because from all accounts, he'd seen his son's enthusiasms for various projects wax and wane before. But Francis was so eager about emigrating, had heard from his cousin in the Swan River Colony, and was being very practical about the whole matter. Well, as practical as such an easygoing man could ever be.

'I don't believe it'll be easy to make a fortune,' Francis went on, 'Why should it be any different there to here? But Paul says there are excellent opportunities for an energetic man, and if we make a decent living, it'll be enough for me.'

'For me, too. I thought your father was softening a little from the way he spoke last night at dinner.'

'So did I. But my mother hates the idea of me leaving England and has begged him not to fund us.'

'She'll miss you.'

'She'll miss controlling me, you mean.'

She heard how bitter his voice was and could only squeeze his arm in sympathy. Francis had been sickly as a child and had been a little spoiled, perhaps. He'd been educated at home and not raised to work or earn money. But he was the youngest son and once their parents died, his brother was unlikely to fund him.

'I'm going to start learning about caring for sheep and cows,' he said abruptly. 'I'll pretend to go out riding in the mornings, but instead I'll be working on a farm. I met a man called Reece Gregory the other day when I was walking on the tops. He's working for his cousin, who is a farmer and has said I can work alongside them, if I want. Reece has even offered to lend me some clothing so that Mother won't suspect how I'm spending my days.'

There. That was truly practical, Livia thought. Could his father not see that this was not a passing fancy? 'I wish I had something to take me out of the house and occupy my time.'

'Why don't you offer to help out with the relief programmes they're setting up for those who have no work?'

She grimaced. 'It'd mean working with the Vicar. I'm not fond of Mr Saunders – or of his band of lady helpers.'

But in the end, desperate to get out of the overheated house and away from her mother-in-law's inanities, she took up his suggestion and volunteered her services to the ladies' committee. And of course they took her up on this offer eagerly, because the county gentry didn't usually mingle with the 'shopocracy', as her mother-in-law called the town's ladies scornfully.

Perhaps she could do some real good until they left England, as she had when she helped her father in his parish duties before her marriage. She hoped so.

When Reece went back to the Blakes' house the following week, he found Edwin ready for a chat, and a book about Australia waiting for him, *Our Antipodes* by a Mr Mundy.

'Cassandra chose this. She said you enjoyed books about travel.'

'I do.' Reece opened it and stared hungrily at the pages filled with information, then realised this was bad manners and closed it resolutely. 'Is she not here today?'

'She and her sisters have gone out for a walk. They'll be back soon to make us a cup of tea.'

Clearly, Reece was expected to sit and chat, and he did, finding Edwin's wry observances about the world entertaining. But what he really wanted was to see Cassandra again, even if his interest in her was hopeless at present.

When the four sisters returned, he accepted a cup of tea but refused anything to eat, knowing how short of food most people were. 'I eat better than most at the farm, even though my relatives can't pay me much of a wage.'

'Shall you stay on there?' Cassandra asked.

'Until I see my way more clearly. I've come to realise that I don't want to go back inside a cotton mill. I like the fresh air and feel healthier for it, and I enjoy caring for animals. My cousin Sam works with wood and he's sharing his skills with me, while Ginny makes cheeses to sell at market and that's interesting too.'

As he walked back, with the precious book tucked inside his jacket to protect it, Reece felt happier than he had for a good while. He'd made some new friends and – an image of Cassandra popped up in his mind and he knew it was more than that. He'd met an intelligent woman with a lively interest in the world, who attracted him in so many ways.

Till better times came, they could at least be friends, couldn't they?

He looked down at the book. It'd be particularly interesting to read about Australia and find out why Francis Southerham couldn't stop talking about that faraway country.

'He's a fine young man, that one,' Edwin said after Reece had left.

His daughters all stared at him suspiciously.

'Are you matchmaking, Dad?' Xanthe asked.

He shrugged. 'No harm in you meeting a fellow or two. How else are you to get wed?'

'A man who isn't in proper employment can't afford to wed,' Pandora protested. 'And anyway, Reece is too old for me.'

'And too solemn for me,' Xanthe said.

'He doesn't take my fancy at all, too dark and serious.' Maia turned to tease Cassandra. 'So that leaves you. Shall you go a-courting Reece, love?'

Her sister surprised everyone, herself included, by blushing. She tried to cover it up by saying loudly, 'Don't be silly!' and clearing up the teacups, but she was only too aware of the raised eyebrows and knowing looks of her family.

To her relief they said nothing more about Reece Gregory. Nor did she.

But in bed that night she admitted to herself that he was . . . more interesting than most. She had really enjoyed talking to him, felt comfortable walking with him as well, because he was taller than her, unlike most men. And what had Maia meant by saying he was 'too dark'? She loved his dark hair and his dark brown eyes. He was actually very good looking, not a pretty boy, but a man grown.

By June of 1862, the Blakes had little left in their pot of money.

'Dad, you can't give any more to people,' Cassandra said. 'Not a single penny. We need all you bring home for ourselves.'

'I can't see a babby starve to death.'

'Can you see us starve to death instead?'

The anguish on his face upset her, but he had to face facts. Without his generosity, their savings would have lasted much longer.

When it was announced that sewing lessons were at last to start up for women who had no work due to the lack of cotton, it seemed like a godsend to the sisters. They would be paid sixpence each if they attended for four hours and worked hard, it appeared.

'Other relief committees offer ninepence,' Pandora grumbled. 'Mary's cousin gets that much where she lives, anyway.'

'We must be glad of anything we can earn,' Maia said, ever the peacemaker.

'I don't see why they can't treat us fairly.' Xanthe was the angriest of them all about their current predicament, unlike her gentler twin, and was fretting over the lack of meaningful activity to fill her days. She wasn't looking forward to the classes, knew she would be shown up for her poor sewing skills. Like her sisters she'd rather read than sew or cook. Their mother had taught Cassandra the basics of needlework, but had been ailing after the birth of the twins and hadn't been able to make the same effort with her other daughters.

After their mother's death, Cassandra had stayed at home to look after the house and once the three younger sisters started work, the long hours in the mills hadn't left much time for sewing. Besides, with five adults working, they'd been relatively well off as a family, and had had the money to pay others to make or alter their clothes.

'Well, at least I'm getting the occasional day's scrubbing,' Maia said. 'I don't know whether Mrs Matterley from chapel really needs me or whether she's just doing her bit to help, but I make sure she gets good value for her money. She says she'll mention me to her friends to help on washing days, just a day here and there, but every little helps. Though I don't enjoy washing. It leaves my hands so red and sore.'

'I'd change places with you in a minute,' Xanthe said with a sigh. Mrs Matterley was very kind to her sister and gave her a hearty meal as well as paying her a shilling for her long day's work.

She helped Cassandra clear away the dirty dishes and made sure the fire was damped down to save fuel. It was strange how most of the time she wasn't hungry, or if she was, she didn't notice it. You just grew used to the empty feeling and the way you had less energy than usual. But then, there wasn't as much to do, and as long as she got something to eat once a day, she'd manage.

★

To her horror, Cassandra found that her aunt was in charge of the sewing class. Beyond an outraged widening of her eyes, Isabel Blake again showed no sign whatsoever of recognising her relatives.

They were set to sewing coarse pinafores for the orphanage, working on material which was unpleasantly rough to the touch and which refused to lie neatly. The beginners were shown how to sew straight seams and set to do this simple work. Those with more experience were to baste the pieces of material together, then sew them up once their work was approved.

Their aunt walked round the room, but kept coming back to criticise her nieces' work, making them unpick what they'd done several times until the other lady helping out with the class stared at her in obvious surprise. Isabel looked down her nose at her nieces, then went across to whisper something to her companion.

After that, the other lady began to pick on them as well and Cassandra wondered what their aunt had said about them. At this rate they'd get nowhere, but continue to work on the same seams, unpicking them again and again, then starting once more on the same crumpled piece of material.

After the sewing class ended, a girl they knew by sight from chapel came across to join them. 'I heard what that old hag said about you.'

They stopped walking.

'What did she say?' Cassandra asked.

'She said you were all known to be immoral and shouldn't be allowed in a class with decent girls.'

They gasped in shock. 'Are you sure she said that?' Pandora asked.

The girl smiled bitterly. 'Certain. I've learned to lip read because of the noisy machinery at work. Why is she telling such lies about you? She's your aunt, isn't she?'

When the other moved on, Cassandra turned to her sisters. 'You two go home. I've an errand to run.'

'What errand?' Xanthe asked. 'We've no money to buy anything today except bread.'

'I've got to see someone.'

'Is this to do with what our aunt said?' Pandora held on to her sister's arm to stop her moving away. 'It is, isn't it?'

Cassandra shrugged.

'There's nothing you can do about that and it doesn't really matter. *We* know the truth and so do our friends.'

'I'm *not* having her say such things about us. The rumours will spread and some people will believe her, so I'm going to see my uncle and ask him to stop her.'

After a shocked silence, Pandora let go of her. 'Will he even talk to you?'

'There's only one way to find out.'

'We're coming too. You shouldn't face him on your own.'

When they got to the shop her uncle owned, Cassandra hesitated. She'd never been inside it before. The name BLAKE'S EMPORIUM sat across the top of the big windows in huge gold letters. A carriage was waiting outside. Her courage nearly failed her. This place wasn't for the likes of them.

But the thought of her aunt continuing to blacken their names gave her the courage to enter. Everyone turned to stare at her but she wouldn't let herself do more than pause just inside the door to get her bearings. There were big mahogany counters on two sides, with a beautifully dressed lady sitting in a chair next to one of them. The walls were lined with shelves piled high with goods of all sorts, unlike the corner shop near their house, where the shelves were nearly empty and only the most basic necessities were now on sale.

Her uncle was standing near a door which must lead into the back. She saw he'd recognised them by the shock on his face. Moving across quickly in case he tried to retreat into the back room to avoid them, she said quietly, 'May I have a word with you, please, Mr Blake? It's very important.' She didn't call him 'uncle' because he didn't act like one and because she didn't want to upset him more than was necessary.

A lady standing nearby was looking down her nose at them, so Cassandra put up her chin and stared right back until the other turned away and pretended to fiddle with something on the counter.

Her uncle hesitated.

'I'm not going away until I've spoken to you,' Cassandra said in a low voice.

'Go round to the side door in the alley.' He pointed to his right.

She nodded and led the way out again, her sisters following. They found the door and waited.

As the minutes passed, Xanthe said, 'I don't think he's coming.'

'If he doesn't, I'll go back into the shop.'

'Is this worth it?' Pandora asked.

'Yes, it is. We haven't got much now, but we still have

our good name and I'm *not* having her telling lies and taking that away from us.' She took three steps in one direction, then came back. 'How long is he going to keep us waiting?'

Just as she was about to hammer on the door, it opened and their uncle came out. He was carrying a canvas sack with something heavy and lumpy in the bottom of it.

'Here. This is what you came for, isn't it?'

She guessed the sack contained food and for a moment was tempted simply to take it and leave. But that wouldn't solve the problem that had brought them here. 'I didn't come to beg for charity, but to ask you to help us with something else.'

A frown creased his brow and he glanced over his shoulder as if making sure no one could overhear them. 'What?'

'It's your wife.' Cassandra saw him stiffen and rushed into speech before he could go inside and shut the door on them. 'She's been telling people that we're immoral. And we're not. I want you to make her stop. We value our good names.' The shock on his face made it clear he hadn't known anything about this.

He looked from one girl to the other. 'You're sure of this?'

Cassandra nodded. 'Certain.'

He sighed. 'No, I know you're not immoral. I'd have heard about it if you were. You find out everything that happens in a town sooner or later when you own a shop. I'll speak to my wife.'

'Thank you.' Cassandra turned on her heel.

His voice followed her, low, as if he was still afraid of being overheard. 'Take the food anyway.'

She turned back. 'If you can't even speak to your brother, how can we accept your charity?'

Another silence while he stared at her as if he'd never really seen her before. 'You're very proud, for folk who're starving.'

'We're not starving.'

'You may not be starving, but you're all very thin and you have that hollow-cheeked look people get when they're not eating enough.'

Still Cassandra hesitated. She hated to accept charity, especially such grudging charity, absolutely hated it.

Xanthe stepped forward. 'I'll take the sack, uncle, and thank you for it, too. We aren't starving, but we are often hungry.'

Cassandra marched away, ignoring the sack. Xanthe picked it up and followed her.

When they were out of hearing, Cassandra said in a low, furious voice, 'Why did you take it?'

'Because Dad's looking ill and needs better food. He's as bad as you, trying to give us his share.'

'We'll have to tell him where we got the food.'

'He'll be pleased. It upsets him to be estranged from his brother.'

Cassandra felt tears come into her eyes. Xanthe was right. With each month that passed, her father was looking older and more weary. Pride wouldn't help him, but good food might. 'I'll take one end of the sack.'

They'd all do anything for their father.

3

The following week their aunt wasn't at the sewing class. Another woman was helping Mrs Burnham run it, a complete stranger who was introduced to them as Mrs Southerham.

Cassandra recognised the name. The Southerhams were rich people who lived on a big estate outside the town, and Reece knew one of the sons. The new lady didn't look down her nose at the young women who filed into the big room, more of them today than previously.

Mrs Burnham ticked off the names of those attending, writing down the new ones while Mrs Southerham handed out the same kind of work as last time.

Cassandra took the pieces of material which would form a pinafore and bent her head to her sewing, doing the best she could with the poor material.

'It's hard stuff to sew, isn't it?'

She lifted her head to see Mrs Southerham standing beside her. 'Yes, ma'am. I'm doing my best, though, truly I am.'

'I can see that. Yours is by far the neatest work. Have you done any sewing before?'

'Mostly mending. My mother taught me and as she died when I was fourteen, I had to take over the family sewing – and everything else, too.' She'd given up mill work for a few years then.

'I've never been inside a mill. The operatives work long hours, I gather.'

'Yes, and it's very hard work. But I wish I was back there earning a living, nonetheless.'

Mrs Burnham came across to join them, giving Cassandra an unfriendly look. 'Is there a problem here?'

'Not at all. I'm just commending this young woman on her neat sewing. Such difficult material to sew, especially for beginners, and that fabric doesn't wear well, either. I wonder who chose it.'

'The Vicar. He doesn't believe in pampering the pauper brats.'

'Is it pampering to provide them with garments that are serviceable?'

'He's in charge of the charity work in this town and I'm sure he knows what's best.'

Mrs Southerham smiled. 'Well, I'm afraid I'm not as sure of his omniscience as you are. I've never yet met a man who truly understands about sewing and dress materials.'

A shocked look was her only answer.

'Anyway, since this young woman already knows something about sewing, I wonder if I could take her to help me with the baby clothes I'm organising? Many of them need mending.'

Silence, then, 'If I may have a word with you first?' Ignoring Cassandra, the haberdasher's wife led the way across the room and the two ladies disappeared through the side door.

Xanthe reached out to give her sister's arm a quick squeeze of sympathy. Cassandra tried and failed to smile back at her. Her aunt might not be here this time, but clearly she'd spread the rumours far and wide. Anger stirred in her at being treated like this, but she held it back. She couldn't afford to lose her place in this class, because it meant a glass of milk and a piece of bread each time she attended, as well as sixpence.

But it was so unfair to be treated like this!

In the small room off the Sunday School area, Livia looked at her companion. 'Is something wrong?' She tried to keep a pleasant expression on her face, but truth to tell, she didn't much like this particular coterie of shopkeepers' wives.

As the daughter of a cleric who didn't have a private income or a rich living, she'd had to be careful with money all her life. And after her marriage she'd still not got money to spare and was shocked sometimes at how carelessly her husband spent their limited resources. But seeing for herself how much suffering had been caused by the war in America, Livia really wanted to help.

'You're new to the town, my dear,' her companion said. 'But you'll soon find out that *that creature* should not be allowed in a sewing class with decent young women.'

Livia stared at her. 'You mean the young woman I was talking to?'

'Yes. One of the Blake girls. Tries to call herself Cassandra.'

'Is that not her real name?'

'It ought not to be, not for a girl of that class. We call

her Cass, which is much more suitable to her station in life. She's not only a Methodist, but her father is a strange man, who has wasted his money for years on Greek lessons. What use has an operative for Greek, I ask you? And he gives those girls of his too much freedom, which they abuse shamefully.'

'How do you know this?'

'My friend Isabel Blake, who is unfortunately related to them by marriage, told me all about the situation.' She shuddered. 'To think I have to associate with them here. If my husband didn't insist I help out, I'd not stay, I can tell you. We can only hope those creatures will realise they're not wanted and stop attending.'

'They're hungry. They need to come.'

'Let them find sustenance elsewhere, then, preferably in another town.'

Livia bit back a sharp response and went to look through the half-open door at the object of all this disgust. 'Cassandra Blake doesn't act in a forward way, nor does she look immoral. Her clothing is modest and clean.'

'She's too cunning to misbehave when she's with decent folk. The ones sitting on either side of her are two of her three sisters – they try to call themselves Pandora and Xanthe – can you imagine folk of that class calling their children by such names? *We* call them Dora and Susan.'

Livia bit back a demand to know what right anyone had to change a person's name, because she knew it'd fall on deaf ears. 'I see. Well, Cassandra doesn't seem forward to me and if she has sinned in the past, our Lord managed to forgive sinners and so shall I.' She didn't wait for an answer but walked back into the room and made her way round it, stopping again by the three sisters. 'Cassandra?'

'Yes, Mrs Southerham.'

'I wondered if you'd like to help me with the baby clothes? We have a big pile of them donated by charitable ladies. They need to be sorted out and mended carefully. Your needlework is better than that of the others here, so would be more suited for dainty work.'

She saw the surprise on the young woman's face, saw too the intelligence there. No doubt that also upset the ladies. 'The baby clothes are in another room. Leave that unfinished pinafore at the front for someone else to work on, but bring the sewing equipment you were given.'

She smiled at the other two sisters and led the way out, ignoring the other lady supervisor's outraged glare.

Wondering what had caused this offer, Cassandra followed Mrs Southerham's swaying crinoline. What would it be like to wear clothes such as these? To have smooth hands that didn't look as if the skin had ever been roughened by scrubbing? Like any young woman, Cassandra did her best to dress as attractively as possible, but she could never look like this.

'In here.'

She realised she'd been so lost in thought she'd nearly walked past the open door and blushed at her own stupidity in letting her attention slip. She mustn't give them any reason to criticise her. Was this talk of baby clothes just an excuse? Was she about to be lectured and told to stop attending the sewing class? If so, she needed to keep all her wits about her. She would *not* let them drive her away.

Heart thumping with anxiety, she followed Mrs Southerham into the room.

'Come and sit down and I'll explain what we need to do.'

As Cassandra moved forward, she realised suddenly that her companion was only her own age and was shorter than she was. You forgot sometimes that behind the beautiful clothes were real people.

Such beautiful clothes, though! The huge bell of a skirt had several rows of flounces round the bottom and even the over-sleeves had two smaller flounces, with white lace-trimmed under-sleeves peeping out beneath them. The bodice buttoned neatly up the front to reveal a white collar edged in lace. On her head Mrs Southerham had a small cap trimmed with lace. And the colour was a rich purple, one of the new aniline dyes, probably.

Cassandra couldn't help a wistful glance down at her own clothes, which were plain and serviceable, a navy blue skirt, ankle length for easier walking, with two petticoats under it. A lighter blue blouse was topped by a short brown jacket and she used a shawl to cover her head when she went outside the house. The clothes hung loose on her now and the jacket was threadbare and shabby. In normal times she'd have bought another one from the second-hand clothes dealer.

'My dear, have you eaten at all today?'

Cassandra shook her head.

'It must be hard going hungry.'

'You stop feeling hunger pangs after a while, but you

don't feel *right*. It slows you down and you can't concentrate like you should. I'm sorry if I haven't worked quickly enough. I—'

'I'll go and get you something to eat before we start.'

'There's no need. I can wait till the others have theirs.'

'I was hoping you'd stay on a little longer afterwards and help me with this task, so you may as well eat now. There are babies being born without a stitch to their backs, so we need to sort things out quickly. Unless you have something else to do this afternoon, of course?'

She couldn't hold back a bitter laugh. 'No. That's one of the problems of being out of work, not having anything to do. With four women in the family, the housework doesn't take all day.'

'Wait here a minute then.'

Cassandra leaned back in her chair, studying the little room, whose walls were covered in well polished wood panelling, and whose floor was covered by bundles of clothing. What was this place used for? There seemed to be a lot of rooms in this building, far more than in the smaller Methodist chapel her family attended.

Mrs Southerham returned with a plate and a glass brimming with milk.

Cassandra's stomach suddenly betrayed her by growling and when the plate and glass were placed in front of her, her hand shook as she reached out for the piece of bread with its meagre scraping of butter. It took all her willpower not to cram it into her mouth.

'Take your time. You'll work better if you're not hungry.' Mrs Southerham moved across to look out of the window.

If she's doing this to give me privacy, Cassandra

thought, as she took small bites, then she's far more thoughtful than the others. She chewed carefully and slowly, swallowing the occasional mouthful of milk to help the food down.

When she'd finished, she cleared her throat and Mrs Southerham turned round, looking at her sympathetically, no sign of scorn on her face.

'Didn't they tell you?' Cassandra asked, surprised by how harshly her voice came out.

'Tell me what?'

'They're telling everyone else that my sisters and I are immoral, so I thought they'd have mentioned it to you.'

'Oh, that. I never give any credence to gossip, and anyway, I don't believe it of you. I've seen enough young women of loose morals to recognise one.'

'You have?'

'Yes. I'm a parson's daughter. I used to help my father and mother visit the poorer parishioners. My mother tried to help girls in that sort of trouble, not make things worse for them, since they carried the burden of shame and the men they went with usually got away scot-free.'

Cassandra hesitated, then asked, 'You speak differently from folk round here. You come from another part of the country, I think.'

'Yes. From Hertfordshire.'

'What's it like there?'

Mrs Southerham smiled. 'Much softer than this part of the world, with no moors.'

'I can't imagine that.' Cassandra realised she was chatting as if to a friend and bit back another question, not wanting to give offence.

'We'd better open the bundles and start sorting out the clothes, but there's no reason we can't chat to pass the time.'

'Why are you doing this, helping me, I mean?'

Mrs Southerham knew what her companion was really asking. 'Because I can't bear injustice. They've even tried to change your names. I think that's shameful.'

Cassandra couldn't hold back a few tears then. Sympathy and kindness were the last things she'd expected.

'Tell me about your father,' Mrs Southerham asked once she'd recovered. 'He must be an exceptional man to be learning Greek.'

'He is. And he's the best father in the world.'

'So was mine. I miss him dreadfully. He died two years ago and I still think of things to tell him.'

'And your mother?'

'She followed him to the grave a few months later, just seemed to lose the will to live after he'd gone.'

When the bell rang to mark the end of the morning session, Mrs Southerham stopped work. 'We'd better tell your sisters you're staying on to help me. I'll come with you in case there are any – er, questions from the other ladies. And you'd better have something else to eat, because we have an hour or two's hard work ahead of us still. I'll get that for you while you speak to your sisters.'

As Livia approached the area where the bread and milk were served, the Vicar approached her.

'Might I have a word, my dear lady?'

'Certainly.'

'I believe you've taken a certain young person out of the group to work with you. I cannot advise this, knowing her background as I do. You must allow me to guide you in your choice of helper.'

'I'm quite satisfied with Cassandra's help, thank you. She's not only a hard worker but she's very intelligent and quick to learn.'

His face became a deeper red. Before he could speak again, she added, 'I think people have been mistaken about her morals, Vicar.'

'The lady who informed us knows the family.'

'The lady who informed you bears a grudge against that family, from what I've heard. And might I say that *my* family will be very surprised that you're questioning my judgement like this.' She didn't often use the Southerhams' superior social status, but was so angry about how they were treating the Blake sisters that she didn't hesitate to do so now.

She watched his desire to have his own way war with his desire to stand well with her husband's family, and the latter must have won.

'Well, if you insist. I must just pray that your trust isn't betrayed.' With an inclination of the head, he moved on.

Why were they all so against those girls? Was it just based on one spiteful woman's word or was there another reason? Perhaps because of the way they spoke, using long words and expressing thoughts that showed an interest in matters beyond domesticity. Livia went across to the table and took some food, together with a glass of milk.

The lady looked at her sharply but didn't protest, and

Livia went back to the small room, where Cassandra was once again at work.

It took another two hours to sort out all the clothes and examine each piece carefully to see which needed mending and which didn't, forming and reforming piles.

At one stage Livia saw Cassandra stroking a tiny embroidered jacket.

'It's beautiful, isn't it?'

'Yes. I've never seen anything like it.' She smiled. 'Our babies don't usually wear such pretty clothes.'

Livia bit her lip but couldn't prevent her expression from betraying her sadness. She saw Cassandra look at her anxiously. 'I lost a child last year and sometimes I feel sad when I see baby clothes.'

'Then why not leave this task for other ladies?'

'Because this is something I can do without their help.' She saw the quick understanding in her companion's eyes and added, 'I'm not very good at gossip and not interested in the town's scandals, real or imaginary.'

'You're kind and that's much more important.'

'I do my best. Now, we've done enough for today. All the bundles are properly labelled. Let me take you home in my carriage.'

'Better not. I've offended those in charge enough for one day.'

Livia chuckled. 'I've enjoyed working with you, Cassandra. Are you coming back tomorrow?'

'Yes. Whatever they say or do, I need the money and the food.'

'Then I'll come back, too. And I'll make sure they let you continue to work with me.'

When Cassandra told her family about Mrs Southerham and how frankly the two of them had spoken, Edwin frowned.

'Be careful, lass. The gentry take sudden fancies, then grow tired of them just as quickly.'

'I don't think Mrs Southerham will. But if she does, I'm no worse off. She's not employing me, after all, just letting me help her with a particular task.'

'Her clothes are beautiful,' Pandora said longingly. 'It must be wonderful to wear clothes like that.'

'Better to have a well-furnished mind,' her father said sharply.

Smiling quickly at one another, they changed the subject. Their father couldn't understand 'female vanity', as he called it, and he never would. But even the clever Blake sisters were interested in pretty clothes.

Maia joined her sisters at the sewing classes on the days she wasn't cleaning or helping with washing. The money they got for attending was a godsend, because the rent still had to be paid if they wanted to stay in their own home.

When the sisters received their money at the end of each week, Cassandra kept it, not putting it in the pot for her father to give away.

'Did they pay you?' he asked that evening.

'Yes.'

'You've not put it in the pot.'

'I've only got enough for the food.'

'There's a family in the next street starving and they have a new baby,' he said. 'Could we not spare a few pence? I'd happily go without food one night to make up for it.'

'Have they applied for relief?'

He hesitated.

'They haven't, have they?'

'The young fellow says he'll starve to death before he accepts charity.'

'Isn't it charity if you give him money?'

'I was going to give it to his wife.'

'You'll help them most by persuading them to go on relief and sending him to break stones.'

'He's not strong enough now to do work like that.'

'Even so, *we* can't afford to help them.'

The glance he gave her was disappointed, but she didn't change her mind. Sometimes their father had to be protected from himself.

A few nights later, after dark, there was a knock on the door and Edwin found a tall young man there with a sack in his hand.

'Mr Blake?'

'Yes.'

'This is for you.' He set the sack down on the floor and hurried off down the street.

Edwin took it through to the kitchen. 'I don't know what this is or why it's been left here, but the young fellow who brought it said my name, so it can't be a mistake.'

They all gathered round.

'It looks like the other sack Uncle Joseph gave us,' Xanthe said.

Sure enough, it contained flour and sugar, potatoes and onions, and even small packages of cheese and ham.

Edwin didn't comment, but his daughters could see how this gift had pleased him. When he looked across at Cassandra pleadingly, she knew what he was asking and she sighed. 'I'll pack a little food for that family you mentioned, but we need the rest, Dad. The rent is still six shillings a week, you know.'

He smiled. 'I knew you'd give what you could.'

He fell asleep after tea, looking tired out. He was helping to do maintenance work at the mill, keeping everything clean and ready for when cotton started arriving again, which meant hard physical work sometimes. He helped in the office occasionally as well, because he wrote a fair hand and there were still letters to write. The previous clerk had now found himself a job in London.

But even so, there was only half a week's work for him, and half a week's wages at the end of it.

As the weeks passed, Cassandra grew more and more worried about her father. He was losing weight steadily, and in spite of eating more than most of their neighbours, he was almost skeletal. In the evenings he tried to hide his weariness, but couldn't.

And yet he had only just turned sixty-one, had been hale and hearty until the previous year. What would they do if he—? No, she mustn't think like that. Once this dreadful war was over, once the raw cotton started arriving in Lancashire again, he'd surely get better. He must.

Reece Gregory's visits were now the highlight of Cassandra's week. She changed library books for him, discussed what he'd read, since she'd usually read it too, and argued sometimes over what the authors meant.

At first her father sat with them in the front room, but after a few visits he left them to chat on their own, and her sisters always found things to do elsewhere.

She wasn't certain whether Reece considered himself to be courting her but was beginning to hope. Then one day he laid one hand over hers and looked at her sadly.

'We need to get something clear, lass. I can't court you, though I'd like to. I've no money to support a wife and I won't bring children into the world to starve. So if my coming here keeps other men away, then I'd best stop.'

For a moment she didn't know what to say, was glad he wanted her but sad that times were against them. 'Other men don't come courting me because I'm too sharp-tongued for most of them, so there's no need for you to stop coming.'

He looked at her, his whole face softening. 'Then they're fools. And when times improve, I will come courting, if you'll allow me to.'

'I'd like that.' There was a warmth inside her and hope was rising that one day, when this terrible Cotton Famine was over, one day ... She cut off the thought. No use putting too much store on what might never happen. Look at how upset Pandora had been when her young man died.

Only when Reece was leaving did she nerve herself to ask, 'You will still keep coming – as a friend?'

He nodded. 'Yes. But don't ask for more yet.'

She allowed herself a few tears after he'd gone, but what was the use of crying? You couldn't change the world, however much you'd like to, and this war and the distress in Lancashire seemed to be going on for ever.

But she felt a warmth at Reece wanting her, and wonder at finding a man to love when she'd given up hope. The thought of him gave her the courage to continue, to hope for better days.

4

Francis Southerham stood to one side as Reece's cousin Ginny milked the first of the cows. 'I think I should learn how to do this,' he said as she finished and prepared to move on to the next animal.

Reece gaped at him. 'Milk a cow, sir? Won't you be hiring a cowman or dairy maid in Australia?'

'I don't know. My friend says they're short of experienced workers, so it seems to me that I need to know everything I can about farming if I'm to succeed there. I may have to take on unskilled workers and show them what to do.' He turned to Ginny. 'Would you mind teaching me, Mrs Dobson?'

There followed a practical lesson which had Ginny in fits of laughter. But by the end of it, Francis was improving and milk was flowing more or less steadily from the cow's teats. Reece got on with his work, but kept an eye on them. He'd never met a gentleman like this one. After a chance encounter on the moors, Mr Southerham had sought him out and they'd chatted. If their lives hadn't been so far apart, they might have been friends because they shared many ideas about the world.

'I'll come back to practise again, if I may,' Francis said as he prepared to mount his horse.

'What's a gentleman doing milking cows?' Ginny asked after he'd left.

'Learning how to farm for when he goes to Australia.'

'He's a strange one, that. He'll soon tire of it, I'm sure.' She dug Reece in the ribs. 'How's that lass of yours?'

He stiffened. 'I haven't got a lass.'

She rolled her eyes and made a disbelieving sound in her throat.

'How can I court any woman when I can't even find work?'

Ginny came across to pat his shoulder. 'This war won't go on for ever, lad. You can court her – just don't marry her yet.'

He smiled at her. She was older than him and treated him in a motherly way. 'It's beginning to feel as if it will never end.' He hesitated. 'I'm thinking I should leave here, Ginny, go down south, see if there are proper jobs to be had there. I'd do anything. I thought coming to you was just temporary, for a few months, till the next cotton harvest came through from America, but . . .' He shrugged.

Her voice softened. 'You don't have to leave. You more than pay your way here.'

He knew that, but it wasn't enough for him just to exist and the desire to change his life was taking a firmer hold inside him with every day that passed. If he did go away, would Cassandra wait for him? Should he even ask her to?

No, it wouldn't be fair. Her father had spoken once of his desire for his eldest daughter to marry and have children before it was too late. Reece had come to love her. It had crept up on him, making him want the best for her. But if this war went on for years, he had no right to make her miss her chance of having a family. Men could father children in their middle years, but women stopped being fertile long before men did.

In the middle of a restless night, he decided to ask Mr Southerham for help in finding a job elsewhere, because the one thing Reece was certain of was that he couldn't continue meeting Cassandra like this. It was like rubbing salt into a wound.

He wanted to marry her, he knew that now, not just for her body, but for her mind, her very self. He hadn't felt like this with his first wife, had learned the hard way what he needed in a wife if he was to be happy.

Damn this Cotton Famine! It destroyed a man's dreams, took away his hopes, made you doubt the future.

When Francis got home, he found Livia sitting in their bedroom, chilly as it was. 'Avoiding my family again?' he asked as he bent to kiss her cheek.

'I hope they don't realise I do that.'

'No, of course not. I know you better, though.'

She hesitated, then asked, 'How are you feeling today?'

He avoided her eyes. 'A little better, I think. The fresh air agrees with me.'

She gave him a long level look that said she didn't believe that. He changed the subject. 'How was your protégée today?'

'Interested in anything and everything I can teach her. I've never met anyone who picks things up so quickly. She's learning to embroider now, and doing it well. All it needed was me to give her a few pointers and she was able to repair the fancywork on some of the garments. She took them home for something to do. She's fretting over the tedium of being unemployed as well as the money side of things.'

'You speak so well of her, I must come and meet her one day.'

'I doubt she'd speak as freely to you. It took her a while to trust me.'

'The fellow I met on the moors is much the same and just as trapped by his poverty as your Cassandra.' Partly to distract Livia, he added with a quick smile, 'Do you want to come and learn how to milk cows?'

She gaped at him, then burst out laughing.

'I'm serious. That's what I was doing today. I know how to care for horses, have felt happy in stables all my life. And we could learn how to make cheese, too – the farmer's wife is noted for her cheeses. Someone must know how to look after hens as well, a task usually undertaken by women. I think we should both know more, just in case we can't find someone to manage the farm for us in Australia. Will you?'

'Why not? At the very least, it'll get me out of the house more. What do you think your mother will say about it, though?'

'I shan't tell her what we're doing. She'd be furious.'

'If only your father would change his mind and help you go out to Australia. I'm longing for a home of our own, however small.'

Francis put his arms round her and held her close, loving the feel of her head resting on his shoulder. He'd fallen in love with her at their first meeting, but his parents had opposed the marriage, since she brought very little to it financially, just a few hundred pounds. 'He will one day. I'll wear him down until he realises I won't change my mind this time, as I did with the other things I tried.'

Francis wasn't as sure about his father capitulating as he tried to sound. He felt ashamed to be living at home at his age, dependent on his father with only a tiny annuity inherited from an aunt. He'd not been feeling well lately, had been coughing a lot, losing weight. He'd have to consult the family doctor if his health didn't improve.

Would Australia be a better place for a man like him? Surely he couldn't be mistaken in what it had to offer. After all, his cousin Paul was living in the Swan River Colony, which some called Western Australia and had written about the opportunities it offered a man like Francis in glowing terms. What reason could Paul have to lie about that?

Joseph Blake endured the sermon, hoping his boredom didn't show on his face. He wondered if the Methodist services were any more interesting. They certainly had some stirring hymns – he'd heard them as he walked past and lingered to listen. And the members of the congregation seemed friendlier towards one another than most of the people at this church were. Why, here they even sat in strict order of social status, with the servants and labourers at the rear.

Saunders was a particularly poor preacher, losing himself in classical allusions and not saying anything meaningful to most of his congregation. Joseph didn't attend every week, couldn't face it.

As they filed out of the church, the Vicar was waiting in the porch to say goodbye to his more important parishioners. He bent forward to say quietly, 'Could you stay behind, please, Mr Blake? I'd like to discuss something with you.'

Joseph went to rejoin his wife and suggested she walk home with some of their neighbours. 'The Vicar wants a word.'

As she walked away he stood watching with a frown. There had been something in her eyes, something quickly hidden, but had it been triumph? What had she been up to now? Her behaviour was becoming increasingly erratic and spiteful. She seemed to enjoy causing trouble far more than helping people, and her animosity towards his family was more than a little . . . unbalanced.

Saunders came across to join him, surplice ballooning out in the wind. 'Chilly day, eh? Shall we go into my room?' He didn't wait for a response but led the way inside. 'Do take a seat. I'll just slip out of this.' He heaved the surplice over his head and tossed it carelessly over a chair back, then sat down on the other side of the desk, frowning, fiddling with a pen, as if unsure how to start.

'What did you want to see me about?' Joseph asked as the silence continued.

'No use dressing it up in fancy words – it's those nieces of yours. The lady helpers are concerned that they're mingling with the other girls at the sewing classes and causing trouble. I was wondering if we could find a way to . . . well, send them away from Outham. There are schemes I know of for rehabilitating young women of loose morals and—'

'Those girls are not of loose morals!'

Saunders lowered his voice, his expression sympathetic. 'My dear fellow, your wife knows all about them, has confided her worries in me. She says you refuse to face facts and I can see she's right when I talk to them. They have no respect for their betters. Why, even the way they look at one is impudent. And they answer me back as if they're my equals. It simply won't do.'

'My wife isn't telling the— She's mistaken. My nieces are decent young women, all four of them. Just ask the Minister at their chapel, if you doubt my word.' He could see his companion didn't believe what he was saying, and he knew no love was lost between the two clerics, so leaned forward and said emphatically, 'And if you try to send those girls away, Vicar, I shall not only stop attending this church but make a few other changes in my life, which will include ending the contributions I make regularly to your various church funds.'

Mr Saunders breathed in deeply. 'I see.'

'I hope you do.' Joseph stood up and left without a farewell, not going straight home because he was too angry to think straight. He had to walk twice round the park before he calmed down enough to deal with Isabel. You'd think he was used to her ways by now. But she'd not attacked his family before, not like this.

When he went into the house, he found Dot waiting to serve luncheon and sent the young maid away 'till I ring'.

Isabel was standing by the window of their parlour and

after one quick glance, she turned her back to him and stayed that way.

Anger that had been held back for years suddenly boiled over and sent him across the room to grab her shoulder and swing her round. 'You've been doing it again, haven't you? Spreading poisonous gossip, this time about my nieces? In spite of what I said to you.'

'I only tell the truth.'

'That's the last thing you ever think of. You say whatever will suit your purpose, not caring whether your lies hurt others. Did you know you're famous in this town for your spiteful tongue?'

'And you're famous for your gullibility where your family is concerned.'

'I know what my brother is like *and* what his daughters are like – decent, honest people, all of them. It's you who aren't decent and you're definitely not honest. I should never have married you. It wasn't worth it.'

They stared at one another for a moment or two, then the ornate clock on the mantelpiece chimed the quarter hour and her face reverted to her usual calm mask.

'I must tell the girl to serve luncheon or the food will be spoiled.'

But he grabbed her arm again, pulling her back as she moved towards the bell pull. 'You're not listening to me.' He gave her another shake to emphasise his words.

Her calm expression was replaced by an ugly scowl. 'How dare you lay hands on me? Let go this instant.'

'I'll let go when I've said what I need to. If you don't stop spreading these lies, I'll—'

She threw back her head and laughed, a shrill sound

which contained no hint of mirth. 'You'll do what? There is nothing you *can* do that will make me stop until I've got rid of your family. It's humiliating to have them living in the same town and I *will not* let it continue. You'll have to lock me up to stop me and you're too much of a coward to do that. You stole my family's money, made my father leave everything to you, but you won't steal my self-respect as well.' Wrenching her arm out of his grasp, she rang the bell and went to sit at the dining table.

He couldn't bear to sit with her, so went downstairs, pacing up and down the long, narrow room at the back of the shop, where his employees packed items like sugar and flour into one-pound bags. He was sick with the realisation that Isabel was right. He wasn't a wife beater and of course he couldn't lock her up. Nothing he said or did seemed to make any impression on her these days.

How could he protect his nieces from her spite?

And why did he care about them when he'd not seen his brother for years and only spoken to his nieces once? He didn't understand why he cared, just knew that he couldn't let Isabel ruin their lives. It would be wrong. They were *family*.

Once he'd calmed down, he went along to the kitchen and asked Dot for a plate of food, taking it back to the packing area to eat.

After that he found a book and tried to read. But the rows of boxes and the shelves full of food seemed to mock him, and his thoughts would not be silenced.

He'd spoken the simple truth. Marrying that harridan upstairs hadn't been worth it. He'd led a miserable life with her for years, and had no one to call his own now, not family, not even a close friend, because she drove people away if she thought they were getting too close to him.

And something had been worrying him lately: what was going to happen to this shop after he died? It was the only child he had and he'd made it a much better shop since he took over, was proud of that, at least.

He was in a good state of health for a man of sixty-three, but even so, he couldn't expect to live for many more years. Twenty, if he were very lucky, probably far fewer in reality.

What was he to do with those years? And how dispose of his shop? He needed to consider that very carefully.

In August a cart rumbled down the street and stopped nearby. When someone knocked on the front door, Cassandra went to answer it. She saw the stableman from the mill and behind him the cart with a man lying on it.

'I'm sorry, love. Your father had a bad turn at work, a seizure Mr Darston thinks, so we've brought him home. The master's sent someone to fetch Dr Turner.'

She couldn't speak for shock.

'Shall we carry him into the house?' he prompted gently.

'Yes, please.' She called out to her sisters, 'Dad's been taken ill. They're carrying him up to his bedroom.' She led the way upstairs, while the others clustered at the back of the narrow hall.

'There. Lay him on the bed.' She looked down at the slack, twisted face. His eyes were closed and he didn't look like her father, somehow.

'We'll undress him for you, shall we?' one of the men said gently. 'Could you get us a nightshirt?'

She nodded and went to wait outside on the landing, hating the way she was worried not only for her father, but for all of them. If he couldn't work, if he wasn't bringing in any money at all, how would they manage? She pushed that thought away. No use facing trouble till it came to sit at your table, her mother had always said.

After the two men had left, Maia went up to sit with their father and Cassandra let her do it, because the younger twin was best at dealing with sickness. The others were left with nothing to do but sit round the kitchen table.

No one said 'What if he dies?' but she was sure they were all thinking it – or trying not to. Impossible to imagine a world without him.

It was a full hour before the doctor arrived. At the sound of the door knocker Cassandra rushed to let him in. She knew him only by sight, because he wasn't the doctor who had attended her mother and since they were a healthy family on the whole, she'd never spoken to young Dr Turner before. She explained quickly what had happened and showed him upstairs.

Maia waited on the landing and the others waited downstairs.

When they heard the bedroom door open and footsteps come down the stairs, Cassandra went to meet the doctor.

He looked up the stairs and whispered, 'Can we go somewhere else to talk?'

She led the way into the front room.

'Your father's had a seizure, as you must have realised, and I'm afraid it's a bad one. He'll probably be dizzy and bewildered for a day or two. The right side of his body has been affected and isn't likely to function properly again. The early days are the dangerous time, when he might have another seizure. That happens sometimes.'

'And if he doesn't have another? Will he get better?'

'A little. I suppose he's your breadwinner as well as your father, but I'm afraid he's not likely to be able to work again.' He pulled his pocket watch out. 'I must go. I have people waiting for me at the infirmary.'

She had to swallow hard before she could speak. 'How much do we owe you?'

'Is anyone else in this house in work?'

She shook her head.

'Then I'll not charge for my visit.'

She could feel herself flush in humiliation, but didn't turn down his kind offer. She knew times were about to get much harder for them and every farthing would count. 'Thank you.'

He patted her hand. 'Keep him comfortable and try to get him to drink as much liquid as he can. I'll be back tomorrow.'

As the day passed, they took it in turns to sit with their father. The best they could say was that he seemed to be holding his own.

Cassandra thought hard about how they were to cope from now on, doing sums in her head, testing out first one idea then another for practicality. One evening she asked Maia to leave their father for a few minutes to discuss their future.

'We're going to be very short of money, so those of us who can must keep going to the sewing classes. It's the only money we can earn.'

'I'll stay at home with him,' Maia said at once.

'Will you be able to lift him on your own?'

'I think I will. I hadn't realised how thin he was till I gave him a drink of water when you were all busy.'

'Is Dad going to die?' Pandora asked, her voice wobbling.

Cassandra repeated what the doctor had told her after his second visit, which was not much different from what he'd said the first time, except that Dr Turner was a little more optimistic about his patient's chances of continuing to live. 'It's not going to be easy, but we'll manage somehow *and* we'll look after him. I'm not letting them put him into the infirmary.'

'Definitely not,' Xanthe echoed. 'I'd not send a dog there to die.' The infirmary was attached to the poorhouse and was a dark, miserable place.

'He'll die in the comfort of his own home. And should he live, he'll do so here as well, whatever it takes.'

Only how to manage that? How to continue paying the rent, buying him nourishing food?

'Do you have any ideas?' Maia asked.

'I'm thinking about it.'

The following day the Vicar stopped them to ask where Maia was, why she was no longer attending the sewing classes. Hating his patronising tone, Cassandra explained about their father.

'So you say.'

There was silence as they stared at the man in shock. 'What do you mean?'

'How do I know you're telling the truth? Who knows what your sister is up to at the moment?'

As Xanthe stepped forward, mouth opened to refute this accusation, Cassandra dragged her back by her skirt. 'Don't.'

She turned to the Vicar and said quietly, 'You can easily confirm that I've told you the truth by asking Dr Turner, who is attending my father. Now, if you'll excuse us, we must get on with our sewing.'

'I shall definitely check that, Cass. I will not be lied to.'

As he walked away, she saw to her dismay that Mrs Southerham wasn't there and another lady had taken her place in front of the sewing class.

'Hurry up, Cass Blake!' the haberdasher's wife called. 'You can work on the pinafores with the other girls today. And make sure you keep your stitches neat.'

Cassandra took the piece of material she'd been given without a word and walked along to a seat near her sisters, bending her head over it. The morning seemed very long, and whatever she did, one of the ladies would come across to criticise her, insisting she pull out the stitches and start again . . . and again.

It was only by regarding it as the best way of fighting back that she was able to keep her mouth closed on angry protests and do as they ordered.

But there was murmuring among the other young

women nearby and in the end, the second lady looked at them nervously and walked away without another scolding.

Afterwards, they ate the food provided, drank their milk and left the hall.

Some of the other lasses gathered round the Blake sisters in the street.

'Why are they treating you like that, Cassandra love?'

'You should stand up for yourself, not act so meekly,' another said. 'They're telling lies. Your work's neater than anyone else's.'

'I'd not take that sort of treatment from anyone,' a third declared. 'Have you heard the things they whisper about you? Where do they get these lies?'

Cassandra said quietly, 'They want me to answer back so they can dismiss me from the classes for insolence. I need the money so I'm not going to do it.'

When they got home she went to sit with her father for a while. He lay so still, looked so pale, it upset her to see him, but his eyes seemed more aware today. 'Would you like me to read to you?' she asked.

He closed then opened his eyelashes, which seemed to be a sign of agreement, so she went down to fetch her library book and sat reading to him for fifteen minutes. Then suddenly his eyes stayed closed and she saw he was asleep.

She stopped reading aloud, couldn't read on at all because the words were blurred by the tears in her eyes, tears she wouldn't allow to fall while he was awake.

When Maia took over she went downstairs. She had nothing to do because she'd been unable to bring home any sewing today, so she said abruptly, 'I'm going out for a walk.'

'Shall I come with you?' Pandora asked.

'No. I need to be on my own, to think.'

As she walked, Cassandra wondered what had happened to Mrs Southerham today and hoped she wasn't ill. The sun shone down, flowers were swaying in a light breeze and birds were singing. The beautiful day seemed only to emphasise her unhappiness.

On her way round the park she met her minister's wife and nodded a greeting, stopping when Mrs Rainey did.

'Is it true, Cassandra dear?'

'Is what true?'

'That the Vicar and his ladies are picking on you.'

'I don't pay any attention to them.'

'It's been agreed that the people from the parish church will run the soup kitchen and sewing classes, while those of us from the Methodist chapel do the home visiting, so I can't really help. But I think it shameful that your aunt has taken advantage of the situation to say such dreadful things about you.' She held up one hand. 'Don't deny it's her, because everyone knows it is.'

Cassandra could feel her cheeks burning. 'I know what she says isn't true, so do my family. That's what matters.'

'And so do your friends. But I'm going to see if I can do something about it.'

'Please don't upset them, Mrs Rainey. The money I get from the sewing classes is too important. I don't know what we'd use to buy food if we didn't get that.' As it was she was already considering which of their possessions they could sell next and how to get the best price for them.

'I shall speak to my husband. This injustice can't continue.'

On the Friday after he finished at the farm, Francis asked Reece to walk with him to the end of the lane. He led his horse and Reece walked beside till they reached the track which led across the moors. 'Let's stop here. We can sit on the milk stone.'

He looped up the reins and as the horse began placidly eating the grass, the two men sat down on the big flat stone on which the churns of milk were left each day to be collected by one of the shopkeepers in town.

'You asked my advice about finding work and I've been thinking about it. I was wondering if I could interest you in coming to Australia with me?' He waited, as if trying to gauge the other's reaction.

Reece looked at him in surprise.

'I could sponsor you, which is necessary, and offer you employment after we arrive.'

'What makes that better than finding work here?' Reece asked.

'My cousin is living there now. He speaks very highly of Australia and has asked me several times to join him. Land is much cheaper there and readily available to buy or lease. You could set up as a farmer one day if you saved your wages, or open a shop or . . . well, anything.'

Reece felt a stir of interest, but shook his head. 'I've no money to get to Australia, Mr Southerham. The fare must cost quite a lot.' He did have a little money saved because he'd lived very frugally since his wife's death, but he wasn't going to admit to having it, or spend it all on the fare and leave himself penniless and dependent when he got there.

'I'd pay for your passage, in return for which I'd ask you to work for me for two years, starting from when we leave England.'

Reece frowned. It didn't sound a good bargain to him. He'd still be poor at the end of those two years. And that would be two more years without Cassandra. No, it'd not do. 'What about wages? If I can't save money, I'll get nowhere.'

'I'd pay wages during those years as well, but I'm not concealing from you that it'd be hard work. I gather one has to clear the land before one can farm it, and since the climate is very different from here, I'm not sure exactly what conditions will be like. My cousin can be a bit vague at times and he's not a farmer.'

Nor are you, Reece thought. Like his cousins, he felt the Southerhams were just playing at farming. How would this man be if he had to get up early every single morning, rain or shine, to milk his cows? The only animals he really seemed to care about were horses. And how would Francis endure hard physical work for days and months and years? Reece wasn't at all sure the other man had the stamina and willpower necessary for that. Indeed, there were days when Mr Southerham looked positively ill.

As for Mrs Southerham, she was a very pleasant lady, who talked to everyone civilly, but her hands were soft and white and she didn't know half of what his cousin

Ginny did, for all she'd fed the hens and helped collect the eggs.

He let the silence continue as he tried to think things through, then said slowly, 'I suppose people still need food, wherever they live in the world. And animals won't be all that different to care for. I've read about Australia. Which part of the country are you going to?'

'The Swan River Colony in the west. It's the smallest of the colonies by far, but my cousin writes that a man of sense who works hard can make a good life for himself there. I was thinking of going to Sydney, but having someone there already to show me how to go on, will be extremely useful. And anyway, I like my cousin. We always got on well.'

'I'll have to think about it.'

'Yes. Of course.'

'There's a young woman I'm interested in here, you see.'

'You could send for her once you were settled. Surely she can wait a year or two?'

Reece didn't like the cavalier way his companion dismissed Cassandra, so said sharply, 'Is your wife going to wait for you here?'

'No. But that's a little different. We're already married.'

'As I said, I'll have to think about it.'

Francis nodded and stood up, reaching out for the horse's reins. 'We'll speak again, then.'

He rode away and when he turned round, saw Reece still standing there, kicking at a piece of turf, hands thrust into his pockets.

Who was the woman Reece cared about? he wondered.

Was she the sort to be an asset or a burden? Should he offer to pay her fare as well? No, he wasn't made of money.

To Cassandra's relief, Mrs Southerham was at the sewing class the next day, but it took a sharp exchange of words between her and the Vicar before Cassandra was allowed to work with her again.

'Was it bad yesterday?' she asked, once they were alone in the cosy little room.

Cassandra shrugged. 'You know what they're like.'

'Yes. I'm sorry, but I shall only be here on Mondays, Wednesdays and Fridays from now on.' Livia smiled conspiratorially. 'Don't tell anyone, but my husband and I are learning about farming. I've been trying to milk cows, but I'm not very good at it, I'm afraid. We're emigrating to Australia next year and we mean to farm out there, so are learning as much as we can.'

Cassandra tried to feel pleased for her, but couldn't help saying, 'I shall miss you. Not just because of the protection you offer me, but because I enjoy your company.'

'I shall miss you, too. But we'd better start work now. I have some lists of families who're in dire need of clothing for their children. We'll begin to visit them from next week onwards.'

'I thought the other churches were doing the visiting.'

'The Vicar wants me to visit those who are members of his congregation.'

'Will I be allowed to go with you?'

'You will if I say so.'

Cassandra had a think about it, then said reluctantly, 'I'm not sure it'd be wise. It'll make the other ladies even angrier.'

Livia shrugged. 'One can't always be wise. But if you'd rather not come, I can find someone else.'

And suddenly Cassandra couldn't resist the idea of getting away from this place. Maybe it wasn't wise but it seemed to get harder each day to put up with the unfair treatment. They were picking on her more than her sisters, she couldn't understand why, but all of them were finding it difficult to keep quiet.

'I'd love to come with you.'

5

On Sunday afternoon Reece turned up at the Blakes' house earlier than usual. 'I heard about your father. How is he?'

'Not well. Do come in out of that rain. It's not stopped all morning.' Cassandra led the way into the front room and gestured to a seat.

'Is he in a state to receive visitors?'

'Not yet.' Her father was still disoriented and weak, unable to speak. They had to do everything for him, which was embarrassing. But she was sure there was a spark of the old intelligence and life in his eyes still, so she stubbornly continued to read and talk to him.

She watched Reece sit staring down at his clasped hands, then sigh and look up at her. 'I'm thinking of going to Australia. Mr Southerham has offered to sponsor me and will pay my fare if I agree to work for him for two years. It's easier to rent or buy land there, it seems. Maybe I can get a smallholding if I work hard.'

She tried to hide her dismay. If he went, she'd lose both him and Mrs Southerham. But it wouldn't be fair to try to hold him back, not with the lack of hope here in Lancashire. With a huge effort she managed to respond calmly, 'It sounds like a good opportunity for you.'

'Yes. There's no sign of cotton coming into the country in any quantity in the near future and anyway, I don't think I could bear to go back inside a mill after working out of doors.'

She'd heard him say that before, felt the same, if truth be told. She tried to say something but could only think how much she'd miss him and struggle to hold back her tears.

'I'd have asked you to come with me, but we're leaving quite soon and—'

She finished for him. 'I couldn't leave my father.'

'I'll write to you if that's all right?'

She nodded, unable to speak for the lump in her throat.

He took hold of her hand. 'Cassandra ... if things work out well for me ... if you're still unattached ... perhaps you could join me there one day?'

'Go to Australia?'

He nodded, then flushed. 'I meant, you'd come out to marry me. You know how I feel about you.' He smiled at her, still clasping her hand tightly. 'And I think you feel the same.'

She didn't try to pretend, not with him. 'Yes, I do.'

'So later on, unless you meet someone else – and I'd not blame you if you did – would you come out and join me there if I send you the money for the fare?'

The idea was exciting but there were other problems too. Everything seemed against her and this man whom she'd grown so fond of so quickly. 'If I went so far away, I might never see my sisters again.'

'I know. That's why I hesitated to ask you. I know how close you all are. And I don't think it'd be fair to tie you down with . . .' he hesitated, then ended up, 'promises.'

'Couldn't you . . . find work in some other part of England?'

'I think this is a better opportunity and I know no one outside Lancashire, so it might as well be Australia. I'm told there are more opportunities for ordinary men out there. Besides, like you, I've always wanted to see the world.'

'I've never expected to, though.'

'No. Life rarely gives us quite exactly what we want, does it?' He kept hold of her hand and put the other arm round her shoulders. 'I can't have you if I stay here, and I can't have you for a long time if I go. But I do want you, Cassandra love. And there is a chance that I can make a life for us in Australia – the only chance for our mutual happiness I can see.'

She looked down at their linked hands and forced the words out. 'You should definitely go, Reece. Don't miss this chance. But do write to me . . . and think about me sometimes. And if it's possible . . . well, I can't see so far ahead at the moment . . . but if I can, I'll come out to join you.'

He pulled her closer and kissed her, first gently, then hungrily. She gave herself up to these kisses, needing his touch just as much as he seemed to need hers. She'd not realised before how strong the need for a man's touch could be, or how much she wanted to caress and kiss him back – had lived too much inside her head, perhaps.

When he broke away, they were both breathing heavily.

He let go of her and she had a sudden urge to pull him towards her, but she didn't. As long as her father needed her, as long as her sisters needed her, she must stay, even if it broke her heart. 'When – shall you go?'

'Not for a month or two yet. I don't know whether that makes it easier or harder.'

She felt the same.

When he'd left, she sat on alone in the front room until Pandora came to find her. She was beyond tears, beyond anything except thoughts of him and mindless wordless protests at what fate was doing to them.

'Oh, there you are. Are you all right, Cassandra? You look – sad.'

She couldn't give them something further to worry about, and anyway, losing Reece was *her* pain. They had another one to share. 'I was just thinking about Dad.'

'He's a little better today, don't you think?'

'Perhaps. But he's not going to be able to work again, is he? We have to make plans. I've been doing the sums and we simply can't afford to rent this house now.'

'You think we should move?'

'That or take in lodgers. More people are sharing houses now to reduce the costs.'

'Let's take in lodgers then.'

'If we do, we'll have to harden our hearts. We can only accept people who can afford to pay for their rooms.'

Cassandra repeated this warning to the other two that evening.

They spread the word that they were letting rooms in their house, which was larger than most houses in the terraces, and within the day, several people came to ask if they could move in.

Cassandra questioned them with Pandora in attendance. They didn't dare let soft-hearted Maia do it, or she'd have given the rooms to people who had no money to pay the rent, and Xanthe was so impulsive you were never quite sure what she'd do.

They'd worked out that they could let two rooms. The large room at the front of the house on the ground floor was taken first by a man who had worked with her father. He brought with him his wife, son and daughter-in-law, plus a newborn baby. All were to fit into the one room and share the kitchen facilities.

But Cassandra knew Harry Grant would be more likely to pay rent than others she spoke to, because he hadn't waited till his money ran out to find somewhere cheaper, and he and his son were both working at stone-breaking.

She told her father what they were doing and he managed a tiny nod. He was so frail now, and so accepting of what had happened, it seemed to her as if the fighting spirit had been knocked out of him by the seizure, as if he was only waiting to die and take the burden of caring for him off their shoulders.

Only she didn't want to lose him. He'd been more than a father to her, he'd been her best friend . . . until she met Reece.

They also found tenants for the largest bedroom, the one at the front that she and Pandora had shared, letting it to an older couple with two lads of fifteen and seventeen. Again, the men were fit enough to break stones. That made such a difference.

They'd had to move their father into the smallest

bedroom and even so, it was a squash to fit four of them into the middle bedroom.

Their Minister's wife organised a roster of people to sit with Edwin or read to him so that all four of them could go to the sewing classes and earn their sixpences. Mrs Rainey was good at organising practical help. Mr Rainey also came to visit Edwin once or twice a week, sitting with him, chatting quietly, offering up a prayer.

Reece still came on Sundays, sitting with Edwin now that he was a little better, talking gently about the week's happenings at the farm or the book he'd been reading. Cassandra joined them upstairs for part of the visit, at least, but it made her sad that Reece no longer made an effort to hold any private conversation with her.

He looked at her, though, devouring her with his eyes. She wasn't fooling herself about that. His looks betrayed what he was feeling, though he held back the words.

She kept telling herself he was right to go. Well, he was in practical terms. She was sure of that. But anything could happen on a voyage to the other side of the world. And who knew how long it would be before they met again – if ever?

She didn't want him to go!

She continued to hold her temper in check at the sewing classes, but it was particularly hard on the days when Mrs Southerham wasn't there.

And one thing troubled her greatly. Even at this time, her uncle didn't come to see his brother. Surely he wanted to make his peace between them before Edwin died? Another sack of food was sent round to the house, but no message. He could at least have sent a kind message with it!

She considered going to the shop and begging her uncle to come and see his brother, but was afraid he'd refuse and send her away. She didn't dare do anything that might stop the food coming. It made such a difference.

And anyway, a visit wouldn't really mean anything unless her uncle came of his own accord.

There was another reason she didn't go. She didn't want to encounter her aunt. She passed Isabel Blake in the street occasionally and the way the older woman looked at her, the hatred in her eyes, filled Cassandra with a nameless dread.

She was quite sure that if her aunt could ever hurt her – or any of her family – she would do so.

Livia walked along the street with Cassandra, looking at her list of people to visit. 'I'm told there's a family here with a new baby.'

'Yes, the Wrights.'

'You know them?'

'My father does. They're very proud people. I'm not sure they'll accept charity, not even baby clothes, though they will occasionally accept a little food from their friends. Mr Wright was injured a while back and can't work at breaking rocks.'

Livia shook her head sadly. Lancashire folk were so independent compared to the poorer folk she'd grown up with in the south. There had already been a few cases in Outham of old people dying for lack of food rather than go into the union poorhouse. She'd had words with her mother-in-law about that, because Mrs Southerham refused to take even the smallest interest in the current problems or make a contribution towards helping the operatives.

'This is their house.' Cassandra knocked on the door and called out her name. 'I've brought Mrs Southerham to visit you. She and I have been mending some old baby clothes that no one wants.'

The room was almost bare, the only furniture left being a rickety old chair and a table made from battered planks. In the corner was a pile of sacks being used as a bed. On it lay a young woman, pale and too languid even to look up. In her arms was a sickly infant, whose head she was stroking gently. It was fretting, its cries faint, as if it had no energy for more than a whimper.

The father of the baby stared at them defiantly. 'If you've come offering charity, you can—'

Livia stepped forward. 'Only a few clothes for the child, Mr Wright.'

The mother spoke. 'Please, John.'

He turned to his wife. 'Did we not agree? No charity?'

'That was before the baby. I've changed my mind now. I want her to live.' She began to weep, another thin, piteous sound. Like her child she didn't seem to have the strength to cry properly.

Cassandra went across to kneel by her, holding her hand and looking up at the young man. 'John Wright, what are you thinking of, letting your wife clem like this? She needs food and so does the baby. Don't you care that your child will die if it's not looked after? That Annie can hardly lift her head and is like to die too?'

He had tears in his eyes and Livia went to catch hold of his arm. 'Please let us help you, Mr Wright. We've brought clothes for the baby, and we can come back with food and tickets for more. Surely there's no shame to accepting the same help as your neighbours do?'

'I'd accept it if I could work for it. But with this –' he gestured to his foot, '– I can't break stones like the others.'

Cassandra swung round, her voice harsh, 'So you've decided that three people must die because of your pride! That's wrong, John.'

'I'll not go into the union.'

'We don't want them to separate us,' Annie said. 'They always do in that place.'

'Then we'll find another way to help you,' Livia said. 'But you must promise to accept what we offer. Please. I can't bear to see you die when I can help.'

There was silence, and it seemed to go on for a long time. He stared first at her then at his wife and child.

Annie called from the bed. 'John, John, do as she says. If this baby dies like the other, my heart will surely break and I'll die too.'

Livia went across to the bed, crouching beside Cassandra, her full skirts billowing around her on the dusty floor. 'What have you called her?'

Annie shook her head. 'Nothing. What's the point? She's going to die. I've hardly any milk.'

'We won't let her die.' Livia stood up. 'I've brought some baby clothes and I'll find some goat's milk for her and food for you. Maybe your milk will come back if you eat better.' She turned to the husband and her voice softened. 'I know it's hard to accept charity, but for their sake, you must, Mr Wright. We'll be back in a few minutes.'

'Have you a jug?' Cassandra asked.

He got it down from the shelf and stared at its chipped rim for a moment. 'It wasn't good enough to pawn but it'll hold the milk.' He thrust it into Cassandra's hands.

As they closed the door, they heard his muffled sobs and his wife's murmurs.

Livia led the way to the baker's on the main street, where she purchased a loaf, then they found a dairyman and bought the goat's milk others used to help feed their babies. It was more expensive than cow's milk, but what did she care for that? It was still only a few pence.

As they came out she said, 'We can get a few other things from Blake's.'

'Don't!' Cassandra warned. 'If you give John too much, he'll not take it.'

'But—'

'We must go slowly.'

When they went back, the door was open so they knocked and went straight in.

John gave them one glance then bowed his head, looking shamed.

Cassandra went up to take his hand. 'It's only bread and milk. We'll bring you tickets for the soup kitchen this afternoon. We're all needing help in these troubled times. I'm doing sewing classes so that I can eat and earn a little money. It's not your fault you can't work.'

'That Vicar fellow said—'

'I don't pay any attention to *him*! You should hear what he says of me.'

For the first time a hint of a smile appeared on his face. 'You're a very determined woman, Cassandra Blake. Your father must be proud of you.'

That brought tears to her eyes. 'I hope he is.'

Annie had pushed herself into a sitting position. 'We've decided to give the baby your name, Mrs Southerham, if you'll allow it. To say thank you.'

'I'd be honoured. No one has ever named a child for me before. My name's Livia.'

'Livia. I like that.' Annie smiled and cuddled the baby closer. But her eyes were on the loaf now.

They left the Wrights to eat in peace.

The other people they visited were not as proud, but it was the memory of the Wrights which stayed in both women's minds.

When they got back to the church hall, Livia went across to the Vicar. 'We need to provide goat's milk for new babies whose mothers can't feed them.'

He stared at her in shock. 'Get them special milk! Don't be ridiculous. There's no money for that sort of thing.'

'I'll pay for it. The man at the dairy knows a farmer who sends goat's milk into town every day. I'll keep a list of those who're in need of such milk and Cassandra can take the milk round to them every day.'

'There really is no need. These people breed like rabbits, you know. If the babies die, it's nature's way of culling the weak. They don't have the same feeling for their children as we do, I promise you.'

Livia closed her eyes for a moment, remembering what

she had seen that morning and praying for patience, because if she said what she really thought, he'd prevent her from helping.

As if taking this action for agreement, he added, 'And how can we trust that Blake female to do the right thing? She'll probably sell the milk.'

Livia had had enough. She drew herself up and glared at him. 'Are you telling me I'm so stupid that I can't recognise a good woman from a bad after I've been working with her for weeks?'

'You're being fooled. You're from another part of the country and don't know these operatives as I do.'

'I've considerable experience of helping the poor. Probably more than you.'

He drew himself up, glaring at her, 'My dear lady, I run several schemes for the deserving poor. And I simply cannot condone this plan of yours.'

'Then I'll do it without you. Our Lord's commandment was to love one's neighbour, all our neighbours, not just those you consider respectable.' She wondered if he'd stop her coming here, but he said nothing.

Once again, she supposed, the Southerhams' standing in the county had helped her.

Who would help those in the direst need, though, once she went to Australia?

Cassandra watched them from the side of the room, but spun round when the lady in charge snapped, 'What are you standing there idle for, Cass? You're here to earn your bread not eavesdrop on your betters.' She said the words slowly and clearly, as if talking to an idiot.

'I'm waiting for Mrs Southerham to tell me what she wants me to do next.'

Livia came across to join them, seeming to sense that someone was yet again trying to find fault with her protégée. 'Thank you for waiting for me as I asked, Cassandra. I'd like you to start sorting out those clothes for older children next. Come with me.'

As Cassandra followed, she saw the lady walk over to the Vicar and the two of them put their heads close together. She wondered what they were planning.

Nothing good, that was sure.

As 1862 wore to a close, Edwin Blake regained some measure of speech, but his movements were very limited and he couldn't negotiate the stairs without help. He'd once fallen down them, taking Xanthe with him and bruising them both badly, so now he mostly stayed in his room. He ate so little they worried about him, wishing they could give him better food than their staples of bread, potatoes and cabbage.

Reece brought them the occasional extra, an egg most weeks, some misshaped cheese of his cousin's making, a flask of milk, bits of ham fat which they could use to fry their bread and once a chicken, a scrawny old bird which they used in a stew. They made it last for several days.

Of course Edwin wanted to share this largesse with the others living in the house, but Cassandra refused, weeping when he tried to insist and she had to deny him.

'I won't do it, Dad. We need the food ourselves.'

'But they need it just as badly.'

'If we had more, I'd share, but we've not got enough for ourselves.'

'I'm disappointed in you.'

She almost gave way then, but the sight of his frail body made her go against his wishes.

She felt even more guilty when he apologised to her later for not trusting her to deal with the food.

6

On 1st January, 1863, President Lincoln emancipated all slaves in America. Later in the month an old friend, who came regularly to sit with Edwin, read about it in the newspapers and brought him the news. Her father was glowing with the joy of it when Cassandra came home.

'It makes it all worth while,' he said over and over again. 'I know we've suffered here in Lancashire, but it's nothing to the suffering of being a slave. I'm quite sure of that.'

She wasn't at all sure, but didn't say anything to spoil his joy. Living his life in his bedroom, visited by people who wanted to cheer him up and who brought only the best news they could find, he'd become very unworldly. Occasionally he'd dip into his Greek books, murmuring the words to himself as his forefinger traced them across the page. His only other reading was the Bible.

He spent a lot of time staring into space and his eyes had a translucent, faraway look to them that she'd seen in others at the end of their lives. That thought cost her a great deal of anguish.

As winter moved into its coldest months, everyone

struggled to keep warm. Since they couldn't afford extra coal, the sisters often went to bed early, lying chatting quietly to one another. They could hear voices in the rooms they'd rented to others, but their lights went out just as early. No one could afford to be extravagant with lamp oil or candles. No one could spare any fat to make old-fashioned rushlights, even. They needed what fat they did get for eating.

Cassandra often lay awake worrying after her sisters had fallen asleep. She felt responsible for them as well as for her father. It was hard, sometimes, being the oldest. And she worried about what to sell next.

One by one pieces of furniture they could manage without went, and at first this didn't matter, because with other people in the house, their stuff was crammed together in the kitchen. These pieces fetched far less than they would have done before the Cotton Famine, which was heartbreaking, but at least Edwin wasn't downstairs to notice the gaps.

The only thing they didn't sell was their mother's locket, which their father kept by his bed and often held in his hand.

'It'll go to you when I'm dead, because you're the eldest,' he told Cassandra. 'She'd have liked that.'

She only hoped she could manage to avoid selling it.

The Prince of Wales got married on the 10th March and a special allowance of an extra loaf to each of the families on relief was voted by the Town Council in celebration of the event. There was also a children's parade, which people watched for lack of something to do, then a meal for the well-fed children who'd been in the parade, all dressed in fancy new clothes, in spite of the hard times.

'The money spent on that parade would fill a lot of bellies,' Pandora said scornfully, watching the scrawny poorer children cluster near the food, one well-fed lad tossing the crusts to the poor ones and laughing to see them fight one another for this largesse.

What had been spent on the marriage celebrations held in town after town would have fed the whole of Lancashire for months, she was sure.

Francis was summoned for an interview with his father after breakfast.

When the two men had left the dining room, his mother glared at Livia across the table. 'I hope you're satisfied now.'

'What do you mean?'

'Don't pretend you don't know. But my Francis has had foolish ideas before, and he's never carried any of them through. This one will be just the same, only he'll be too far away for us to help him. You'll see. You'll end up begging on the streets.'

'He's very eager to go to Australia. And besides, the doctor advised him to move to a warmer climate.'

'He persuaded the doctor to say that. Francis has always been delicate. That's a reason to *stay* not go. He's *not* the sort of man to make a success of farming. He's a dreamer. And *you* encourage him. I hate you! Hate you!' She burst into tears and fled the room, pressing her handkerchief to her eyes.

Livia went up to the bedroom to wait for Francis. The

early morning fire had died down now and she didn't bother to put more coal on it, but sat worrying. Her mother-in-law was refusing to see the truth. Francis was definitely ill.

He came into the room beaming and swung her into his arms, dancing her round the bed. 'The doctor's persuaded my father to help us, so father's going to give me some money to help me set up as a farmer. Isn't it wonderful?'

'Yes, it is. But your mother is very upset, Francis. She won't admit that you're ill and she thinks she'll never see you again.'

'Of course she will. In a few years, once we're established, we'll come back to visit. People do it all the time. And I'm not ill exactly, just have a weakness of the lungs and am being sensible about it. I shall be fit as a fiddle in no time after a long sea voyage and then living in a warmer climate. You'll see.'

She hoped he was right but didn't want to destroy his hopes – or her own. 'I'd better start packing in earnest then, hadn't I?'

'Yes and I'll tell Reece to get ready as well.'

When he'd left, she sat motionless on the bed. Francis was so enthusiastic, so happy. Surely this was the right thing to do? His mother was wrong. The other projects had failed because they weren't right for him. But look how happy he was working at the farm.

No, she couldn't believe it was wrong to go to Australia. And Francis would be stronger, act more sensibly once he was away from his mother's influence, Livia was quite sure of that.

★

What kept Cassandra's spirits up most of all during this difficult time was Reece, who continued to visit them, trudging into town each Sunday through snow, rain or hail.

It was Mrs Southerham who told Cassandra the news first.

'We're leaving soon,' she said one day. 'We've booked passages on a ship called the *Eena*, sailing to Fremantle in Western Australia. I gather the passengers will be mainly colonists nominated by people already living there, plus the families of some convicts out there who've served their time and been given their tickets of leave. It must be dreadful to be separated from one another like that, but they've paid for their crimes now.'

What crime had she committed, Cassandra wondered, to be parted from the man she loved, and from a lady who was almost a friend. But she was well practised now in keeping such thoughts to herself, even when she was with Reece.

Livia stopped walking. 'I shall miss you.'

'I shall miss you too, Mrs Southerham. I'm sorry you're leaving.'

'I'm worried about what will happen to you without my protection.'

'I'll endure what I must. This war can't go on for ever. We'll get cotton and be able to work again one day.'

'There's no sign of an end to it yet and my husband doesn't think the South is going to win. I don't know what'll happen to the cotton supply if they lose.'

'They'll get the cotton through to us again because they'll need the money it earns, and people all over the world need cotton to make their clothing.' Cassandra kept saying that to herself regularly. She had to believe things would improve one day.

'Will you let me leave you a little money?'

'No. From what you've said, you'll need all you've got to set up your farm. Besides, we're managing.' She didn't let herself think of what they would do once they'd run out of pieces of furniture to sell, didn't dare. Even with the rent money from their tenants, and what they earned at the sewing classes, it was hard to feed five of them and pay the rent.

'Things have changed a little. Old Mr Southerham is giving Francis a little money, so I insist on leaving you just a little, for emergencies only.'

Cassandra bowed her head and struggled with her conscience. What use to tell others they must accept charity if she didn't do it herself? 'Very well. But I'll only use it for emergencies.'

'Good. I shall feel better if you have something. There's another thing . . . Reece Gregory is going with us. I gather you and he are – friends.'

Cassandra couldn't hide her sadness. 'Yes. But we both know it can't be more. I have my father to look after, my sisters are here and he has a new life to make in Australia.'

'And if he succeeds out there?'

'If he does, we'll see what happens. He'll be at the other side of the world and there will be plenty of other young women to catch his eye, I'm sure.'

'If he loves you, he'll wait for you.'

Cassandra shook her head. 'I'd not ask him to, and he's said the same to me.'

'You're both being foolishly noble.'

The anger spilled out then, just for a moment. 'What's noble about it? We're not *free* to make promises – either of us.'

Noble, indeed. Her heart was near to breaking with the agony of losing him and she didn't even have the privacy to weep about it in bed now.

When Reece came to visit them on the Sunday before he left, Cassandra steeled herself to stay calm and wish him well.

After saying farewell to her father and sisters, he turned to her. 'Would you come out for a walk with me? It's quite a fine day, feels like spring.'

'I'd like that.' She got out her mantle and bonnet, ashamed that they looked so faded, that the darns showed in the mantle, that the ribbons on the bonnet were limp and frayed.

He took her to the churchyard, as she'd known he would. 'You have three sisters,' he said as they stood looking down at his wife and child's grave. 'Can you not leave your father's care to them? There might still be time to get permission for you to come with us – as my wife.'

A tear betrayed her, rolling down her cheek, followed by others.

He pulled her into his arms and held her while she gave in to her emotions. He murmured soft words into her hair, then kissed away her tears and folded her in his arms.

She couldn't bear this for much longer. Best to say their farewells and be done with it. 'He's been the best of fathers. I *can't* leave him like this, knowing I'll never see him again. And my sisters need me too. I've always been the one who organises things, copes, minds the money. Perhaps later . . . we could all come out to Australia. From what you've said, they need servant girls there, and we'd be willing to do anything.'

But she didn't feel hopeful. When she'd mentioned that Reece and the Southerhams were going to Australia, her sisters hadn't been able to understand it, had said they'd not leave their homeland like that. Pandora in particular had hated the mere idea of leaving Outham.

'I'll write to you.' He traced a finger down her damp cheek.

Her words came out choked. 'I'll write to you, too, as soon as I have an address.'

He drew her into his arms again and for a few moments they forgot the rest of the world as they embraced and showered one another's faces with kisses and caresses, murmuring words of love.

Her voice was shaking as she pulled away from him. 'We must stop. I daren't risk – doing anything else.' Ah, but she wanted to, understood fully now what drove men and women to lie together heedless of the consequences.

His voice was rough with emotion. 'I know. And I wouldn't do anything to put you at risk, though heaven knows I want you.'

The Town Hall clock struck just then and he took another step backwards, waiting for her to tidy herself. 'Come on. I'll walk you home, then I must get back to the farm.'

★

When they'd disappeared from view, Isabel Blake, who had been standing behind a marble angel watching them, gave a triumphant smile. 'I knew it. She *is* immoral. I was right to follow them today.'

Her smile faded as she stood thinking. It was even more urgent now to get rid of her nieces, all of them, before they blackened the family name, the name she shared. There had to be a way. Especially now that the Southerham woman was leaving. Without a protector, Cassandra would be so much more vulnerable.

She'd take action when the right opportunity presented itself. Or make an opportunity. Yes, she couldn't risk waiting too long.

She'd walked out at dusk and seen streetwalkers waiting under lampposts. She knew which narrow alleys were frequented by the criminals of the town. Well, every lady knew to avoid such streets.

If she went to those streets now, surely she'd find someone who would help her? She'd enough money to pay them well.

The next day, without Livia Southerham, the sewing classes were a lesson in endurance. But Cassandra wasn't going to allow the ladies to provoke her into what they'd call 'impudence'. They were not going to find any excuse to drive her from the classes and deprive her of the two shillings and sixpence she earned from them each week.

The other girls were again furious and wanted to protest on the four sisters' behalf, but they begged their friends not to cause trouble. They'd agreed with one another that if they gave way to their anger or resentment, then their aunt would have won.

What gave them the strength to do this was the thought of their father. Without the money they brought in, he'd have to go into the poorhouse. And he'd die very quickly in there, they were sure. They'd faced the fact that nothing they could do would save him, but they were determined that he would die in the comfort of his own home.

When spring began to brighten the year, Cassandra heard of a group of young people going into Manchester and singing on the streets to earn money. It was said they came back with enough to last a month, pay the rent and feed themselves decently. She decided to try the same thing. People said begging was shameful, and indeed she hated the thought of it, but she had run out of furniture to sell, had rent to pay and an invalid to feed.

She broached the idea to her sisters, who were horrified, but willing to do anything for their father.

'After all, we've sung for years to amuse ourselves,' she said bracingly. 'And we're better at it than most. We may not have strong voices, but we can hold harmonies and people say they enjoy our singing.'

'Except mine. I can't hold a tune even,' Pandora said.

'Which works out well because you can stay here to look after Dad.'

'What about the sewing classes?'

'We can say we ate something that disagreed with us.'

'Will they believe that?'

'No. But then, they don't believe anything else we say,

either. Don't tell anyone what we're doing, though. Better we keep this to ourselves.'

So they set off well before dawn to tramp the dozen miles into Manchester, because they didn't have enough money for train fares. They hoped to get a ride or two, and to their relief, succeeded, travelling for about three miles in the back of a farmer's cart, though that meant picking bits of straw off each other afterwards. The rest of the time they simply walked, hungry and cold, but determined.

As they approached the city a carter bringing vegetables in from the country stopped. 'Cotton lasses?' he called.

They nodded. They'd deliberately chosen to wear their shawls and working aprons, knowing they'd be recognised for their trade, that some people at least would understand why they were doing this.

'We're going to sing for our supper,' Cassandra said as he told the horses to walk on.

'How about you sing to me now, for your breakfast? I'll buy you a cup of tea and a piece of bread and butter each when we get there.'

'We'll sing a few songs, but we have to save our voices.'

'Aye, lass. I know. Just a few to cheer us all up.'

So they sang, letting their voices echo out. He joined in after the first couple of songs.

'You sing well,' he said with a smile when they finished.

'So do you.'

'Aye, I love a good song. Have you ever been to a music hall?'

They shook their heads. 'Outham's too small to have one,' Cassandra said. And anyway, the Town Council seemed determined to keep the modern world at bay for as long as it could. It was run by people like the Vicar, who didn't want to better the lot of the poorer inhabitants. Their father said there had been a huge fuss over the coming of the railway in the early days, and the council had refused to allow a co-operative store to be set up because the shopkeepers thought it'd take away their trade.

The city was covered by a dark haze of smoke and looked anything but welcoming. They fell silent as the horses clopped in through street after street of dwellings, manufactories, warehouses. Some of the buildings were so grand they took the sisters' breath away. Others were so tumbledown, you wondered whether they even kept the rain off their occupants.

Their driver drew up next to a street stall and called out, 'Feed my three friends, will you, Nell? I'll pay you when I come for my breakfast. Give them the same as me.' As the girls got down, he pointed to the next turning. 'After you've eaten, go down to the end of that street, turn right and that'll bring you to Deansgate.'

The food was a wonderful boost to their spirits. As they took up their stand on the corner of Deansgate, one of Manchester's major thoroughfares, Cassandra pulled out a sign she'd painted on a piece of white material torn from an old sheet, saying *Cotton Workers grateful for your help*.

Xanthe clutched her twin's hand. 'I don't think I can do it.'

Maia surprised them by saying firmly, 'You have to. Think of father. It's for him.'

So they began to sing tunes everyone knew well. They

started with 'Home Sweet Home', easily slipping into the harmonies they'd practised over the years, then went on to 'Jeanie with the Light-Brown Hair', a favourite of their father's, and then 'O for the Wings of a Dove!'

When people stopped to listen, Cassandra watched them anxiously. Would they give anything? Or would they simply walk on?

Relief shuddered through her when some dropped coins into her father's cap. That gave her the confidence to sing better and she sent her voice echoing down the street, wanting to give good value for the money that continued to clink into the cap.

Suddenly a boy darted out from a doorway, snatched up the cap and its contents and ran off with it.

They stopped singing abruptly and Xanthe was the first to run after him, skirts flying, yelling, 'Stop, thief! Stop him!'

No one moved and the lad began to increase his lead. Then suddenly a young man further down the street stuck out his foot and tripped up the thief, grabbing him by the back of his shirt and causing him to drop the cap.

As coins rolled everywhere, the lad's shirt tore and he jerked out of the man's grasp, haring off again.

Desperate not to lose the coins, they didn't try to chase him but plumped down on their knees and began to pick the money up in frantic haste.

When passers-by who'd seen what happened also began to pick them up, Cassandra worried that they might pocket the coins. But they dropped them into the cap, sometimes adding another and wishing the girls luck.

Not until every single coin had been picked up did Xanthe turn to the young man and thank him properly.

'I was glad to help, miss. I've seen other groups like yours singing in the street and pitied them, knowing why they were so desperate.'

She flushed, because it was embarrassing to be pitied.

'There's a pie stand on the next street,' he said. 'Perhaps you'd let me buy you all something to eat?'

'That's very kind of you,' Xanthe said. 'We're grateful.'

It worried Cassandra to see how admiringly the young man was looking at Xanthe.

'I'm Harry Needley.' He looked at them expectantly.

She could see no way of avoiding giving him their names, not when he was going to buy them pies. This was a problem she hadn't thought about when planning to go out singing. Pandora might be the prettiest but Xanthe was also lovely.

'We can only stay for a few minutes,' she said abruptly. 'We need to earn as much money as we can before we start walking back.'

'Where do you come from?'

Xanthe told him before Cassandra could stop her.

They could smell the pie stall before they got there and all three of them fell silent because it was a long time since they'd tasted meat. 'Eat slowly,' she warned the others.

He looked at her in puzzlement.

'We're not used to such rich food and a drayman bought us breakfast. We only usually eat once or twice a day at the moment.'

'I'd heard people were starving, but I didn't realise it was literally true.'

'They're starving to *death*, those who're too proud to accept charity.' She wondered what other meaning there was to the word 'starving'. Perhaps people simply didn't want to believe it was happening in Britain, that many thousands of people could be lacking food. 'We've managed so far, but our father's ill, so we're not too proud to accept any help that's offered.'

His voice grew gentler. 'You can't be eating enough, though. You're all very thin.'

She shrugged. She hated to see herself in a mirror these days. Her nose had always been prominent, but it seemed like a beak now, her cheeks and eyes sunken, her skin no longer rosy and her neck stringy, like an old woman's.

He turned to order four pies and four cups of tea, standing eating his own food with every appearance of relish, though he was a gentleman by his dress and speech, not a working man.

When they'd finished, Cassandra said firmly, 'Thank you, Mr Needley. We'll get back to our singing now.'

He hesitated but with murmurs of thanks, they all walked away.

The next two hours gave them as much money again.

'Could we catch a train back, do you think?' Xanthe asked. 'It looks like rain and I'm so tired, I don't think I can walk all that way.'

Cassandra hesitated, then nodded. 'It'll save shoe leather. My shoes have a hole in them.'

'Mine too.'

'We'll use some of this money to get them repaired.'

They were quiet as they sat in the train. They might have earned good money today, but they'd all hated singing in the street. Dress it up as you might, it was a form of begging.

What would Mrs Southerham have said? And Reece?

They'd never know. She'd probably never see either of them again. She had to resign herself to that possibility, stop hoping. With the best of wills, Reece probably wouldn't be able to send for her.

It was dark when they got back but by the light of the street lamps, they could see some of their neighbours standing in front of their house, the way people usually did when there was trouble.

Cassandra immediately started running, thinking it must be her father. He couldn't have died! *Please let him not be dead*, she prayed. *Let him stay with us a little longer.* She thought she'd have to push her way through the crowd, but they moved quickly aside, murmuring to one another.

Her neighbour from across the road thrust a lamp into her hand. 'Here, lass. You'll need this.'

'Thank you.'

Inside the front door, she stopped in dismay, holding up the lamp to inspect gouge marks in the walls. The bottom of the banister was hanging loose and the door that led to the kitchen at the back was also battered. There were no marks on the door of the front room, though.

'Dad! Pandora!' she called as she ran up the stairs.

Someone was weeping in the front bedroom. Its door

was unmarked but the door of the girls' bedroom was hanging off its hinges.

The rear bedroom door looked as if it too had been attacked by an axe. It opened and Pandora appeared, her face bruised, her sleeve torn off her bodice.

'What happened?'

'Some men burst into the house just as it was getting dark. Luckily I was at the top of the stairs. They started smashing things, so I barricaded myself in Dad's bedroom and called for help through the window. Only they broke the bedroom door down before anyone could come to our aid.' She began sobbing. 'They hit me and said if we didn't leave town they'd hurt *him* next time. I thought he'd die, he was so upset at being powerless.'

Cassandra put her arm round her sister and moved into the bedroom. Her father was lying in bed, his expression dark and angry on the half of his face which still had flexibility. 'Do you know who they were, Pandora?'

'No. I've never seen them before.'

Her father shook his head when she looked at him.

'I heard some of our neighbours come to the front door,' Pandora went on. 'They yelled at them to be off. The men threatened to hurt anyone who got in their way, so no one tried to stop them leaving. One was carrying an axe and the other a club.'

Maia went to sit on the bed, holding her father's hand, tears running down her cheeks.

'They haven't touched the rooms where our lodgers live,' Xanthe said. 'There's not a single mark on those doors.'

As the implications of this sank in, they looked at one another, then Cassandra put it into words. 'There's only one person in this town who wishes us ill and wants us to leave Outham.'

'But how would our aunt find men to do something like this?' Pandora asked. 'And what does she think to gain by it? We've nowhere else to go.'

Anger was surging through Cassandra. 'I'm going to see our uncle.'

Her father shook his head, but she went to his side and raised his hand to her cheek for a moment. 'I have to tell him, Dad. It's my guess he doesn't know about it. He's been sending us food, not trying to hurt us.'

His words were even more slurred than usual. 'Don't – beg.'

'Dad, if we don't stop her, she might do worse next time. I'm sure our uncle will help us if he can. He's the only one with any chance of stopping her.'

A tear rolled down her father's cheek, then another. She wiped them gently away, kissed him then left the bedroom without another word.

Pandora and Xanthe followed her down the stairs.

'The men might still be waiting outside. They might attack you if you go out on your own,' Pandora said.

'Let them try!' Cassandra was so furious that anyone would attack a sick, helpless man like this, she felt herself to be burning up. She'd been tired when she got off the train but energy was surging through her now.

Before she left, she went to check the kitchen, which had also received its share of attention, then turned to Pandora. 'Will you come with me? You were here. You can describe exactly what happened.'

'Yes, of course.'

7

They stopped outside Blake's Emporium, which stayed open until nine o'clock. It was brightly lit, with gas lights flaring outside, as well as illuminating the inside and the goods in the window.

'There's only one customer,' Cassandra said. 'We'll wait till she leaves.'

When the lady came out of the shop, Cassandra led the way inside before the lad holding the door open had time to close it again.

Her uncle was standing behind the counter, talking to a rather short young man who was wearing the long white apron common to shop workers. A taller young man, with a plain but kindly face, was dusting some shelves.

As the door bell tinkled, her uncle stared at them in surprise.

She didn't dare call him uncle. 'Could we speak to you in private, please, Mr Blake? Something dreadful has happened.'

The door behind him banged open and his wife came out. 'I saw them loitering outside the shop. Get those creatures out of here this minute, Joseph! *This minute!*'

The young men moved aside and the lad went across

to the far corner, turning his back on them and pretending to tidy a shelf.

Her uncle grabbed his wife's arm as she tried to push past him. He looked at Cassandra. 'Please wait outside. I'll be with you in a few moments.'

Isabel struggled to get free of him, failed, then yelled, 'You trollops would do better to go away from here, and the further the better! I'll call the police if you come here again. You don't fool me. I've seen you with my own eyes fornicating with a man in the churchyard.'

With an exclamation of annoyance, Joseph pulled his wife into the rear of the shop. She fought him all the way, shrieking, scratching his cheek and clawing at his eyes, seeming to have lost all self-control in her fury at seeing his nieces.

Pandora shuddered as they went outside and stood in the shadows to one side of the shop. 'She looked like a madwoman.'

'What did she mean by saying she'd seen you in the churchyard?'

Cassandra sighed. 'I was kissing Reece goodbye, that's all she could have seen.'

'Oh. I'm sorry he left.'

She didn't answer that. It'd make her tearful and she needed all her wits about her now.

After a few minutes, the taller of the young men came out. 'Mr Blake says he's sorry to keep you waiting and if you'll go round the side, I'll let you into the packing room.'

He went back into the shop without waiting for an answer, but he'd spoken kindly.

The sisters did as he asked. The side door opened almost immediately and he beckoned to them. 'Please wait here.'

They found themselves in a long narrow room lined with shelves loaded with packages, boxes and bottles. There was a square white sink at one end, a bench all along one side, empty bottles waiting to be filled with vinegar or other liquids. Bulging sacks and wooden crates stood underneath the bench. The room smelled of tea, sugar and spices. Everything was immaculately clean. How good it must be to work here, Pandora thought wistfully, much more pleasant than inside a noisy mill.

They had to wait longer than a moment or two, but at last the door opened and their uncle joined them, looking dishevelled and harassed, dabbing at the scratch on his cheek. 'I'm sorry to keep you waiting. My wife is – well, you saw that she's not – um, not herself today. What's happened? Are you in trouble?'

'While three of us were away today, our house was broken into by two men,' Cassandra said. 'They destroyed our furniture, smashed doors and threatened my father, who is bedridden. They said they'd come back and kill us if we didn't leave town.'

As he listened, his expression went from politeness to shock. 'Is my brother all right?'

'They didn't touch him but he's badly shaken. Because the seizure has left him partly paralysed, he was helpless to stop them and could only lie there while they manhandled my sister.'

'They didn't touch the rooms we've let to other families,'

Pandora added. 'So someone must have planned this carefully to hurt us . . . and only us.'

He didn't say anything for a moment, closing his eyes with an expression of anguish on his face. When he looked up, he said quietly, 'Wait here. I'll close the shop early and get my coat and hat. I want to see for myself.'

Cassandra looked at him in surprise. 'You're coming to our house?'

'It's more than time I made peace with my brother, don't you think?' Looking upwards to the rooms above the shop, he added, almost to himself, 'And then afterwards I'll talk to *her*. I'll find some way of stopping her from hurting you again.'

When they reached the house, Joseph looked at his nieces. 'I'd like to speak to Edwin alone, if that's all right with you?' He felt the things they had to say to one another after all these years of estrangement were best said in private.

'You won't do anything to upset him?' Cassandra asked.

'I promise I won't.'

Inside the house, he inspected the damage with a feeling of sick horror, then followed his oldest niece up the stairs.

She opened the bedroom door, beckoned to Maia to come out, then said, 'Here's someone to cheer you up, Dad.'

His brother's face lit up at the sight of him and Joseph tried hard to conceal his shock at how old and worn Edwin looked. To his dismay, his brother had the translucent look that often meant a person was close to death. Somehow he knew he was only just in time to say goodbye.

He moved towards the bed, glancing round the room. It was furnished only by a narrow bed with ragged blankets, a hard wooden chair and a battered chest of drawers. 'I've been a fool, Edwin, a greedy fool. I was wrong to marry Isabel, wrong to abandon my family.'

'That – doesn't matter – now.'

As Edwin stretched out his good arm, Joseph went to embrace him, shocked all over again by how insubstantial his brother's body felt. He sat down on the bed, keeping one of the wasted hands in his own, listening to the slurred, halting words.

'I'm so glad – you came, Joseph. I've wanted – many times – to speak to you.'

'And I you. But my wife went into hysterics if I so much as mentioned your name, and I'd promised to sever all connection with my family when I married her, so I kept my word. I thought she'd change her mind later about that, but she never did.'

'Does she know – you're here now?'

'Yes.' He touched his scratched cheek. 'I think she's gone mad. *She* must have arranged this attack on you. It could be no one else, because you're well liked in the town, and anyway, you have nothing now to tempt a thief. I'm sorry, so very sorry.'

'It was worth it if it brought you to see me again.'

They were both silent for a few moments then Edwin said, 'Joseph, I need – your help.'

'Anything.'

'I've been worried – about what's going to happen to my girls after I die. There's no end in sight to this war – and they're getting thinner and thinner.'

'I'll send more food. Maybe that'll help *you* get better, too.'

'Don't pretend. I'm not long for this world – and we both know it.' He searched his brother's face and seemed to see something there that reassured him. 'You'll look after my lasses?'

'Of course.'

As Edwin pulled him into a hug, Joseph couldn't prevent tears from running down his face. They held one another for a long time, then sat and talked quietly.

When the Town Hall clock struck half past nine, Joseph pulled out his pocket watch and squinted at it in the dimly lit room. 'It's later than I realised. I must go now. But I'll be back, I promise.'

'I know you will. And you've taken such a weight – off my mind. I'm glad my girls will have you – to keep an eye on them once I'm gone.'

It was over an hour before Cassandra heard footsteps coming down the stairs. She went out to say goodbye to her uncle.

He smiled at her and took one of her hands in his. 'I think my brother and I have mended our relationship now. Edwin's forgiven me, though I don't deserve it.'

'I'm glad. He'll rest easier because of that. You'll come and visit him again?'

'Of course. And I'll send food more often. Um – I gather Isabel's friends have been picking on you at the sewing classes.' As she nodded, he sighed. 'It's yet another thing she's done to hurt you.'

'It doesn't matter.'

'It does. It matters very much to me. I hadn't realised until recently that she was still telling everyone you're immoral . . . which I know you're not.'

'We and our friends know we're not, which is what counts most.'

He patted her hand. 'I think it'll help your reputations if I take you walking in the park on Sunday after church. That'll show the world I think well of you.'

She hesitated to accept. 'Is it worth it? It'd upset your wife even more and you have to live with her.'

'Do I? I'm going to see the doctor on the way home. I think she's insane and if necessary, I want her locked away. I'll call for you and—'

Could things really be that easy? Somehow Cassandra doubted it. He'd not stopped his wife maligning them, seemed as gentle as her father under that affluent exterior. 'Let's wait until you've dealt with your own situation before we make any further plans. If your wife is still living with you, your life won't be worth living if you take us walking.'

'Perhaps you're right. Edwin said you were all clever lasses. He's very proud of you. I'll send a message when I know how things stand.'

She nodded.

After he'd gone she ran lightly up the stairs and found her father looking far more at peace than he had for a long time.

He smiled at her. 'Thank you for bringing Joseph to visit me. I didn't want to die without seeing him again.'

'We'll not talk of dying, if you please. We earned some money today singing in Manchester and with the food our uncle gives us, we can afford to feed you properly from now on.'

His smile vanished. 'You went singing on the street *like beggars*? Oh, Cassandra, did you have to?'

She met his gaze without flinching. 'Yes. There was no other way. And we sang well, too, gave them pleasure in return for their money. I don't regret doing it. We all have to eat. We've been selling furniture and other things, but there's very little left now except for Mum's locket and I'll never part with that.'

He shook his head sadly. 'Well, you must do what you think best, my dear girl – who am I to judge? – but I can't like the thought of you doing such a thing.'

She didn't want to prolong the discussion. 'I'll fetch you some supper now.'

'I'm not hungry.'

'You have to eat.'

He sighed. 'A small piece of bread, then.'

'How about pieces of bread in hot milk with sugar? We bought some food with the money we earned. A bowl of pobbies will slip down easily.' Her mother had always given them pobbies when they weren't well.

'All right.'

But he ate only half before pushing the bowl away and saying apologetically, 'I can't force myself to eat any more, love.'

When Cassandra went downstairs, exhaustion struck her and suddenly she could hardly move one foot in front of the other. Her sisters fussed over her, persuading her to eat the rest of the soggy pieces of bread he'd left before she went to bed, because you couldn't waste good food.

But like her father, she wasn't hungry, just wanted to lie down and sleep. She forced the cold mush down stoically then left them to clear up and went to bed. She would be at the sewing class as usual in the morning.

It had become a point of honour not to let her aunt's friends drive her away.

And if her uncle stopped his wife from hurting them and sent food for her father, surely things would improve a little?

Joseph called at Dr Turner's house on the way home, explained what had happened and asked him to come and examine Isabel. 'I truly believe she's gone mad.'

But when they got home, they found her sitting sewing. She shot one quick glance at the doctor and sighed. 'I'm sorry I lost my temper, Joseph. I don't know what came over me.'

His heart sank. He knew she hadn't changed but when she behaved like this, in a gentle, ladylike way, no one would consider her mad enough to be locked away. 'I asked Dr Turner to come and see you, I was so worried.'

She took out a handkerchief and dabbed at her eyes. 'I'm ashamed of myself, having hysterics like that. I think perhaps I need a tonic, doctor. This war in America is getting everyone down. To see the operatives looking so hungry and hopeless – well, none of us can escape the worry of what will happen to our town, can we?'

Joseph escorted Dr Turner downstairs and couldn't resist saying, 'She's play-acting. She doesn't care about the operatives and she hates my nieces so much that I'm afraid for their safety.' He hesitated, but had no proof

Isabel had arranged the attack, so said nothing more about that.

'I don't think she's mad, but she is at that age when women get upset easily, hysterical even. I'll send round a tonic for her, and you must try to keep her quiet and happy, if you can. The irrationality is only temporary, however. In a year or two this stage of life will have passed and she'll be calmer again.'

'I'll try to do as you say.'

But Joseph moved his things to another bedroom that night, something which made her curse and throw an ornament at him. He also decided to lock the door before he went to bed. A faint squeak woke him with a start some time later and he saw the door handle turning, then turning back again.

He'd been right not to trust her. And he'd be very careful from now on. One day she'd betray herself and he'd have her locked away.

Until then, it would be better not to be seen with his nieces in public. But he'd go round to visit his brother again. He'd not let anything stop him from doing that. He had a lot to make up for and, if he judged correctly, very little time in which to do it.

He fell asleep trying to work out how to help his nieces without driving his wife to do something desperate. And he must make sure they'd be all right if anything happened to him. At his age, you didn't know how long you had left, whatever your state of health.

In April things improved suddenly for the sisters. Because the numbers of people out of work were now so high, it was decided by the local Relief Committee that the ladies of the Methodist Chapel were to run another soup kitchen and hold sewing and reading classes for members of their own congregation.

One of the few things on which members of every denomination were agreed was that it was better not to leave young people idle, far better to make them earn their relief money by attendance at classes than just have it handed out.

Able-bodied men were breaking stones or helping make better roads between Outham and its neighbouring towns. Men who were less capable physically were required to attend reading classes, and did so willingly, even though the Vicar's patronising attitude was greatly resented.

'He treats us like childer,' some grumbled. 'Naughty childer at that. We're grown men, skilled in our trades, whether we can read those damned spider tracks in books or not.'

'Ah, never mind him. It helps pass the time,' others said. 'I just laugh at that pompous fool.'

Cassandra agreed with the latter viewpoint. She saw older men wandering the streets like lost souls, trying to fill the empty hours, and when she came out of the free library, where she sometimes went to read the newspapers, men who couldn't read would ask her what the news was and if the war looked like ending soon.

She went along to the sewing class at her chapel the first day feeling almost light-hearted that she would not have to face a constant barrage of criticism. And indeed, the morning passed very pleasantly for everyone. More work was got through in a happier atmosphere and the food they were given at lunch time was better too.

Pandora volunteered to help with the cooking, which got her out of sewing, an activity she still detested. But Cassandra enjoyed sewing and here, her neat stitches were praised. She didn't have to pull her work back once.

When a real dressmaker came to give the more skilled girls lessons, they were all delighted to learn about cutting out and putting clothes together.

But nothing filled the gap left in Cassandra's life by Reece, nothing ever could, she was sure. She missed him even more than she'd expected. The two of them had talked and talked. Just being with him had made her quietly happy. The mere sight of him had lifted her spirits.

Now she had no one to talk to in the same way, because her father grew breathless so quickly and slept a good deal of the time.

Reece would be well on his way to Australia now, because it took about three months to get there, she'd read. She hoped he wasn't seasick, hoped he would make a success of his new life. And the Southerhams too, of course.

Hoped he wouldn't forget her . . . . couldn't help praying for that.

On board the *Eena*, Reece often thought about Cassandra too, missing her dreadfully, far more than he'd expected. He'd been wrong to come on this journey, he knew that now, but it was too late to do anything about it. With her, it'd have been an adventure. Without her, it was a bleak exile from the one he loved.

He had been so stupid! But he'd been desperate for work, had hated accepting charity, even from his family.

Cabin passengers were kept separate from emigrants like him and he had to share the crowded quarters below deck with other men. These had poor access to fresh air and the hatch leaked when it rained. He felt very alone because he couldn't go and visit the Southerhams, who lived and slept separately from him.

However Francis came across to chat to him when they were all on deck, sometimes bringing his wife with him. It was strange how Reece felt about his employer. As he got to know him better – because like many others they filled in the long hours by chatting – he realised Francis needed practical guidance if his dreams were to become reality. His employer seemed to have little common sense, however kind he was. After a while Reece even thought of him by his first name, though he didn't *say* it, of course.

Perhaps it was just an effect of the voyage. Or perhaps it was one of the first signs of his new life, of the independence he was hoping for.

Francis asked one day, 'Is something wrong? You look sad sometimes.'

Reece hesitated, then the unexpected sympathy brought it pouring out. 'I'm missing Cassandra, shouldn't have left her without at least getting engaged to show her I won't forget her. How could I have been so *stupid*?'

'My wife has spoken about your young lady. She thinks well of her.'

'So does everyone who knows her. I used to visit her and her family every Sunday, wanted her to come with me to Australia. Only her father is dying and she has three younger sisters, all out of work like her. She can't leave them at a time like this. She's very devoted to her father. He has a fine mind, was learning Greek till he could no longer afford the lessons.'

Francis looked at him in surprise. 'An operative learning Greek?'

'Working people aren't necessarily stupid.'

'I'm sorry. I didn't mean to sound patronising. I just wondered why he'd do that.'

'He said it was one of the world's great civilisations and we could learn a lot from studying its people and ways.' Reece found it a comfort to share his thoughts. 'I could have stayed and tried for a job in the south, I suppose. But what sort of job would I have got? They've no cotton mills there, so probably work as a labourer. You can't build a decent future on the wages you get from that. I need something to offer Cassandra. She's a wonderful woman, with a fine mind like her father's.'

Francis laughed. 'I've never before heard of a man admiring a fine mind in a young woman.'

'I was married to a stupid woman once, and though I was fond of poor Nan, who was the kindest soul on earth, it was tedious at times living with her. With Cassandra, there's never a dull moment. Once I'm sure I can earn a living in Australia, I'm sending for her. And her sisters too, if she won't leave them. I'll do whatever it takes to make a life with her.'

When Francis left him, Reece went to chat to some of the men who were in his mess. They had all been assigned to groups for their daily life. He was in charge of provisioning his own mess of eight single men. He had to draw the weekly food rations for them all, after which they ate together. And he had to cook the extra food allowances each group got as best he could under the watchful eye of the cook, who did the main meals only. Some of the men grumbled about having to do that, but Reece quite enjoyed the novelty of what was usually a woman's job.

Those not assigned to cooking had to clean their bunks and the space around them, airing bedding regularly. There were strict rules about cleanliness on board ship.

He was lucky in his group. They were all young and friendly, and none was a trouble-maker.

To pass the rest of the time, there were reading groups set up, a class in astronomy, which taught them to recognise the different stars in the southern hemisphere, and lessons on agriculture in Western Australia, offered by a farmer returning after a visit to his relatives in England.

The latter was one of the rare classes which both emigrants and cabin passengers were allowed to attend, because the farmer, James Havercock, wasn't in the least snobbish about a man's background. Francis was the only cabin passenger who continued to attend, however. The others dropped out when they found that James wanted them to work with his animals to learn the practicalities. Some of the poor beasts were penned below and were very unhappy about that, while the smaller ones were in crates on deck.

What sort of farmer didn't want to get his hands dirty? Reece wondered. Did these gentlemen think the work did itself? Didn't they realise that skilled labour was in short supply in the colony? He'd learned that now, knew his own worth and realised that Francis was lucky to have him for two years.

Like him, several of the emigrants from steerage went to every talk on farming. And some of the ways they learned to do things were different from in England. But when Reece asked the farmer about cheese making, the man laughed, said he didn't bother with that, hadn't the time or the skill. Folk didn't eat a lot of cheese when there was meat to be had so easily.

That made Reece thoughtful. He'd helped his cousin make cheese and it wasn't all that difficult. Maybe that was something he could do later to make money.

As people got to know one another better, he found out that most of the passengers had relatives or acquaintances who had sponsored them, because you had to have permission to settle in the colony of Western Australia. They thought he'd be allowed to sponsor Cassandra if she was coming out to marry him.

Some men were relatives of expirees who had been transported for various crimes, had served their time and either gained a ticket of leave or a conditional pardon. As long as they didn't re-offend, they could work for wages or set themselves up in business, according to their backgrounds. And if they could afford the fares, could send for their families.

To add to the complications of life in Australia, it seemed respectable people didn't associate with ticket of leave men and their families socially, but then the gentry wouldn't associate with Reece socially, either. As one young Irishman said, as long as he, his mother and two sisters were able to be with his father again, they wouldn't care about what anyone else thought of them.

One moonlit night, Reece talked about Cassandra to this man, because Patrick knew what it was like to be separated from someone you loved, even though a father wasn't the same as the woman you wanted to marry.

'You should definitely send for her,' his new friend advised. 'Don't wait. Do it as soon as you can afford to pay her fare. If she loves you as you love her, she'll not mind facing hardships at your side.'

As the voyage progressed, the cool weather of the English Channel and the Bay of Biscay gave way to the heat of the Tropics and then to cooler weather again. As they drew closer to their destination, Reece waited impatiently to arrive and get on with things.

In June the sisters could all tell that their father was failing fast and wept together about this, but not where he could overhear them.

One evening Edwin lay back on his bed and gestured to Cassandra to take away the bowl, from which he'd had only a few spoonfuls.

She blinked away the tears she couldn't hold back as she put it down, hoping he'd not noticed. But he had, of course.

'Don't cry, lass.'

'How can I help it, Dad? I don't want you to leave us.'

'We all die, love. No one can avoid that.'

She didn't trust her voice and tried in vain to hold back the sobs.

'How many times have I told you not to worrit about things you can't alter?' he chided in a fond tone.

That made her smile fleetingly. 'More times than I can remember.'

'It's my time to die – I feel that. And if it wasn't for leaving you girls – well, I'd be glad to go. This is no sort of life for anyone, lying in bed day after day, useless to myself and to you. I've missed your mother, shall be glad to see her again. I've done my best, my very best, to live a good life – and to look after those I love, so I doubt I'll be going to hell.'

He stared into the distance as if he saw things Cassie didn't. He'd been doing this often during the last few days and he looked so peaceful she sat quietly, not wanting to disturb his dreams. Gradually the tears dried on her cheeks and when he reached out for her, she placed her hand in his.

'I've spoken to my brother and Joseph has promised he'll not let you girls want, my dear one.'

'That's kind of him.' She looked down at their clasped hands, both thin, the long, elegant bones showing clearly.

'Cassandra . . .'

'Yes, Dad.'

'Remember how happy you were when they started fighting to free the slaves in America? How hopeful for those poor souls?'

'Yes.'

'Well, this war's achieved that, so it's not all been bad. Now you must wait just a little longer for the fighting to end. You've been so brave . . . haven't complained. I'm proud of you . . . proud of the others in Lancashire, too.'

Another silence, then, 'And I want to thank you for all you've done to help me since your mother died. You looked after your sisters better than anyone could have expected, young as you were – though at the expense of your own happiness, I fear.'

'I love them. I don't regret the choices I made.'

'I'm glad to see such love between my children. But now – go and find your own happiness if you get the chance. You've earned it. Reece is a good man. I trust him to be a fitting helpmeet for you.'

'If he sends for me, I'll go.' She didn't dare let herself hope for too much, though she doubted her feelings for Reece would ever change. Life had a way of turning your plans upside down.

Joseph continued to worry about his wife and to be wary of her. She'd begun muttering to herself when she thought she was on her own, often stared at him blankly when he spoke to her, as if she didn't understand what he was saying. Then she'd jerk to attention and ask him to repeat what he'd said.

When others were around, Isabel was much more careful, though, speaking softly and flattering the women she called her friends. She still visited them regularly and picked up all the gossip. She must have eavesdropped on what was said in the shop as well, because she seemed aware of everything that was going on in the town.

'It won't be long before your stupid brother dies,' she said one evening, beaming at him as if this was good news.

Joseph clamped his lips together and ignored the remark,

determined not to let her provoke him. He turned the page of his newspaper, though he hadn't taken in a word.

She ripped it from his grasp, tearing it to shreds and laughing shrilly as she did so. 'When I speak, I expect you to listen to me. I bought you with this shop –' she waved one hand in a wide gesture, '– and you must pay the agreed price, Joseph Blake, which was to abandon your family. You must and shall pay the price.'

'I've paid too dearly already.'

'So have I. And am still paying. Do you think I don't know about the food you send them, food paid for with *my* money? I've let you do it, let my friends think I approve. But I don't! It's stealing from me.'

'You'd see them starve? My sick brother too?'

'I'd laugh as I watched them starve to death. Laugh, I tell you.'

As abruptly as she'd started ranting, she sat down, picked up some needlework and gazed down at it. But she didn't set a stitch, merely stared at it fixedly for the next hour.

And though he cleared up the fragments of newspaper, picked up a book and turned its pages now and then, he had no idea of what he'd read.

Things had reached an impasse between them, he decided. That was the word. One day something would happen to break it – but who would be the winner, himself or his wife, he couldn't tell. She was cunning as well as vicious.

And he was very tired of dealing with her.

8

In July the *Eena* arrived at Fremantle, which the steward said was the port for Perth, the capital of Western Australia, which lay a few miles up the river Swan. Reece could smell the land long before they reached it. The livestock must also have realised something was different because cocks began to crow, sheep to bleat and cattle to low. This all added to the sense of excitement rising in him.

The first land to come into view was a low-lying island called Rottnest, seen first as a smudge on the horizon.

'Rat's nest, that means in Dutch,' one passenger said.

Reece couldn't hold back a wry smile. The man had been showing off his knowledge throughout the voyage till people were sick of him.

'There are animals on that island that look like rats, but they're not. They've got pouches to carry their young, like kangaroos. Quokkas, they're called.'

'I don't believe him,' another passenger muttered. 'Who'd call an animal by such a stupid-sounding name?'

Reece stayed near the boaster, wondering if all he said was true.

To the passengers' surprise there wasn't a proper harbour at Fremantle and because of a sand bar across the Swan River, the ship dropped anchor in Gage Roads. And there it rested opposite the town, which looked more like a child's drawing to Reece than a proper town. Houses were dotted here and there as if at random. The largest building to be seen was the prison, a long white building on a hilltop, though it was only a low hill not even as high as the moors back in Lancashire. In fact, there was nothing grand or beautiful about the scenery and he couldn't help feeling disappointed. When you came so far, you expected . . . more than this, something exotic – special.

To add to their disappointment, the ordinary passengers were unable to disembark until the following day and could only crowd at the rail, staring longingly at the land and speculating about what they saw.

Because he was there as a servant of the Southerhams, Reece was one of the earliest of the emigrants to leave the ship. Francis's cousin Paul had come to meet them and he shook hands with Reece as well as his relatives, which was a surprise. A gentleman wouldn't do that in England.

They went for a short walk to get used to being on land again. At first it felt as if the ground were still moving beneath them like the deck of a ship, and Livia clung to her husband's arm, laughing at herself. But that sensation gradually wore off.

A short thoroughfare led up from the water to the main street, where there were a few handsome houses set cheek by jowl with others of a meaner appearance.

'Most of the bigger houses belong to the government,' Paul Southerham explained. 'Or to the few men who've made fortunes here or brought money out to the colony. Our own house isn't nearly as grand as these, I'm afraid. It's only rented, though fortunately there is a spare bedroom for you and Livia.' He turned to Reece. 'There's a small room at the end of the veranda, which I hope you'll find comfortable.'

There were a few shops, but Reece noticed Paul called them 'stores'. Further on they stopped for a moment to study a church, situated where two streets divided. The building wasn't at all beautiful but was bigger than he'd have expected for such a small town.

'The other church is Roman Catholic.' Paul turned up his nose in scorn even as he pointed it out.

Reece hid a smile. Even here, it seemed, people had to stay separate for their religious observances, though they were worshipping the same god.

Fremantle, he decided, looked unfinished more than anything, with unpaved footpaths and streets that had houses here and there, as if waiting for the gaps to be filled in by other buildings.

They strolled back to the Swan River and boarded a small paddle steamer which took them up to Perth, some fourteen miles away by water. The river widened out almost immediately and there were some fine vistas of forested land and then some even wider reaches of water, which could have held a large fleet of ships. This scenery was a pleasure to look at.

Reece left the Southerhams to themselves and got chatting to a man who lived in the Colony. He found out that Perth lay on the north bank of the river and beyond it, further up the river, was a small town called Guildford.

As they approached the city, he saw it was most attractively situated. It contained some large buildings and when he asked about the most imposing of these, he found it was the new Roman Catholic cathedral. He was delighted to have fig trees pointed out to him, as large as the horse chestnuts he'd obtained conkers from as a lad. Some shrubs full of pink blossoms were oleanders.

'You get flowers everywhere in the spring,' his companion told him. 'Just wait till you see it then. There's nowhere as beautiful. Look! That's a flock of white-tailed black cockatoos.'

A shrieking cloud of the parrot-like birds wheeled and dived around some trees and then disappeared, sounding as if they were squabbling.

Even the air tasted different here, fresh and untainted by anything other than the occasional drift of woodsmoke. Reece remembered the sooty air of Outham and thought of Cassandra, still breathing that air. What was she doing now? Sleeping probably. It'd be night in Lancashire.

The rest of the capital city seemed little more than a higgledy-piggledy collection of buildings. The street leading up from the river was covered with soft sand, making walking difficult, especially for the ladies of the party.

'You'll grow used to it,' Paul said. 'It's very sandy here but at least that helps the winter rain drain away quickly. Our home is a little out of town and it's getting late, so I've taken rooms at a hotel for tonight.'

'It'll be wonderful to sleep in a proper bed again,' Livia said feelingly. 'Those bunks on the ship were dreadfully narrow.'

Reece supposed he was lucky that they remembered to include him in their conversations from time to time, but he was very conscious that he was merely a servant.

He felt full of energy – ready to go out and make his own life, not help another man make his.

When they got to the hotel, it looked to Reece more like a house, and not a particularly large one, either, though it had a sign outside saying it was a hotel. There was no comfort of a proper bed for him. He found himself relegated to a dormitory in a shed at the rear. Here were men on their own, both gentlemen and servants, to his surprise.

The roof and walls of the shed were made of tin, rusty in patches. But it was waterproof at least, which was a good thing, because that evening the rain poured down heavily, bouncing up a foot off the ground and misting the world with grey.

'Does it always rain so hard?' he asked the man occupying the next bunk.

'Not always. Don't worry. It doesn't usually go on for long, so when it pours down this heavily, just find some cover and wait for it to pass.'

Reece went to bed early because he wasn't the sort to go out drinking. He found it hard to get to sleep and lay thinking about his situation. He'd promised Francis two years' work of whatever sort was needed in return for his passage being paid. At least he'd had the sense to include the passage time in that, but still, only three months had passed. It was very frustrating to be tied to another man like this, especially one who didn't seem very practical, for all his fine words.

Stretching his tired body, Reece grimaced as his head hit the wall at the end of his hard bed. When he turned over carelessly a short time later, he nearly fell out of the narrow bunk. The rain sounded to have stopped now, but the air was still heavy with moisture.

As soon as the Southerhams found a home and he had a proper address, he'd write to Cassandra and tell her all his news. He'd kept a diary of sorts on the ship, just occasional jottings, but it had helped pass the time, and it'd provide him with a record of what had happened. He might even copy some of it out for her.

But it would take so long to communicate. Three months at least to send a letter to England once a ship departed, another three months to get a reply. For the umpteenth time he asked himself why he'd been so stupid as to leave her.

Was Edwin Blake still alive? He didn't think it likely. But surely the girls' uncle would look after them if their father died? Perhaps if Cassandra agreed to marry Reece, Joseph would lend his nieces the money for their fares and they could all come out here. That would make her happier, he was sure. Her sisters would soon find husbands. Already, from the men's talk in this bunkhouse, Reece had found out how short they were of women in this colony. One woman to every ten men, someone said, if you counted the convicts.

They even brought women out to Western Australia on what were jokingly referred to as 'bride ships'. Imagine that.

He was just starting to feel drowsy when he heard voices outside in the back garden. He'd have ignored them, but came fully awake when he realised it was Francis and Paul Southerham – and they were arguing.

Should he find out what it was about? It was wrong to eavesdrop, but he was on his own in Australia with only his wits to rely on, so he rolled out of the bunk. Creeping across the dirt floor to the door, he opened it quietly and slipped outside on to the rough planks of the veranda, sitting on a bench in one corner, hidden behind a shrub, to listen to what the two gentlemen were saying as they stood nearby on the veranda of the main hotel.

Francis saw his wife up to bed, making the excuse that he wanted a breath of fresh air before he retired. He contained his anger until he and his cousin Paul were outside, standing at the end of the back veranda of the hotel. Then the words would no longer be held back.

'You lied to us about Western Australia!'

'What do you mean?'

'You know damned well what I mean.'

Paul shoved his hands deep into his trouser pockets and kicked out at a black beetle creeping past, missing it but sending it scurrying into a crevice. 'This colony will be a thriving place one day, I'm sure.'

'Well, it isn't thriving now! I don't even call this a city. How many people are there in Western Australia?'

Silence, then, 'About 15,000 if you include the convicts.'

'Dear God! Less than a tenth of the population of Manchester.'

'The colony will grow, and you and I with it. The convicts have made a big difference to the place, more than doubled the population. I don't know why they didn't send convicts to the west from the start, as they did to Sydney.'

'They've stopped sending out convicts to the other parts of Australia now, so it can't be that much of a good thing. From what I've learned talking to others, this colony in the west seems to be behind the times in every way. And there are *as many* convicts as free settlers, if what that man was saying was correct! Don't you worry about the danger such men may represent?'

'Many of them are political prisoners, Irish, and quite respectable, though of course no one deals with them *socially*.'

'You still haven't said why you lied to me and dragged me out to this god-forsaken place. How can I make my way in the world here? The Swan River Colony doesn't look or feel at all prosperous.' He waited, then repeated impatiently, 'Well, why did you do it?'

'Charlotte was pining, but I don't want to go back, don't dare.' Paul patted his chest. 'I've felt so much better since I came here. That dreadful wheezing has stopped and I'm getting stronger all the time.'

'So you brought my wife and me out for company, not caring whether it would be for our own good or not? You always were a selfish devil. I don't know why I thought you'd have changed.'

'You can make good money here if you work hard . . . if you get allotted good land. And I've a friend who'll advise you about that.'

'You'd better be right about it, because unlike you, I can't afford to go back now. I need a warmer climate for my health and besides, I'm not only a younger son with nothing to go back to, but I've upset my parents by insisting on coming here. My father gave me some money but says that's it. He'll not give me any more to waste, and I'm to consider that my inheritance.' He breathed in deeply. 'I'd have gone to Sydney or Canada but for you. Damn you, Paul!'

Reece saw Francis turn round and walk inside without a word of farewell. The other man stood there, shoulders slumped, staring down at the ground with his hands in his trouser pockets. Then it began to rain again, a light spatter, which grew steadily heavier. Paul followed his cousin back inside.

Reece stayed out on the veranda of the hut, watching in the intermittent moonlight as the slashing rain refilled the puddles. It wasn't really cold, not like an English winter. But he felt a chill inside himself at what he'd heard. It wasn't Francis alone who'd been fooled. Reece too would suffer for Paul Southerham's selfishness.

The shower only lasted a few minutes and he watched in mild surprise as the water drained away quickly through the sandy soil. How did you farm that sort of soil? he wondered. Mere sand couldn't possibly be fertile enough to grow crops. It'd be like planting vegetables on a beach.

Even after he'd returned to his hard, narrow bed, he lay awake for some time worrying about his own future. Clearly the information he'd found about Australia didn't necessarily apply to this colony on the western side of the country.

Surely there would be opportunities for a hard-working man to make a decent life for himself even here, though? People still needed feeding, after all.

He'd find some way to succeed, he vowed grimly, if he had to work every hour of the day and half the night too. If he didn't, he'd not *deserve* Cassandra's love.

But what he'd overheard meant he didn't dare send for her straight away, not till he was certain he'd have a future to offer her.

Men didn't cry, but he could feel moisture on his cheeks.

What a mess he'd made of things!

Edwin died on a warm day in late August, having lived much longer than any of them had expected. It seemed afterwards as if he'd waited for them to come home from the sewing classes that day before he let go of life, because when he heard the front door open, he turned to Maia and said in a thread of a voice, 'Good. Fetch your sisters to me.'

She looked at him anxiously, but he was staring into space with a faint smile and didn't appear distressed in any way, so she did as he'd asked.

Only when the four of them were gathered around his bed did he seem to bring the room into focus again.

'There you are. I was just telling your mother I was waiting to say goodbye to you before I joined her. Give me a kiss, my dears.'

One by one they bent to kiss his cheek, each with eyes brimming with tears.

'Such lovely daughters, aren't they, Catherine?' He looked up at the empty air beside him. 'We can be proud of them.'

And he was gone – so quickly, so quietly, it was a minute or two before they realised.

They wept a little, then Cassandra pulled herself together. 'We can't stand here crying. We have things to do, must see him laid to rest properly.'

'I hate to see him go to a pauper's grave, no stone to mark his resting place,' Pandora said.

'We could ask our uncle for help,' Xanthe suggested. 'I'll go and do it if you like. He always speaks kindly to us.'

Cassandra frowned, wondering whether to use some of the money Mrs Southerham had given her to pay for a modest funeral. But that felt wrong, somehow, like stealing. It hadn't been given to her for her father's burial, but for her own use if she was ever in dire need, so she'd hidden it and resisted the temptation to dip into it. For some reason she didn't understand, she hadn't even told her sisters about it. 'I'll go with you.'

Once again they went to the shop, entering it openly and waiting till their uncle had finished serving a customer before they moved forward.

'I'll see to these young ladies,' he told the shorter of the two young men who served there and was hovering nearby, staring avidly at Pandora. Joseph raised his voice so that everyone in the shop could hear. 'Good evening, my dear nieces, how can I help you?' But his smile faded as they came closer and he saw their reddened eyes.

'Father died today,' Cassandra said. 'I thought you'd like to know.'

Joseph closed his eyes for a minute, pain on his face, then said, 'Come through to the back.' Opening the flap in the counter, he ushered them into the same storeroom as before.

With a quick gesture of the head he dismissed the lad who was weighing out sugar and putting it into neat cones of blue paper.

When the door had closed, Joseph asked, 'How did it happen?'

'Very peacefully.' Cassandra explained, then hesitated as she tried to find the words to ask the favour they needed.

He didn't wait for her to ask, but said immediately, 'I'll pay for the funeral, of course. That's what you came to ask, isn't it?'

'Yes.'

'It'll be my pleasure to do this last thing for him. I couldn't bear Edwin to lie in an unmarked pauper's grave. I'll just get my hat and then we'll go round to Studdard's.'

'Dad wouldn't expect such an expensive funeral!' Cassandra exclaimed. Studdard's dealt with the better class of people, not operatives' families.

'No, but it'll please me to send my brother off in comfort. And I shall, of course, pay for a headstone. You must decide what you want written on it.'

They walked through the streets, one on each arm of their uncle, ignoring the surprised glances they got.

From the window above the shop, Isabel watched them go, clenched fists resting on the windowsill. She'd seen them come into the shop, because she watched all the comings and goings in the street below. Furious that *those creatures* would dare to come here again, she'd crept down the stairs to listen to what they were saying.

It was the signal she'd been waiting for. Time to take action.

She rejoiced to think that the old fool was dead, clasping her hands together and twirling round in joy. She ran lightly down the stairs to tell Dot to make her a pot of tea and send up some cake, because she was suddenly hungry. Still filled with joy, she twirled round again as she reached the bottom of the stairs, nearly bumping into the shop lad, who had come out of the packing room and was staring at her in amazement. 'Get out of my sight, you fool!' she snapped and gave him a shove. When he tripped over a box and fell, she kicked him a couple of times and laughed as he scrambled away.

She walked slowly back up to their quarters, forgetting the pot of tea, thinking how best to get rid of *those creatures*, drive them right out of the town. She had to tread carefully, though, didn't want Joseph telling the doctor any more lies about her.

It was her husband who had run mad, not her. Fancy a leading shopkeeper associating with females who were not only paupers but immoral. She remembered the churchyard, how the oldest one had pressed herself against a man like the wanton she was. No doubt the others were as bad.

Isabel knew she had a duty to her dear parents to make sure Joseph did nothing to bring shame to their name. She was the only surviving Horton, after all. And the shop should still be called Horton's Emporium. He'd had no right to change its name, no right at all.

She'd change it back once she was in charge. She'd change a lot of things. She wasn't sure how she'd manage to gain control, but she'd find a way.

She'd go and talk to the man and woman who'd helped her before. Rough creatures, but useful.

The four sisters dyed their clothes black so that they could be turned out as decently as possible to farewell their father. But their shabby clothes looked even shabbier after they'd been dyed.

On the evening before the funeral there was a knock on the front door.

Pandora went to open it and found the taller assistant from her uncle's shop, together with the young lad. Both had large bundles in their hands.

'Miss Blake?' the older one asked.

'Yes.'

'These are for you and your sisters.'

'But we didn't order anything. We can't afford—'

'They're from your uncle. And I'm sorry about your father.' He thrust his bundle into her arms. His companion deposited the other one on the floor inside the door.

'Good night, miss.'

She watched them stroll down the street, chatting to one another. The taller man had a kind face. She'd noticed him before when she went to the shop. With a sigh, she shut the door and hurried into the kitchen.

When they opened the parcels, they found skirts, bodices and jackets in black, together with simple black bonnets, each with wide black ribbons.

Maia found an envelope and opened it. 'Please accept these from me.' It was signed by their uncle.

In spite of their grief, they were thrilled with the clothes, which were plain enough, without the wide skirts necessary for crinolines, but better than anything they'd ever owned before.

'I wonder if *she* knows about these,' Xanthe said, craning her neck in an effort to see how she looked in the broken piece of mirror which was all they had left to check their appearance in.

'I hope she doesn't.' Cassandra shuddered and felt suddenly apprehensive. Her aunt would be furious, she was sure. And she wondered what people would say about them wearing such fine clothing. She dreaded to think what the ladies who organised the relief work would think.

Then she put up her chin defiantly. It didn't matter what people said. This was to honour their father.

The funeral of Edwin Blake caused a lot of talk, not only because it was done in such style, but because the people who had known and respected him attended en masse. Some were in ragged clothing, some in decent garb. His former employer was there as well as his former workmates. No one could remember such a turn-out for a mere operative.

The Minister at his chapel delivered a touching eulogy. He spoke of Edwin's high intelligence and love of all things Greek. He finished with a few words in Greek, his voice breaking on the final phrase.

Others stood up in the church to say how Edwin had helped them, how highly they'd thought of him.

Sitting at the front with his nieces, Joseph listened in amazement. How well liked his brother had been! How many people he'd helped in his modest way! Shame filled

Joseph that he'd stayed estranged for so many years and his determination to look after his nieces grew stronger by the minute.

Isabel didn't attend the funeral, of course. He'd have stopped her if she'd tried, but she didn't. She dressed in her brightest colours that day, hummed cheerful tunes as he got ready, and kept saying what a lovely morning it was and how glad she was to be alive.

He made no comment. She'd find out what he intended soon enough.

After the funeral, he saw his nieces home and when they got there, he accepted an invitation to share a cup of tea with them.

'What are you going to do now?'

'I don't know,' Cassandra said. 'We're still thinking about that.'

'I have a cottage on the north side of the park, a very comfortable dwelling. I wondered if you'd like to live there. I'd not charge you rent and I'd help you with the food.' When they said nothing, he added, 'I promised your father I'd look after you and I know that would set his mind at rest. I really *want* to do something to help you, make your lives easier.'

'What about your wife?' Cassandra asked. 'Won't that upset her even more?'

He shrugged. 'Everything upsets her these days. I'm quite sure she's insane, but I can't prove it because she's very cunning. Beware of her, accept nothing from her hands. Even I keep my bedroom door locked at night.'

They looked at him in shock, then Maia went across to kiss him on the cheek. 'You look so sad sometimes,

Uncle Joseph. But you've got us now. We'll be happy to live in your cottage and see you as often as we can.'

One by one they went to kiss him.

He could feel their kisses on his cheeks as he walked home, wished he'd had a child of his own to love. But would any child of his wife's have been lovable? He doubted it, so perhaps it was for the best that their baby hadn't survived. The Lord worked in mysterious ways.

Of course Isabel was waiting for him at home, foot tapping, cheeks flying red signals of anger. 'Is he got rid of now?'

'We've buried my brother, if that's what you mean.'

'Good riddance. Perhaps now you can attend to the shop and pay *me* some attention. You've been neglecting me lately.'

He was upset enough to tell her the truth. 'I wish I need never see you again!'

She froze then her face seemed to set in even grimmer lines. 'I'll make you sorry you said that.'

'I can't be sorrier than I am now. And by the way, the girls are moving into Brook Cottage in a few days' time.'

'*What?*'

'I shan't be charging them rent and I'll help them in any way I can from now on. You're wrong about them, so wrong. They're fine, decent young women.'

She threw back her head and laughed, on and on, till the shrill sound drove him down to the shop.

He passed Dot on the stairs and stopped her to say, 'I'd wait before going up, if I were you.'

She nodded and went back down again.

It seemed as if the sound of Isabel's laughter echoed

around him for days, because she seemed very happy about something, he had no idea what. And she was talking to herself more and more. He'd never seen her as bad as this before and he knew Dot had noticed her mistress's increasing strangeness too.

Even the people working for him in the shop had noticed that something was very wrong, he could tell. But she'd not given them incontrovertible proof that she was mad. She was too cunning for that. She still went to tea with her friends and invited them to tea with her, behaving perfectly normally then.

He didn't think he could go on like this for much longer.

In early September, a group of solemn gentlemen came to Outham, calling on the Vicar, who summoned the clerics of the other denominations to a meeting in the church hall.

What was said there was kept a secret, but it sent the Vicar's wife whispering to her friend Isabel, who stared at her in delight.

'Would you help me?' she begged. 'My dearest Sylvia, would you help me take advantage of this opportunity to get rid of those creatures? I feel so weighed down by the humiliation of seeing them flaunting themselves around the town. I'm constantly worrying what they'll do next. And now Joseph is going to move them into our cottage near the park. Can you believe that? They'll be spreading their poison among decent people.'

'Near the park? Why, they'll be just round the corner from us if they live there! Creatures like that! You can certainly count on my help. I'll make sure my husband does whatever is necessary to get rid of them. It'll take a week or two to arrange, though.'

'That's all right. There are things I need to do first to persuade them to leave.'

When the Vicar's wife had left, Isabel sat and thought for a while, then put on her bonnet. She walked out through the shop, saying airily as she passed her husband, 'I need some fresh air.'

Joseph didn't protest, even though it looked like rain. He watched her leave, a little worried by the smug smile that curved her lips slightly, the air of suppressed triumph that hung about her. Something had changed since this morning, he could tell.

What was she plotting now? He'd have to keep a careful watch on her, for his nieces' sake.

Isabel went to find the woman she'd contacted before, a woman of the streets who'd do anything for money. She made sure no one was nearby who knew her before she entered the noisome narrow alley behind the main street.

When the doorman let her into the house and took her up to his mistress, she asked to see the man she'd seen before.

The woman frowned. 'Why?'

'None of your business.'

When the man was found, Isabel sent the woman away before she told him what she wanted doing.

'It'll cost you more than the other.'

'I'm prepared to pay generously.'

'Come back tomorrow with fifty pounds. I'll make arrangements once I've seen the money.'

Isabel was glad to leave *that house*, turning up her nose at the smell in the alley behind it. She hurried past lounging figures at corners and on doorsteps, her veil pulled down over the front of her bonnet.

It was *his* fault she'd had to come here, but soon she would be free of him, free of them all.

But it had to be done right. Not only did *he* need dealing with, but those nieces of his had to be punished, especially the oldest one, who was the most impudent and immoral of them all.

She smiled. She'd just arranged a very fitting punishment.

The four sisters went to inspect Brook Cottage and were delighted with it. There were only two small bedrooms, but there was also an attic, one of the old handloom weavers' rooms, with a long row of small windows to front and rear to give more light for weaving. They decided Cassandra should have this for her bedroom and the twins would share the larger of the two bedrooms.

Their uncle watched them exploring the house, a fond smile on his face. It made him look like their father, which both hurt and yet brought him closer.

'When shall I send a cart to move your things?' he asked.

'As soon as you like,' Cassandra said. 'One of the families who's renting a room from us is going to take over renting our house. They can manage if people move into our rooms.' She looked at him sadly. 'We've had to sell most of our furniture, so there's not a lot to move.'

'I'll buy you more. I can't have my nieces going short, can I?'

It was as if he felt he must buy their affection, Cassandra thought. She must show him that wasn't necessary.

The next day two men arrived with a cart and two empty wooden tea chests containing straw. They carried out the battered furniture, the pitifully ragged bundles of bedding and clothes, while the sisters filled the tea chests with their remaining crockery and cooking ware, packed in straw.

Within the hour they'd left the house they'd lived in all their lives.

'It feels strange to have left,' Maia said as they walked across town behind the cart.

Pandora was almost dancing along, her face alight. 'It'll be wonderful living so close to the park! Isn't our uncle a lovely man?'

'Yes. But he always looks sad,' Maia added.

'Who wouldn't look sad with a wife like that?'

'You don't think she'll . . . try to hurt us? She frightens me, she looks so fierce.'

'What can she do? We don't even go to the sewing classes at her church any more, and Mrs Rainey and the ladies from our own chapel know we're not immoral.'

Then there was no time for chatting as they began to set the new house to rights. It looked quite bare, but they didn't let that upset them. They were making a new start here and knew their father would be happy to see it.

★

Joseph got ready to go out at nine o'clock that evening, having closed the shop a little early. He was looking forward to a walk across town because it'd been a fine day and the late evening was still warm.

As he put on his hat and coat, his wife came to bar his way.

'I know where you're going,' she said. 'To see those whores.'

'My nieces are not whores.'

'I've *seen* one of them with a man in the church-yard.'

He didn't even bother to answer, but tried to push past her.

She clung to his arm. 'I'm giving you one last chance. I'm your wife. You should stay with me, not go to them. I beg you, Joseph, don't go.'

He had to fight to get past her.

Isabel stood there for a moment or two, panting, then straightened her clothing, muttering, 'It's his own fault.' Before she went up to their living quarters, she told the maid to go to bed.

Dot was so relieved to be given an early night, she didn't question this, but nodded and began to bank the kitchen fire. 'What about the master?'

'Oh, he can let himself in. He has a key. I'm not waiting up for him. I'm exhausted.'

Impatiently Isabel waited for the girl to go to bed. It seemed to take a long time for Dot to finish her tasks and yawn her way upstairs.

Then Isabel sat down. She didn't try to embroider or read, just sat and waited, feeling very peaceful.

She'd tried to stop him. Whatever happened now was his own fault, not hers.

As Joseph was passing the park, two men burst out of the bushes and attacked him with cudgels and knives. He yelled for help, then felt a sharp pain in his chest and looked down to see a knife hilt protruding.

'He's done for,' one of the men said and pulled the knife out.

The pain was excruciating but Joseph couldn't even cry out as he fell to the ground.

'Easiest money I ever earned,' the other man said as they walked away.

Joseph lay there, unable to move. The pain had gone now and he felt as if he was floating. He was quite sure his wife had arranged this attack and suddenly it came to him that he'd been mortally wounded.

His greatest regret was that he wouldn't be there to help his nieces. But he'd still kept his promise to his brother, as Isabel would find out. He prayed she wouldn't harm them. If there was a God up above, surely he'd look after those fine girls?

Blood seeped out, feeling warm on the fingers Joseph had pressed instinctively to his chest. Slowly the night grew darker, much darker . . .

9

When her husband hadn't returned by midnight, Isabel knew it was done. Calmly she got undressed and went to bed. She slept soundly and woke early to a chorus of birdsong from the nearby park, smiling at what the day would bring. Freedom, that's what. She'd be free to do anything she liked from now on.

She rang for the maid and when Dot brought up the cup of tea and the ewer of hot water, Isabel sipped the warm sweet liquid in a leisurely way before getting dressed.

When she went down to the kitchen, she asked casually, 'Has my husband gone down to the shop already?'

'No, ma'am. He hasn't even rung for his tea and hot water yet.'

Isabel looked at the clock. Time to start taking action. 'That's strange. He's usually up by this time. Go up and peep into his room, make sure he's all right.'

'But he always locks the door.'

'Then knock on it till he answers, you fool.'

Dot clattered up the back stairs. She was down again within the minute, eyes wide with astonishment. 'The door wasn't locked, ma'am. The master isn't there and his bed hasn't been slept in.'

'*What?*'

Isabel hurried upstairs, not complaining when the young maid crept up after her. She walked into her husband's bedroom and checked it. The bed was untouched. He'd definitely not returned.

'Where can he be?' She waited. What a stupid fool that girl was! Why didn't she suggest sending for the police? Impatient to get it done, Isabel clapped one hand to her head and feigned a stagger. 'I don't know what to do. I feel faint.'

'Let me help you into the parlour, ma'am.'

When she was sitting there with the smelling salts and a handkerchief pressed to her face to hide the smile that would keep creeping back, Isabel said in a faint voice, 'Go round to the police station. Tell them Mr Blake didn't come home last night. Tell them I'm worried about him. Then call at the Vicar's and ask if Mrs Saunders can come round to see me. Tell the Vicar why. Is that clear?' She made the girl repeat her instructions to be sure.

Only when the back door had slammed did Isabel allow the smile to settle on her face. Just for a few minutes. After all, it was her first day of freedom.

Before the maid came back there was a knocking on the front door of the shop and she tiptoed to the window to peer out. The boy was there and the two young men who served in the shop. She couldn't leave them waiting outside. It'd cause comment and stop customers coming in. She went down and drew back the bolts.

They looked at her in surprise, so she said in a failing voice, 'Mr Blake went out for a walk last night and didn't come back. I've sent for the police. You'd better open the shop and carry on as usual.'

They goggled at her but she didn't stay, pretending to stumble on her way through to the house.

'Do you need any help up the stairs, Mrs Blake?'

It was one of the two young men who worked in the shop. Prebble was quite short, a sharp-faced fellow, and she was never quite sure whether his respectful attitude was genuine, but he'd been working there long enough to know how things were run. If he behaved himself, she'd appoint him manager. The other senior assistant was so tall he towered over her and she didn't like that. Besides, she'd seen Carr being polite to *those girls*. He would pay for that.

'Thank you. I do feel rather faint. I'm so worried about my husband.' She allowed Prebble to help her up the stairs, then sent him down to the shop again, with instructions to behave normally and not say a word to the customers about what had happened.

Feeling very peaceful, she sat waiting for the police to come.

Cassandra and her sisters went to their sewing classes the morning after they'd moved into the cottage, because they didn't want to be more of a burden than was necessary on their uncle. They'd not only continue to earn money by coming here but it would help fill the time. Maia hadn't been to the classes since their father fell ill, but was warmly welcomed back by the Methodist Minister's wife. Mrs Rainey was a wonderful woman, kind to all, well liked by her husband's congregation.

Towards the end of the morning a young man came into the room and went to whisper to the ladies running the class that day. From their shocked faces, it was bad news.

By now, everyone in the room had stopped work.

Mrs Rainey walked along the aisle to where the four sisters were sitting. 'Could you please come outside? I have some bad news for you, I'm afraid.'

They looked at one another in surprise and followed her quietly out.

'Your uncle was attacked and killed near the park last night. His body was found this morning under some bushes.'

Maia burst into tears, the others stood stiff with shock, then Cassandra managed to ask, 'You mean – he was murdered?'

'So the messenger said. Do you want to go to your aunt?'

Cassandra shook her head. 'She'd not want to see us. I don't quite know what to do, Mrs Rainey.'

'Why don't you get something to eat now and go home? It's nearly the end of the class, after all. She may send a message to you there.'

They did as she suggested, walking silently back through the streets, not stopping to talk to anyone, not even speaking to one another.

Inside the house, Pandora began weeping. 'Poor uncle. Just as we were getting to know him.'

'We've no time to weep,' Cassandra said sharply. 'She'll throw us out of here. I'm quite sure of that.'

They all gaped at her.

'I think we'd better pack our things and be ready to leave at a moment's notice.'

'But where would we go?' Xanthe asked.

'I don't know. I think we should ask Mr Rainey for his advice.'

'I'm not going into the poorhouse,' Xanthe said at once.

'We may be able to find a room to rent.'

When Cassandra went up to her bedroom to sort out her few remaining possessions, she looked round regretfully. It was such a lovely bright room. Was nothing ever to go right for them? Her thoughts kept going back to her uncle. He hadn't deserved such a death and she still couldn't understand why anyone would want to kill a kind man like him.

She hoped the police would find the murderer before he attacked anyone else.

She hesitated about whether to pull her money and locket out of its hiding place, but decided to leave them there. They'd be safer than in her pocket, she was sure.

For the rest of the day they waited for a message from their aunt, but it didn't arrive until after nightfall.

A lad knocked on the door and said, 'Mrs Blake wants to see Cassandra. She doesn't want to see the others.'

'Did she give you a note?'

He shook his head.

'When does she want to see me?'

'Right now. She's waiting for you at the shop.' He turned and ran off into the darkness.

Cassandra took her shawl off the hook in the hall.

'You can't go out on your own,' Xanthe said. 'Not after what happened to our uncle.'

'I must follow her instructions in case there's a chance—No, I'm sure she's going to tell us to leave the cottage.'

'Why does she want to see only you?'

'I think she hates me most of all, though I can't understand why.'

'We're coming with you anyway,' Pandora insisted. 'We can wait round the corner from the shop and she'll not see us. But we're not risking you getting murdered like our uncle.'

Cassandra and Pandora were walking ahead of the other two when suddenly, a man called out, 'Get the tallest one.'

Men pounced on them and tried to drag Cassandra away. She and Pandora fought their attackers and the twins came running to their help, screaming at the tops of their voices.

In the mêlée, Maia was knocked unconscious, Pandora was sent flying and Xanthe was punched viciously in the stomach, collapsing on the pavement, fighting for breath. The men quickly dragged Cassandra away, one of them thumping Pandora when she ran back and tried to cling to her sister.

By the time Pandora had stood up and Xanthe had caught her breath, there was no sign of the men . . . or of their sister.

It had happened so quickly, Pandora thought as she stared at the surrounding darkness. She couldn't think what to do, was still shocked by the speed of the attack. The men had clearly been after Cassandra from the start and only one other person had known her sister was going out tonight: their aunt. Had Isabel Blake arranged this? Why?

She heard footsteps and for a moment fear held her motionless. Then she realised that this wasn't more attackers, but people coming to their aid. Soon they were surrounded, explaining what had happened, seeing the shock on their rescuers' faces.

A man immediately offered them shelter in his nearby house. Maia was still unconscious, so had to be carried there.

No one even tried to pursue the attackers, though Pandora begged them to. The men kept assuring her that the police would soon find them, or else the men would let their captive go when they found she had no money.

But Pandora had heard someone say 'Get the tallest one'. She knew this wasn't a random attack, only she couldn't think why they wanted Cassandra.

Maia recovered consciousness but seemed dazed, and all three of them were terrified for their sister.

When the policemen came, they questioned each sister in turn, but dismissed Pandora's idea that the men had set out to capture Cassandra.

'You must be mistaken. Why should anyone want to hurt your sister? No, they saw you and seized their chance,' the sergeant said. 'It's never safe for decent young women to walk out at night, or men either. I'll send my men to search the slum streets. You'd better stay here till we've done it, if that's all right?' He looked at the householder, who nodded.

But the two policemen on night duty didn't find any

sign of Cassandra, nor could they find anyone who had
seen the men carrying her away.

After that even the sergeant couldn't pretend the missing
woman would come back safely.

Isabel sat in her parlour after the shop had closed for the
night, rang for the maid and asked for a tea tray. When
it came she poured herself a cup she didn't really want,
realised some time later that it had gone cold. She tipped
it into the pot in which a plant was struggling to grow.
She hated having plants in the house, but one of her
friends had given this one to her, so she'd let it stay there
for a while. It'd soon die. Plants always died when you
didn't look after them.

At half-past nine she rang for Dot to take away the tea
tray and went to stand by the window. A short time later
a lad walked along the street, picked up a stone and shied
it at a lamppost. That was the signal they'd agreed on.

Smiling, Isabel sat down again. The men had done it,
captured her eldest niece, the one who was the most
immoral of them all. Now they'd be punishing her as she
deserved.

The Bible said that the wages of sin was death, but
that was too easy. Isabel wanted Cassandra to suffer for
a long time to come, suffer as she herself had done, for
years and years, married to a soft-hearted fool, with no
children, no future.

If the other girls did as she wished, she'd not have
them punished in the same way. She'd have to force them
to leave, of course, but they'd do anything to help their
sister, she was sure.

It was wonderful what money could buy. And she'd be in charge of all the money from now on. She'd not have to scrimp and save her pin money to gather enough to pay for the services she needed.

For a moment her thoughts went to Joseph, lying dead at the undertaker's because she'd refused to have his body at home, saying the customers wouldn't like it to lie above the shop.

She kept thinking she saw him, standing in the corner, looking at her in that sad, reproachful way he had. There he was again.

'It's your own fault you're dead!' she told him. 'Go away!' When he didn't, she screamed, 'Go away!' Still, he didn't move from the corner.

She refused to look at him any more, picking up a book and holding it in front of her face.

Downstairs, Dot stopped when she heard the scream. But the bell didn't ring and she didn't go near her mistress if she could help it, so simply got on with her work.

If only she could find another job! She'd leave here tomorrow. But jobs were scarce at a time like this.

At eleven o'clock there was a knock on the house door.

Isabel went to answer it herself, because she'd sent the maid to bed an hour ago.

At the door stood the Vicar, his wife and a policeman. She stared at them, trying to look worried and shocked. 'What's the matter?' She pressed one hand to her chest.

'Could we come inside, my dear lady?' the Vicar asked.

Isabel led the way upstairs, allowed Sylvia to sit beside

her on the sofa and listened as they told her about the attack on her nieces.

Hiding her delight that the others had been hurt in the struggle, she fell into hysterics and had to be helped to bed. Dot was standing at the foot of the attic stairs, staring at them. Could the maid see Joseph too? Was that why the girl kept staring at her?

'Go away!' she yelled, unable to bear the sight of the girl. 'Leave me alone.' When this was all over, she'd get rid of Dot and find an older maid, one who didn't stare at her as if she knew what was going on.

She didn't let the Vicar send for the doctor, just asked for a dose of her calming medicine.

Sylvia insisted on staying the night and when Isabel couldn't persuade her to go away, she tried to sound grateful and told her to use the spare bedroom.

As her bedroom door closed she sighed happily, smiling at the window, its shape illuminated by a nearby gas lamp in the street. She hoped that immoral creature was suffering, that the men were doing what she'd asked them to, that they'd *hurt* her.

Tomorrow she'd tell the other girls they had a week to get out of the house. They weren't *her* nieces, after all.

Only after they'd left town would she bury her husband. She wasn't having *them* at the funeral.

It took her a long time to get to sleep because she kept thinking she saw a man's dark outline at the foot of the bed.

Cassandra fought desperately against her attackers, but there were several of them and they were far stronger than her. They gagged her quickly and efficiently, then tied and blindfolded her. She was carried by two of them, one at her head and one at her feet.

Where were they taking her? Why?

After a while they stopped and she heard a door open. She was sure they were now inside a building. Carrying her down some steps, they dumped her on what felt like a mattress.

Bound and helpless, she could only lie there while the men spoke in low voices nearby. She had heard someone cry, 'Get the tallest one.' Could this be her aunt's doing? Were these men going to murder her? Had her uncle been murdered at his wife's behest?

It was unthinkable. Only . . . it was happening.

Shuddering, terrified, she could only wait to find out what they would do.

Footsteps came towards her and someone fastened her arms to the bed head. He untied her legs and lifted her skirt. She knew then what they intended. When she tried to kick out at him, he slapped her so hard, her head rang with pain.

He didn't say a word the whole time he was raping her, didn't seem to notice or care how much he was hurting her or that tears were running down her cheeks.

When he'd finished he left and she lay there weeping.

Someone else grunted and climbed on to the bed and to her horror, it started all over again.

She thought she'd die of it, but she didn't, could only endure.

When the second man had finished she hoped they'd

release her, but they didn't. They simply left her lying on the bed, humiliated and helpless.

The tears stopped, but the fear didn't go away.

Nor did the men.

The Minister and his wife came to the house where the three remaining sisters had been offered refuge and tried to take them to their home.

'What if Cassandra comes back to the cottage?' Xanthe asked. 'We have to go there and wait for her. She may be hurt.'

'We can't leave you alone there,' Mr Rainey protested. 'Maia is still dizzy. You're both badly bruised. What if you're attacked again?'

But they refused to go anywhere else, walking through the dark streets with the Minister, his wife and a policeman. The town was quiet. They met no one. It was as if the darkness had swallowed up their sister, and everyone else too.

'We'll come round first thing in the morning,' Mr Rainey said. 'Don't open the door to anyone but the police or me.'

When they were alone, the sisters went to sit in the kitchen, waiting for they knew not what.

The clock ticked away a long, slow hour, and then another, but Cassandra didn't come back.

'We should get some sleep,' Pandora said at last. 'Maia, you look as if you're about to collapse.'

'We can't just – go to bed. We must be here for when she comes back.'

'I'll stay up and keep watch. I may doze but I'll hear if anyone knocks.'

But no one did. The house remained quiet until morning brought people into the streets again. Before the Cotton Famine, the mill hooters would have woken everyone and the streets would have been full of hurrying footsteps. It was quieter now, far too quiet at the cottage.

As they were preparing breakfast, Maia burst into tears suddenly.

'Stop that!' Pandora said as she continued to sob. 'What good will it do to cry?'

But her own eyes kept filling with tears. Something terrible had happened to Cassandra, she knew it.

The morning following the attack, the police sergeant went to see Isabel to talk about her nieces again. Her friend Sylvia was still there to support her.

Isabel looked at the sergeant in feigned outrage. 'You mean my husband's nieces were walking the streets after dark?'

'They said you'd asked Cassandra to come and see you.'

'*After dark?* My husband was *killed* walking after dark. Do you think I'd have asked any decent young woman to risk being attacked?'

'But – they all said a lad came to the door with a message from you.'

'Where is it? Show me the note?'

'There was no note, he just passed on a verbal message.'

She drew herself up. 'I did not send a message. Not after my dear Joseph—' She broke off, burying her face, and her smile, in her hands.

'Really, Sergeant, have you no consideration?' Sylvia said.

'I'd better leave. I'm sorry to have upset you, Mrs Blake.'

After he'd gone, she sat dry-eyed but pretended to shed a few tears, then allowed her friend to coax out of her what the matter was.

'It's those *creatures*. I'm so ashamed of being related to them. Oh, Sylvia, I worry all the time about what they're going to do next. We all know why young women walk the streets after dark.'

'We do indeed. It isn't your fault, though. No one could blame *you* for what happened.'

'They're related to me. They have the same name. Oh, the humiliation! What dreadful thing will they do next?'

'I'll speak to my husband again. The matter we discussed before is still under consideration. This incident might ensure that your nieces are selected, though they might not agree to go.'

'Oh, Sylvia, you're a wonderful friend to me. I don't know what I'd do without you. And I'll make sure they agree to it.'

By lunchtime Isabel was fed up with pretending to be so upset and persuaded her friend to go home for a while.

Only then did she allow herself to smile and give in to the temptation to waltz round the parlour, crying, 'I've done it, I've done it! What do you think of that, Joseph Blake?'

The maid, who had come up to ask about lunch, watched in amazement from the landing outside. Her mistress was growing stranger with every day that passed.

She crept back downstairs, not wanting Mrs Blake to know she'd seen or heard anything, and found something to keep herself busy. There was always something to do. If the mistress wanted anything to eat, she'd ring the bell.

But the upstairs bell remained silent. Which was one mercy, at least.

Later, Mrs Blake rang for her and gave her a note for the shop lad to deliver.

In the afternoon a note arrived for the three sisters from their aunt.

> *In view of your troubles, you may stay in the cottage until the end of the week, after which you must find somewhere else to live.*
> I. Blake

Xanthe would have thrown the piece of paper into the fire but again Pandora took charge and stopped her. 'Don't! We may need to prove we have a right to stay here.'

'If it weren't for Cassandra, I'd leave today. Surely we must be able to find a room to rent somewhere?'

'We'll ask around, but we're not moving out till we have to. This place is rent free and besides . . . it's where she'll come.'

So they stayed at the cottage, waiting, praying – and as the hours of that long, weary day passed, despair pressed even more heavily on them. If Cassandra was alive, surely she'd have come home by now?

In the afternoon Mr Studdard came to see Isabel to make arrangements for the funeral. 'My dear lady—'

'I'm not burying my husband until his nieces have left the town.'

'But – you can't leave him unburied.'

'You can preserve the body, can you not?'

'Um – yes. But it'll be more expensive.'

She waved one hand dismissively. 'That's not important.'

'And your nieces may not want to leave Outham.'

'I'll make sure—' He looked at her strangely and she hastily amended it to, 'I'm sure they will. The dear Vicar knows of a scheme which will give them a new chance in life. I'm not fond of them but it's my duty to see that they're not in want. I'm certain my dear husband would have expected me to do that.'

'And the funeral, when we do hold it . . . shall we discuss the arrangements now?'

Suddenly she'd had enough of him. 'No. I'm arranging nothing until they've left town. I bid you good day.'

She buried her face in her black-edged handkerchief, not raising it till he'd gone. Then she smiled. It was working just as she'd planned.

Mr Studdard went round to see the Vicar and tell him what had happened.

Mr Saunders shook his head. 'The poor lady is taking her husband's death very badly. And as for his nieces, well I gather they're an immoral lot. She's terrified they'll bring shame to his name.'

The undertaker didn't contradict him, but he remembered the four young women from the funeral of the other Mr Blake. He'd thought them polite and well-spoken. Most of the young women who worked in mills were raucous and bold; these four had seemed different, had spoken differently too. He realised the Vicar had spoken. 'I beg your pardon. What did you say?'

'I said, I'm fairly sure the Blake sisters will agree to leave next week, then we can bury Joseph Blake.'

When the undertaker had left, the Vicar went to his desk and took out a letter he'd just received, writing a quick reply and giving them the names of three suitable young women.

Those Blake girls would be getting an opportunity to make a new life for themselves. They would be grateful for this one day. The other one must be dead by now – or lost to decent society.

The new life Reece had expected on their arrival in Australia was slow in arriving. The house Paul took them to was small, rented only, and once again Reece was expected to sleep in a shed-like construction out at the back because the two maids were occupying the sleep-out on the veranda.

He shared this space with a convict, who tended the horses and did the minimum work he could get away with on the garden. The other man wasn't at all talkative, seeming to regard the newcomer with suspicion.

Reece didn't complain, kept his thoughts secret and made himself useful. He was badly bitten by mosquitoes, so requested a mosquito net like those used inside the house.

'I never thought of that!' Francis said. 'My dear fellow, I'm so sorry. We'll go and buy you one this very afternoon.'

He muttered as he turned away, 'I need to get away from this house for a while, anyway.'

On the way into Perth, Francis said quietly, 'You must have noticed that I'm not – um, best pleased with what I've found here, Reece.'

'It's not what any of us expected, sir.'

'My cousin has bought himself a plot of land on the coast, about thirty miles south of Fremantle at a place called East Rockingham. He says it'll be a fine little town one day and he intends to build a spacious new home there. His land is close to the ocean, but from what he says, there's nothing much there at present. *He* has the money to set up as a gentleman and he's never been strong so doesn't mind idling around, but *I* need something to occupy my time – and earn me some money. My father wasn't as generous as he could have been.'

He breathed in deeply and let out a sigh that was nearly a growl. 'I was misled about the Swan River Colony, Reece, and I apologise to you.'

'We've not started finding our feet yet, have we? Happen things will look better once we're settled in.' Reece didn't intend to take sides or criticise his employer's relatives, but he'd been talking to passers-by, servants from other houses, anyone he met, trying to find out what the situation in this colony was really like. He hoped he'd be left on his own in Perth today, so that he could gather yet more information. People talked to him as they wouldn't to his master.

'Will you be all right?' Francis asked when they arrived. 'I feel we should look elsewhere for our land, so I'm going to ask about sites. Buying you a mosquito net was a good excuse to come into Perth and ask around.' He thrust a piece of paper into Reece's hand. 'I've a list of things the ladies want, if you could purchase the items, and your net, of course. We'll leave the horse and gig at the livery stables and you can have the parcels sent there.'

Reece studied the list grimly. Women's stuff. What did he know about that?

Francis fumbled in his pocket and handed over a small purse. 'You'd better buy yourself something to eat at midday. A florin should cover that. I'll meet you again in three hours' time at the livery stables.'

Reece did the shopping first, lingering if he found anyone to talk to, taking careful note of the amenities Perth offered and the types of stores that were there.

He found it cheaper to buy some bread and ham from a street seller, would have preferred bread and cheese but the man said gloomily that cheese wasn't easy to obtain. He washed the food down with a cup of strong black tea, leaving himself with half the lunch money still. Tucking the change into his pocket, he smiled wryly. Every penny counted, every halfpenny even. People like the Southerhams would never understand that.

He had some money of his own, not much but from what he'd found out, enough to set up some sort of business. But what?

When Francis joined him at the livery stables, he looked thoughtful.

'What did you find out?' Reece asked, listening carefully to his employer. Farming, if done well, if the land was fertile, could apparently provide a decent income. Horse

breeding was also good business, with many mounts being
sent to India.

'I shall probably breed horses,' Francis said. Almost as
an afterthought he added, 'Oh, and they said that there's
a need for timber, so if you can get land with well-grown
trees on it, you can profit from clearing it, too.'

Which gave Reece a lot to think about. He didn't share
his conclusions with his employer because Francis didn't
ask him.

Servants, it seemed to him, were not only invisible
to their employers most of the time, but not expected
to have opinions or ideas of their own. Francis was
friendlier than most, but still used Reece mainly as a
sounding board for his own thoughts. Didn't these
people realise how much servants saw and heard? The
two maids discussed their mistress freely over kitchen
meals.

He was glad he hadn't been brought up a servant. It
was no way to live. At least when he'd worked in the mill,
his time after work had been his own.

He smiled up at the clear blue sky, enjoying the gentle
warmth on his skin in between the downpours. If it was
like this in winter, what would summer be like? Hot,
people told him. But he enjoyed warm weather.

The more he learned about this place, the more
determined he became to make good here. But he didn't
feel it fair to write to Cassandra until he had some future
worth offering her.

It was a few days before the men set off to view the plot
of land Paul Southerham had bought to build his house

on. It was on the coast, south of Fremantle. They travelled in a wagon drawn by oxen, which made for slow progress, and they were going to camp there for a night or two, fishing and swimming in the sea if the weather was good enough.

In East Rockingham, Reece looked in amazement at the block of sandy land they'd come to see. Even to his inexperienced eyes, it had clearly been bought for the view, not because it was fertile land.

'The soil doesn't look very promising for growing things,' Francis said at last.

'I'm not going to be *farming* it,' Paul said huffily. 'I bought it for the views and because it's exactly the right size. I'll have a fine garden here one day.'

'I can't buy here. I need land suitable for horse breeding.' Francis's voice was flat and his displeasure came through.

'I thought – didn't you say my uncle had given you some money?'

'Only enough to set me up for earning my living.'

'Oh.' Paul avoided his eyes, kicking a tuft of wiry looking grass. 'I'm sorry.'

'Never mind. Let's go and walk along the beach.'

The two days of camping allowed Reece to chat to the drivers, who owned their own team and were doing well, already saving to buy a second team and wagon.

As they relaxed with him, they shared their scorn of gentlemen immigrants who didn't want to get their hands dirty.

'There aren't as many rules here,' one said that night as they sat round their own camp fire some distance away from the gentlemen's camping spot. 'You've a better chance of making a go of life than you'd ever have in England.'

'If you want to be your own master, that is,' the other driver said quietly. 'Some don't.'

'I do,' Reece said without hesitation.

'There you are, then. You've come to the right place. Y'need a wife, though. Makes a big difference, a good woman does.'

When they all sought their beds, the gentlemen lay in a tent and Reece lay under a tarpaulin one of the drivers attached to the side of the wagon. He looked out at the stars twinkling in the clear night sky. Had he ever seen stars as bright before he left Lancashire? He didn't care about the hardness of the ground, or the nip in the winter air that had him snuggling under the rough blankets. The drivers had produced rolls of bedding, which they called 'swags' and had shown him how these could be carried on the shoulders if you were on the tramp.

He'd have liked to spend a few weeks exploring the colony on foot. He'd have liked lots of things, and even though he couldn't see how his future would turn out, he felt happier than he had for a while. Men like these drivers gave him hope for the future. Surely if he worked hard, chose his land carefully, he'd make a success of life here?

He'd do his best at whatever his employer wanted him to do for the time agreed, though. That went without saying. He'd always honoured his promises.

10

Cassandra woke with a start as a woman's voice said, 'I'm going to help you feel more comfortable, but if you make any attempt to escape, my friend will hit you on the head.'

The bonds were untied and when she reached up automatically to pull off the blindfold, they let her.

There were two women, one on either side of her, and a man was standing nearby. The older of the two women pointed to the door. He grinned and left.

Cassandra let them do what they wanted, grateful for being cleaned and allowed to put her clothes on.

'I'm sorry about this,' one woman whispered. 'I thought they were only going to hold you prisoner or I'd not have let them bring you here. I don't care what they do to men – I hate men! – but I won't help them to hurt other women.'

'Poor bitch,' the other said. 'It ain't right what they're doing, Jane. They've gone too far.'

The door banged open just then and a voice Cassandra knew only too well said, 'What the hell's going on here?'

She shivered uncontrollably.

'We're making sure it's not murder,' the woman in charge said, hands on hips.

'What does it matter if she dies?'

'It matters to me. I've done a lot of things people think wrong, but I won't let you kill her in my house. And if you go on like this, it *will* be murder. You never said you were going to treat her so badly. What are you, animals in rut?'

'Be careful how you talk to me, Jane.'

'And you be careful how you treat *me*, Pete. I've got friends too.'

There was silence for a few seconds and Cassandra could hardly breathe as she waited to see who won the encounter.

His voice turned sulky. 'Why shouldn't we enjoy ourselves with her? It's what the old biddy asked us to do. We don't usually get *paid* to do it.'

'You won't carry on like this in my house because I say so.' Her voice became cajoling. 'If you leave her alone from now on, I'll make sure one of my girls sees to you every day while this one's here. My girls are a lot more fun anyway.'

There was silence then he laughed. 'All right. She lies there like a dead fish anyway now she's stopped struggling.'

When he'd gone, the second woman said, 'I'm not doing it with them. He's turned rough, Pete has, lately.'

'I'll pay you double the usual fee and make sure someone's standing by in case you need help. Or are you going to let them kill her?'

A long silence then, 'Oh, all right. I'll do it. I don't know what's got into Pete lately. He used to be a decent enough fellow, even if he was a thief.'

'Who knows what changes people? Come on. Let's get

her up to my room.' Jane turned back to Cassandra. 'If you give us any trouble, they'll bring you back here and I won't be able to stop them.'

'No! Please, no. I'll do anything, *anything*.' She heard her own voice break and couldn't stop sobbing.

Jane shook her hard. 'Stop that! It does no good.'

It took her a few minutes to calm down, however hard she tried.

'Poor bitch,' the other woman said again.

'She'll get over it. She's still alive, isn't she?'

'Thanks to you, Jane. And they might still change their minds.'

'I'll make sure they don't.'

'I don't know why you bother.'

'Because I hate men and I know what it's like to be forced – and hurt. So do you.'

'Yes.' There was silence for a minute or two, then she said, 'As long as I get the extra money.'

'Have you ever known me break my word?'

'No, Jane. You're a good 'un. I like working for you. You treat us fair.'

'I'm a "good 'un" as long as you do your job well.' She turned back to the bed. 'Come on, you. I've not got all day.'

Cassandra made a huge effort, unable to believe that the horrors which had nearly destroyed her were over. If it started again, she'd lose her reason, she knew she would.

They helped her up three flights of stairs and into a well-furnished sitting room, where they told her to sit on a chair. There were two oil lamps here and she blinked at the brighter light, her eyes watering after being blindfolded for so long.

Jane picked up some scissors. 'I need to cut your hair off.'

'*What?*'

'The person who's paying them wants your hair to prove to your sisters that they've got you prisoner.'

Instinctively Cassandra's hands went up to her head.

'I'll tie it back and chop it off, then tidy up the ends for you. It'll grow again in no time.' Jane studied her, eyes narrowed. 'You're not going to give me any trouble about this – or about anything else – are you? I've risked a lot for you.'

Cassandra swallowed hard. 'No. I'll not give you any trouble.'

'Sensible. I thought you would be. I've seen you around town, couldn't help noticing, you being so tall. You never did look stupid.'

The scissors snipped and Cassandra felt cold air at the nape of her neck. Strange to have short hair like a man, but a small thing compared to what else had happened to her. How many days had passed since she'd been here? She'd lost count, couldn't even be bothered to ask.

Would they let her go eventually? Or would they kill her?

She didn't know. And for all Jane appeared friendly, Cassandra didn't really trust her. The woman had allowed the men to keep her prisoner here and this was clearly a brothel.

★

No word came about Cassandra for five days. The sisters spent much of the time looking out of the window, watching passers-by, waiting for a knock on the door, crying now and then, unable to settle to anything.

One morning another note from their aunt was delivered.

I shall be coming to see you this afternoon at four o'clock precisely. Make sure the house is clean and tidy.
I. Blake

'What do you think she wants?' Xanthe wondered.

'I don't know. Probably to throw us out.' Pandora walked round the ground floor of the cottage, but was soon satisfied that all was in order.

After that, there was nothing to do but wait.

At exactly four o'clock footsteps tapped along the path and the front door opened without the courtesy of a knock.

Isabel walked in, staring round, surprised to find it immaculate. 'Well, at least you don't live like pigs.' She took a kitchen chair and waved a hand to the others to sit. 'I don't intend to crick my neck looking up at you. Such maypoles you are! Men don't like women to be that tall. It's no wonder you've none of you married.'

She waited until they'd sat, pleased to note how pale they were, how reddened and puffy their eyes were, how anxiously they were looking at her.

'I've made arrangements for you three to go to Australia. You're to leave town on Monday and will be taken to stay at a migrants' hostel in London until the ship leaves.' Glee danced through her at the utter shock on their faces.

'Why should we go to Australia?' Pandora asked.

'Because there is nowhere in the world further from Outham and because once and for all I wish to be rid of the embarrassment of having you living here.'

'We can't go anywhere. We're waiting for Cassandra to come home. And anyway, we don't want to go to Australia.'

Isabel allowed herself to laugh, but it nearly got out of hand and it was an effort to control it. 'Oh, dear. Oh, dear me. Don't want to go, they say!'

'How can you laugh? Our sister's missing. We don't know whether she's dead or alive. We're not going anywhere till we have her back.'

Isabel stared at the beautiful one, wishing she could slice into that flawless skin and mar it for ever. 'You won't get her back, but I can assure you she's alive.'

They looked so astonished, another chuckle escaped her.

'How do you know that?' the gentle-looking one asked.

'Because she was taken prisoner on my orders and won't be released till you three have left the country.'

The silence went on for a long time, then the beautiful one asked, 'Why?'

She had to admire that, Isabel admitted. Straight to the point. No hysterics. This one was sharper than the others. 'Because I needed to find a way to force you to leave Outham.'

'I don't believe you.'

She smiled and let them wait for her answer, then reached into her bag. 'Do you recognise this?' She waved the long piece of hair in front of them, tied at one end with the ragged piece of ribbon they all recognised.

They gasped and one moaned.

'You cut off her hair?' the gentle-looking one's voice was a scratchy whisper.

'I ordered it to be cut off. It'll be her thumb next time if you still need convincing. Your sister has a scar on her thumb and a birthmark on her belly, does she not? You'd recognise that thumb and we could slice off the piece of skin with the birthmark as well.' She smiled. She had them now.

'How do we know she'll be safe if we agree to do as you wish?'

'Because I'll give you my word, hand on the Bible, and since I'm not an immoral trollop like you, *my* word means something.'

'Not to me, it doesn't,' the one who did most of the speaking said. Isabel couldn't remember their stupid, fancy names and didn't intend to try.

She leaned back. 'My word is all you've got, all that'll save your sister. Shall you wait for the thumb then? It's easily chopped off.'

'I'll go and get the Bible,' the gentle one said.

Isabel smiled. She actually meant what she was promising, but they didn't know why. She wanted Cassandra to live with what had happened to her, to have nightmares about it for the rest of her life. That would teach her to be so impudent towards her betters, to come between man and wife.

Calmly, she swore on the Bible that if these three went to Australia, their sister would be released. 'But only,' she added with her hand still on the book, staring at each one in turn, 'if you give me your word to say nothing to anyone of why you're going.'

'You mean we mustn't tell anyone you're forcing us to leave?'

She nodded. 'If you value your sister's life and want to see her freed.'

'What will Cassandra do then? How will she manage?'

'She can do whatever she wants as long as she leaves Outham.' She didn't tell them she'd make sure circumstances would keep the other one away from the town. 'Now, this is what you're to do . . .'

When she'd gone, Maia burst into tears, stroking the tied bunch of hair still lying on the table as she sobbed. 'They've killed her, I know they have.'

'I don't think so,' Pandora said slowly. 'I think that horrible creature meant what she said and will keep her promise – but for reasons of her own.'

'Do you really think Cassandra is alive?'

'We have to believe that.'

'But we'll never know for sure, will we?'

'Perhaps one day. We can tell the Minister where we're going. If she comes back, she'll go to Mr Rainey, I'm sure. Then he can write and let us know she's safe. There is a mail service to Australia, even if letters take months to get there.'

'We have no choice,' Xanthe said at last. 'But I don't want to go to Australia.'

Pandora's eyes filled with tears. 'Neither do I. I love living here, love the moors, can't imagine being anywhere else.'

They sat in miserable silence for a few more minutes, then Pandora stood up, 'She said we have to go and see that horrible Vicar at six o'clock. Let's make ourselves as tidy as we can. And whatever he says or does, you're not to cry, Maia. You're not to give him that satisfaction . . . or *her*. We've done nothing to be ashamed of. They're the ones who should be ashamed.'

The Vicar left them standing in front of his desk and looked scornfully at them as he took his seat behind it. 'Since it's now obvious that your sister must have been murdered, your aunt has kindly made arrangements to give you a new start in life. You'd better make sure that from now on you behave in a respectable manner and are polite to your betters.'

He looked at them, clearly expecting a response, so Pandora murmured, 'Yes, sir,' and nudged her sisters, who echoed her words. It was strange, she thought, how the other two kept turning to her for guidance, even though she was the youngest. Everything was strange lately, strange and horrible.

'You will leave Outham in two days' time and be taken to the migrant hostel in London. From there you will sail to Australia on the *Tartar*. They're taking a group of female paupers from Lancashire because they're very short of servants in the colonies, apparently. So that's what you'll become once you arrive there, servants. See that you make the most of this wonderful opportunity your aunt has given you for a fresh start. You should be thanking the Lord on your knees for it.'

Pandora again forced herself to say, 'Yes, sir.'

'I gather you can all read?'

This time Maia had to pinch Pandora because the scornful way he had said this, as if he expected them not to be able to, made her so angry she didn't dare speak for a moment or two.

'Yes, sir. We can all read.'

He thrust the newspaper at her with another scornful look. 'Read this, then. Show me how well you can read.'

She picked it up and began at the top of the page, reading easily, long words or not. Then she passed it to her sisters, who continued to read the piece just as easily.

'Enough, enough.' He made a note. 'You will have to undergo a medical examination before you go on board the ship. I trust none of you is diseased.'

What had their aunt been saying about them? '*No . . . sir.*'

'I hope you're telling me the truth, because if you *are* diseased, you'll not be allowed on the ship and you'll be thrown out on the streets. You're not to come back here, whatever happens. If you even try, I shall have you committed to the Reformatory for immoral behaviour.'

He stood up. 'Very well. I shall send someone to escort you to the railway station on Monday in time to meet the train that stops here at twelve minutes past ten in the morning. The lady supervising the trip to London will be on board with some of her other charges and she will look after you from then onwards. This is a list of what you should take with you. If you don't have it, your aunt has said she'll supply you with what's needed. She is a very Christian, generous woman. Make sure you thank her for her help.'

None of them could force out words of acquiescence to that.

After they left the Vicarage, they didn't stop to talk, just walked home in grim silence. Only when they were indoors did they spend a few minutes letting their emotions out, furious at the injustice of what was happening to them.

'This is doing us no good,' Pandora said in the end. 'Let's plan what to do.'

'I'm not applying to *her* for help,' Xanthe said.

'I am. I want to make her pay as much as I can, so even if we already have what's needed, we'll ask her to buy it for us, then sell our other things. We have enough friends to help us do that. We don't want to arrive in Australia penniless, do we?'

'I never thought of it that way,' Xanthe said admiringly.

'Cassandra would have.'

That silenced them again. Maia wiped away a tear and the others stared down at the floor.

After they'd sorted through their clothing and other possessions, they went to leave a note at the Vicar's house asking their aunt for what they needed for the journey and giving a list, as well as asking for trunks to put it in.

'She'll be more likely to provide it if he knows about it,' Xanthe said.

'She won't care. She'll do anything to get rid of us.' Pandora realised she'd screwed her hands into fists and unballed them. She mustn't let her anger rule her. Or her pain at the thought of saying farewell to Lancashire and all she knew.

'Do you think it's true what I heard when I nipped out to the baker's for a loaf?'

'What, that she's not going to bury her husband until we've left town?'

'Yes.'

Xanthe sniffed back a tear. 'She wants to prevent us from attending it. She's even denying us a proper farewell to our uncle. I didn't know him for long, but I really liked him.'

'It's no use dwelling on that. Come on, we must let Mrs Rainey know we're leaving.'

The Minister's wife looked at the sisters in horror. 'You can't mean it?'

'We do.'

'But – what if your sister comes back? What will Cassandra think if you're not here? No, no. I can't allow this. Your aunt is wrong to urge you to go.'

Pandora swallowed hard, couldn't dredge up a lie and pleaded desperately, 'Please. We have no choice.'

Mrs Rainey stared at them. 'What do you mean by that?'

'We can't tell you anything else.'

'Is that woman *forcing* you to go?'

'We're going,' Pandora said quietly. 'That's all we can tell you. We gave our word not to say why. We wanted to ask you if you'd keep Cassandra's clothing and sell our furniture and other household possessions, then keep the money for her. We've not got time to do that ourselves.'

She hesitated and allowed herself to say, 'We've been assured she's alive. If she comes to you . . . you'll tell her where we are, why we had to go?'

Mrs Rainey looked at her sharply. 'Of course I'll do that. And we have some clothes donated by the more affluent members of our congregation. Probably some of those will fit you. You'll need to take a few extra things, apart from what's on that list. And you'll need trunks.'

'Our aunt is providing those.' Pandora's voice broke and she dashed away a tear with the back of her hand. Mrs Rainey's sympathy was nearly her undoing.

Her sisters moved closer, put their arms round her. She didn't know what she'd have done without them. How would Cassandra feel about them leaving her on her own? It broke Pandora's heart every time she thought of that.

'Let me fetch my husband and you can tell him what you've told me.'

So they repeated to the Minister what they'd already said.

Mr Rainey tapped his fingers on the arm of his chair. 'You're quite sure you can tell me no more? I wouldn't betray a confidence, you know.'

They shook their heads.

He sighed. 'I won't press you. I've been told about this scheme and if I didn't believe this to be a good opportunity for you and the other young women who're going, I'd not give in so easily. I promise you faithfully that my wife and I will look after your sister. Write to us once you arrive and we'll write back.'

'It's all happening too quickly,' Xanthe said as they

walked home. 'How can we go so far away without being certain that Cassandra's all right?'

'We have no choice,' her twin replied.

'I never wished anyone ill before, but I wish something terrible would happen to *her*.'

'It won't. Look what she's done so far, and no one suspects a thing.'

'We're not sure she had our uncle killed.'

'I am,' Pandora said with such quiet certainty their steps faltered for a moment or two, then they started walking again in silence.

When they'd gone, Mr Rainey looked at his wife. 'What hold has that woman got over them? And why is the Vicar helping her to send those poor girls away? For a man of God he is singularly unsympathetic towards our poorer brethren.'

'There's nothing we can do about it. The whole arrangement looks like a good deed. People will praise Isabel Blake for helping her nieces. We're the only ones who know she's doing it to separate them from Cassandra. Heaven knows why.'

'I can't begin to guess. I never did understand why she hated them so.'

She hesitated, then said, 'I don't like to speak ill of others, but I'm beginning to think Mrs Blake is – well, deranged.'

'I too, though as we have no proof, we'd better not say that to anyone else. What do you suppose has happened to Cassandra?'

She looked at him with tears in her eyes, 'I'm afraid

to think about that. She's either dead or . . .' She didn't dare finish that sentence, but they both knew what happened to some women who were abducted. She let him put his arms round her, then joined him in a heartfelt prayer for Cassandra's safety.

The following week Francis wanted to go into Perth again and this time he allowed Reece to come with him to the Land Office and listen to the discussion about which blocks of land were available for buying or renting. They were given the locations of three which sounded suitable.

'We'll ride out to see them,' Francis decided.

'I've not ridden before,' Reece said mildly. 'Though I'd like to learn.'

'I'll be happy to teach you. You'll be a bit sore at first, but it'll be worth it. The roads are so bad here and there are no railways, so it's the best way to get around quickly. Besides, you'll be looking after the horses when we find our own land.'

'You'll have to show me how to do that, as well. But I'm usually a quick learner and I got on well with the animals on my cousins' farm.'

When they'd finished at the Land Office, they went to buy some horses, leading them back to the livery stable Paul used and arranging to have them cared for there when they were not in use.

'Reece and I will go and inspect the blocks of land tomorrow,' Francis told his wife and cousins as they sat drinking cups of tea on the veranda.

'You'll tire yourself out, doing so much,' Paul said.

'I think I'll come with you,' Livia said.

The men looked at her in surprise and Charlotte in horror.

'I don't think that would be suitable, my dear,' Francis said. 'We'll be camping out.'

'Suitable or not, I'm coming. I want to help choose where we live and I want to see more of Australia. So you'd better arrange to hire a horse for me. And I'll need one of those – what did Reece say they were called? – swags.'

'It may be raining,' Paul protested. 'You'll get wet.'

'I shan't melt.'

She eyed them so challengingly Francis let out a crack of laughter. 'Very well.'

The thing he liked best about the Southerhams, Reece thought, was how much they loved one another.

He hoped one day he and Cassandra would be as happy together as they were.

11

The Vicar himself came to escort the three sisters to the railway station two days after their interview with him, walking along beside them with a grim expression. He'd sent a cart for their trunks.

People they passed in the street called out to wish them well. Some tried to stop them to shake their hands, exchange a few final words, but he hurried them on, calling 'Stand back, if you please!'

When they got to the station, they saw their aunt standing just outside the entrance. She made no attempt to speak to them but followed them far enough inside to watch them leave. She had a smug smile on her face.

The Vicar stayed with them till the train arrived, not speaking, then handed them over to an older woman who got off the train to collect them.

'These are Susan, May and Dora Blake,' he said.

'Those are *not* our Christian names,' Pandora said at once.

The woman looked from them to the Vicar in puzzlement.

His face went red and he glared at them. 'Their father called them by highly unsuitable names. It was thought better to change them. Don't pander to them, it gives them ideas above their station.'

When they got into the compartment with her, they found four other young women sitting there. They smiled wearily at the newcomers, looking thin and tired, as if it was a long time since they'd eaten a decent meal.

Maia burst into tears as the train pulled out of the station.

'Sit upright. Don't give her the satisfaction!' Pandora snapped. But her eyes were brimming with unshed tears as she stared stony-faced at the last sight of their aunt, standing beside the Vicar now, still smiling.

'What are your real names?' the lady asked once they were out of the station and rattling through the countryside.

When they told her, she smiled. 'I think they're very pretty names. I'll make sure the other ones are corrected on the ship's manifest.'

At any other time the sisters would have been excited at the long railway journey into parts of England they'd never seen before, not to mention visiting the capital city. Today they watched tiredly, did as they were told and said little.

Pandora changed seats to watch the moors disappear into the distance, to be replaced by towns and softer countryside.

'I hope Cassandra is all right,' Maia said once in a low voice.

Xanthe reached out for her hand. 'She will be. She must be. Once our aunt hears that we've left England, she'll let our sister go. She promised.'

'Who are you talking about?' the lady asked.

'Our sister. She wasn't able to come with us. She wanted to, but our aunt wouldn't let her.'

'You'll be able to write to her.'

Maia burst into tears again.

Cassandra sat staring listlessly at the fire burning low in the grate of the room where they kept her now. There was always a woman with her, but none of them would speak to her, though one or two looked at her in a pitying way. She felt soul-sick, and hadn't been able to sleep properly at night, suffering nightmares that woke her whimpering and struggling against the brutal men who peopled those nightmares.

How many days had she been here? She couldn't work that out, couldn't think clearly about anything. And she shivered every time *that man* came into the room to check that she was still there, which he did several times a day.

The door opened and Jane nodded dismissal to the one now sitting with her. 'You're leaving in the morning.'

'Where am I going? What are they going to do to me next?'

'I don't know. A lady's coming to see you tonight, the one who arranged all this.'

It was as if Cassandra's brain suddenly started working again. 'She's my aunt.'

'*Your aunt?*'

'Yes. She hates me, hates us all.'

'Well, don't say a word about who she is to anyone else. I'm to inform you that if you tell anyone her name, she'll have you killed. And if you'll take my advice, you won't say anything except yes and no when she speaks to you. She's – not a kind person and she has enough money to get people to do whatever she wants.' Jane hesitated then added, 'If you say a word about what I'm going to tell you next, I'll let *him* have you again before you leave.'

Cassandra shuddered and said hastily, 'I won't. I promise I won't.'

'I thought you should know that your sisters have already left England. She's sent them to Australia.'

The room spun round Cassandra and she couldn't breathe properly.

'It's all round the town that they're sending about sixty young women from Lancashire out to Australia, ones who have no family left. They need servants there, apparently. And your sisters are among them.'

'My sisters have left the country?' She wanted to scream and protest, beg her companion to say that it wasn't true. It was a struggle to say quietly, 'I can't understand why she didn't send me with them.'

'Nor I. I shouldn't really have told you. You'll never be able to keep it to yourself.'

It was as if the apathy and dullness that had surrounded Cassandra like a cloud for the past few days had suddenly lifted. 'I'll not say a word, I promise you, Jane. And I'm grateful for that information. Very grateful. It'll help me stay in control of myself when she taunts me with it.'

'I can't do anything else to help you. I've my own safety to think of.'

This was, Cassandra thought when the other woman came back to sit with her, like one of the Greek tragedies her father had so loved. Only now was she beginning to understand how deeply such events affected people, how scarred you could feel inside from the things that happened to you.

And she still didn't know what was to become of her, whether hers would be a tragedy that ended in death – or whether her aunt had something else in store for her. It'd not be pleasant, whatever it was. Of that at least she was certain.

When her aunt was shown in, Cassandra said nothing.

Radiating triumph, Isabel sat down. Her eyes were fixed on her niece as she adjusted her full black skirts and leaned back in the chair.

'Leave us alone,' she told Jane.

As the door closed, she turned back to Cassandra. 'If you wish to live, you'll do exactly as I say. Your sisters were wise enough to obey me.'

It would look better to say something, so she did. 'What do you mean? What's happened to my sisters?'

'They're on the way to Australia. I've got rid of them once and for all.'

Cassandra gasped, murmured, 'Oh, no!' and clapped her hands to her face. She was grateful that Jane had given her this information earlier, that she had been able to plan how to respond.

'It only remains to get rid of you.'

Cassandra pretended to wipe away tears, found that there really were tears. She looked up at this. 'Are you going to have me killed?'

'No. That'd be too easy.' She waited, clearly enjoying her power.

'What are you going to do with me? Send me to Australia, too?'

'No. You're the worst of them all and you don't deserve that chance. You'll be left in Manchester and you'll have to do the best you can to make a living for yourself. You'll probably enjoy being on the streets. I saw you pressing yourself against that man in the churchyard, you slut! No, don't say another word. Just listen.' She leaned forward and said slowly, emphasising the words. 'If you *ever* come back to Outham, I'll have you killed. These people will do anything I ask if I pay them.' She laughed and went on laughing for a long time, hiccupping and gulping as if she found it hard to control the laughter.

Cassandra and her sisters had suspected that their aunt had had her husband killed and now, seeing the expression on the older woman's face, she felt sure of it.

'Well? Aren't you going to plead with me to send you to join your sisters?'

'Would it do any good?'

'No.' Isabel smiled.

'How did you persuade them to go?'

'Showed them your hair, told them it'd be your thumb next.' She laughed at the sight of her niece's shock, another shrill laugh, but this one cut off suddenly as she clapped one hand to her mouth and muttered something.

Cassandra prayed for the strength to keep silent, wondering how long the taunting would go on.

'The men will come for you tomorrow afternoon,' that hateful, gloating voice continued, 'and take you into Manchester. You'll be left there with nothing but the clothes you stand up in.'

She glanced at her fob watch and stood up. 'Well, I must go. My maid will be wondering where I am.'

She turned the door handle. 'I shall remember the sight of your face today, the horror on it, how white you look. I shall enjoy that memory as I live my comfortable life and run my shop.'

Without another word she left.

As one of the other women came back in to sit with her, Cassandra closed her eyes and tried to think. She still had trouble believing this was happening, that her aunt was able to do such things. It was like a gothic novel from the library, but without the haunted castles and ghosts. Only it was much worse than those tales, because it was true – horribly, painfully true.

Why did no one else realise her aunt was mad? She was sure her uncle had known. Perhaps that was why he'd been killed?

And how was Cassandra going to manage on her own in Manchester?

When he'd shown the old hag out and pocketed the guinea she always slipped him, Pete went to see Jane. 'I'm to take your guest into Manchester and leave her on the street with only the clothes on her back.'

'Poor bitch.'

'Proper waste, that'd be, if you ask me. She's not bad looking and she's almost a virgin.' He laughed heartily at his own joke. 'I don't see why I shouldn't take a little more benefit from this. There are whore houses who'd pay good money for a fresh young woman like her.'

'You'd not sell her into one of those places!'

'Of course I would. She's worth ten guineas at least, perhaps more. I want you to find her something nicer to wear, though, something that shows off her attractions.'

'All right. But I'll want a share of the money.'

He smiled. 'I'll pay you two guineas, that's all.'

'You're a mean sod.'

'You're no different. You'll do anything for money.'

'I like my comforts.'

Jane came into the room and again dismissed the woman guarding Cassandra. 'Listen carefully.' She explained what Pete intended to do.

'I'll kill myself first.'

'They won't let you once they get you into one of those places. They have ways of taming young women who don't behave, drugging them, beating them till they beg for mercy.'

'And you'll let Pete do this to me?'

Jane glanced at the door and raised her voice slightly. 'I can't stop him so I might as well make myself some extra money. Now, I'll find you some nicer clothes to wear than those rags. If you look pretty and behave yourself, you'll be treated better.'

Cassandra looked at her in horror, terror roiling inside her belly. She thought she'd experienced the most dreadful thing possible for a woman, but it seemed there was worse to come.

Two hours later one of the young girl servants brought up a tray of food and Jane followed her carrying a pile of clothes. She waited till they were alone and moved closer to Cassandra, whispering as she took a piece of cake from the tray, 'If you want to escape, this is the time to do it.'

Cassandra shot her a puzzled look. Was this another way to trick her?

'Take something to eat. You need to keep up your strength,' Jane said loudly, then lowered her voice to add, 'Do you have somewhere to go, someone who'll hide you until you can get out of town?'

Cassandra nodded.

'When I give you the word, you must hit me on the head and make your way out of here.'

'I can't *hit* you.'

'Mmm. Good cake, this,' she said loudly, then whispered through a mouthful of crumbs, 'Unless you do, I shan't let you escape. If they think I've helped you, they'll make me sorry. You'll have to hit me hard enough to raise a bad bruise then I'll pretend to be unconscious.'

Cassandra swallowed a mouthful of cake that felt like grit going down her throat. 'All right.'

Jane took another bite. 'Once you're out of the room, turn left and use the back stairs. It's up to you after that. I can't tell whether the stairs will be clear, but at least I can give you a chance of getting away.' She raised her voice, 'Eat up! We don't want you fainting on us.'

Cassandra swallowed another mouthful, giving a tiny nod as she did so.

Another whisper. 'One more thing. After you've escaped, stay hidden. Don't try to bring the police into this. They'll believe your aunt rather than you. She's great friends with that fat Vicar and he believes whatever she tells him.'

'That'd mean letting her get away with it.'

'People like them do get away with things, especially ladies who seem respectable. You should see the *gentlemen* who come in here. Pillars of the church, some of them. Now, we've no time to argue. Eat something else and I'll ring for the tray to be taken away.'

'I'm not hungry.'

'You don't know where your next meal is coming from. Eat.'

As the maid cleared away the tray and left, Jane went to open the door for her, saying loudly before she closed it, 'Change into these clothes now. I'm sick of seeing you in rags.' She almost closed the door, listening intently as she peered through the narrow gap. 'Right. He's gone. But he'll be back. So be quick about it.'

Cassandra took off her clothes, glancing nervously towards the door. The bodice she'd been given was cut very low and she hesitated to put it on.

'Do it quickly before I regret my generosity.' Jane was back at the door, keeping watch. When Cassandra was dressed, she came across to her. 'Now hit me from behind so I can't see it coming. Quick, before I change my mind.'

Cassandra picked up an ornament and took a quick swipe at Jane, who crumpled to the ground and didn't stir. She looked down at herself, horrified at the sight of her half-exposed breasts. She couldn't go out like this. She pulled the shawl from around Jane's shoulders, but the other still didn't stir. Out in the street Cassandra would need to put it round her head to hide the short hair that people would be bound to notice. But inside here, she needed to look like the others, so she draped the shawl over one arm.

With a last regretful glance at Jane, she moved quickly to the door, listening to make sure no one was outside, opening it slightly to look, then slipping out and down the narrow back stairs. At the bottom a door shut the back stairs off from the next landing. She started to open it, heard voices and jerked back, peeping through the gap.

A man walked past, fondling a young woman and they disappeared into a room.

Her heart pounding so hard she had difficulty breathing, Cassandra listened to check that no one else was coming then crept down the next flight of stairs. This time there was no door at the bottom and to her horror a man came out of a room just as she stepped on to the landing. Somehow she found the courage to force a smile and walk past him as if she had a right to be there.

He strolled down the front stairs, hardly giving her a second glance. She could hear voices and laughter below. The sounds seemed to echo in her head and for a moment she froze from fear of going further. Then she pulled herself together and hurried down the final flight of back stairs.

At the bottom she paused again to get her bearings. The kitchen area was to one side and people were bustling around, one tired-looking man pouring wine into glasses, an old woman drawing a jug of beer from a barrel in one corner. They saw her but didn't give her a second glance.

A young woman came in from outside and walked into the kitchen, saying, 'That's better. I was bursting.'

Cassandra guessed the door led out to the privy. She

wanted to run, but forced herself to walk slowly towards it. Almost sobbing with relief that no one had tried to stop her, she opened the heavy outer door and stepped outside.

The chill of the night air made her brain feel more alert and as another door nearer the front of the building opened, she moved quickly across the yard into the shadows. There she waited until a man had gone across to a low building which smelled like the privy.

She went in the same direction but opened the back gate and went out into an alley between the rows of houses. Only then did she give in to the temptation to run, moaning in her throat and stumbling along like a drunkard.

At the end of the alley, where it met the next street, she stopped, out of breath. Recognising where she was, she pulled the shawl tightly over her head and round her shoulders then set off walking through the streets. The skirt was fuller than she was used to, the petticoats swishing as she walked, and she was petrified of meeting someone she knew. Or worse still, meeting someone who thought she was a streetwalker. She was sure she looked like one.

She was going to the Raineys. They would help her and surely her sisters would have left a message for her there . . . if they'd been able to.

She had no idea what she would do after that, where she would go, but she believed Jane, that it wouldn't be safe to involve the police. She intended to go as far away from Outham as she could. And one day, somehow, she'd find her sisters again.

*

Pandora sat by the window in the big single women's room of the migrants' hostel, still angry at the embarrassing examination the doctor had made of her person. But it was no use complaining. They were here now and it was better to do as they were told and not make a fuss.

'Do you suppose they've let her go yet?' Maia said from beside her.

'No. Our aunt said they wouldn't do that till our ship had sailed.'

'Do you believe her promise not to harm Cassandra?'

'I don't know. Sometimes I do, other times I don't. What other choice had we but to do as she ordered? I'm quite sure she'd have carried out her threat and cut off Cassandra's thumb.'

'She'd have done it herself without flinching. She's . . . very strange.'

'Mad, don't you mean?'

'Yes.'

A group of young women who slept in the corner bunks on the other side of the room burst into raucous laughter. Others sat quietly. Some looked so thin it was amazing that they could walk, and though the food provided was unappetising, they'd fallen on the evening meal like wolves, eating every scrap on their plates, gristle and fat included.

About sixty young women were to sail on the *Tartar*, they'd been told, including the three sisters. It would take three months or so to get to Australia.

The hardest thing was that they'd not know whether their eldest sister was safe.

12

Halfway to the Minister's house, Cassandra remembered the money and locket she'd hidden in the cottage. She'd kept it for an emergency, as Mrs Southerham had intended, and this surely was one. It must still be there.

Could she retrieve it? Dare she?

She drew in a long, shuddery breath. She had to try. Without money you were utterly helpless.

Changing direction, she walked towards the cottage, keeping to the shadows, her feet in the soft indoor shoes making no noise except when she trod in a puddle by mistake. Whether her feet got wet or not seemed so unimportant she didn't even try to avoid other puddles. The important thing was to move as quickly as possible, retrieve the money and get to the Minister's house before anyone discovered she was missing.

The cottage was dark. Had it been let again? Would there be people inside it sleeping? If so, the money was lost to her.

She went to peer into the front window, but could see nothing, because the slender crescent moon had gone behind some clouds. The air was damp with the promise of more rain. Taking a deep breath, she crept round to the rear and fumbled on the lintel over the back door where they'd kept the spare front door key. But it wasn't there any more. She felt her way along the lintel a second time, to no avail.

Did that mean there was someone living here again?

Should she give up? No. It was her money and she needed it desperately. That thought made her stiffen her spine. She found a stone, used the shawl to muffle the sound and smashed it against the kitchen window. Even so, the noise of breaking glass seemed very loud and she waited before moving again, just in case someone was inside the house.

But no one came to investigate. Shaking her shawl carefully to get rid of the bits of broken glass, she reached inside for the window latch. A sliver of glass stabbed into her but she managed to get the window open. She felt the warmth of blood trickling down her arm but ignored it.

She carried an old wooden tub across to the window and stood on it, managing to squeeze through the small opening only with difficulty. She landed on the slopstone, jarring her hip on the tap that dripped into it.

Relief shuddered through her as she looked round. There was no furniture so the house must be empty. But just to be sure, she waited again.

She heard the soft pattering of a rat above her then a floorboard creaked, making her stiffen in fear. Her heart pounded in her chest as she listened but there were no other noises that might indicate people. Floorboards creaked all the time, she told herself. If there was no furniture there'd be no one here. She had to believe that.

Trying to make no sound at all, she crept across to the stairs and climbed them slowly, all her senses alert.

The second flight of stairs leading to the big attic room were even harder to climb. It was so dark here that she'd not have seen anyone standing at the top. She felt a jolt of terror as one stair creaked beneath her foot and pressed one hand to her chest as if that would still her pounding heart.

As she came up into what had been her bedroom, tears filled her eyes. She had only slept here for a few nights, but she'd loved this room.

Fool! she told herself. *Get this done quickly.* If they'd found she'd escaped they'd already be out looking for her. She hadn't long to find a hiding place.

She went across to the loose floorboard in the corner and tried to pry it open. It was harder without a tool of any sort, but desperation made her use her fingernails, heedless when they broke or splinters stabbed into her. She got it open enough to pull out the little leather bag of money and the locket, clutching them to her breast, unable to move for a moment or two as relief shuddered through her.

What was wrong with her, standing here like a fool? She should be hurrying away. She hung the locket round her neck and stuffed the bag between her breasts. Turning, she made her way outside again, still moving quietly, even though she knew now there was no one inside the house.

Not daring to run because that would look suspicious, she hurried through the streets, muffling a sob of relief as she reached the Minister's house without meeting anyone.

She didn't dare knock on the door because that would wake the maid, but she knew which was the Raineys' bedroom so flung clods of earth from the flower bed up at the window. Someone came to look out. It seemed dangerous to call out, so she looked up and waved, praying whoever it was would recognise her.

There was just enough moonlight to see the pale blur of a face staring down at her. Mr Rainey, she thought. She put one trembling finger to her lips, hoping he could see it and realise he needed to be quiet.

He waved one hand and vanished.

It seemed a very long time until the front door opened and by then she was wondering whether they'd even want to help her after what had happened to her. People called women who'd been used by men in that loathsome way 'soiled doves'. Were you still a soiled dove if you'd been forced? She didn't know, was only holding on to her wits with the greatest of efforts.

When she heard the bolt slide and the key turn in the lock, she staggered forward, feeling dizzy now.

'Don't let anyone know I'm here.' She started to sob, muffling the sound with the ends of her shawl, her whole body shaking.

Was she safe now? Would they help her?

If they didn't, she had no energy left to continue, could think of nowhere else to turn.

Mrs Rainey took one look at her and put an arm round her shoulders. 'You poor thing. What's happened to you? Gerald, light the gas.'

'No, don't! The people who captured me will know I came here if they see lights on in the middle of the night.'

'They wouldn't dare break into my house!' Mr Rainey protested.

'No, but they might wait for me to leave it, follow me and snatch me later.'

'I can't believe they would risk that.'

'I've seen their faces. They'll want to make sure I can't tell anyone who they are.'

'We must send for the police, then. They'll know what to do.'

'I can't *prove* anything. My aunt will claim I'm immoral and say I went to that place of my own accord, I know she will. The person who helped me escape said that if I valued my life I should just – vanish. Only I don't know where to go. I want to be with my sisters but she's sent them to Australia.' She burst into tears again, at the end of her tether.

Mrs Rainey patted her arm. 'Shh now. Don't cry. We'll find you somewhere to go.'

'You won't tell anyone I'm here?'

'We'll have to tell our maid. You can't hide anything from Phyllis. But she's been with us for over twenty years and she's never betrayed a confidence yet.'

Cassandra drew up a mental image of their elderly maid, who attended chapel sitting at the back on her own, very prim and proper, looking as if she disapproved of the world. 'She won't want to help me when she knows where I've been.'

'Tell us.'

It was hard and her voice faltered as she told them what had been done to her.

Part way through the explanation, Mrs Rainey unclenched Cassandra's hand from the bunched skirt material and kept hold of it till she stopped talking. 'Were you thinking we'd turn you away for something that's not your fault?'

She could only nod.

Mrs Rainey stroked her short hair. 'You're wrong. Is she not, Gerald?'

His answer was slow coming and Cassandra waited, holding her breath, but at last he said, 'We'd never turn anyone away.'

'And Phyllis will want to help too, my dear, I promise you. In fact, I'll go and wake her so that she can help me care for you.'

While his wife was away Mr Rainey said nothing, standing in front of the fireplace looking at Cassandra sadly. When he caught her staring at him, he looked down at his feet as if he didn't know what to say.

If *he* couldn't bear to speak to her or look her in the eyes, what would other people be like? Few people were as warm and caring as his wife.

Mrs Rainey brought the maid downstairs with her and Phyllis said gruffly, 'There's enough warm water to give you a quick bath, if you'd like. I don't need a lamp to find my way round my own kitchen.'

'Yes, please. Oh yes! There's nothing I'd like more than a bath – and to get out of these horrible clothes.'

The fact that Phyllis was prepared to help rather than scorning her gave Cassandra her first real hope. She let the two women take her into the kitchen and with only the moonlight to help them, they got the tin bath from the scullery and filled it.

She lay in the warm water, glad there were no lights

because she couldn't stop more tears from rolling down her cheeks. Where did they come from, all these tears? Would they ever end?

Mrs Rainey's voice intruded into her thoughts. 'You'd better get out now, dear. The water's going cold.'

She obeyed without a word, surprised to find they were offering her some nightclothes. She hadn't noticed either of them leaving the room to get them.

When they had helped her dress in a flannel nightgown and wrapped her in a soft shawl that smelled of fresh air and sunshine, they took her up to the attics and made up a bed in the unused bedroom that was meant for a second maidservant.

She climbed into it, feeling as if her limbs were made of lead.

'No one will know you're here.' Mrs Rainey stroked her forehead with one hand. 'And I've brought your money and locket up. You'll want to know they're safe, I'm sure.'

'Thank you. I—' She gulped, not knowing how to put into words her relief that they hadn't scorned her.

'Shh now. Try to get some sleep. And stay here once you wake because people often come to the kitchen door. Either Phyllis or I will fetch what you need. I'll say goodnight now.'

When she'd gone, Cassandra turned to the maid. 'I'm sorry. I don't want to be a trouble to you.'

'I'm happy to help you, lass,' the other said gruffly. She clasped Cassandra's shoulder tightly. 'I'd shoot those devils myself if I had a gun. Treating decent young women like that! Men may invent railways and who knows what else they'll invent before they're through, but they haven't found a way to stop such wickedness. That's what I pray for when I go to chapel, for the wickedness to stop.'

These words comforted Cassandra hugely. Neither of the women had recoiled from her. She'd thought they'd despise her . . . now.

She still felt dirty, though, in spite of the bath. The word 'besmirched' came into her mind and exactly described how she felt. She sniffed back a tear, snuggling down and pulling the soft blanket right up to her neck.

She'd expected to find it difficult to sleep but she was so tired, it seemed natural to let her eyelids close.

Jane realised she was lying on the floor and couldn't for a moment understand why. Then she remembered and winced as she moved her head. Cassandra must have hit her hard enough to knock her out. Some would think she'd been stupid to help their prisoner escape, only she never could abide men selling women as if they were toys. It was one thing to choose a life like this, and for her, it'd been the only way to escape a life of poverty. But it was quite another to be forced into it and not paid at all for what you did. That was very wrong.

Her head throbbed but she didn't dare move. She wished they'd hurry up and find her.

It seemed a long time until the door opened.

A man's voice exclaimed, 'What the hell—?' and someone knelt beside her. 'Jane!' He rolled her over as roughly as he did everything these days, muttering, 'She's alive, at least.' There was a pause, then, 'The bitch has escaped. Well, she'll not get far.'

Jane judged it time to start regaining consciousness and moaned.

He was back beside her. 'What happened?'

She blinked her eyes, stared at him and shut her eyes again.

He shook her. 'Wake up, dammit.'

She groaned loudly. 'My head hurts. What happened?'

'That's what I'm asking *you*. Where's that girl you were supposed to be looking after for me?'

She judged it wiser to moan than try to answer.

Someone else came to the door of the room and screamed. Thank goodness, Jane thought.

The girl who'd been due to keep an eye on Cassandra next rushed across and helped her sit up. When Pete tried to question Jane again, the newcomer said fiercely, 'Can't you see she's not regained her wits yet? Someone must have hit her very hard. Look at her poor head.'

His voice came from further away. 'That bitch must have taken her by surprise. But she'll pay for this. She can't have gone far. We'll find her, wherever she is.'

Jane let the other women fuss over her, pretending she had no idea what had happened. And actually, she was glad to be put to bed because her head was aching fiercely. It was worth the pain, though, to have foiled Pete and that horrible Blake woman who'd hired him.

The main thing was, he didn't realise she'd helped his prisoner escape. She was safe.

She looked at the clock. An hour had passed since she last looked at it. Maybe Cassandra really would escape.

She hoped so. Women like them had to stick together because it was a hard world.

In the morning Phyllis and Mrs Rainey woke Cassandra before it was light.

'What's the matter? Is something wrong?'

'My husband couldn't sleep, he was so worried about you. He got up early and did some calculations. You know that he and the other ministers of religion in the town were consulted about sending young women who'd been affected by the Cotton Famine out to Australia?'

She nodded.

'Well, he studied all the information he'd been given, and realised that the ship carrying your sisters hasn't sailed yet. If you leave today, you may be able to catch up with them, go to Australia with them.'

Cassandra's breath caught in her throat. 'But will they allow me on the ship?'

'I don't know. We can but try.'

'How am I to get away from Outham?'

'By wearing your mourning clothes. We have all your clothing and some of your other possessions here. Your sisters left them with us. I can lend you a taffeta overskirt to wear with those mourning clothes your uncle bought you. I can give you a full veil too and they'll not look at you twice. Phyllis will go to the railway station with you and you can get on the train together. Lean on her arm and pretend to be overcome with grief. Can you manage that, do you think? I'd like to give you longer to recover, but we need to leave straight away.'

'I'll manage it.'

'My husband and I will travel on the same train, but separately. They might suspect us if they saw us escorting a young widow, but I doubt they'll know who Phyllis is, and she'll be wearing mourning too.'

Cassandra flung the covers off the bed. 'I'll do anything to be reunited with my sisters. I can't thank you both enough.'

Isabel was woken early by someone knocking on the door. She let the maid answer it, wondering who could be calling at such an hour.

When Dot came up to tell her that a man wanted to see her urgently, she was tempted to refuse, but suddenly wondered if he was here to say Cassandra had been taken to Manchester, as she'd ordered.

'I'll get dressed. Ask him to wait.'

When she went down to her parlour, she found Pete pacing impatiently to and fro. 'I thought I told you not to visit me here.'

'I needed to see you urgent, Mrs Blake.'

'What about?'

'That niece of yours has run off.'

'*What?* I thought you said she'd be carefully guarded.'

'Last night she hit my lady friend over the head, knocked her out of her senses, she did, the bitch, and then ran off. We've hunted all over town, but she's gone to earth. We'll find her, though.'

'You'd better, if you want the rest of your payment. Make sure you watch the railway station and that you keep her away from the police station. I don't want her reporting this to the authorities.'

'I've a man outside both places already, and they know her by sight.' He grinned. 'She won't get past them. They've instructions to hit her on the head and pretend she's fainted. But she's got no money and none of her friends will have the fare, not in times like these, so I don't see how she can buy a ticket. We'll find her. She won't get far on foot.'

'She may have gone back to the cottage she used to live in. I'll get you the key and you can check that she's not hiding there.' Isabel went across to the drawer of her writing desk and took a key out. 'Check there on your way back.'

When he'd gone, she began pacing up and down, furious that Cassandra had escaped. She had no doubt that her niece had gone to a friend's house and was staying hidden. But who could it be? The Minister and his wife? Perhaps. Or one of the trollop's men friends. That was more likely.

Well, if Cassandra tried to follow her sisters, she'd be intercepted. Isabel already had someone watching the ship to make sure the others got away safely and that Cassandra didn't join the other pauper lasses emigrating from Lancashire. She wasn't leaving anything to chance, not one single thing.

And she wasn't burying her husband until after the *Tartar* had sailed, no matter what anyone said. She was quite determined about that. She wasn't going to have *those creatures* interrupting the funeral, acting as if they were related to her.

Within the half-hour, the maid came back to say the man wanted to see Mrs Blake again.

She waited till the door had closed behind Dot. 'Well?'

'Your niece must have been at the cottage. The kitchen window's been smashed, so she'll have gone in that way. We checked every room but she's not there now. I reckon she spent the night there.'

'Why would she go back there?'

'Wasn't that where she lived before?'

'Yes. But I checked to make sure they'd left nothing behind and she was told her sisters had left the country.'

He shrugged. 'Well, missus, she can't get out of the town without us seeing her, especially if she didn't start out last night.' He grinned. 'We'll find her and make her sorry, don't you worry.'

After he'd left Isabel went to stare out of the window, anger churning inside her.

A little later it occurred to her that if Cassandra had been helped to run away, she'd not dare to come back to Outham, so although her niece wouldn't be left penniless in the slums of Manchester, a punishment which had rather appealed to Isabel, the creature would still be on her own, still have memories of what had happened to her, still be separated from her sisters.

She smiled. 'They're gone now, all of them. I always get what I want – in one way or the other.' She saw Dot staring from the doorway and scowled. 'What do you want? I'll ring when I want something. Go away.'

'Yes, ma'am. Sorry, ma'am.'

The three Blake sisters sat at the long table that ran down the centre of the single females' quarters on the ship, not speaking just getting used to their temporary home. The sides of this area had been divided off into tiny chambers with four bunks in each and a rough curtain for a door.

They were sharing theirs with a young girl of fourteen, who'd been sobbing since she came on board because of being separated from the rest of her family. At her age she wasn't allowed to stay in the married quarters and had been put with the single women.

'I wish the rain would stop,' Xanthe sighed. 'We didn't get a chance to look round on deck, they rushed us straight down here.'

Pandora pulled a face as she heard someone being sick at the other end of the long room. 'If people are sick now, what will they be like when we get out on to the open sea? The ship's only rising and falling a bit. Matron says it gets much rougher than this.'

'I don't feel very well, either,' Maia said. 'I think you'd better get me one of those buckets, just in case I can't reach the water closet in time.'

They'd been pleasantly surprised to find a water closet for their use. It emptied its contents into the sea and you used sea water to clean it.

One of the other women had protested about that, wanting the familiar comfort of a chamber pot next to her bed, but Matron had told her sharply not to be silly. A chamber pot would spill its contents everywhere in rough weather.

Maia dashed off suddenly and Xanthe followed her twin. A few minutes later a white-faced Maia went to lie down.

'She was sick,' Xanthe said unnecessarily.

'Poor thing. I feel fine. Don't you?'

'Yes. But it's not much fun sitting here below the deck, is it?'

'Matron says the weather's not looking good and we may be locked down for days. I do hope it won't be stormy.'

An hour later Matron came and clapped her hands for their attention. 'Gather round, please. Come out of the bedrooms.' She waited till the group of young women had gathered.

Pandora studied her travelling companions. The Lancashire contingent were thin, looking peaky. There were one or two with suspiciously short hair, women with hard expressions, maybe they'd been in prison, where women's hair was cropped short. If so, what were such people doing here? She turned her attention back to Matron, who was speaking again.

'We need to organise you in messes, groups of eight. The mess leader will get your food from the cook and share it out. Sometimes she will be required to help cook the extra allowances of food. The easiest way is to take two cabins to one mess.' She pointed out the pairs of cabins and asked for volunteers to be mess leaders.

Since the other members of her own mess were looking woebegone and avoiding Matron's eyes, Pandora volunteered. If it hadn't been for her worries about Cassandra, she'd have been enjoying the novelty of this, though she still wasn't reconciled to leaving Lancashire for good.

She was sure her father would have approved of them seeking a new life for themselves, though. His life had been so restricted, yet he'd never complained. She had one of his Greek books in her luggage. She couldn't understand a word of it, but she stroked it sometimes and thought of him.

The twins were so close to one another, seeming to know what the other was thinking half the time, that Pandora felt left out a bit. She'd always felt closer to her eldest sister.

'Right. Mess leaders come and get the food. It's just a simple cold meal today. There won't be proper cooked meals until we're under way.'

Pandora followed Matron up to the deck and was shown the cook's area, waiting in line for food, which turned out to be a generous supply of bread, butter and jam. Her spirits lifted. She felt hungry all the time these days, hated to see her thin face and dull hair in the mirror, and couldn't wait to eat her evening meal. She was told how much to serve and to keep the rest of the bread for breakfast, but there was plenty, so that would be no hardship.

She sighed as she set the loaves down on the long table. If only Cassandra were here, perhaps it wouldn't be as bad. She kept worrying about her sister. Was Cassandra even alive? Would they ever see each other again?

Pandora didn't want to leave England. Something deep within her felt it was home as another land could never be.

13

Two ladies dressed in rustling black silk and the deepest mourning got down from a cab and walked into the station. Both were heavily veiled, the younger one leaning on her companion's arm and raising a black silk handkerchief to her eyes from time to time. A porter fussed over them and the older lady left her companion drooping on a bench while she went to buy their tickets.

Mr Rainey came into the station separately, bought tickets for himself and his wife and then escorted her across to the W. H. Smith's bookstall to buy her a magazine and himself a newspaper. They stood beneath the clock, chatting quietly as they waited for the train to arrive.

An obliging porter had wheeled the luggage of the two bereaved ladies on to the platform and was now leaning on it, waiting for the train to arrive. When it did, he found them a first-class compartment, lifted their carpet bags up into the rack then loaded their trunk into the luggage van at the end of the train. When he came back from doing this, the older lady gave him a tip and he touched his cap to her, whistling as he pocketed the money and walked back down the platform.

A man lounging near the entrance had studied the

ladies as they went into the station, but his eyes didn't linger for long on such well-dressed people and he went back to scanning the others entering the station. He stared at the Raineys rather more carefully, recognising the Minister and his wife. But they were alone. In fact there was no one like the young woman he was seeking.

As the train left the station Cassandra felt shuddering relief sweep through her. 'We did it, Phyllis. Did you see the man by the entrance? He was one of them.'

'I noticed him, but he hardly looked at us.'

'Are you sure? I was having such trouble walking so that I'd look shorter that I had to concentrate on that.'

'You did well, dear. Now, why don't you have a rest? Mr and Mrs Rainey won't be able to join us in this compartment until the next stop.'

But Cassandra couldn't rest. She wasn't only escaping, she was saying farewell to Lancashire, probably for ever. The rhythmic clacking of the train wheels seemed to pound into her head and she found herself putting words to it: *Saying farewell, saying farewell, saying farewell . . .*

At the first stop, Mrs Rainey came to join them in the compartment while a porter transferred their luggage and Mr Rainey went to purchase a hamper of food for the journey.

'Three shillings!' he exclaimed as he brought it back. He looked inside it and scowled. 'Highway robbery. It's nothing but sandwiches and cakes.'

Cassandra had lifted the mourning veil from her face and tucked it back over her bonnet, but as people walked past their carriage on the platform, she kept her face averted, wishing she could continue to hide behind the veil. She hated how her hair looked now, wondered what people must think of it being so short.

'How are you feeling?' Mrs Rainey asked gently.

When she tried to answer, her throat thickened with tears and she could only shake her head blindly.

As the train rattled along again, Mr Rainey turned to another point of grievance. 'Did you see that fellow at the station entrance in Outham, staring at everyone? Did he expect to abduct you from there in broad daylight?'

'He might have done if I was alone. It's very easy to hit someone on the head and knock them out.' Cassandra shuddered. She hated the thought that she'd hurt Jane.

'I'd never have believed it if I'd not seen it with my own eyes! You were right, Cassandra. They were indeed trying to recapture you. The effrontery of these people! I shall take a greater interest in law and order from now on. It's no use saving people's souls unless their bodies are safe.'

By the time they reached London, Cassandra was so numb with tiredness and reaction to her ordeal that she could hardly force her wobbly legs to move. She reached up to pull her veil across her face.

'No need for that now,' Mrs Rainey said.

'I'd rather keep it on.' She still felt as if people could read what had happened to her from her face, still felt sick at the thought of it.

'You do what you want, dear,' Phyllis said, offering the support of her arm again, gruff as ever, but there.

Everything was happening with such bewildering speed

Cassandra hardly knew what to think. Would she really find her sisters again, go to Australia with them?

Could she really make a new start?

When they arrived in Gravesend, it was quite late and they could do nothing but find a hotel until the various offices opened the following morning. Again, Cassandra slept like the dead in the room she was sharing with Phyllis, but it was a heavy, unrefreshing sleep and she woke with a dull headache.

She and Phyllis joined Mrs Rainey for breakfast.

'There's no time to waste, with the ship leaving tomorrow, so my husband is already out making enquiries about a passage for you.'

Cassandra nodded. She didn't feel hungry but ate a little to please her companions, both of whom were worried about her, she could see. Her main feeling was of numbness. She didn't seem to know herself any more so for once, she let the others guide her.

Mr Rainey still hadn't returned by ten o'clock, so they waited for him in the guests' sitting room.

Her companions tried to make conversation, but soon gave up the attempt to include her, for which she was grateful. She was having trouble concentrating.

Gerald Rainey went first to the docks to make sure the *Tartar* had not yet sailed, and an obliging old sailor, who was leaning against a bollard smoking a pipe, pointed it out to him.

'Have they taken the emigrants on board yet?'

'Yesterday.'

'Who must I see about getting passage on that ship?'

The old man laughed. 'Can't just buy a passage, sir. It's an emigrant ship. You'll have to see the agent.'

Gerald slipped the man a shilling and hurried off to the address given him, only to find the office wasn't open yet. A card in the window said it would open at nine. He went to find a stall to buy some food and was fortunate enough to find one that sold cups of tea and hearty sandwiches, so was able to satisfy his appetite before returning to the office. There a clerk allowed him to sit and wait for the agent, who didn't come in until later.

When the man did arrive, he shook his head decisively at a request to take another young woman from Lancashire on the *Tartar*.

'My dear sir, all the places are taken. There simply isn't any sleeping accommodation left.'

'Then could we pay for her passage?' He explained about Cassandra's sisters, the urgent need for her to get on that ship, pretending she'd just lost her husband, which was the story they'd agreed on briefly the night before.

'It's a sad story but I don't allocate the other places, so I can't help you. I did hear, however, that the cabins have all been taken by paying passengers. I can't see there being room for another passenger, whatever the circumstances.'

'Could you at least tell me if the sisters are on board?'

'What did you say they were called?'

Gerald told him.

The agent frowned. 'Young women called Susan, May

and Dora Blake are on the ship. They tried to claim other names, but we had been warned by the Vicar who recommended them not to give in to such fancies.'

'But the names they claim are their real ones. I christened them myself.'

The agent shrugged. 'Too late now.'

Gerald felt angry all over again at the way the Vicar trampled on everyone from the lower classes. That was no way to spread the Lord's message. He sat down in the waiting room for a moment to try to calm himself and work out how to break the bad news to Cassandra. As usual when there was trouble, he prayed to his Maker for help.

When he'd finished, he saw another gentleman sitting opposite him, looking annoyed.

'How long is that agent fellow going to be?' the other asked.

'Is something wrong?' Mr Rainey asked, since his companion seemed bursting to confide in someone.

'Yes, very wrong. That stupid maid of my wife's has changed her mind and now refuses to come to Australia with us, says she's too old for such junketing and she doesn't want to leave her family. I've heard there are some young women being sent out to the colonies and I want to find out if one of them can do the job temporarily. That is, if they're respectable. I'm not having a slut tend my wife, who is in a delicate condition. She needs a woman's help on the journey. *I* can't do the sorts of things she requires.'

Dear Lord, thank you, Gerald thought. 'Actually, I may be able to help you.'

'Oh?'

'A young friend of ours has been suddenly widowed. Her sisters are on that ship and she's desperate to go out to Australia with them. I'd come here to try to persuade the agent to take her as well, but they have a full quota. And he says there are no passages to be bought, either. If she were to take your maid's place . . .' He looked at the other.

The man slapped his hand on his leg. 'It could be the answer. I'd need to meet her. Is she respectable?'

'She's very respectable, has been a member of my congregation all her life. She's with my wife and our housekeeper in a nearby hotel. She is, as you will appreciate, very upset. Her husband was taken from her suddenly in an accident. But I'm sure she'll do her best to help your wife if you pay for her passage. She's a capable young woman.'

'How old is she?'

'About thirty, I think, perhaps a little younger.'

'Just the ticket. Much better than a flighty young female or a timid older one. My name's Barrett, Simon Barrett.'

They shook hands and Gerald introduced himself.

'Tell me where you're staying and we'll come to meet her as soon as I can fetch my wife. You *are* sure she's respectable?'

'I can not only vouch for Cassandra, I knew her father and mother well. Sadly, they too are dead and her sisters are the only relatives she has left in the world.'

'Very sad.' But Mr Barrett spoke absent-mindedly.

Gerald hurried back to the hotel.

★

'Here he is!'

Cassandra looked up to see Mr Rainey stride into the sitting room.

'We should go up to our bedroom and talk privately,' he said. 'Please hurry.'

The ladies looked at one another in surprise and followed him up the stairs.

As he explained what the migration agent had said, Cassandra closed her eyes in despair. 'I may never see them again. And what am I going to *do*? I can't go back to Outham.'

'If you'll let me finish, my dear . . .' He told them about the Barretts.

Cassandra stared at him as if she'd not understood a word he'd said and he looked at his wife for guidance.

'Are you all right, my dear?' she asked gently.

'Yes. I was just so – overwhelmed. If they'll give me the position, I promise I'll work very hard indeed, though I've no experience of being a maid.'

'Tell them that. Don't pretend.'

'Why do I need to say I'm a widow? Surely I can become myself again now?'

Mr Rainey exchanged another glance with his wife and edged towards the door. 'I'll – um, leave you ladies to have a quick chat about this. I'll be waiting for you downstairs.'

When he'd gone, Cassandra turned in puzzlement to Mrs Rainey.

'Have you not considered that there may be – results of the way you were treated?'

She couldn't think clearly, felt dull and weary, so shook

her head. It was over now, wasn't it? Except for the nightmares.

'My dear, what if you're expecting a child?'

Cassandra looked at her in horror. 'I hadn't even considered that,' she said, her voice a mere whisper. 'Is this nightmare never going to end?'

'It may not happen, and we'll pray that it doesn't, but you said they used you many times.'

The silence seemed stifling. She couldn't breathe.

There was a knock on the door and Phyllis answered it to find a maid there to summon them downstairs to meet the Barretts.

Mrs Rainey looked doubtfully at Cassandra. 'My dear, you must pull yourself together, difficult as it is. This may be your only hope of joining your sisters.'

As the words sank in, Cassandra nodded and took a shaky breath.

'Remember, you're recently bereaved. Your husband died of . . . what?'

'He was knocked down by a runaway horse and cart,' Phyllis said. 'We need something sudden and shocking.'

Mrs Rainey nodded. 'Yes, that's a good idea. What was his name?'

Cassandra could only think of John.

'And his surname?'

'John Lawson.' Phyllis again offered a suggestion. 'Tell them you'd only been married for a few months. They'll be even more sympathetic then. And there's your hair to consider. How do we explain that?'

Cassandra reached up to touch the short, jaw-length hair. It still felt strange. 'There's nothing I can do about it.'

'You'd better tell them you were ill just before your husband died and they cut your hair short to conserve your strength. It looks well enough, even now, being so thick and wavy.'

She nodded. What did it matter? Everything seemed so unreal and this was yet another chimera that had arisen to bedevil her. Perhaps this was a nightmare and she'd waken soon.

But she knew it wasn't, and although she called it a chimera, it was not a product of her imagination nor a mythical beast. The beasts had been men. The unthinkable had really happened and its consequences were still affecting her life, driving her to extreme measures.

She hated to lie. But if lying would reunite her with her sisters, then she'd do it. She took a few deep breaths and gave the two older women a shaky smile. 'I'm ready.'

'I'll stay here,' Phyllis said. 'I'm only the housekeeper. Most employers aren't like Mr and Mrs Rainey, who treat everyone kindly. They won't like me being there with you. And remember, you can't expect the same friendliness from them.' She hesitated, then went across to give the younger woman a quick hug.

Cassandra hugged her back and then, feeling as if her main support in the world had been taken from her, followed the Minister's brisk wife down the stairs.

In the sitting room they found Mr Rainey chatting to a young couple. Mrs Barrett looked wan and puffy, and her husband's eyes kept going to her anxiously.

Mrs Rainey put one arm round Cassandra's shoulders

as they moved across the room and waited for her husband to introduce them.

Mrs Barrett eyed Cassandra's black clothing doubtfully and then her short hair. 'When did your husband die?'

'A few days ago,' Mrs Rainey said for her. 'He was killed in an accident, a runaway horse and cart. It was very sudden, and our young friend was just recovering from pneumonia when it happened.'

Mrs Barrett's eyes filled with tears. 'Oh, how sad!'

'Are you sure you should be making such a big change to your life?' Mr Barrett asked, looking at Cassandra doubtfully. 'It's very early days. And we need someone who can work hard and help my wife.'

'I have only my sisters in the world now,' Cassandra said. 'I want more than anything else to go to Australia with them.' She turned back to Mrs Barrett and spoke from the heart, 'I'm not trained to be a lady's maid, but I promise you I'll do my very best if you show me what you need. I'm a quick learner and a hard worker.'

'Can you sew?'

'Yes. Well, I can mend and I've been learning to embroider and make clothes.'

'I hate mending,' Mrs Barrett said. 'But I love embroidering.'

She smiled suddenly at Cassandra, who concentrated on the thought of her sisters and dredged up a smile in return. 'I'm sorry about your husband. If you'd like to work your passage as my maid, you can come on board with us tomorrow. We'll pay you wages, of course.'

'But not as much as a fully-trained maid,' her husband said quickly.

'The cabin passengers board later than the emigrants and you won't be sleeping with them on the ship. You'll share a small cabin near us with another lady's maid.'

But Mr Barrett was still frowning. 'What happened to your hair? Why was it cropped?'

She knew they cropped the hair of women who went into prison and stiffened. 'They cut it short when I was ill, to conserve my strength.'

'We keep telling her it looks well enough,' Mr Rainey said. 'But young women care about these things, do they not?'

Mr Barrett was still frowning. 'You know about it, then, why it was done?'

'Of course I do. And I'll not mince my words. There isn't time. I appreciate that you're worried it might have been done because she was imprisoned.' Mr Rainey laughed. 'That was definitely not the case with Cassandra. I give you my solemn word on that.'

Mr Barrett's expression lightened.

'What about the emigration agent?' Mr Rainey asked. 'What will he say about the changes?'

'I don't think we'll tell anyone she's not Hilda until after the ship has sailed. They probably won't even ask, so we won't actually have to *lie*. I don't want to risk my dear wife having no help on the voyage, not in her condition. You'd better move to our hotel today, Lawson. We'll need to get up very early in the morning.'

'I wonder if Cassandra could stay here and join you tomorrow as you board the ship.' Mrs Rainey smiled apologetically. 'It's the last time we'll see our young friend and we'd like to be with her for as long as possible.'

Mr Barrett looked annoyed. 'I don't want my wife troubled with packing the luggage and overseeing its removal to the ship. That sort of thing is part of a maid's job.'

'I'll come now, if you wish,' Cassandra offered quickly, terrified of losing this opportunity. 'I'm sure my friends will understand. I just need to pack my night things.'

'I'll come up with you,' Mrs Rainey said.

When the luggage was packed, Cassandra burst into tears. 'I can't believe how generous you've been. I don't know how to thank you. What I'd have done without your help doesn't bear thinking of.'

'"Love thy neighbour,"' Mrs Rainey said. 'We don't need thanks for helping you. But when you're more comfortably circumstanced, perhaps you could try to help others who're in need?'

'I shall. I promise you.'

Cassandra sat in a cab with her new employers, listening to Melissa Barrett prattle about nothing and watching Simon Barrett smile at his wife fondly. Neither of them spoke to her, or even seemed to notice her during the short journey to their hotel.

Once there, she helped her mistress finish her packing and was given a lesson in laying out clothes for the evening. She found she was to eat with other servants in a separate dining room and felt shy as she made her way there. How different these people were from the Raineys, who treated Phyllis more as a friend than a servant and who had been so kind to Cassandra.

She found that the group of servants at the hotel had

their own hierarchy and looked down their noses at her when she said she was only a temporary lady's maid. She felt very out of place with them and couldn't summon up the energy even to chat to them. She forced food down, knowing she had to keep her strength up.

The sense of unreality persisted but she tried hard to pay attention as she helped Mrs Barrett change into her nightclothes. She must have given satisfaction, because her new mistress said approvingly, 'You do learn quickly. That's going to be a big help. And I shall enjoy teaching you to be a lady's maid. It'll give me something to do on board the ship.'

'Yes, ma'am. Thank you very much.'

Melissa sighed. 'To tell you the truth, Lawson, I wish my dear husband hadn't been sent out to Australia. He's to work for the government out there, you know. He has no need to work because I have a private income, but he says a gentleman must make his mark upon the world. We're only going to be there for a few years, thank goodness. But I'm not looking forward to the long voyage. So tedious.'

This time when Cassandra went to bed in a tiny comfortless room in the attics, she didn't fall asleep easily. She didn't feel safe until she'd pulled her luggage across the door. And even so, her thoughts churned round in circles. In the middle of the night, she woke from a nightmare to find tears on her cheeks.

This was doing no good, she scolded herself. She must look forward not backward. But that was easier to say than to do, because you couldn't control nightmares, could you?

She was relieved when one of the chambermaids knocked on her bedroom door while it was still dark and told her it was time to get her mistress ready for an early start. She quickly packed her own nightclothes and took her bag down with her.

Mrs Barrett was yawning over a cup of tea and there was no sign of Mr Barrett. 'Is that all the luggage you've got?'

'I have a trunk as well, but I packed in a hurry and may not have all that's necessary.'

'Well, Simon says there's no way of getting Hilda's trunk off the ship, so I shall give her things to you.'

'I couldn't take them!'

'They'll just be thrown away if you don't. *I* certainly don't want them.'

'Oh.'

'Besides, how would it look to have a maid who didn't have the proper clothes? You must take the trunk and make up your own deficiencies from it.'

'Very well, ma'am.'

Mrs Barrett nodded approval. 'Now, please help me dress. We don't want to be late or Simon will be annoyed. I'm not used to waking so early.'

She prattled the whole time, talking of nothing worthwhile, in Cassandra's opinion. But at least it filled the silence. Being a maid clearly involved a lot of listening and agreeing with her mistress.

It was raining hard as they went on board the *Tartar* and Mrs Barrett kept up a steady commentary as she and her husband were shown to their cabin, complaining about everything she saw. Cassandra walked behind them in silence, carrying her own portmanteau. She stared round, fascinated by this new world and felt her spirits lift a little at the novelty of her surroundings. She'd always wanted to travel, hadn't she?

Because of the bad weather there were no passengers on deck, so she couldn't see her sisters yet. She must trust Mr Rainey's assurances that they were on the passenger list, even if under incorrect names.

The Barretts' cabin was small but well fitted out. It had two bunk beds and enough room for a small table and sofa. These were screwed to the floor and the dining chairs were attached to the wall by leather straps until needed.

When the cabin trunks were brought in, they were set upright in a space at the inner end of the cabin. They opened to show drawers full of everything the Barretts could need during the journey.

Mrs Barrett flung herself on the sofa, dabbing at her eyes. Her husband went to her side, tossing over his shoulder, 'Perhaps you'd show my wife's maid where she's to sleep?'

The steward touched Cassandra's arm. 'If you'll come with me, miss?'

'It's Mrs,' she corrected. 'Mrs Lawson.'

After closing the cabin door, he said, 'They don't usually have married maids.'

'I'm a widow.'

She was shown into a very narrow chamber without a porthole. It contained two bunk beds and not much else.

He looked at her, grinning. 'Ever been on a ship before?'

'No, I haven't. I'd be grateful for any advice you can offer me.'

'Well, we have to work together, so the sooner I teach you what to do, the easier my job of looking after your employers will be. Which bunk do you want?'

'I don't mind. Who is the other person?'

'Another maid, according to the list. She's not come on board yet.' There was a call of 'Steward!' and he looked over his shoulder, sighing. 'What do they want now? I'll be back as quickly as I can.'

A few minutes later he returned accompanied by a scrawny older lady. 'This is Miss Pershore. Mrs Lawson.'

The newcomer paid no attention to the introductions, too busy staring round in horror. 'I can't spend three months in a tiny space like this! You must find me another cabin immediately, one on my own. My mistress will pay whatever is necessary. She can't have understood what was involved when her brother purchased our passages. She'd *never* have expected me to put up with such a – a cupboard.'

The steward's face lost its friendly smile and turned into a polite mask. 'I'm afraid there isn't anywhere else, Miss Pershore, however much your mistress is willing to pay.'

She moaned and sagged against the door frame.

'Actually, it's not a bad little cabin. You two are private, at least. The female emigrants are all crowded together below, but there's only the two of you here. I'm sure you and Mrs Barrett's maid will get on well and be able to help one another.' He indicated Cassandra again.

'I should refuse to go,' Miss Pershore said with a doleful sniff. 'And I would, if I wasn't so fond of my mistress. I've worked for her for thirty years, but she's never asked me to do anything like go to Australia before, never! Her younger son is out there and she's determined to visit him. I'm sure it'll be the death of us both.'

'Well, let me show you how to stow your bags when they're not in use. Which bunk do you want?'

'I must have the bottom one. I can't possibly climb up there, not at my age.'

'I'm happy to take the top bunk,' Cassandra said.

'There,' said the steward in an over-hearty voice, 'Didn't I say you ladies would get on well?' He winked at Cassandra. 'Now, let me show you the amenities, then I have to check on my passengers.'

The passengers were to relieve themselves in cupboard-like water closets, one for the gentlemen and one for the ladies. 'You can't be going down to the emigrants' quarters, so you'll have to use these,' the steward told them.

Miss Pershore nodded, tight-lipped.

'You can get as much sea water as you want to wash yourselves with, but fresh water for drinking is obtained from me. You'll need to be careful with that, and so will your mistress. We can't afford to waste it.'

'I shouldn't have to carry the water at my age!' Miss Pershore said faintly.

Cassandra had intended to ask him how she could get to see her sisters, but she didn't like to do that in front of Miss Pershore. And anyway, the steward seemed very busy, poor man.

When he'd left, the older lady sat on the lower bunk,

dabbing her eyes and muttering that she didn't know what the world was coming to, she really didn't.

Cassandra climbed up to her own bunk and decided it was much nicer on top, without someone lying above you. But it was still a very small cabin and she didn't think Miss Pershore was going to be a pleasant companion.

Still, she was going with her sisters to Australia. That's what mattered most. The bad times were over. She must put them behind her.

14

When word came from the watcher Isabel had hired to say the ship had sailed and that Cassandra Blake had definitely not joined the group of emigrants from Lancashire, Isabel beamed at the letter and danced round her parlour. 'I did it! I did it!'

Dot, who had brought up the morning tea tray her mistress had ordered, backed down the stairs and came up again, pretending to bump herself on the landing post and exclaiming a little more loudly than was necessary. When she went into the parlour, she found Mrs Blake seated by the window, looking flushed, her eyes glittering, her fingers plucking at her skirt.

'Set it down there.'

'Yes, ma'am. Is there anything else you need, ma'am?'

'Yes, you can send for Mr Studdard. It's time to bury Mr Blake.'

'Yes, ma'am. I'll find a lad and—'

'Go yourself. You're looking pale. A walk will do you good.'

Dot went, but wasn't happy, because although she liked to get out of the house, she'd still have to get through her work once she got back.

★

'Mr Studdard to see you, ma'am,' she announced an hour later.

'What? Oh yes, show him up.' Isabel stood up, waited for the undertaker to come in and gestured to a seat.

'They've left now, so it's time to bury Mr Blake,' she said.

He smiled and nodded.

'A small funeral. I shall only be inviting a dozen or so guests.'

His smile faded a little.

'And as cheap as we can decently make it. As a widow, I dare not waste my money. After all, a fancy funeral won't bring my husband back, will it?'

'No, Mrs Blake.'

After he'd left Isabel went back to staring out of the window, talking to herself and even arguing with herself at one stage.

Dot rapped on the half-open door.

'What do you want now?'

'The Vicar is here to see you, ma'am. About the funeral.'

'Oh. Right. Show him up.'

Isabel watched the Vicar approach her with the smile he always adopted for his better class of parishioners, and was nearly betrayed into laughing at the thought of what he'd say if he knew what she'd done. She composed her face into a suitably sad expression, gestured to a chair opposite hers and waited for him to speak.

'Mr Studdard has arranged a funeral for tomorrow, my dear lady. Is that not a little rushed?'

He reminded her she'd have to send out invitations. 'I

let my grief overwhelm me,' she said in a soft voice, 'and now realise Joseph should have been buried before.'

'But not in such a rush. Shall we say the day after tomorrow? That will give you time to send out invitations.'

She didn't see why she should change things to suit him. She was only going to suit herself from now on. 'Unless *you* are not able to officiate – I won't be put off with a curate – I'd rather get it over with tomorrow.'

He opened his mouth as if to protest, so she stood up. 'I've made my mind up,' she said firmly. 'Tomorrow.'

When he'd gone, she rang for Dot. 'Tell the shop boy I need him to deliver some letters in half an hour or so. I must send out invitations to the funeral tomorrow.'

'Tomorrow, ma'am? But—'

'Are you daring to question my orders?'

'No, ma'am, certainly not, ma'am. Tomorrow. Do we – um, need to provide refreshments?'

'No. Just a glass of sherry for each mourner and some of those fancy macaroon biscuits. Get Harry Prebble in the shop to send them up.'

'Yes, ma'am.'

'I'll ring when I have the invitations ready.'

She took out some notepaper and scribbled notes to those she regarded as friends, blotting each one carefully, remembering as a girl having to use sand to dry the ink. Modern inventions like blotting paper made life a lot easier.

When the invitations were ready, she handed the envelopes to Dot, and went to get out the new mourning clothes she'd had made, stroking the heavy twilled silk with a loving hand. *I'm enjoying being a widow, being in charge here, doing as I please,* she thought, and swished the skirt to and fro for the pleasure of hearing it rustle.

It was a pity they couldn't have the reading of the will for a few days yet. Why the lawyer had to choose this time to go to London, she didn't know. But that was only a formality. Who else could Joseph have left the shop and other properties to but her? They'd gone to him from Isabel's family and now they'd be returning to a Horton again. She'd change the sign on the shop back to 'Horton's Emporium', in big gold letters.

'You'll like that, Father, won't you?' she murmured, smiling when he agreed with her. 'And I'll make you proud of me. I'll work very hard. You should have let me go into the shop. You would have done if I'd been a boy. That wasn't fair. But better late than never.'

Humming, she went to stand by the window.

Dot worked hard to get everything straight in the kitchen, glad her mistress only wanted a chop and a boiled potato for tea. She ate her own chop afterwards with relish. Mrs Blake didn't even tell her what to eat these days, so Dot had decided to have the same as her mistress.

Her meal was interrupted by responses to the invitations and she sighed as she took the notes upstairs. Her feet were killing her.

She wasn't looking forward to the funeral tomorrow. It'd be nothing but hard work for her but she hadn't dared ask her mistress if they could hire extra help to serve the sherry and open the door to guests. The master would have thought of that. He'd been a kind man and she missed him.

★

As Isabel got ready the following day, Dot brought in a note from the Vicar's wife, asking if she would like the loan of a maidservant to help with the guests after the funeral.

Isabel dashed off a quick reply, thanking her for this generous offer of help. *'But I'm bringing up one of the shop men to help.'*

Harry Prebble had been very helpful and it had suddenly occurred to her that she needed someone to serve the sherry. He'd been properly grateful when she offered him the chance to run the shop. He was twenty-five, after all, old enough to have a bit of sense. Joseph had thought more of the other young man – what was his name? Zachary, that was it. Zachary Carr. Such a tall, lanky creature, he didn't *look* like a manager. But Joseph had always said he was a good worker, so she'd let him stay on.

The funeral went well and was over quickly, thank goodness. She kept the veil over her face during the short ceremony to hide the fact that she couldn't even pretend to cry. And when she bent to pick up a handful of earth to scatter on his grave she felt such triumph, such joy in her new status that it was a minute before she could let go of it.

When they returned to the house, she managed to contain her emotions until the guests had drunk a glass of sherry and left.

Thanking Harry for his help, she closed the door on them all.

Then she could hold it in no longer. She began to laugh and couldn't stop, laughing on and on until she cried.

★

Downstairs, Dot and Harry from the shop were each raising a glass of sherry in a toast to their dead master when the noise started. They stopped drinking to listen.

'She's laughing!' he said in astonishment. 'Today of all days!'

'She laughs a lot. Though it's not real laughter, is it?'

'Is she hysterical with grief?'

'Not her! *I* think she's glad to be rid of him.'

'She's asked me to be the manager. But she said she was going to keep a close eye on things.'

'If you take my advice, you won't cross her. She's mean when she's crossed.'

He topped up their glasses from the decanter and passed hers back. 'We've more than earned this today.'

With a giggle, she accepted it.

'He's bound to have left it all to her, isn't he?' Harry sipped thoughtfully.

'Who else is there?'

'What about those nieces of his?'

'He'd never dare leave anything to them. Anyway, they've gone off to Australia, haven't they?'

'Three of them have. Who knows where the other one is?' As the laughter upstairs stopped abruptly, he drained his glass and took two mints out of his pocket, handing one to Dot. 'Don't want her to smell it on your breath, do you?'

When he'd gone, Dot chewed her mint thoughtfully. By the time Mrs Blake came down to check on her, she was washing the glasses, setting them on a linen cloth on the wooden draining board after she'd rinsed them.

Mrs Blake stood in the doorway watching her. 'Take good care of my glasses. They're the best ones.'

She turned and left without giving any other further orders.

I don't need telling that, Dot thought resentfully. *I know my job.* As she got on with her work, she glanced uneasily upstairs from time to time. Silence wasn't a comfortable thing in this house. It meant she didn't know where the mistress was. She felt uneasy today and couldn't help glancing over her shoulder from time to time.

She'd write to the employment agency a friend had told her about in Manchester, she decided. It didn't matter where they sent her, she couldn't stay here, not now. Who knew what her mistress would do next?

For the first few days after the ship set sail, the weather was either stormy or further storms were threatening. Whenever she was allowed, Pandora went up on deck for a breath of fresh air, holding tight to the rail and laughing as the wind whipped her hair out of its tidy bun. She saw the Isle of Wight disappear behind the *Tartar* several times, only to see it reappear a short time later. It seemed as if they'd never be able to leave the English Channel. She wished they didn't have to, was already missing Lancashire.

There was much grumbling among the single women, who had been locked down in their quarters for a good part of the time.

On one occasion the weather was so bad that no one needed to tell any of them they were in danger. Some women were violently ill, others quarrelled or prowled up and down the narrow area between the long table and the tiny cabins. The air smelled foul when you came down from the deck and the mood was equally unpleasant.

Pandora didn't suffer from seasickness and since Maia did and Xanthe was looking after her, she was left mainly to her own devices. She was very bored. She'd been told there was a small library on the ship for the use of passengers, but nothing had yet been organised and the books were stored in the purser's area, so she couldn't borrow one yet.

She watched as the doctor came to attend to the sick people, though he wasn't able to help them much. He, it seemed, was in charge of the emigrants and Matron fussed over him as if he was a god.

A clergyman who was travelling to the Swan River Colony also came to visit the single women and prayed with those suffering as much from terror as from seasickness. Poor Mr Millett had something wrong with his face, which twitched horribly, but he was of a kindly disposition, so everyone soon learned to ignore his strange appearance.

The cabin passengers were allocated a different part of the deck for exercise but Pandora only saw one or two people using that area during the bad weather, mostly gentlemen. And few of the other women came up, either, on the rare occasions they were allowed out of their quarters.

It was with great relief that they heard, ten days after they'd first set sail from England, that the ship had left the Channel behind.

'At last we're on our way,' Xanthe said.

'And we're going to be even further away from Cassandra,' Maia added.

Pandora didn't say anything. She'd tried to catch a last glimpse of the land, but failed, and now she felt bereft. She'd never have left England if she hadn't been forced, never! The others didn't seem to care about leaving Lancashire, only about leaving Cassandra, but she cared about both those things.

Mrs Barrett was so seasick that for the first week Cassandra's time was mostly occupied in looking after her. Mr Barrett was also affected, but not nearly as badly as his wife. Even Cassandra felt a little nauseous at times. It wasn't too bad, just came and went, so she tried to ignore it. She had to repay the Barretts for bringing her, so couldn't give in to any weakness.

It wasn't until they left the English Channel that she had a chance to ask if they'd told the Captain yet about her taking their maid's place.

'No. And I've been wondering if it's really necessary,' Mr Barrett said.

She stared at him in astonishment. 'Of course it is! I want to see my sisters.'

'Can't you just – pretend to make friends with them?'

'No, I can't.' She didn't even have to think about that. It was bad enough that she had to pretend she'd been married and use a false surname. It was unthinkable to deny her relationship with her sisters. And anyway, she was years younger than the maid she'd replaced. It would be bound to come out at some stage that she wasn't Hilda.

Mr Barrett breathed in deeply, looking like a bird with its feathers ruffled. 'You're being very uncooperative, Lawson.'

'I'm sorry, sir, but it's important to me. My sisters are the only relatives I have left now.'

'Very well, then. I'll seek an interview with the Captain. You'd better hold yourself in readiness to be questioned by him. I hope you realise the risk you're taking with this. What if they send you back to England?'

That made her think again, but she still came to the same conclusion. She was tired of deceit. As much as she could, she wanted to be herself again, openly and freely. And anyway, from what she'd heard since she came on board, they were short of women in the Swan River Colony, and desperately needed maids and wives. Why would they get rid of a perfectly respectable female?

She often wondered how Reece was getting on there, hoped things were going well for him, hoped he'd be glad to see her. Seeing him again was a wonderful thought and sustained her through some dark hours.

As the two women waited for Mr Barrett to return, Cassandra tidied the cabin and Melissa watched her.

'I won't let them take you away from me,' she said suddenly. 'I can't manage without a maid, not in my condition.'

'Thank you, ma'am. I appreciate that.'

Melissa pulled a face. 'You talk meekly enough, but your eyes aren't meek. You'd be better to keep your eyes down and speak softly to the Captain. He's used to being king of this small world.'

Cassandra looked at her in surprise. 'Thank you for

the advice, ma'am. I'll do what you suggest. I've been hoping to see my sisters, but the single women have mostly been kept below.' She thought the steward might help her contact her sisters but didn't dare ask his help until the truth was out.

It was a full half-hour before Mr Barrett returned. He ignored his wife and scowled at Cassandra. 'The Captain wants to see you. He's not pleased with our deception.'

Melissa swung her legs off the sofa and stood up. 'I think I'd better go with her.'

'I think you'd better stay here, my dear. I don't want you upset.'

'Do *you* want to be the one who empties the slops and helps me when I'm sick in the mornings, Simon?'

He threw up his hands. 'Oh, do what you want, then. You always do anyway. I'll never understand women.'

The steward was waiting outside and didn't see Mrs Barrett behind Cassandra. 'I'm to take you to the Captain, Mrs Lawson. He's not in a good mood. What have you been doing? Oh, Mrs Barrett! Sorry. I didn't see you there.'

Melissa smiled sweetly. 'I've decided to go with my maid. She needs someone to speak up for her. Do you think that's a good idea, steward? You know the Captain better than I do.'

He winked at Cassandra. 'I think it's an excellent idea, Mrs Barrett.'

He led them to the door of the Captain's cabin, knocked and when a voice called to come in, he opened the door, waved them inside and closed it behind them.

The Captain looked up from his desk, frowning as he saw two women.

'Please forgive me for coming with Lawson,' Melissa said, 'but I'm worried you'll be angry with her. It's my fault we kept her identity secret, you see. As I'm in a delicate condition, I was afraid to go on such a long voyage without a maid to help me.'

Cassandra watched her mistress blush and lower her lashes on to her cheeks. How could anyone blush on demand? she wondered. And would it make a difference?

The Captain stared at Mrs Barrett, his expression softening a little. 'Nonetheless, you should have informed me of the change at once.'

'I know. And I do apologise for that. But I was so ill when we came on board that I wasn't thinking clearly. Lawson's been wonderful, she's such a hard worker. And all in the middle of her own tragedy. Did my husband tell you about that?'

'No, but—'

Melissa rushed into an explanation of the death of the supposed husband, the fact that her maid's only relatives in the whole world were on this ship. 'So you see, she and I helped one another. And we both crave your forgiveness.' She nudged Cassandra.

'I'm really sorry, sir. I don't like being deceitful but I was desperate.'

'Hmm.' He looked her over carefully. 'It's no use pretending to be meek. You don't look at all meek to me. None of those women from Lancashire do. I'm having a lot of trouble with them. Why the Migration Agents always send out the sweepings of the gutter, I don't know.'

Cassandra opened her mouth to protest hotly at this description being applied to her or her sisters, but a poke in her ribs brought her to her senses about that.

'I'm sure Mrs Lawson's sisters are as well-behaved as she is, Captain,' Mrs Barrett cooed.

'I shall check that with Matron and let *her* arrange when it's convenient for you to see your sisters, Mrs Lawson. Do not disobey me in this. And I'll have to lay this case before the Governor when we get to Perth. There's no avoiding that. You've not been authorised to go to the colony.'

'No, sir.'

'You'd better be on your very best behaviour if you want a good report from me.'

She spoke from the heart. 'Yes, sir. I'll do anything to stay with my sisters. They're all I have left in the world.' The tears in her eyes were all too real.

He harrumphed and dismissed them with a wave of the hand.

Outside, Cassandra turned to her mistress. 'I'm so grateful for your support, ma'am.'

Melissa shrugged. 'I need a maid. What's more, I expect that when we arrive in Western Australia, you won't leave me until I can find someone else to replace you.'

'I'll do my best to help you in any way I can, I promise.'

But if what she suspected was true, Mrs Barrett wouldn't want her help.

And then what would Cassandra do?

Isabel decided to receive the lawyer sitting at the dining table which occupied one end of the long, narrow parlour.

Everything would be very straightforward, she was sure, and she'd get rid of Mr Featherworth as quickly as she could. She was looking forward to taking charge of the shop and would have started making changes before now, but the lawyer had sent word after the funeral that until the legal situation was settled, it was not possible to give her money from the estate and she shouldn't do anything differently from usual.

This made her suspect that her husband had left something to his nieces and the thought of that infuriated her. She'd found it difficult to sleep since the funeral, because Joseph kept haunting her. Well, he could wander round the bedroom and stare at her all he liked. He couldn't touch her, could he, not now?

She heard the door knocker and waited until Dot brought up the visitor, having already told the maid to deny entrance to everyone except the lawyer.

'You always were a fool,' she told Joseph when he came to stand in the corner of the room, arms folded. 'Well, you've lost everything and it's all mine, now. *Mine!*'

She swung round to see Dot and the Vicar standing in the doorway, both looking at her strangely.

She glared at the stupid girl then turned to the Vicar. 'I'm afraid I'm not receiving visitors at the moment, Mr Saunders. I'm expecting my lawyer, who is to go through the will with me.'

'Er, yes. Mr Featherworth asked me to join you, I'm not sure why. I do hope you don't mind.'

She held back her anger. It wouldn't be wise to make an enemy of the Vicar, but really, this was no business of his. 'As long as you keep what he says today to yourself.'

'I shall do whatever the lawyer advises, I promise you, my dear lady.'

She wasn't quite satisfied with that response, but before she had time to ask exactly what he meant, the door knocker went again.

Mr Featherworth came in, looking distinctly nervous. He sighed with relief as he saw the Vicar.

Joseph *had* left something to those creatures! Isabel decided, looking across at the corner again. He was smiling smugly at her. With an effort she turned back to her two visitors. 'Don't waste time in civilities. Get on with the reading of the will.'

Mr Featherworth took out some papers, arranging them in two piles on the mahogany dining table. 'This is the last will and testament of my client, Joseph Henry Blake,' he said. 'Shall I – um, read it to you or shall I summarise it first, then leave you to read your copy of the will at your leisure?'

'Summarise it.' Still he hesitated, so she added, 'Well? Get on with it.'

'I'm afraid that your husband has left everything he owned to his nieces, Cassandra, Xanthe, Maia and Pandora Blake. He stipulated that—'

Before he could speak again, Isabel let out a scream of pure rage. 'No! Noooo! *He can't have done that!*'

'I'm afraid he could and did.'

'But I'm his *wife*! And the shop belonged to my parents. He *can't* leave it to anyone else but me.'

'I'm sorry, but he has.'

She stared at him, bereft of words, feeling as if she was choking. 'Do you mean I shall be thrown out of my own home, become a pauper?'

'No, no, dear lady. If you'll allow me to continue? Your husband included a provision for you to receive twenty per cent of the profits of the shop for as long as you shall live, on condition that you move away from Outham. In addition, he has set aside a sum of money to purchase a modest house for you – possibly in some seaside resort – the house to revert to his nieces upon your death and—'

Joseph was laughing. He was laughing at her! She jumped to her feet and rushed to the corner, trying to scratch his eyes out.

Mr Featherworth stopped reading to stare open mouthed as she began to scream. She went on and on, flailing about with her arms as if she thought someone was there, as if she was trying to hit someone.

'No! No! You shan't do it, Joseph Blake! The shop's mine! Mine!'

Both gentlemen were on their feet now, looking at one another in shock, uncertain what to do about this.

The screams brought Dot running up the stairs.

The Vicar recovered first. 'Fetch Dr Turner!' he yelled to the maid. 'And send for my wife.'

When Dot didn't move, just stood staring at her mistress, he gave her a push. 'Did you hear me?'

'Yes, sir. Sorry, sir.'

Sobbing, Isabel began to tear at her hair, reeling across the room, bumping into furniture, still shrieking. 'They shan't have it!' She sent a row of ornaments crashing off a shelf with one deliberate sweep of her hand, and then turned to do the same to the ornaments on the piano.

'She's gone mad,' the lawyer whispered.

She spun round. 'What are you two whispering about? Are you in league with him? Why are you all trying to cheat me?'

The Vicar moved forward. 'My dear lady, you're not yourself. Please calm down and—'

She picked up the poker and brandished it at him.

The lawyer darted forward. 'We can't let her do this, Saunders. Help me!'

As they attempted to restrain her, she fought back, scratching and biting, managing to leave a deep gouge mark down the Vicar's plump cheek and the imprint of her teeth in the lawyer's soft, well-manicured hand.

There was no reason in her eyes, just hatred and the wild light of madness. They both clung to her for grim life, panting and struggling to hold her down, certain she'd attack them if they let her go. She nearly shook them off a couple of times, for they were both plump and nearing sixty, but they caught her again and held her fast, face downwards.

When Dr Turner came running up the stairs, he paused for only a moment in the doorway to take in what was happening. Opening his bag, he took out a small blue-glass bottle. 'Hold her down!' he ordered. 'I need to sedate her.'

But it wasn't until Dot lent her aid that they were able to hold Isabel still for long enough to force her mouth open and pour some laudanum down her throat. Even then it took a full half-hour before she calmed down and they could carry her into her bedroom.

'Has your mistress ever shown signs of madness before?' Dr Turner asked the maid.

'Yes, sir. She talks to herself all the time when she thinks no one can hear her.' Dot hesitated and looked at them.

'You must tell us anything you know.'

'Well . . . I've heard her telling Mr Blake he should have listened to her then she'd not have had to get rid of him. She acted as if he was still there.' Dot shivered. 'I kept to the kitchen when she was like that.'

All three men froze.

'Are you sure she said that, girl?' the Vicar asked.

'Yes, sir.' She put up her chin. 'I am sure, sir. She said it more than once.'

'Why did you not tell someone?' Dr Turner asked.

'Who'd have believed me? Mrs Blake was clever. Never did nothing when her friends were here. But I'm knocking about the house all the time and I couldn't help overhearing things. Fair made me shiver, it did. I wasn't eavesdropping, sir, honest I wasn't.' She began to cry.

There was silence, then the doctor said quietly, 'Her husband was also worried about her sanity. He brought me round to see her once, but she was quite calm when I arrived.' He nodded to the maid. 'I do believe you, Dot.'

'She has – a disordered mind?' the Vicar faltered. 'But she and my wife were friends. She visited our house regularly.'

The doctor looked down sadly at the woman. 'She won't be visiting anyone from now on. She'll have to be locked away, I'm afraid. She's dangerous as well as insane.

Shall I – make the arrangements?' He led the way out of the room.

'Yes.' Mr Featherworth hesitated then asked, 'Do you think she'll recover?'

'I doubt it. They don't usually, not when something has tipped them over the edge like this.'

'There is some money for her. Can you find – somewhere decent? I don't like to think of a lady being put into a common asylum.'

'I know a place where they look after such people carefully as long as you can pay for the privilege.'

'What am I going to do about the bequests?' the lawyer wondered aloud.

'What bequests?'

'He left everything to his four nieces.'

Dot clapped one hand across her mouth to hide a smile. Serve the old hag right. Then she realised she'd be out of a job and her smile faded as she continued to listen to the men talking. They seemed to have forgotten that she was there.

'I shall have to send a message to Australia,' the lawyer said. 'Though how long it'll take for a letter to get there, I don't know, or even if it'll arrive safely.'

The doctor shook his head. 'Letters can go astray. I have a cousin in Australia who writes to me regularly, but once or twice his letters haven't arrived. You'd better find someone who's going there – a man would be best – and pay him to deliver the message to the Blake sisters in person. And you'll need to find someone to run the shop in the meantime.'

The doctor went back to check on Mrs Blake, but she

was still asleep. 'I know a married couple who'll come and look after her here until we can make the necessary arrangements. He's very strong. And careful. I can promise you they won't ill-treat her, however strangely she behaves. I'll warn them that she can seem quite rational at times.'

Mr Featherworth pulled himself together. 'It'll take time, but it'll all be sorted out eventually, I suppose.' He suddenly became aware of the maid, standing by the door, wide-eyed. 'You, girl. Make sure you don't talk about this to anyone.'

'No, sir. And – please sir, what about my job?'

'You'll be needed till we've got her safely locked away, then I'll pay you any wages owing and you can leave.'

She began to cry. 'I'll need references, sir. I can't get another job without them.'

'Is this a time to fuss about that?' She continued to cry noisily, so he said impatiently, 'I'll get my wife to write them for you. Now carry on with your normal work. The Vicar and I will stay with your mistress until the doctor sends help.'

'Shall I bring you up some tea and biscuits, sir?'

'Good idea.'

When she'd gone the Vicar sighed. 'This is most unfortunate. If it had only happened a few days sooner, we could have got the Blake sisters back. But their ship has already sailed for the Antipodes.' Then he frowned. 'Well, three of them went on the ship. I fear the oldest sister must be dead. There has been no word about her.'

A dreadful thought came into his mind and he dismissed

it hastily. Surely Mrs Blake could not have been behind her niece's death as well?

Well, whether she had been or not, it was too late to do anything about it, and it was no use prosecuting a madwoman.

15

After they'd finished cleaning out their quarters, something Matron insisted on them doing every morning, the single women went up the companionway, as they'd learned to call the steep wooden steps that led up to the deck. By that time, they were more than ready for a breath of fresh salty air. Some pushed to the front; others waited their turn patiently.

Even Maia was now well enough to enjoy the thought of a stroll and pulled a face when Matron asked the three of them to stay behind for a few moments.

'I believe you have an older sister . . .' she began.

They looked at each other in surprise, then Pandora nodded.

'You left her behind because she was married and—'

'But—' Xanthe began.

Pandora interrupted. 'Let Matron finish telling us.'

'Sadly, the very day after you left, your brother-in-law was killed in an accident. With the help of your Minister, Mr Rainey, your sister tried to join you on this ship as an emigrant, but there were no places left.'

Maia gasped. 'Oh, no!'

'Fortunately, Mrs Barrett's maid had changed her mind at the last minute about coming to Australia with her, so that lady has kindly employed your sister instead and—'

'You mean – Cassandra is on this ship,' Xanthe exclaimed, unable to bear this slow telling a second longer.

'Indeed she is.' Matron gave them a look which was as close to a smile as she ever came. 'If you'll wait here, I'll fetch her and you can have your reunion in private.'

Before she'd even left, Maia opened her mouth again and Pandora quickly put a hand across it, then put a finger to her lips and went to check that no one had lingered in any of the cabins.

They heard someone coming towards the companionway and then a woman's skirts came into view, so they rushed to that end of the single women's quarters. Weeping and laughing they flung themselves at Cassandra, hugging, kissing and hugging her again.

'Let's sit down and talk,' she said at last, her arm still round Pandora's waist.

When they were at the table, Xanthe asked in a low voice, 'Why do they think you were married?'

Cassandra's joy vanished abruptly and she bowed her head. 'After those men captured me, they . . . used me as they would a street woman . . . on *her* orders.' Tears rolled down her cheeks, but she daren't allow herself to sob, as she ached to do, because someone might hear her.

There was dead silence, then Pandora put her arm round her sister's shoulders. 'I hope she rots in hell. Oh, Cassandra, was it – very bad?'

She could only nod. It was a few moments before she asked, 'How did she force you to leave?'

'She showed us your hair and told us she wouldn't set you free until we'd left England. Did she change her mind? How were you able to join us?'

'I escaped. I went to the Raineys and they helped me get to the ship in time.'

Maia still looked puzzled. 'But that doesn't explain why you're pretending you were married.'

Cassandra saw Pandora and Xanthe roll their eyes at their sister's naiveté. She had to force the words out. 'Because there may be ... results of those days. I may be – expecting a child.' She couldn't stop more tears rolling down her cheeks and shame sat leaden in her belly, though she couldn't have prevented what happened.

'When shall we know?' Pandora asked gently.

She'd said 'we' not 'you', Cassandra thought wonderingly. Then she truly knew she was back with her family again, not struggling alone in a hostile world. It seemed as if the weight on her shoulders shifted slightly and grew a little lighter. 'We'll find out quite soon. I should be starting my monthly any day now or ... not.'

They sat in silence, but Pandora kept hold of her hand and Cassandra clung to it, feeling she could cope with anything if only she wasn't alone. 'I'd better tell you about my imaginary husband. We named him John Lawson and said he was killed in an accident, a runaway horse and cart. We may as well make him a drayman.'

'Why didn't you come to see us before now? We've been under way for days.'

'I only got passage on the ship because Mrs Barrett needed a maid. Her husband insisted I pretend to be their former maid Hilda until after the ship had got well away from England, so that there would be no possibility of me being sent back. Mrs Barrett is pleasant enough but she never lifts a finger to help herself. And then with the rough weather, they were both ill, so I had to look after them. He wanted me to keep pretending I was Hilda. But I refused.'

'That was cruel. He must have known you wanted to see us.'

'He doesn't think about me, just how well his wife is served. Neither of them has even asked whether my quarters are comfortable or how I'm feeling, though they think I've recently been widowed.' She sighed. 'So only you three and the Raineys know what really happened to me.'

'And I suppose those involved know too,' Xanthe said. 'If I ever meet our aunt again . . .'

'That's not likely.'

'If you are – you know, expecting a child, we'll look after you,' Pandora added.

'I pray I'm not.' She couldn't hold back a shudder.

They heard footsteps on the companionway and one of the younger girls came down, stopping near the bottom to call, 'Matron says you're to come up and get some fresh air now.' She went back up on deck without waiting for an answer.

'We'd better do it,' Xanthe said. 'Matron's word is law down here. On this ship, she, the doctor and the Captain are like a trio of those Greek gods Dad loved so much.'

They went up and gradually edged into a place by the rail, staring out across the sunlit water.

'To think we'd never seen the sea before,' Xanthe said.

'Isn't it beautiful? We were always promising ourselves to go on an excursion to Blackpool, but we never did.'

'We spent too much time with our heads in books,' Cassandra said grimly. 'And Father was so generous to those in need, we never had much money to spare. I'll never make that mistake. I'll always make sure I have some money saved from now on.'

They couldn't speak too frankly because the decks were crowded, single women and families in one area, single men in another, with Matron sitting between the two groups. This didn't stop the younger men looking, and as usual, they kept staring at Pandora, who always seemed unaware of her startling good looks.

But with her new-found knowledge of what men really wanted, how little some men respected women, Cassandra wondered if she would ever be able to trust a man again, even Reece. She banished that thought, angry at herself. Hadn't she promised herself not to dwell on things that couldn't be changed? She wouldn't let *that woman* ruin the rest of her life.

'How do you pass the time?' she asked. 'Mrs Barrett is so fussy, she keeps me quite busy. I'm always having to fetch her something or mend things she's torn, or read to her. She's like a spoiled child, kind if she gets what she wants from her husband, but irritable towards me if he crosses her. But though I've got work to do for her, there are still hours to fill.'

Xanthe grimaced. 'It's been very boring until now. Because of the bad weather they're only just starting to organise group activities. But we can read already, so why should we join a reading class?'

'I heard there was going to be a singing group,' Pandora said. 'You three would enjoy that, I'm sure. Would your mistress let you join it as well, Cassandra?'

'I don't know. She's in a delicate condition and is friendly one minute, then snaps at me the next. I can ask her, though.' She looked up and saw her mistress staring in her direction from the area set aside for cabin passengers. Mrs Barrett beckoned and Cassandra sighed. 'I'll have to go back to her now.'

'She didn't let us spend much time together, did she?' Xanthe grumbled.

'Never mind. Once we reach Australia, we'll stay together.'

'Not if they send us to different places,' Pandora said. 'I overheard Matron talking to the doctor last night, telling him about the last group she brought out here, how some maids were sent to country homesteads a long way from Perth. And there are no railways in Western Australia – can you imagine that? – so travel isn't easy. From the way she talks, it sounds like the Dark Ages there. I wish we hadn't come.'

They looked at one another in dismay.

'Surely they wouldn't separate us?' Maia said.

Xanthe moved closer to her twin. 'They might try. Will we even have a choice of what jobs we take?'

'Of course we will,' Pandora said. 'We don't have to accept a job if we don't want it. We're not *slaves*.'

'But there are four of us. No one will be looking for four maids. And how will we live if we've no work?' Xanthe asked. 'We've only a few coins between us.'

'I've got some money,' Cassandra said. 'Mrs

Southerham gave it to me. And she'll be in Western Australia. Surely she'll be able to help us?'

'Reece is there, too,' Pandora said slyly. 'I doubt you'll have to find a job at all once he knows you're there.'

Cassandra flushed. That was her dream, but she couldn't marry him without telling him what had happened to her. It wouldn't be fair. And anyway, she still had nightmares, so she wouldn't be able to hide it.

Mrs Barrett beckoned again, so she gave each of her sisters a hug, then hurried across to her mistress, who didn't really need her but was bored and wanted fussing over.

Mr Rainey was shown into the Vicar's study. After exchanging greetings, he came straight to the point. 'I've been hearing rumours about Mrs Blake.'

'Ah. Yes.'

'Is it true she's gone mad?'

'I'm afraid so.'

'What about the shop? There's also a rumour that it wasn't left to her.'

Mr Saunders stiffened. 'How did that news get out?'

'So it is true!'

'I really can't discuss the poor lady's affairs.'

'I'm not interested in her. It's her four nieces who are my concern. They were my parishioners, after all.'

'We fear the oldest one has been killed.'

'No. She escaped from her captors and came to us. But we felt it better for her to get away from her aunt, so we hid her.' He hesitated, then decided it was time for the truth to be told. 'It was Mrs Blake who arranged for her to be kidnapped, you see.'

The Vicar goggled at him, opening and shutting his mouth, and it was a few moments before he could string a few words together. 'You're sure Cassandra Blake is alive?'

'Didn't I just say so?'

'What a relief! That'll solve the problem of what to do with the shop.'

'Not quite.'

'What do you mean? Surely she can come and take charge of it on behalf of her sisters till they return from Australia?'

'She's on her way there with them.'

Silence, then the Vicar stood up. 'We'd better go and tell the lawyer about this. Featherworth is the one who'll have to send word to Australia. I just pray we'll find all four young women safe and sound. You never know what'll happen on such a long and perilous journey.'

Mr Featherworth listened to what Mr Rainey had to tell him, asking a few questions, then shaking his head. 'It's a terrible business. The doctor tells me Mrs Blake is still out of her mind and very violent, has to be restrained for her own safety. Tomorrow we're taking her to a place in the country near Halifax. It's been strongly recommended by the doctor and is run by people who will care for her properly. I'm going with them to make sure everything is all right. I've got an order from the magistrate to take charge of everything until the heirs can be found.'

'What are you going to do with the shop until then?' Mr Rainey asked.

The lawyer sat tapping his fingers on the desk for a

moment or two. 'I shall have to employ someone to manage it, I suppose. I know nothing about shopkeeping.'

'What about the senior man there?' the Vicar asked. 'Won't he do?'

'Well, he's been very helpful and is keeping things going, but I'm not sure. He's very young for such responsibility. I'd prefer an older man.' And there was something about Prebble that Mr Featherworth didn't quite trust. He couldn't put his finger on it, but you got that feeling sometimes about people – and his judgement had never let him down before.

'Why not give the young man a chance?' the Vicar said. 'I've known the Prebbles for years. They're members of my congregation, regular attenders. I married the parents and christened young Harry. Decent folk, they are, from humble beginnings, but making something of themselves. You'd have to pay him more than he's getting now, of course.'

'I'll talk to him before I make my mind up. Then there's the maidservant, Dot. I'd thought to dismiss her but now I'm not sure.'

The Vicar pursed his lips, then passed judgement. 'I don't like to think of a housemaid having that place to herself. Who knows what she'll get up to without proper supervision?'

Mr Rainey cleared his throat. 'My wife has a cousin who works as a governess, but is between jobs at the moment and is coming to us next week for a rest before she seeks a new post, because she's had the influenza and is run down. We could ask Alice – Miss Blair – to live there and keep an eye on things, if you like. You could trust her absolutely. She'd only ask for food and board, and perhaps a small honorarium.'

'I was going to suggest a parishioner of my own, a widow,' the Vicar said in an aggrieved tone.

Mr Featherworth stepped in hastily. He wasn't fond of the Vicar and didn't want him poking his nose into the Blakes' affairs, which he would be able to do if one of his parishioners was installed above the shop. On the other hand, he did respect and like the Methodist Minister and his wife, who were both well thought of in town. 'Perhaps you could introduce me to your wife's cousin when she arrives, Mr Rainey? If she's free, it may be just the thing. In the meantime I'll have to consider how to contact the Blake sisters in Australia.'

The Vicar frowned. 'You're definitely sending someone to find them, then? Won't that be rather expensive?'

'It'll be more expensive, yes, but I believe it's essential. I've been considering asking the young man who works in the shop to go, not Prebble, but Zachary Carr. He knows the sisters by sight and he's always been very helpful when I've dealt with him.'

'That's an excellent idea,' Mr Rainey said warmly. 'They'll need more help in the shop, though.'

'Prebble's already asked about appointing someone. He tells me he knows a suitable young man. He'll have no trouble finding more help in these troubled times.'

'Have you asked the young fellow if he's prepared to go?'

'Not yet. I wanted to make enquiries about him first, to make absolutely sure that he's reliable.'

★

Pandora hated sewing, so let the twins join that particular shipboard class without her. But she did join a group to whom one of the ladies was reading a book aloud. She'd rather have read the book for herself, but didn't say that. At least it passed the time. And some of the other young women from Lancashire who hadn't joined groups were misbehaving, so she didn't want to be thought like them. Safer to participate in some quiet activity and keep out of the others' way.

When the lady reader was unwell one day, Pandora volunteered to take her place, wanting to know what happened next in the story, as well as to fill in another hour or so.

Matron looked at her in surprise. 'Can you read well enough?'

She bit back a hasty answer. 'I think so. Let me show you.' Finding the place they'd reached in the book, she started reading.

Matron stopped her after a couple of paragraphs. 'Excellent. I'll let you take charge today, then.'

'Thank you. And Matron?'

'Yes?'

'Someone said there was a library on board. Could I borrow books from it, do you think? I'll be very careful with them.'

Matron gave one of her rare smiles. 'Not just a library. A benefactor has donated a box of writing materials and diaries, and those who know how to write can apply for a diary and keep a record of the voyage. Some people make two copies and send one back to their families. I've been waiting till the weather calmed down to distribute them.' Her frown returned. 'Unfortunately, the single women on this ship have been more difficult to settle than usual.'

Pandora beamed at her. 'Oh, I'd love to keep a diary.'

'You didn't join the sewing class, though.'

She grimaced. 'I don't like sewing.'

'Nonetheless, it'll be helpful for you in your new life. There are no cotton mills in Western Australia and you young women were brought out as maids. Employers will think more of you if you can at least do the mending. Perhaps you could reconsider the sewing class?'

'I'm not good at it and I doubt I ever shall be.' And she hated sewing, would far rather use her brain.

'There's nothing like perseverance for improving a skill. Mrs Barrett says your eldest sister is quite a good needlewoman. I must say it's very kind of her to instruct her maid as she is doing.' She cocked her head, waiting for an answer, and when it didn't come, she added, 'Besides, the busier you are, the more pleasantly the voyage will pass.'

Pandora looked at her pleadingly, because this sounded like an ultimatum.

'Didn't you hear what I said? Sewing is a valued skill in a maid. You *need* to be able to do it. Besides, by joining the class, you'll gain an item of underwear. There's a box of underwear cut out and ready to sew, donated by a group of ladies who care about the welfare of young women sent out into the world on their own.'

Knowing it wouldn't be wise to defy Matron, and bearing in mind the fact that she wasn't so well supplied with clothing that she could ignore a free gift, Pandora gave in. 'Oh, very well, I'll join the sewing class, then. But I'll ruin anything I touch. I just don't seem able to sew a straight seam, however hard I try.'

'I'll teach you.' This was said very confidently.

She hid her doubts and was given a diary and writing implements that very afternoon, something which thrilled her. She stroked the crisp, clean paper of the first page and considered how best to begin.

One thing Pandora did enjoy was organising their mess's meals, but she was thankful they hadn't got any of the more unruly single women in their group to disrupt things.

Food was plentiful and many of the young women from Lancashire put on weight quickly, acquiring rosy cheeks again. There were some startling transformations. One woman, who'd seemed middle-aged, grew young again before their eyes.

Well, it was no wonder. For breakfast they had tea or coffee with bread and butter, and there was as much as anyone could want. Occasionally they had molasses or jam to spread on the bread, or ship's biscuits instead of bread. Pandora didn't care what they were given. She'd been hungry for so long, she enjoyed every mouthful now.

Dinner was usually meat and potatoes, with preserved pork or beef being the most common meats, though occasionally there was fresh meat when one of the ship's animals was slaughtered. None of the Lancashire contingent complained if the preserved meat was a little salty. They'd all known hunger.

With the food they were sometimes given preserved

cabbage or pease pudding made from dried peas. The preserved cabbage wasn't to some people's taste, but Matron urged them to eat it to ward off scurvy.

A few girls hid the cabbage in their handkerchiefs and tossed it into the sea, others refused point-blank even to touch it. They were stupid, Pandora thought. It stood to reason Matron knew what she was talking about, as she'd done the voyage several times now. It seemed a strange way to earn a living, but the older woman obviously enjoyed ship life and was often to be seen gazing out at the ocean, her expression content.

The women were given flour, suet and sugar for each mess every alternate day, and were allowed to make cakes of any sort from it, which the cook would bake for them.

Pandora asked his advice and learned a lot about cooking in difficult conditions. Xanthe took an interest in this, too, but some of the mess leaders only made simple things to which they were used, not showing any interest in extending their skills.

Others were too busy stealing things from one another to care what they ate, as long as there was food. The more they recovered from the famine days, the worse some of the girls' behaviour grew. The objects they liked most to steal were photographs of the others' sweethearts or brothers. Then they'd pretend that these were *their* sweethearts. This caused a lot of distress among the victims.

When she found her father's book gone from under her pillow, Pandora reported it to Matron, who searched all the single women's cabins, with the Purser standing by. The book was found and many other small articles too that people had missed.

Afterwards the Captain himself gave them all a scolding and threatened to lock the ones who'd done it below instead of allowing them on deck. But even that didn't stop the pilfering.

In the end some girls took their little treasures to the Captain and asked him to keep them safe till the voyage was over.

The Blake sisters gave their more precious possessions to Cassandra, the main one being a photograph of them and their father, now without its frame, which they'd had to sell. She'd shown them their mother's locket, which had photos of their mother and father as young people in it. They hadn't expected to see that again.

Not until the trunks were brought up at the end of the first month, as was usual, to allow for a change of clothes and access to their other possessions, did Cassandra get a chance to see what she'd 'inherited' from Hilda.

The missing maid's trunk was placed in her cabin next to her own and Miss Pershore's. That left them barely enough room to squeeze past to get to the tiny washstand fixed to the wall.

'Why don't you sort out your box first?' she suggested to the older maid. 'My mistress wants me to help her go through her things.'

'I will then, thank you. *My* mistress will leave what is taken from her box to my judgement. I've got everything ready for a quick exchange.' Miss Pershore looked down her nose at Cassandra, because she'd quickly learned that her companion was not a real maid and lost no opportunity to emphasise her own superiority.

'I'm sure you have. And any hints you can give me for packing my mistress's things again will be most welcome.'

Somewhat mollified, Miss Pershore spent ten minutes outlining her way of organising things, which involved making packages of clothing for each stage of the journey, each bundle wrapped in clean sheets. These could be removed from the trunks quickly.

Cassandra tried to look interested, because life in the tiny cabin was easier if Miss Pershore was not in a bad mood, but she had other things to worry about at the moment and it was hard to concentrate. Her monthly had not come and though she'd never been as regular as her sisters, there were changes in her body which signalled her condition all too clearly. Her breasts were tender and she felt slightly nauseous in the mornings.

She'd been trying to tell herself that the huge changes in her life had made her late, but this morning she'd had to rush to the water closet to be sick. It was no longer impossible to deny the facts: she must be expecting a child.

She shuddered every time she thought of that, couldn't even bring herself to tell her sisters. She'd wanted children, of course she had, but not one forced upon her by men like that. Why, she'd never even know which man was the father.

And what about Reece? She'd dared hope he'd not hold what had happened against her, that they'd be able to marry, but this was far worse. No man could be expected to take on the child of such a coupling.

That thought made her cry sometimes after she went

to bed. She muffled her sobs under her blankets, not daring weep for too long in case it made her eyes red.

There was no denying that her future was looking bleak.

Soon she would have to tell her sisters. They were looking at her with the question in their eyes already. Only she didn't want to admit it to anyone yet, because she felt deeply ashamed of her condition.

After an hour's earnest perusal of the contents of her trunk, Mrs Barrett sighed and waved one hand languidly. 'You can close that thing. I don't want anything else out of it. We have enough to manage with in the cabin trunk, really. Why don't you go and sort out your new possessions?'

Cassandra hesitated. 'I still feel guilty about taking them. What if there are some personal items in the trunk?'

Mrs Barrett shrugged. 'Serves Hilda right. She should have thought of that before she changed her mind. My husband paid for that trunk to be transported to Australia, but he doesn't intend to pay for it to be sent back. So it has to be disposed of and you might as well benefit.' She waved her hand again. 'Go away. I need to have a nap. I've never been so sleepy in my whole life. The things we women have to endure to provide an heir!'

Her attitude to the trunk seemed very heartless and Cassandra was thoughtful as she went along to her cabin. If Mrs Barrett could dismiss the feelings of a woman who had been her maid for years, it seemed likely that she'd be equally cavalier in her attitude towards Cassandra once they arrived in Australia, especially when she found her new maid was also expecting a child.

She sighed as she went into the tiny cabin, relieved that Miss Pershore had finished dealing with her things and gone back on deck. Feeling like a thief, she opened Hilda's trunk and took out the contents one by one. As she'd feared, there were some very personal items, things which couldn't be replaced. The one which she felt most guilty about was a photograph of a family group in a silver frame, obviously a treasured possession. They were all staring at the camera, glassy-eyed. No wonder, she thought with a smile. When she and her family had had their portrait taken, they'd had to stay motionless for over a minute. It wasn't easy to keep a smile on your face for that long.

On the back of this one was the name of the photographer, and the address of his studio. It had been taken in a place called Linforth, near Kendal. She wondered if she dared ask Mrs Barrett whether this was the place Hilda had come from. She'd have to catch her in a good mood, because her mistress was very sharp-tempered at times and you couldn't please her whatever you did.

There were also some books, a volume of famous poems and two novels. She'd enjoy reading those. A package wrapped in an old piece of cloth revealed a square of material for an embroidered tablecloth, with a thread-counted design carefully drawn on a piece of paper attached to it, the numbers given and faint marks for where to position the design on the cloth itself. Wrapped in a shawl was a small watercolour of a rural scene showing a village in the distance. On the back of the painting was the same name: Linforth.

At the bottom of the trunk she found some letters, tied up with a blue ribbon. She unfolded one and found the full address of Hilda's sister and husband – and the first page, which she read guiltily, showed her the Suttons were a close, loving family. That must be why poor Hilda had run away rather than go so far from them.

If it was possible, Cassandra would return the personal items to the poor woman one day, but as she desperately needed some extra clothes and underclothes for such a long voyage, she'd have to use the clothing. She was relieved to find that all the skirts and bodices were in dark colours which would suit her supposed widowhood, but of course the skirts were far too short. The bodices and blouses were too wide as well, so everything would need altering.

Well, that would give her something to do, wouldn't it? She'd ask Mrs Barrett's advice about how best to do the alterations. Her mistress knew so much more about sewing and fashion than she did. Mrs Barrett spent a lot of time talking about clothes, growing animated as she described in detail the outfits she'd worn on special occasions, some of which were packed in one of her many trunks. And she occupied some of her time with sewing and embroidering exquisite little garments for her baby, when she could be bothered.

Cassandra was glad Hilda had been quite stout, because she would need fuller clothes to wear later as she grew bigger.

When her mistress woke up and rang for her, she confided her worries about how best to alter the clothes and to her surprise, Mrs Barrett bounced out of bed at once. 'Bring the things you've chosen here. I'll work out how to alter them and supervise your sewing. If I'd been born a poor person, I'd have become a dressmaker, and I'd have been a good one, too.'

If only the rest of her life was as easy to change as the clothes, Cassandra thought as she sat on deck later, within call of her mistress, sewing a flounce on the hem of one skirt to make it longer. She'd sacrificed a navy blue skirt to lengthen two others of the same colour, and Hilda's best outfit had had so much material in the skirt, they'd been able to take some fullness out and make a band for the hem from that.

As she sewed, she listened to the choir practising at one end of the deck. She'd have liked to join in, but Mr Barrett hadn't thought it proper for her to do so. She wasn't going to look for work as a maid when she got to Australia. It was horrible being at someone else's beck and call, having to accept unreasonable decisions.

Francis and Reece spent the next few weeks going to inspect pieces of land which were for lease, mostly without Livia, who hadn't enjoyed her first trip. Gradually they got to know something about how people farmed here, and what constituted good land or bad.

Poor land, most of it was. But some blocks had fine stands of timber and you could make good money from felling trees and selling the wood. One man had told him that if you took the trouble to saw the timber into planks and let it stand for a year or two, so that it was seasoned, you could make even more money from it.

His informant offered him a timber felling job on

the spot, and if he'd been free to accept the offer, he would have accepted so that he could learn how to do it properly.

'Any time you want work, even if it's only for a few weeks at a time,' the man said, 'come and see me. I pay well, and I feed my men well too.' He grinned at Reece. 'If you don't mind working for an ex-convict, that is.'

'As long as you deal honestly with me, I'd not care if you had feathers instead of hair,' Reece threw back at him.

But he knew by now how scornfully people regarded ex-convicts. Even Francis, usually friendly enough towards his fellow men, whatever their station in life, had become very stiff when he'd discovered his neighbour if he took one place would be an emancipist. 'Not a suitable place for Livia,' he muttered.

Reece lay in bed that night fretting that they were getting nowhere and that coming here might have been just as bad a mistake as coming without Cassandra. Then he scolded himself. Surely Francis would find some land soon?

Maybe it was time for Reece to write to Cassandra, asking her to come out and marry him.

No, he'd better wait till they were settled, till they'd found some land. A few weeks wouldn't make that much difference . . . would they? And letters might take a long time to get to England, but they went regularly. Ships didn't come to Fremantle all that often, but the post was often taken down to Albany on the south coast, where it was picked up by ships coming from Sydney or Melbourne on the eastern side of the continent.

No, he'd wait just a little longer. He couldn't ask the woman he loved to come here and suffer the hardships involved in clearing and settling land.

16

About a week after the *Tartar* crossed the Tropic of Capricorn, there was a shout of 'Man overboard' and sailors began running.

Cassandra stood watching in horror as one of them flung a life buoy overboard, then others lowered a boat. Cork jackets were found for those going after the poor fellow and they set off on their search. Already the man had disappeared from view. As they rowed away, the boat looked so small against the vast mass of water she feared for their safety too.

The ship changed course to come about and they lost sight of the small boat, which had now disappeared from view. The cabin passengers muttered to one another, fearing for its safety and somewhere a woman was sobbing.

The emigrants were so curious to see what was happening that some of them pushed their way on to the poop, which was forbidden to them, and the cabin passengers began to complain about this invasion of their territory.

The Captain ordered the emigrants to leave the poop, and when they didn't obey his orders, he grew angry and ordered them to be locked down in their quarters.

The boat eventually came into view again and there

were murmurs of 'Thank goodness!' as it made its way slowly back to the ship's side. But it was soon clear from the men's expressions that they'd failed to find their companion.

The clergyman, Mr Millett, led them in a prayer for the man's soul. The poor fellow was the second person to die on this voyage. A child from the steerage quarters had died earlier and they'd had the sad experience of a burial at sea. The mother had been so distraught, she'd had to be restrained from following her child's body into the water.

Cassandra found it hard to get to sleep that night. The sailor who'd died had been very young, some mother's son. That had reminded her of her own child, and she found herself laying her hand protectively on her belly until she saw Miss Pershore frowning at this gesture.

But the incident had a profound impact on her. She was alive, wasn't she? And this child she was carrying was just that – a child – not a monster.

After that she felt calmer, more resigned to her condition and even began to wonder what the baby would be like. Would it be a boy or a girl? Would it look like her family?

Next time she managed to be private with her sisters, she'd tell them. She wasn't alone in the world now, nor would the child be. It'd have three aunts. If anything happened to her, they'd care for it, she was sure.

She wished her father had known about his first grandchild. He'd have loved the baby, she was sure, whatever its origins. In that last year he'd spoken many times of his wish for them to marry and have families, had kept insisting that children were precious. *I will treasure it*, she promised him in her thoughts as she tossed about. *I will, Dad.*

Of course that turned her thoughts to Reece. She tried hard to imagine how he'd feel, but the only thing she was sure of was that it wouldn't be fair to burden him with another man's child. Nor would it be fair to the child, because he would surely regard it as a cuckoo in the nest. Children should grow up with unconditional love, as she and her sisters had.

She remembered all too clearly Timmy down the street whose mother had married a man who treated the little boy coldly. She couldn't bear the thought of her child spending its life on sufferance, unhappy, barely tolerated.

But oh, it hurt so much to think of losing Reece! One of her secret hopes in coming to Australia had been to be reunited with him.

As she made a very difficult decision, she realised her cheeks were wet with tears, though she hadn't realised she'd been crying. She couldn't ask Reece to take a child fathered in that way, couldn't risk it being unhappy.

She'd never loved a man before and didn't suppose she would again, but she could still love her child. Something inside her had eased today. She was sorry it'd taken the death of the young sailor to bring her to this point of accepting her condition, to make her count her blessings. But good had come out of bad, at least.

From now on, she must take strength from the knowledge that she was alive and well, and that, against all the odds, she'd been reunited with her sisters.

On that thought, even before the tears dried on her

cheeks, she slipped into the deepest, most peaceful sleep she'd had since she'd come on board.

Francis heard about a piece of farming land to lease a little further south of Perth than they'd looked before, in the foothills. It had been settled by a family who'd had a run of bad fortune and were moving to New South Wales, so it had a house of sorts and he would be entitled to a couple of convicts to help him work the land.

As usual, he took Reece with him to inspect the place. 'What do you think?' he asked after they'd been shown round the tiny shack by the current tenant, whose wife looked thin and unhappy and whose children were subdued.

By now, Reece had learned enough to say decisively, 'Not much.'

'Couldn't we make something of it, though? It has a pretty outlook and—'

'Pretty isn't as important as fertile,' Reece said impatiently because they'd had this discussion before.

Francis kicked a piece of fallen branch out of the way and a spider scurried from its underside into the litter of dry, leathery gum leaves. 'I need to move away from my cousin's house, and the sooner the better if we're to remain on speaking terms.'

Reece didn't need telling that. All the servants were well aware that the two Southerham men had had several quarrels lately. Indeed, this stay in another man's house had taught Reece that you could have no privacy at all with servants around, and he wondered if it was worth it.

'Let's go and see the other block of land we heard about before we decide anything,' he suggested.

'It's further away from Perth and I don't want Livia to be in such an isolated place. What if some of the natives attacked us?'

'They don't sound very warlike. I should think if you treat them kindly, you'll have no trouble. This is their country, after all, even though they don't seem to farm it. They must know more about the land and plants than we do.'

Francis looked at him in shock. 'How can you possibly say such a thing? This is *not* their country now. It belongs to the Queen, is part of Her Majesty's empire. And what can savages possibly know that we don't?'

They'd disagreed about this before as well, so Reece bit his tongue. For all Francis's wish to treat all men well, at times he still showed the innate arrogance of his upbringing, seeming to feel that he was superior to most other people.

Reece was growing increasingly frustrated. He wasn't cut out to be a servant. Even with a liberal master, there were certain lines a servant didn't cross. How would he face nearly a year and a half more of keeping quiet and doing things in ways he considered unwise, or sometimes downright sloppy? Even the hunt for land was being conducted haphazardly, not systematically.

That night he began his long-postponed letter to Cassandra, describing the voyage, which she'd surely find of interest, and his early days in the Swan River Colony. He found himself pouring out his heart and feelings to her, remembering how they'd talked and talked, their minds as in tune with one another as their bodies.

When his fingers cramped with holding the pen and he grew tired of the smell of ink, he screwed the cap on the ink bottle and put his writing materials away. He'd write about the prospects here another night. He'd be very honest ... but he'd definitely ask her to come out and marry him. He'd learned enough during his time here to feel that together they'd stand a good chance of prospering, a far better chance than they would have had in England.

He looked down at the pile of pages. At least he'd made a start on the letter now.

Was she thinking of him? Would she come out to join him?

What would he do if she didn't?

It was a long time before he got to sleep and he dreamed of her, dreamed of the smile that lit up her whole face, the way her eyes sparkled when she was interested in something, the way she was just – Cassandra.

Unfortunately, there was nowhere on the ship for the young women emigrants to find complete privacy. Cassandra waited till she and her sisters were standing at the rail, then spoke in a low voice, hoping no one would bother to listen to their conversation.

'I'm ... expecting a child,' she said at last, not finding any softer way of breaking the news. As she stared out at the ocean, the sunlight glinting on it was turned into a blur of light by the tears in her eyes. She cried so easily now, had heard other women say they'd been like that when they were carrying a child.

There was silence, then Pandora's arm went round her shoulders. 'Oh, Cassandra.'

The tears would fall, try as she might to hold them back.

'We'll manage, love,' Pandora said quietly. 'We three will find employment and look after you.'

'Yes.' They knew she had some money, but she didn't tell them how much, because other people were too close. It was safely locked in the trunk, thank goodness.

'Do you – feel well?' Maia asked.

'Most of the time. Not in the early mornings, but that soon passes if I take things slowly when I first get up.'

'We're going to be aunts,' Xanthe said, forgetting to keep her voice down.

'Shh!' Pandora nudged her.

'Sorry. I'll start sewing for the baby. There are all sorts of scraps of material in the sewing box. I'm sure Matron will let me have some when I tell her why.'

Cassandra spoke more sharply than she'd intended. 'Don't say *anything*! I don't want anyone to know. Let's get this voyage over with first. I don't seem to be putting on much weight. I'm sure I can continue to hide my condition.'

Some of the more rowdy young women pushed in next to them and Pandora quickly changed the subject. 'We seem to have been travelling for such a long time. Still, they say we should be there in December. It'll be summer in Australia then. Just imagine that!'

They all stared out across the water. It was hard, Cassandra thought, to imagine what things would be like in Australia, what it would look like, what their daily life would be – and how they'd earn a living.

Mrs Barrett had shown her pictures of the Swan River

Colony in a book, but they'd seemed very unreal, with trees that looked like a child's drawing, so sparse of foliage and the wrong colour of green. There were little figures of black men standing beneath the trees, some with spears.

Her employer had already said she wanted to keep her on as lady's maid once they arrived, and Cassandra was quite willing to do that for a time. She could work for another couple of months after their arrival, at the very least, without her condition showing, longer if it was permitted.

'Are you coming to the concert tonight?' Maia asked. 'The choir's been practising some really nice songs.'

'If Mrs Barrett doesn't need me.'

'It's like being a slave, working for her,' Xanthe said. 'You hardly have a minute for yourself and they decide everything for you. I don't know how you stand it. I couldn't.'

'They've paid my fare to Australia. In return I try to do everything they want.' She smiled. 'And anyway, even if she doesn't let me come, I'll still hear the singing. I've heard you rehearsing, too. There's nowhere out of hearing on a ship.'

But she'd have liked to be part of the concert group, to sit with the others and listen to the concert.

Reece jogged along on the old mare Francis had hired for him. He was, he felt, an adequate rider now, because the Southerhams had taken the time to teach him. That was one of the few things they did superbly, ride.

'You're wishing you hadn't come to Australia, aren't you?' Francis said suddenly.

'Sometimes, yes.' He glanced at the other man's expression and cursed himself for betraying his feelings. 'Sorry. You've been very kind, but I feel just as unsettled as I was in England because there's no purpose to my life yet.'

'If you want to return to England, I'll pay your passage,' Francis said huffily.

Reece took a few moments to think about this, glad when his employer didn't say anything. 'Thank you for that kind offer, but no. I've not given things a fair chance here yet, have I? However . . . I'd appreciate your help in securing a small parcel of land after you've found yours, even if I can't settle on it until my two years' service with you are over. If it's near yours, I can work on it during my free time, clear it a little, perhaps.' A quick glance showed that his companion was startled by this.

'So you're not intending to stay with me after the two years are over?'

'No.'

'Did you ever intend to?'

'No.'

'I see. Well, I'm not best pleased with that attitude, I must say.'

'But you just offered to send me back to England!'

Francis let out an angry snort. 'I didn't expect you to take me up on the offer.'

'And if I change my mind now and accept it?'

'We Southerhams always honour our word.'

As if others didn't, Reece thought, half-amused and half-irritated. He decided to say something he'd been thinking for a few weeks. 'It seems to me that there's little difference between master and man here, the ones who aren't convicts, anyway – except for the money. You'd be better working in *partnership* with me than using me only as a servant, because I *do* know something about farming, and I'm a good worker. If I had some share in the land, something of my own, I'd work every hour I could stand upright to look after it and make it productive.'

Francis stared at him in shock, breathed deeply and said, 'I'm afraid that's not what *I* want, however.' He immediately began to talk about something else.

Reece followed suit. He hoped he'd given the other man – he hated to call anyone his 'master' – something to think about, hoped Francis would see the sense in it.

But he doubted it.

He still intended to get some land of his own, though.

As the *Tartar* drew closer to Australia, they began to see sharks and sea birds of all kinds. During the journey they'd all enjoyed the sight of the giant albatrosses soaring over the ship, seeming to be keeping an eye on them. Near the Cape of Good Hope, they'd seen cape pigeons and flying fishes, too, which had caused great excitement.

In Australia they were all eager to see kangaroos hopping about and Matron said parrots flew about everywhere, were common wild birds.

'So many wonders to come,' Maia said one day, dreamy-eyed.

Pandora didn't reply. She was enjoying the new things she was seeing and doing, but she was still homesick and it wasn't getting any better. She missed the moors dreadfully, even missed the soft, clinging rain of

Lancashire. It was no use dwelling on that, though. Even if they did go back to England, they'd never dare return to Outham, because of their uncle's wife.

'You're thinking about home again, aren't you?' Cassandra said, linking her arm with her youngest sister's.

'Yes. Does it show?'

'There are times when you get a sad expression and you look into the distance as if you're seeing something else.'

'You look sad too sometimes. Cassandra . . . what about Reece? He'll be there. How do you think he'll feel about – your condition?'

'I couldn't ask any man to take on this child. He'd never be able to forget how it had been conceived, and what sort of life would the child have then? It'd be like little Timmy. Remember him?'

'Yes. Poor little thing. But you should give Reece the chance to offer, surely? He'd not be unkind to a child.'

'No. I've thought and thought about it, and now that I'm used to the idea, I feel very protective towards the baby and love it already.' She smiled wryly. 'I hadn't expected that.'

'Well, I'll stay with you, help you look after the baby. You won't be on your own.'

Cassandra smiled. 'You've never been the sort to cuddle babies!'

'I can learn, can't I? It can't be that hard. Other women do it all the time. And anyway, you'll need someone. You can't manage on your own.'

'Thanks, love.'

★

In November, at long last, Francis found a piece of land he really liked, one which had a reasonable chance of providing a living one day, even in Reece's careful estimation. It was in the foothills near a place called Serpentine and was well forested, with some of the lower land on the block cleared. There was a spring behind the house, a small affair, but they were told it didn't run dry even in the height of summer. A rudimentary shack had been built there and abandoned.

Before he agreed to lease it, Francis took Livia to see the block, making the journey there by horse and cart, with Reece in attendance on horseback. The roads were mere dirt tracks but it was the dry season, so there was no chance of getting bogged down.

They stayed one night at a small inn, because of Livia, though Reece would rather have camped out.

On the second day they arrived at the farm.

The land was tinder-dry, which worried Reece, who had heard about bush fires. What would they do if one burned through here? People had told him they moved more quickly than a horse could gallop if it was windy. He mentioned this to Francis, but his employer was so eager to get away from his cousin's house and start his own life, that any objection was waved away. In the end, Reece stopped trying.

There was no land nearby for him, but he too liked the district, which was more attractive than the flat land near Perth. Francis didn't think of his servant's needs, but Reece decided to keep searching for his own place, however small.

They camped at the farm for two nights, Francis and

Livia sharing the shack, which Reece had insisted on checking for spiders and snakes, something his employers hadn't even thought of. He couldn't believe how careless they were, or how little they seemed to have learned about Australia compared to what he'd found out by talking to anyone he could.

He was only too aware that this wasn't England and you had to be more careful about insects and other wildlife, because he'd found a redback spider in his bed one day. Its bite wouldn't have killed him, but it'd have made him very uncomfortable for a few days. And then there were snakes. Their bite could kill you. But if you didn't attack them, his informant had said, they usually slithered away.

In his opinion you could learn a lot from those whom the Southerhams considered inferior. He was prepared to defer to the superior knowledge even of convict workers, whereas Francis turned up his nose at speaking to the latter, let alone allowing his wife to do so.

'You're entitled to two convicts to help you,' Reece said one day. 'Shouldn't you apply for them?'

Francis wrinkled his nose, as if he'd smelled something distasteful. 'I shall wait until I have somewhere safe to lock them up at night, for Livia's sake.'

Reece bit back angry words. You couldn't force a man to be sensible. Didn't Francis see that the two of them couldn't turn mainly uncleared bush into a farm without help?

They moved to the block on a searing hot day. It took two big carts to carry all the furniture and boxes the Southerhams had brought with them from England.

The horses pulling the carts went slowly, needing regular rests, so Francis and Livia went ahead in another, much smaller cart he'd purchased, with their riding horses tied to the rear of it and Reece's horse, a much less spirited animal, pulling it. They left him to oversee the transportation of all they possessed in the world.

Fancy leaving all their worldly possessions in others' care like that! He'd not have done that. And fancy spending so much on two high-bred riding horses instead of working animals. But the Southerhams were both horse mad.

'Run things for them two, do you?' Jack asked.

'I don't know what I'll be doing yet,' he said ruefully, and explained the terms under which he was employed.

'Had it easy in life, they have. You can see it. Things ain't easy here, though, ain't easy anywhere for most folk.' He spat over to one side to show what he thought of that. He drove along in silence for a while, except for encouraging his horses to keep moving forward and yelling the occasional remark about the state of the road to the two men in charge of the second wagon.

'What brought you to Australia?' Reece asked.

Jack grinned. 'The government, when I was a nipper. Landed in Sydney, I did, in a convict ship.'

'What had you done to deserve transportation, if you don't mind me asking?'

Jack's face went grim. 'Stole some food to keep my family alive. Stole a shawl for my mum, too. We was starving after Dad died and she was blue with cold that winter, her clothes were so thin. Didn't help her much, did I?'

'I'm sorry. Have you heard from your family since?'

'No.'

'That must have been hard to bear.'

The man shrugged. 'Nothin' I could do about it.'

'But you own this cart now?'

Jack nodded, failing to hide his pride in this. 'Got an early pardon, I did, for saving the life of a guard who fell into a river. Best thing I ever done, hauling that fat sod out of the water. I got a job as drayman's helper afterwards and he taught me to drive. Good bloke, Matt was. And then I met my lass. She'd been brung out here too. Stealing as a servant. Same reason as me: her family was hungry. Anyway, I married Nellie, was lucky to find her.'

'You seem to have prospered.'

Jack shrugged. 'Me and Nellie worked all the hours God sent and built up gradual to owning our own business. I'm doing all right now and she's never gone hungry since we met. That's my son on the other wagon, the big chap. Tommo. He's never gone hungry in his life, my son hasn't. And he owns that cart. Good worker, he is.'

'I admire what you've done and hope to follow your example. I've a lot to learn about Australia, though. If you've any advice about how to get on out here, I'd appreciate you sharing it.'

The driver thought hard for a while, then shrugged. 'If you've got what it takes, an' you don't get no bad luck, you'll get on by working hard and not drinking away what you earn. You're the sort to get on, I reckon.'

'How can you tell?'

'You're a worker. You didn't stand and watch us load stuff on the cart like your master did, you helped us.'

When they were a few miles away from the farm, there was a yell from behind, and they turned to see that one of the wheels of the other wagon had hit a half-buried piece of rock and was skewed at an angle.

Cursing, Jack yelled at his beasts to stop and thrust the reins at Reece. He jumped down and ran back to look at the damage.

'Good thing we always carry a spare wheel!' he called to Reece. 'Some don't, but it can cost you days if a wheel gets damaged when you're out in the bush.'

By the time they'd changed the wheel it was fully dark and Jack decided to make camp and spend the night here, since there was a farm nearby where they could get water for the horses.

Reece had no choice but to stay with them, but wondered how Francis and Livia would get on overnight without anyone to help them.

As the sun sank slowly in the west, sending long shadows across the bare earth in front of the shack, Francis paced up and down. 'Where are they? They should have been here an hour ago.'

Livia, who was sitting on the edge of the tiny veranda, shrugged. 'Perhaps one of the horses went lame.'

'That'd only account for one wagon. Reece should have brought the other one here. How are we to manage without proper beds?'

She smiled. 'It's not going to be cold. We have a rug in the cart, and food. We can have bread and cheese for supper.'

But the butter she'd brought had melted, which made

Francis pull a face, and the cheese had sweated and looked unappealing.

'No use worrying,' she said cheerfully. 'It's not poisonous and I'm ravenous. Light me a fire to boil some water, Francis, then go and check the shack for spiders and snakes.'

A few minutes later there was a yell from the shack and he erupted out of the door, standing staring back into it.

She swung round. 'What's wrong.'

'Snake. I think there's a shovel on the cart. I'll chop its head off. Watch the door in case it comes out.'

It took him several minutes to corner the snake, then he brought its separated head and body out and tossed them to one side with a shudder. By that time she'd brewed a pot of tea and had their simple supper laid out on the blanket.

'I'm sorry,' he said as he sat beside her on the ground.

'What for?'

'Bringing you to such a primitive place, with no comforts or servants. I didn't think it'd be this bad.'

'We have Reece to help us, though he's not like a servant, is he? But he's very capable. And anyway, I'm not helpless. I can milk cows, thanks to our lessons with Reece's cousin, and feed hens, and cook bread. Come and eat your food. We shall do fine. Your health is far more important than living in luxury.'

'We'll get you a maid as soon as we possibly can. They say there's another ship due soon, so we'll see if we can hire one of the women from it.'

They sat by the fire for a while, and then, as there was

still no sign of the big carts, they made up a bed inside the shack and settled down for the night.

'It's nice, really,' she said.

'What is?'

'Being on our own. We've not been on our own for months.'

'We'll build a shack for Reece away from this house,' he said, taking her in his arms. 'I'd welcome a bit more privacy to make love to my wife.'

She snuggled up against him. Maybe this time they'd manage to make a child. They'd been trying for a while now, without a sign.

Reece and the two big carts arrived at the block about ten o'clock the following morning. He explained about the wheel but could see that Francis wasn't happy about him failing to arrive.

'They should still have sent one cart on! I don't like my wife roughing it.'

'They needed all three men to change the wheel, and even if I'd had a horse, I'd have stayed with them. Not only were *your* possessions on those carts, but everything I own in the world, too. And the roads round here aren't good enough to travel in the dark. There was no moon last night.'

Jack slouched across, his face impassive, as if he hadn't heard the conversation. 'Where d'you want us to put your things, Mr Southerham?'

'We've brought a big tent to use as a storeroom, and for Reece to sleep in. If you could help set it up first then unload into it, I'd be grateful.'

'Yeah, right. Cup of tea would be nice to start us off, missus.'

Reece could see Francis bridling at this casual way of treating his wife, so said quickly, 'I'll make the tea.'

Livia smiled at them all. 'No, I will. You men get on with unloading things and I'll call you when the tea's ready.'

She had more sense than her husband, Reece thought as he turned to inspect the terrain and ask Jack's advice about where to site the tent.

'I thought to put it over there,' Francis said.

'You'll get a river running through it come winter if you do that,' Jack said. 'Up to you. We'll set it up where you want.' He winked at Reece.

'A river?'

Jack pointed to the ground. 'Come winter, you'll get run-off coming down here.' He saw Francis's puzzled look. 'Rainwater. Got to go somewhere, hasn't it? Most of the rain comes in winter and runs away downhill. Don't want it going into your stores, do you?'

'Where would *you* advise us to put it?' Reece asked.

'Billy will know.' He pointed to the man who'd sat silently for most of the journey next to Tommo. He was clearly part-aboriginal, but dressed and acted like his companions, and they seemed to treat him as an equal. 'Good lad, Billy is. We'll get the tent unloaded while he looks round.'

By the time Billy had chosen a piece of land that rose a little, about a hundred yards from the shack, the tea was ready. The men drank it with loud appreciation, after which they set to and erected the tent.

'Is there anything you don't know how to do?' Reece asked, watching how capably the other three worked, compared to himself and Francis.

'Y'have to be able to look after yourselves when you're on the road,' Jack said. 'Poor sort I'd be if I couldn't put up a shelter and cook my meals when I'm away from home.'

It was well into the afternoon by the time they'd unloaded everything and put it in the big tent, making space in a corner for Reece to sleep behind some boxes.

'Do you three want to stay the night here?' Francis asked. 'It's all right by me if you do.'

'Got a friend nearby. I'll go and see him. Didn't realise you were moving next door to old Kevin. If you've time, I'll take you across to meet him. Doesn't hurt to meet the neighbours.' He looked sideways at Francis. 'He's an ex-convict like me, though, so perhaps you'd rather not.'

Francis looked at him in shock. 'An ex-convict is allowed to lease a block of land?'

'He was a *gentleman* back home. Irish. Fell foul of the government because he wanted to free Ireland, so they sent him out here. He's a good fellow, but.'

'I'll go and meet him with you,' Reece said, seeing by his expression that Francis was going to refuse. 'How far away is his place, Jack?'

'An hour for us. But if you cut across the slope on foot, it won't take you more than a few minutes to get back.'

Reece didn't wait in case Francis refused but joined Jack on the cart. A neighbour who knew this area would be able to help them in these new conditions, whatever his background.

Kevin Lynch was older than Reece had expected, his face lined, his hair white. He was very thin, his skin tanned but with a yellowish undertone, as if he wasn't well.

When Reece offered his hand, Kevin shook it and grinned. 'Not frightened to touch an ex-convict, then, Mr Gregory?'

'Terrified. And my name's Reece.' Ordinary Australians didn't stand on ceremony with one another. He liked that. 'I'm general servant to the Southerhams next door until a year next April, then I'll find a piece of land and set up on my own.'

'Know about farming, do you?'

'A bit. I worked on a farm for a couple of years after the cotton mills shut down. I've still got a lot to learn, though, so if you've ever got any advice about conditions here, don't hesitate to share it. I'll listen gratefully.'

He didn't stay long, but left with a standing invitation to ask for advice any time or simply to come visiting.

He wished it was his land, and that he was working for his own future not the Southerhams'. But he'd served several months now, and the rest of the time would soon pass. And maybe by the end of it, he'd have a wife. He hoped so.

He'd work on that letter to Cassandra tonight. And he'd put it in the post next time he went to Perth, however much it cost to write to England. They charged by weight, he'd heard, and he'd written a lot of pages, but he didn't want to take out any of them. She had to know what she'd be facing here.

He prayed she'd come and join him. He missed her so much.

17

Early in the morning of the 13th December, Cassandra heard someone call out that land had been sighted. She got up, throwing on her clothes any old how, eager to go up on deck and see her new home. But her body betrayed her, rebelling at such haste. Clapping her hand to her mouth, she fled to the water closet.

When she returned to the cabin, she found Miss Pershore sitting on the edge of the lower bunk, staring at her as if she'd grown two heads.

'You're expecting a child, aren't you?' she demanded in a tone of both triumph and disgust.

'Yes, I am.'

'I've wondered all along whether you really did have a husband, because you never talk about him, and that's not natural. I think you're just saying you're a widow to escape the consequences of fornication!'

Cassandra drew herself up to her full height and stared down at the scrawny, scowling woman. She'd tried in vain to get on with Miss Pershore, to stay polite, but if she let this accusation go unchallenged, her child would be labelled a bastard and the stigma of that would ensure the poor little thing would be treated badly throughout its life. 'I was brought to join this ship by a clergyman and his wife, who vouched for me and who knew what my married state was. Do you think they'd have done that if this child was the result of my immorality?'

Silence, then Miss Pershore let out a loud sniff. 'Does your mistress know about it?'

'None of your business.'

'She doesn't, I can tell. And she won't want you as a maid once your condition is known. They never do.'

'Then I shall find myself another job.'

'You won't get one as a lady's maid.'

'I shan't want one if it turns people as sour as you.'

She regretted the hasty words as soon as she'd spoken them. It never paid to make outright enemies. There was a long, fraught silence, then Cassandra picked up her shawl and went up on deck. Why hadn't she remembered to take things slowly this morning?

She stood by the rail and felt better for the fresh air blowing in her face. Narrowing her eyes against the sun, she saw a faint smudge in the east that could only be land. A little closer to the ship was a lighthouse standing on another piece of low-lying land. It must be Rottnest Island. And beyond it, Matron had told them, was the port of Fremantle, where they'd disembark.

Cassandra had a sudden desperate longing to stride out on dry land, to walk for hours on her own and not just shuffle her way round the deck, afraid of bumping into someone.

Sighing, she went back below to tidy her hair and wait for a summons from Mrs Barrett. There was no sign of Miss Pershore, which was unusual, because her mistress wasn't an early riser and didn't normally summon her maid until later.

When the steward knocked on the door and said Mrs Barrett wanted to see her, he was frowning.

'Is something wrong?'

He looked at her stomach openly then. 'I gather there is.'

Miss Pershore must have been gossiping. Cassandra raised her chin defiantly. 'It's not wrong for a married woman, even one who's been widowed, to be carrying her husband's child. Some would say it's a good thing and wish me well.'

He shrugged. 'I suppose so. I forget sometimes you're not really a lady's maid. You've learned the job quickly.' He moved away, tossing a 'Good luck!' over his shoulder.

Why should she need good luck? Cassandra's heart sank. What had Miss Pershore *done*?

When she was bidden enter the Barretts' cabin, she found Mr Barrett there with his wife, both of them frowning, their eyes going immediately to her stomach.

'Why did you not tell us you were with child?' he demanded. 'Whose is it?'

She didn't reply at once, standing very still and telling herself to answer quietly and confidently.

'I'm recently widowed, so whose do you think it is?' she countered. 'My husband's.'

'So you say.'

'I'll remind you that I was introduced to you by a clergyman. You didn't pick me up off the street.'

He ignored that remark. 'Why have you said nothing about your condition?'

'I didn't know at first, then I wanted time to grow used to the idea. I hadn't expected a child, felt sad it would never know its father.'

'I can't possibly have a maid with a big belly like mine!' Mrs Barrett said pettishly. 'Think how people would laugh at the pair of us.'

'My condition isn't showing yet, and won't for a while. It hasn't made me work any less hard, nor will it.'

'I shall have to inform the Captain about this,' Mr Barrett said.

She'd had enough of people telling her what to do. 'Why? What business is it of his?'

'He must inform the authorities when we land. They may even send you back to England. They won't want you to be a charge on the public purse.'

'I have some money to tide myself over and I'm a hard worker. I'll be a charge on no one. I also have my sisters, so I won't be alone. This baby is no one's business but mine.' She had a fleeting thought of Reece as she spoke, because it affected him too, but knew she mustn't let herself be distracted so clamped her lips tightly together.

'Leave us alone, Simon. Please? There are things women can only say to one another when men aren't present.'

When he'd gone, Mrs Barrett looked at her and sighed. 'I'm sorry you won't be able to stay with me after we land, Lawson. You've worked hard and I've grown used to you.'

Not much of a compliment, thought Cassandra mutinously. 'Can I not stay with you until my condition begins to show, at least, to earn a little more money?'

Mrs Barrett hesitated. 'We'd decided not, but it must

be dreadful to face this alone, so I'll think about it. I don't know what I'd do without Simon to look after me at a time like this.'

Cassandra bent her head, feeling tears well in her eyes. 'I'd not expected to be having a child on my own, either. But I'll look after it carefully and love it, because it'll never know its father.'

Mrs Barrett dabbed at her eyes. 'How sad. And that Pershore creature is a mean old stick. It was she who approached my husband on deck and told him. She didn't even have the courtesy to come to me first.'

'She's not been an easy woman to share a cabin with, but I don't understand why she wishes me ill. I've done nothing to harm her, have always treated her politely.'

'Have you looked in the mirror lately?'

'I beg your pardon, ma'am?'

Mrs Barrett waved one hand towards the mirror that stood on top of the cabin trunk. 'Look at yourself.'

She moved across the room. 'I don't see anything different.'

'You're glowing with health and though you'll never be pretty, not with that nose, you look handsome.' She came to stand beside the maid and studied their reflections. 'I'm pretty and have a husband who loves me, so *I* don't need to envy you. Miss Pershore is ugly and has never been loved, so she envies you greatly.'

'Oh.' Cassandra cast another quick look at herself. She'd never spent a lot of time in front of the mirror, but had to agree that she was looking well. The sunny days on board ship had lent colour to her cheeks and the good food had given her back her womanly figure.

'You never talk about your husband.'

'It's too – painful. If I dwell on the past, I'll be lost.'

Mrs Barrett sighed. 'How brave you are! I'll give you a good reference. And you can still keep Hilda's trunk. I don't like to think of a child wanting. Since I shall still need help, you can stay with me for a few weeks after we disembark. But I can't have you as a maid once your condition shows. It'd make me a cause for ridicule if there were two of us in the family way.'

What a strange reason on which to base a decision! Cassandra thought. But she thanked her mistress, saying how grateful she was for this generosity.

It was terrible to have to be so deceitful, in large ways as well as small, but she was fighting for her own and the child's future now, and would do whatever she had to.

As for Miss Pershore, she would ignore the woman completely. It might make things uncomfortable in the cabin, but it wouldn't be for long now.

When she went back to the Barretts' cabin in the afternoon, Cassandra found Mr Barrett waiting for her again, his expression no more friendly than it had been last time. His wife looked sulky.

And in the middle of the floor was Hilda's trunk.

'Open it, if you please,' Mr Barrett said, pointing.

'Could I ask why?'

'Because we never did check what was in it, which may have been hasty of us. I want to look through it now, before you take it away. There may be things of value in it.'

She felt outraged. 'I don't think that's necessary, sir. There was nothing valuable. I'd have told you if there were.'

He glared at her. 'If you don't open it, I'll send for the Captain and get him to do it.'

Furious, she pulled out the key, which was on a chain round her neck. 'There are some of my own things in that trunk.' She'd put her money there because Hilda's trunk had a better lock.

When she opened it, he pushed her aside, pulling out the contents and tumbling them on the table and floor, not caring whether they got creased or dirtied by this rough treatment.

'Aha!' He pounced on her purse.

'That's mine, sir.'

'So you say.' He poured out the coins it contained on the table and counted them, then stared at her. 'No wonder you wanted to keep me away from this. I'm sending for the Captain. You're nothing but a thief.'

'We gave her the trunk, Simon.'

'Not Hilda's savings, though. It isn't right to take them.'

'The money is *mine!*' Cassandra protested again.

'So you say. But I don't believe you.' He rang for the steward and then they waited for the Captain to arrive.

The message about theft brought him quickly, even at a busy time like this, and he stared in surprise at the mess in the cabin.

Simon pointed to Cassandra. 'This woman is a thief!'

'I'm not! That's my own money and *you* gave me the trunk.'

Mrs Barrett went to stand by Cassandra. 'We did give her the trunk, Captain.'

'But not the money,' Mr Barrett insisted. 'We said if there was any money in it, that would have to be returned to our former maid.'

'But there wasn't any money in it. That's my savings!'

'Can you prove it?'

Her mind wasn't functioning and for a minute she stared at him, then desperation made her rack her brain and she suddenly cried, 'Yes! The woman who gave me most of that money is in Western Australia. She'll tell you.'

'How can she have given you the money if she lives there?' the Captain demanded.

'She sailed out on the *Eena* earlier this year.'

'A fine tale!' Mr Barrett scoffed.

'Wait!' The Captain held up his hand. 'There is a ship called the *Eena* and it did sail for Western Australia earlier this year. What's this woman's name?'

Cassandra gave him the details, praying that Mrs Southerham would still be in the colony.

'In the meantime, I'll keep the money,' the Captain said, putting the bag of coins into his pocket.

'If you please, sir, I'd appreciate it if we could count the money and you could give me a receipt.'

He gaped at her. 'Impudence! Do you think I'm going to steal it?'

'No, sir. Of course not. But it's simple good sense. That money is all I have in the world. It's safe with you, I know, but if anything were to happen to you, who would know the money belonged to me?'

'Hmm. Very well. You have a point. Count it out again.'

After this had been done, he looked at her thoughtfully, then said, 'When the others disembark, you are to stay behind, Mrs Lawson. You'll be escorted to the Migrants' Home and will stay there until we hear from this Mrs Southerham.' He nodded to the Barretts and took his leave.

Mr Barrett pointed to the contents of the trunk. 'Put this stuff back, Lawson, then we'll lock up the trunk and send it back to the hold. You're not to come into our cabin on your own from now on.'

Cassandra deliberately took her time repacking her things and in the end he grew bored and left her to it, with his wife supervising.

'It is your money, isn't it?' Mrs Barrett said.

'Yes.'

'I'm sorry. He – gets the bit between his teeth sometimes.'

'I'm sorry too. I've served you well, worked hard and this is a poor reward for my efforts.'

'It was that Pershore creature again. She told him she'd seen you counting money and was worried you'd stolen it. And indeed, there has been a lot of pilfering by the single women during this voyage.'

'I've never stolen anything in my life. Never.'

When she'd finished repacking her things, Mrs Barrett rang for the steward, but he said the sailors were too busy preparing for arrival at Fremantle and the trunk must stay where it was.

Mrs Barrett yawned. 'I need a nap. You may go, Lawson.'

Cassandra went up on deck. Her sisters found her and

at last, with them, she gave in to the tears she'd held back in front of her accuser.

They were horrified about what had happened, murmuring words of consolation. None of them knew what would happen after the ship docked and they were all anxious about the future.

Would nothing ever go right for her? Cassandra wondered. And would this accusation once again separate her from her sisters?

And what if Mrs Southerham couldn't be found and she lost her money? How would she manage to get her money back then?

Or would they send her back to England?

The first few days at the new farm passed very quickly. Livia made light of having to do the household chores, but Reece could tell Francis hated to see his wife doing such menial work.

He held his tongue about their current situation, but in his opinion, his employer was going about everything wrongly. They'd need to build additions on to the shack before the winter came, but Francis had said nothing about doing that and seemed more concerned to make sure that shade was provided (in the form of a tarpaulin strung between trees) for the two horses and was talking about building them a stable for the winter.

It was Reece who cobbled an outdoor table together from pieces of the wooden crates holding the furniture. Livia needed something to prepare food on, and they all needed it for eating. The shack itself was too full of boxes and packing cases to be used as a dining room, and even the small veranda was crammed with boxes still to be unpacked.

He just prayed people he'd talked to were right and it wouldn't rain until about March or April.

As the first week drew to a close, he waited until they'd finished a meal, then said, 'I presume it's still all right for me to take Sundays off? I've an invitation to visit our neighbour tomorrow.'

'Are you sure you're doing the right thing, associating with a convict like Lynch?' Francis asked. 'You don't want people thinking you're one of them.'

'I like Kevin and he's an emancipist now, with his full freedom,' Reece said. He'd walked over to visit their neighbour a couple of times in the evenings without telling them, and today he was going to ask Kevin's help in finding a piece of land to lease. Reece definitely couldn't afford to buy anything. He hadn't said anything to the Southerhams about that either, though. Time enough if he decided to take the risk.

He set off after breakfast, feeling relieved to get away for a while. He'd asked permission to take a chunk of kangaroo meat for his host. They always had to throw away part of the carcass because it went rotten so quickly in the heat, so Livia had been happy to give it to him.

He was finding it harder and harder to think of them by their surnames when they all lived so closely. They'd probably be annoyed if they knew that. They were always pleasant and polite with him, but it never seemed to occur to them that he might be lonely. Or that he too would like to sit and rest near the fire in the evenings without being asked to 'just' do this or 'just' fetch that.

Which was why he went to bed early, lying in the narrow space in the stores tent, feeling as if he was stifling.

If he'd stayed around on his day off, they'd not have left him in peace, he knew that.

Kevin was waiting for him, sitting on the veranda of his small but comfortable house.

'Are you all right?' Reece asked. 'You look pale.'

'I'm feeling my age. And I never did like the hot weather. I'll revive like a flower once it starts raining.'

Reece wasn't so sure. The other looked ill, not tired. He wondered how old his neighbour was. Nearer sixty than fifty, he'd guess. 'I brought you some meat.'

'Now that'll be useful. I'm not so spry with the hunting as I used to be. Will we be having a cup of tea before we set off to look at the land round here?'

'Good idea.'

Kevin had a small trap and an ugly but willing horse to pull it, so Reece harnessed it for him, another skill he'd learned in Australia.

After watching to make sure he was doing it right, Kevin slapped the little mare on the shoulder. 'You're a good girl, aren't you, Delilah?' She nuzzled him and when he pulled a piece of sugar out of his pocket, she licked it up delicately from his hand.

'Delilah?' Reece teased. 'What sort of name is that for a horse?'

'She tempted me to buy her when I'd intended to buy a bigger, stronger horse. Her owner was ill-treating her. They're terrible hard on horses in this country. And it turned out all right. She's got stamina, that one has, for all her lack of looks, and will pull her heart out if you ask her.'

'Are we going far?' Reece asked.

'Not very far.'

The land they saw was as parched as the rest of the countryside round here. Kevin pointed out advantages to look for, like a permanent stream or spring, and some good timber that could be felled and sold.

'I don't call these streams,' Reece said at one of their halts. 'They're mere trickles.'

'They'll gush along fiercely once the winter rains start. See how this one's eaten away a gully for itself. Worth a lot, a stream is. Does your master have one?'

'No. But there's a spring and we found a well the other day at the lower end. Nearly fell into it, just looked like a pile of old planks. But I fixed up the roller again and made a wall of the planks. We had some rope and a bucket. The water's a bit brackish, but it's all right.'

'Southerham's not a farmer, is he?'

'No. It's horses he likes, and the outdoor life. I think he confused the two things in his own mind.' They were silent for a moment or two, then he asked, 'How much will I have to pay for land?'

'You lease it by the acre.'

'And I'd need to put a dwelling on it.'

'You can make do with a bark hut at first. I'll show you which trees to strip.'

Reece hesitated, but felt comfortable to confide in his neighbour. 'I'm hoping to bring out my young lady, so I'll need some of my money for her fare. A man needs a wife and . . . she's a wonderful woman. But I still owe over a year of service to the Southerhams.'

'I've got a few ideas you might like to consider. Shall we go back to my place to discuss them? I'm growing tired and this heat is getting me down.'

'Shall I take over the reins?'

'That'd be grand. And if you'd pass me that old umbrella, I'll shade myself from the sun.'

When they were sitting on Kevin's veranda, sipping tea from big half pint mugs, he said, 'I could do with some company here, Reece lad. I'm having a bit of trouble keeping up with things, I must admit. It's more than the heat. It's old age. It's not good to grow old alone.' He let the words sink in then added quietly, 'I could lease you some land. We'd do it properly. I'd lease it you for five years, and I'd not do it for money, but in return for you looking after me.'

Reece stared at him, taken aback by this.

'I've got a spare bedroom, had some hopes once that one of my nephews might come out here, but he didn't. And we can push out the living room a bit to give us more space for the winter. It's not hard to add on to a wooden house. It rains awful hard in the winter. I've got some rough slabs of timber lying there ready. They'll do just fine if you trim them up a bit.'

Reece answered obliquely, because it seemed so sad that a man had to pay someone to look after him. 'Do you hear from your family still? Would they not send someone out to care for you?'

'No. My wife died before she could come out to join me. We didn't have any children and my other relatives, even those I felt close to, aren't very proud of being connected to a convict.' He sighed and stared into space for a few moments. ''Tis a cruel thing to do, transporting a man for the term of his natural life.'

Reece waited a minute, watching Kevin stare into the distance. When the other looked back at him, he said, 'It's a kind offer. Are you sure?'

'I am.'

'I wonder . . .'

'What?'

'Well, it's only a few minutes' walk to your place across the side of the hill. Could I come and stay with you straight away? I've only got a corner of a tent at the moment.'

Kevin studied him, then smiled. 'I'd like that fine.'

'I'll help you round the place in return.'

'Will they let you do it?'

Reece smiled. 'I don't think they'll dare refuse. Help isn't easy to find. And there's no law saying servants have to live in.'

But when he got back and told them what he intended to do, Francis did protest.

'But we need you here.'

'I'm a servant, not a slave,' Reece said mildly.

'But . . . servants usually live in.'

'Would you leave an old man to struggle on his own? And am I not to have any time off?'

There was an uncomfortable silence then Livia stepped in. 'Is Mr Lynch really struggling?'

'Yes, he is, Mrs Southerham. He has no one to help him.'

'Why you?'

'He and I get on well, have done from the very first meeting. Sometimes you do take to a person easily, don't you?' As he had with Cassandra. He banished the thought of her and added, 'And a tent isn't the most comfortable place to sleep. What's more, if I move out of it, you'll have more room to store your own things and can make a bit of space in your house.'

It was a gross exaggeration to call the place a house. Even 'shack' was a polite word. But Francis still wasn't making plans to repair it, kept saying he'd keep that job for the convicts he was going to put in for when he was ready for them. He did mark out the timber he wanted to fell to earn money, or rather he and Reece started marking the trees and Reece finished it when Francis grew too hot and sweaty.

He spent most of his time with the horses, who were surely the best cared for in the colony. Reece suspected Francis was already finding he'd made another mistake.

What he couldn't make the Southerhams understand was that the winter rains would find every leak in the rusty tin roof.

After watching Livia struggle to work in the hot sun without complaining, Reece suggested to Francis that they string up a tarpaulin to make a roof over the area round the rough wooden table. He'd only to say, 'Mrs Southerham needs the shelter' and Francis immediately turned his attention to the task. But Reece had to take charge of doing it, because Francis had no idea how to set about it and his suggestions would lead to a structure that would blow down in the first strong wind.

They worked in heat that was like a hammer striking down on you in the middle of the day. None of them had ever experienced weather like this.

'You're a very practical man,' Livia said as Reece waited under the tarpaulin for her to serve his midday meal. She gestured above them. 'This has made a big difference to me.' She glanced across at the horse shelter where her husband was checking on their two steeds and smiled. 'My Francis isn't as practical as you, but once we get our convict servants, I'm sure we'll get more things done round here. He's hoping to arrange that while we're up in Perth.'

Reece had his doubts about how that would work out. From what he'd heard, convict servants were not particularly skilled at building, or anything else, and had to be carefully watched. Men forced into doing things were never the best workers. 'Well, at least Mr Southerham keeps us in meat with his shooting.'

'And even then, you were the one who thought of digging a pit and keeping the meat in the cooler layers of soil underneath the surface.'

'Kevin told me about that.'

'Our neighbour?'

'Yes. He's an intelligent man, born a gentleman. If he wasn't an ex-convict, you'd like him.'

'But he *is* an ex-convict.'

He knew better than to push the point. For them, there were gentry and others in the world. They might be friendly towards those they considered inferior, but they'd not deal with ex-convicts if they could help it, even if it was to their advantage. He preferred to judge each man on his own merits – and each woman too.

Francis came across to join them, washing his hands in the bucket, and she served the food: damper and kangaroo meat stew from the previous day's kill. The potatoes were starting to sprout and she'd talked about throwing them away.

'Why not plant them,' Reece suggested. 'There's nothing like growing your own food.'

'With potatoes so cheap, it's not worth it,' Francis said with a grimace.

'Then give them to me once they're useless to you and I'll plant them on Kevin's block.'

Francis shrugged. 'Take them if you wish.' He ate another mouthful, sighing as he stared down at his plate. 'I heard before we left Perth that there's a ship due to arrive in mid-December. I'm going up to see if I can find a maid from it to help Livia, and I'll collect my convicts at the same time.'

'I'm coming with you, then,' she said at once. 'I'd rather choose my own servants.'

'Can you look after things here while we're gone, Reece? We'll take the cart and leave you with one horse.'

'I need to go into Perth too. I've a very important letter to post and I need to buy a few things. I'm going to be leasing some land from Kevin and I want to build a house on it.'

They both stopped eating to stare at him.

'Are you sure that's wise?' Francis asked. 'It won't be your own land. You could be wasting your money.'

'I'll use mainly bark. The house won't cost much. Kevin's going to show me how.'

'When will you do that?'

'On Sundays.'

'I hope you won't come back exhausted to your main job.'

'Have you had any reason to complain so far? I've been working to level the building area already.'

'I thought you were living with Kevin. Are you not getting on with him?' Livia asked.

'I need to have somewhere for my wife to come to – if she'll have me. That's why the letter is so important.'

'Cassandra?'

'Who else?'

'I'm sure she'll accept you,' Livia said warmly.

'It'll be at least a year till she can join me, perhaps more, and I'll have to work out how to send her the money for her passage. I've been saving my wages carefully.'

Livia smiled. 'I left her some money, enough to pay for her passage. Maybe she'll come a bit sooner.'

Reece wished he felt as certain that his proposal would be accepted. He alternated between doubt and hope. Sadly, Edwin Blake would have died by now, must have done, so surely Cassandra would allow herself to think of her own future? Or would she refuse to leave her sisters?

It made him sad to think how long it would take for his letter to reach her, and then for her reply to reach him. He'd heard the phrase 'the ends of the Earth' but he'd never expected to find himself there, hadn't realised how isolated the Swan River Colony was, how few people were living here.

Francis's cousin had a lot to answer for, writing lies about this place.

On the other hand, Reece liked it here, enjoyed the freer life and felt excited about the opportunities he was starting to see for himself. He even liked the warmer climate, something he'd never experienced before. The sun shone day after day and you never needed a coat. Something in him responded cheerfully to that bright warmth. He'd already known he could never go back to working in a mill again, now he knew he would never want to go back to cool, rainy Lancashire.

18

A few hours after passing the island of Rottnest, the *Tartar* anchored in Gage's Roads, a sheltered stretch of water about half a mile from the shore. The town of Fremantle lay before them, tantalisingly close, yet still out of reach.

'There isn't a harbour!' Xanthe exclaimed in surprise. 'Just long piers.'

'I heard there's a sand bar at the mouth of the river, so only smaller ships can go up to Perth.' Pandora sighed. 'Isn't it frustrating? I'm dying to see our new – home.' It was an effort to call it that. Home to her would always be Outham. She couldn't even discuss the pain of leaving it with her sisters. It still hurt too much.

'There's a lot of forest and not many buildings,' Maia said. 'I thought it'd be much bigger than this. And what's that big white building on top of the hill?'

'A prison.'

'I suppose they would need a big prison if they send convicts here, though Matron says most of them aren't locked away, but are out working on new roads and other improvements. Or they've been given a ticket-of-leave, as long as they behave.' She frowned. 'Do you suppose such men are dangerous?'

'They'd not be let out of prison if they were, surely?'

Three other ships were anchored nearby and as they continued to watch, a boat was rowed slowly out to theirs. It was carrying the health inspector, they found.

A smaller boat came out next and took off two of the cabin passengers, while the emigrants were left to crowd on deck and gaze longingly at the shore.

There was a lot of grumbling that night when they were locked down at their normal time of eight o'clock.

Cassandra was summoned to the Barretts' cabin the next morning, as usual, and almost refused to go, she was so angry at Mr Barrett. But she couldn't afford to be proud because they still hadn't paid her the wages they'd promised.

Mrs Barrett was there alone and hurriedly slipped her a letter. 'It's a reference. Simon says we shouldn't give you one, but I don't agree. You've worked hard, done everything I've asked. Put it away quickly. Now, help me do my hair and finish my packing.'

'Could I ask – about my wages, ma'am?'

She began fiddling with her wedding ring. 'I'm afraid Simon thinks paying for your passage was enough, given the circumstances.'

'He agreed to pay me wages as well!' She drew herself up. 'I shall find a lawyer and sue you for those wages, if necessary. I need every penny I can get for my child. Mr Barrett has already taken my money from me – *every penny of my savings!* Is he going to refuse to pay my wages as well? How does he expect me to live once I'm ashore?'

Mrs Barrett burst into tears, but Cassandra didn't try to comfort her, nor did she start work.

When the door opened, she turned to see Mr Barrett standing there, scowling at her.

'What are you doing to upset my wife?'

'Asking for my wages.'

'The impudence of you! Stealing money and then asking for more.'

A phrase Cassandra had read came into her mind. 'In English law, there is a presumption of innocence until someone is proven guilty. When I'm proven innocent, what are you going to do about the wages? Will you still be in Perth even? I call *that* stealing.'

'How dare you accuse me of such a thing! And you can stop using fancy words that you don't understand and aren't suitable for a maid.'

'I understand exactly what I'm saying. I may not have as much money as you, but there's nothing wrong with my brain.' She watched as his wife tugged his arm.

'Pay her the wages, Simon! She's worked hard, deserves them. Indeed, I don't know what I'm going to do without her.'

He turned in shock to his wife. 'But we agreed!'

'No. *You* said that's what you were going to do. You didn't even listen to my answer. And if you don't pay her, I shall.'

There was a pregnant silence, then he fumbled in his pocket. 'I'm only doing this to stop you upsetting my wife!'

He tossed some coins at Cassandra and she had to bend to pick up the ones that fell on the floor. She counted them carefully. 'This is a pound short. Are you intending to cheat me?' She held out her hand with the money lying on it to show him.

He glared as he fumbled in his pocket and drew out another coin, this time deliberately dropping it on the floor.

She picked it up, because a pound was a lot of money, but it made her angry that he'd behave in such a petty and vindictive manner. She turned to Mrs Barrett. 'Thank you for your help, ma'am. Now, what did you want me to do for you this morning?'

He stalked out and Mrs Barrett closed her eyes and shuddered. 'Men! Did your husband always think he knew best?'

It took her a minute to think of an answer. She kept forgetting that she was supposed to have had a husband. 'No, ma'am. Nor did my father.'

'You were lucky, then.'

They didn't say much as Cassandra arranged her mistress's hair and finished the packing. 'There. And I want to thank you for teaching me so much, especially about embroidery. I love doing that.'

'I enjoyed it.' She laid one hand on her belly. 'I wish you well with your baby.'

'And you with yours, Mrs Barrett.'

When Cassandra left the cabin she wasn't sure what to do with herself and stood for a moment outside it, relieved to have some time alone.

Then the steward's voice made her open her eyes again. 'Captain says you're to wait with the other single women once you've finished here.'

She'd have preferred a few moments of peace, but knew better than to argue.

★

It was two days before the ordinary emigrants could disembark and when they did, the single women were taken up to Perth, Cassandra among them.

She was sent with her sisters to the Poorhouse-Home, which had been newly renovated and here again the single women would be under the care of a matron. Why did they always treat single women like children, Cassandra wondered rebelliously. She wasn't a single woman, officially, but a widow. She sighed but didn't make a fuss, not wanting to gain a bad reputation.

Xanthe grew anxious when she heard that they were being put in a poorhouse, especially when they saw that this one was surrounded by a high stone wall with broken glass set in the top. 'Are emigrants so eager to escape that they have to be locked in?' she muttered to her twin. 'I don't like this place, Maia.'

But to everyone's relief, they found that the pauper inmates were lodged on the upper floor, while the emigrants had decent, if crowded quarters on the ground floor.

The long room they were shown into had been divided by wooden partitions into smaller spaces, and the sisters shared one with some other young women from Lancashire. To everyone's relief, the bedsteads were new and the bedding was clean.

Cassandra was sternly warned not to try to run away by the new matron.

'I'm not likely to leave without my trunks,' she replied. 'They contain all I own in the world. And I want my money back before I go as well. Mr Barrett stole it from me.'

'I've been told *you* could have stolen that money,' Matron said bluntly.

'Well, I didn't. And I shall prove that when I find Mrs Southerham, who gave it to me in the first place. She came out on the *Eena*.'

'No one of that name has ever been lodged here.'

'She wouldn't need to have lodgings provided. She was gentry. They were going to stay with Mr Southerham's cousin till they could buy some land.'

'Hmm. Well, we'll see if you're proved correct. And in the meantime you've clean lodgings and food, so what are you complaining about?' She looked at Cassandra as if daring her to try. 'Now, I must get on. Already there are employers coming to see if they can find suitable maids, though how I'm expected to know whether you girls are suitable when I've only just met you all, I don't know. You'd better not line up with the others, Lawson, not till your case is decided.'

Matron insisted on her sisters going out to talk to potential employers, however, and wouldn't take no for an answer. 'I'll fetch you some sewing,' she told Cassandra. 'We expect people to earn their keep here. You can sew, can't you?'

She stifled a sigh. 'Yes. I've had plenty of practice during the past year.'

'Good. Come with me and I'll give you a petticoat to piece together.'

When she returned with the bundle of sewing, Cassandra sat on her bed, hearing others talking nearby in the garden, feeling very alone and apprehensive about the future. What if she was unable to prove the money was hers? What would she do without it once she was unable to work?

And what sort of job would she be able to find anyway? There were no cotton mills here. Anyway, she couldn't accept a job without telling employers about her condition and they might not want her for only a short time.

After the baby was born it would be even more difficult to find work, but she didn't intend to let anyone take her baby away from her. She'd seen what happened when young women from the mill sent their babies away to be cared for 'in the country'. A lot of those babies had died from neglect, that's what.

Pride had kept her head up and her expression calm while she spoke to Matron, but now, with no one to see her, she couldn't hold back the tears, which plopped on to the material as she threaded her needle and sorted out the pieces.

Reece drove the cart up to Perth for the Southerhams and they rode their horses, since they couldn't leave the poor animals to fend on their own without a stream and meadow. The grass was beige and tinder dry with the summer heat.

By setting off very early, they managed to give the horses a good rest during the heat of the day and find a place to stay for the night.

The following day they pressed on, leaving the horses and cart at a livery stable and taking a ferry across to the north side of the river. In Perth they went to the hotel where they'd stayed previously because at least it was clean.

'It wasn't too bad, was it, my dear?' Francis said to his wife.

Neither of them thought to ask Reece what his accommodation at the small hotel had been like and he didn't say anything. He was getting hardened to sleeping in rough places. Same old shed for me, he thought with a wry smile as he stowed his bag of clothes under a lower bunk bed.

In the morning, however, Francis was unwell, so Livia sent for Reece and asked him to postpone his own business and go with her to the Poorhouse-Home, where the new arrivals were lodged. 'I'm afraid all the maids will be hired if I wait until tomorrow. There's such a shortage of good servants here.'

They walked through the streets as soon as Livia had had breakfast, leaving Francis in the bedroom nursing his upset stomach.

'I think it was the crab,' Livia said. 'I didn't eat any, but Francis had two helpings. I gather another of the guests is also unwell. Francis has stopped being sick now but he was bad during the night and he's not fit to walk anywhere yet.'

There was a crowd of people at the Home and Livia stopped for a minute in dismay at the sight of them. 'I was right to come today. Oh dear, I hope there are still some maids left to hire.'

'If you stay behind me, I'll push my way through the crowd,' he offered.

They edged their way towards the area where the young women were standing, some talking to prospective employers, others to one another. Before Livia could talk to anyone, there was a shriek and one of the young women ran across to throw herself into Reece's arms.

He stared in blank astonishment at Pandora. 'What the—' Even as she stepped back, flushing as if embarrassed at what she'd done, two others ran up to join them and hugged him as well. 'What are you doing here?' He looked round. 'Where's Cassandra?'

'It's a long story. Not for public telling and—' Pandora began, then stopped as she saw the lady behind him. 'Mrs Southerham! Oh, I can't believe our luck! You're just the person we need to see.'

Livia smiled at her and looked round, also asking, 'Isn't Cassandra with you?'

'They won't let her come outside. They think she stole some money. She says *you* gave it to her.'

Matron came across to them. 'Is this man a relative?' she demanded frostily. 'I'm not having you girls throwing yourselves at men who are not.'

Livia stepped forward. 'Mr Gregory works for me. We both know these young women. We all come from the same town in Lancashire.'

As Matron relaxed a little at the sound of a lady's cultured accent, another man came up to them, eyeing the sisters in a way that annoyed Reece.

The stranger pushed into the group. 'You can't hog them all, my dear lady. I'm looking for a maid too. My wife and I live out at York and we'll pay well.'

The sisters stepped away from him instinctively.

'You found a maid only a few months ago, Mr Searle,' Matron said. 'What happened to her?'

'She's gone and got herself married, the ungrateful

bi— um, creature. You can't keep female servants for
more than a few months here.' He stared at Pandora. 'I'd
not hire one as beautiful as you, though. The men would
be round you like bees round a honey pot. You'd not last
a week.'

'I'd not work for you.' She glared at him. 'I don't like
the way you look at me.'

Matron gasped and choked back what sounded like a
laugh.

Reece didn't bother to hide a smile at the outrage on
the man's face. Pandora was right, though he'd never
heard a young woman say it so bluntly. The way the
fellow looked at women was an insult in itself. He despised
men like that. He'd bet that the previous maid had left
her job for more than one reason.

'Nor would I work for you,' Xanthe added, linking her
arm in her twin's.

'I'd not hire uppity maids like you. In fact, these
Lancashire females don't know their place.' The man
walked off, muttering to himself.

Matron turned to the sisters, her smile fading. 'I can
understand you not wanting to work for Mr Searle, but
be very careful in future how you reply to people offering
you jobs. Remember, you're here to find yourselves
employment, not to be a burden on the government.'

'We need to find jobs near to one another,' Xanthe
said.

'You'll have to take what's offered, young woman,'
Matron said. 'It's not likely anyone will want to hire two
of you. Now, I must—'

Livia stepped forward. 'Excuse me, Matron, but

Pandora said there was some problem about Cassandra and money.'

'Yes. She claims that a certain lady gave her the money in question in England, but the employer who brought her out here thought she'd stolen it, so it was taken from her. The Captain was going to give the money to the Governor for safe keeping.'

'I'm Mrs Southerham and *I* gave her the money. What must I do to prove that?'

Matron gave her an assessing look.

'Never mind the money, where is she?' Reece asked. 'I need to see her urgently.'

'We don't allow men into the single women's quarters,' Matron told him frostily.

'Then bring her out. I need to see her.'

'Who are you?'

'Reece Gregory.' He was looking anxiously beyond her, desperate for a sight of Cassandra.

'What is your interest in Mrs Lawson?'

'What? I'm not interested in Mrs Lawson. It's Cassandra Blake I want to see. She's the woman I want to marry. I thought she was still in England. I've just written to her.' He beamed at them all. 'I've never heard such wonderful news in my life.'

Matron looked at him in puzzlement. 'Is it a while since you saw her?'

He nodded. 'A very long time.' It seemed an eternity. Out of the corner of his eye, he saw Xanthe nudge Maia, but didn't look at their faces, too anxious to persuade this woman to take him to Cassandra. If she was here, he'd ask her to marry him immediately. Surely she'd say yes? She could share his room at Kevin's and— He realised Matron was speaking again and tried to concentrate on what she was saying.

'You can come as far as the rear of the garden, Mr Gregory. I'm sure Cassandra will explain the – um, circumstances. But first I must write a quick note to the Governor's office. One of his clerks will no doubt come to speak to you, Mrs Southerham, to verify that the money does belong to Miss Blake. May I ask where you're staying? Right.' She turned back to Reece. 'You must be patient for a few more moments. After I've written the note I'll send Mrs Lawson out to speak to you.'

Pandora poked him in the side when he opened his mouth to protest again that it was Miss Blake he wanted to see.

Matron turned to add sharply, 'As for you three, remember it'd be most unusual for two of you to find jobs close to one another, let alone three. This is the Swan River Colony, where settlements outside the capital city of Perth are small and widely scattered. We don't have crowded towns like those in England.'

When Matron had left, taking Reece with her, Livia cleared her throat. 'Actually, I'm looking for a maid to do general work, and would be happy to employ one of you, but I can't afford to employ all three. Still, it'd mean one of you was living near your sister, who will no doubt accept Reece's proposal of marriage.'

Their faces fell as they questioned her and discovered how isolated the place where she lived was, how far out of Perth.

Livia frowned. 'What did Matron mean by calling your sister Mrs Lawson? Is Cassandra married?'

Pandora hesitated then whispered, 'We can't explain here.'

Before she could pursue the matter, others came up to make enquiries as to whether the sisters were seeking employment and it was impossible to talk about private matters.

Livia couldn't understand why the three kept looking anxiously in the direction Reece had gone, or exchanging worried glances. It was as if they were expecting something to go wrong. Surely Cassandra's feelings towards Reece hadn't changed? He was a kind and good-looking man, would be an excellent provider, and he clearly still loved her. What more could any girl ask?

Cassandra sewed steadily, enjoying the warm air blowing through the window and the bright sunlight. She looked up as someone came in and saw Matron frowning at her again. 'Is something wrong?'

'Could you please describe the appearance of this Mrs Southerham who is supposed to have given you the money?'

She did so and saw Matron's stern expression relax.

'Then I'm happy to tell you she's outside and has confirmed that she gave it to you. Don't drop that sewing on the floor! Put it on the bed.'

Cassandra's hands were shaking as she did this. She couldn't believe it could be so easy to prove that the money was hers. Surely this was a sign that things would start to go better for her from now on?

Matron waited for a moment then continued, 'Of course the Governor will have to approve the purse being given back to you, but I can't see any great difficulty in that. Mrs Southerham is clearly a lady.'

Did that mean that only ladies could be trusted to tell the truth? Cassandra wondered. This was another world from the cotton mill and narrow streets where she'd grown up. She'd never had any close dealings with gentry like the Southerhams before, or been treated so openly as an inferior being – which wasn't how she regarded herself. But she was in another world now in more senses than that, she reminded herself, and kept her mouth closed on the angry response that nearly escaped her.

'There's something else.'

'Yes?'

'She's got her servant with her, a fellow called Reece Gregory, and— *Are you all right?*'

Cassandra dropped on to the bed, unable to speak for a moment, and sat there shaking, clasping her arms round herself in a vain attempt to stop the tremors. She'd known Reece was here in Australia, but to be confronted with him so soon . . . She wasn't ready for the encounter, hadn't yet been able to work out what to say to him.

And would she ever be ready for the look of scorn on his face when she told him?

'He seems very eager to see you, so I've said you could meet him outside in the rear of the garden. But do not go out of sight. I'll take you to him. Hurry up. I've a thousand things needing my attention today.'

Cassandra stood up, feeling numb with panic and terror. How was she to tell Reece something so important with other people nearby, able to overhear them, able to see him walk away from her, as he surely would?

She couldn't do it.

Only . . . if he still wanted to marry her, she would have to tell him, to explain why she couldn't do so. It would be wrong to try to deceive him.

Her thoughts in a tangle, she followed Matron outside and there he was, standing in the sunlight, his dark hair gleaming, his skin tanned, looking better than she'd ever seen him. His eyes raked her from head to foot and a smile blossomed on his face as he strode towards her. Before she'd realised what he intended, he'd pulled her into his arms.

'Cassandra! Oh my darling, I can't believe you're here!'

For a moment she allowed herself to lean against his strength, then Matron's voice cut through the haziness in her brain.

'Mrs Lawson! Mr Gregory! Kindly behave yourselves.'

Cassandra tore herself out of Reece's grasp and waited until Matron had walked away. 'I didn't expect to – see you so soon.'

He looked at her in puzzlement. 'What's wrong?'

She looked round desperately, but there were people on every side. 'I can't tell you here.'

'And why did she call you Mrs Lawson? Have you married someone else?'

'No. It's not that. Shall we – move across to that far corner? What I have to say is not for others' ears.'

In the corner was a bench and as they sat on it, she searched desperately for words and once again failed to find ones that would soften the blow.

'What is it, love?'

The gentle way he spoke was her undoing. Tears began to trickle down her face. She pushed words out in spurts, not finding anything but the bald truth to offer him.

'After you'd gone, Dad died.'

'I knew he hadn't got long to live. He'll be sorely missed. Are you still grieving for him?'

'No. It's not that. Our aunt – uncle Joseph's wife – no one realised, but she was quite mad. She had our uncle murdered and—'

'Murdered!'

She rushed on. 'And she had me kidnapped.' Somehow he'd taken hold of her hand and she held his tightly, unable to pull away from him. He'd spurn her soon enough.

'What happened? Did they – hurt you?'

'Yes. They—' She couldn't force the words out, only cover her face with her hands and sob, heedless of who saw them.

He stood up and pulled her into his arms. 'Did they – use you?'

She didn't dare raise her eyes, couldn't bear to see the disgust in his face, as she nodded.

'Did you think that would make me scorn *you*?'

She risked a glance and saw grief and pain, but no disgust.

'That won't change my mind, Cassandra love. It's over and done with now and I still want to marry you.'

She had to press her lips together for a moment or two or she'd have been wailing, because it wasn't over, would never be over. 'That's not all. Because of what they did . . . I'm with child.'

He didn't speak, but horror was etched across his face. 'Cassandra, no!' His hands dropped from her arms and he took a step backwards.

Words failed her and she ran for her quarters, heedless of who saw her weeping.

She wept even more bitterly because he didn't try to follow, because he *had* looked at her in disgust at the thought of her carrying a child.

19

Reece walked blindly out of the Home, bumping into people, oblivious to the four women watching him. What had happened, Livia wondered, to drive a strong man to this state of anguish.

'She's told him and he's walked out on her,' Maia said in a low voice. 'I thought better of him.'

Livia swung round. 'Told him what?'

They looked at one another, then shook their heads.

'It's Cassandra's secret.'

'If I'm going to help you – and them – I need to know.'

That held them silent for a few moments, then she saw them look at one another and nod.

'I'll tell her. You wait here. Matron will be angry if we all vanish.'

Pandora took her outside and a little way down the street. There, standing at a distance from passers-by on a dusty plot of land, she explained what had happened to Cassandra and exactly why they'd all had to leave England.

Livia stared at her in horror. 'Dear heaven! Your aunt was more than mad, she was wicked beyond belief.'

Pandora nodded. 'After all that, Cassandra needs us, so we can't accept jobs that take us away from her. She was like a mother to us, gave up her own life to bring us up. And once the baby's born, she'll need us even more.'

'She can come to us with you,' Livia offered. 'It's very primitive, I'm afraid. You'll have to sleep in a tent, but two of you can be together, at least. I can't take the others, though, and I can't pay her wages, only her keep. My husband and I have less money than we'd hoped and no chance of making more for a while.'

'It's very kind of you. We'd hoped Reece would . . . forgive her. No, not forgive. She's done nothing wrong. But accept what happened. Accept the child. I don't think *she* ever believed he would, though.'

'It's – difficult.'

Pandora sighed. 'Yes. I think we'd better go back. I'll tell Cassandra about your offer. Perhaps if the twins could find somewhere not too far away . . . Oh, I just don't know.'

Livia didn't wait for Reece to return, but walked slowly back to the hotel on her own. There she told Francis what had happened and sent him out to look for Reece. But there was no sign of their servant.

'I'll go and see Cassandra tomorrow,' she said. 'We must offer her shelter. I can't see any other solution. No one's going to have employment for four of them.'

'I know how you like and respect her, and I'm happy to offer her shelter,' he said at once.

'She's a very intelligent young woman. You don't meet many of her calibre. She'd make him a good wife. Why did he walk away from her, spurn her like that?'

He frowned. 'It's a lot to take on. Has it occurred to

you that if she comes to us, she'll be seeing Reece every day? That may be the last thing she wants.'

'She may not have any choice but to come to us. She and her sisters know no one else here. And he may change his mind about her.'

'I don't think I could accept another man's child, especially one conceived in that way.'

Reece strode through the streets without thinking where he was going, rage burning hotly within him. How could anyone have done such a thing to Cassandra? And what cruel fate would leave her with a child?

If he married her, he'd be taking on the child of a brutal abuser of women. He didn't think he could bear to do that.

When he found himself by the river, he stopped walking and sat down on a piece of rising ground, staring at the water as he tried to think through what had happened.

I let her down, he thought, as his fury began to subside. *I just walked away and let her down. What must she be thinking of me?*

It was the shock, he supposed. He wasn't proud of himself. He'd go back and apologise, tell her . . . what would he tell her? That he didn't want the child, but he still wanted her?

Would she give the child away? Of course not. He'd seen her smile at little children in the street, chat to neighbours' children, slip food to that unhappy looking boy who lived nearby. She had been a mother to her own sisters, and a good one, too. No, Cassandra would never abandon or give away her own child, however it had been begotten.

Could he take the child, raise it as his own?

He didn't know. Only . . . if he didn't, he'd not have Cassandra.

He put his head in his hands and groaned.

'You all right, son?'

He looked up to see a ragged old man standing beside him. 'Just had some bad news.'

'Ah. Sorry, mate.'

The fellow looked so thin and hungry, Reece took out sixpence and gave it to him. 'Get yourself a decent meal.'

'Thanks. Much obliged.'

Reece watched the old man walk stiffly back towards the town and wondered whether he would spend the money on a meal or on booze. What did it matter? He didn't usually give to beggars, but the old fellow had stopped to make sure he was all right and he'd appreciated that.

Sometimes you could feel very alone.

How alone was Cassandra feeling now?

He began to walk slowly along the water's edge till he came to a garden fence blocking the way. Turning, he walked back.

Nearby he saw a young couple walking along, not touching but still so close and loving as they talked and smiled and gesticulated that it was a pleasure to watch them.

The baby hadn't asked to be born, had it?

He shouldn't have run away like that. He'd let Cassandra down badly . . . and hurt her. She'd been crying.

He wanted to cry now, sob his heart out. Why were men not allowed to weep?

He'd been longing to see her for months, regretting leaving her, wishing he'd stayed with her. And when she'd come to him, he'd walked away and left her.

Was he going to throw all his hopes and plans away because of what had happened?

A bird landed nearby, pecking at some debris. A warm breeze wafted around him. A boat went past far out on the water.

But could he do it? Could he take on the child?

He straightened up. He'd have to. He'd not get Cassandra if he didn't.

He shouldn't have left her like that.

He needed more time to calm down, though, before he faced her, so continued walking aimlessly, not really noticing his surroundings until he realised with a jolt of surprise that it was getting dark.

He went back to the Home, but was refused admittance because of the late hour and couldn't persuade them to relax the rules.

In the end he went back to the hotel and lay on his bunk, not hungry, just desperately sad.

When someone came into the sleeping quarters, he didn't look up until Francis said, 'Are you all right?'

It was dark and Reece was glad of that. 'No. Not really. I – had a shock this afternoon.'

'I know. Her sisters told my wife. Bad luck, that. She'd have made you a perfect wife.'

Reece jerked to his feet. '*Would have made a perfect wife?* She *is* going to be my wife.'

'You're still going to marry her?'

'Of course I am.'

'Very noble of you.'

'Not noble. Selfish. I want her.'

'High price to pay, though. Still, perhaps she'll lose the child.'

Reece stood motionless as these words sank in. They were no doubt meant to be comforting, but instead they brought back memories of how he'd felt when his wife and baby had died. 'I hope she doesn't. I've lost a baby myself and it tears you apart. And what harm has that baby done anyone?'

'Livia thought you'd say that.'

Reece closed his eyes for a moment, trying to pull himself together.

He heard the door closing and realised he was alone again, alone with his thoughts and his memories – and an even firmer determination to go back the following day and ask Cassandra to marry him, child and all.

He'd lost one child. Now another had been given to him.

He'd get up early and leave a note for his employers. If they chose to get angry about him absenting himself again, let them. His whole future was at stake.

When she heard her sisters come back to their sleeping area, Cassandra tried to stop weeping but couldn't. Pandora sat down on the narrow bed to comfort her and after a while she managed to stop. This was the last time she'd allow herself to weep. It changed nothing.

'I'm all right.'

'Of course you're not,' Pandora said.

'I've cried it all out. Now I must make plans for the future.'

'I'm disappointed in Reece. I thought he'd have stuck by you.'

'It's a lot to ask of a man.' She hesitated then added quietly, 'I realised on the ship that it was too much to ask anyone to do, taking on such a baby. But I'm not giving up my child. I thought about what Dad would say and I knew—' Her voice broke for a moment or two, but she pulled herself together and continued. 'I knew he'd say it wasn't the child's fault and every child needs loving. I can't take the risk that a man might make such a child feel – different, unloved. Like Timmy. I dare not marry Reece, whatever he says.'

'Oh, Cassandra.'

She saw the twins sitting on the next bed. Xanthe's eyes were brimming with tears and Maia was crying openly. 'I'll be all right. I'll feel much better once I have my money back. I have to look for work.'

'Mrs Southerham has offered me a job,' Pandora said. 'She says you can come too and earn your keep, but she can't afford to pay you wages.'

'Then why did she give me the money in England?'

'She must have thought your need was greater than hers, or that they'd get more from Mr Southerham's family than they did.'

'It's kind of her, but I can't go to their place! Reece will be there.'

'Then I'll tell her we can't take up the offer and we'll try to find another job where we can be together,' Pandora said. 'If we can't all find work near one another, the twins can stick together and so will you and I. We three have already decided that and you won't change our minds.'

Cassandra smiled at them. What would she do without her family? 'Thank you.'

One of the other single females came into the bedroom. 'I've got a job!' she said cheerfully and began to pack her things. 'It's in a lady's house, working as a general maid. I don't mind what I do as long as I get plenty to eat. She seemed very nice and Matron says she knows the family, so it's safe to go with her. Oh, and tea's being served, so you'd better go and get some food.'

'I'm not hungry,' Cassandra said.

Her sisters were insistent that she couldn't go without her tea so in the end it was easier to go with them and nibble a little food. She was sure her eyes were red, and people were staring at her, so looked mainly at her plate. She couldn't have said what she was eating. It seemed tasteless, but eating it satisfied her sisters, stopped them bullying her.

She didn't sleep very well, didn't expect to. Night was the best time for thinking and she had a lot to think about.

The following morning, Matron came across the dining room to Cassandra. 'Mrs Southerham has vouched for you, Mrs Lawson. I've received word that your money will be returned to you this morning.'

Cassandra closed her eyes in relief before thanking her.

'Please eat more than that, love,' Pandora urged after Matron had moved on to speak to another group.

She looked down at the plate she'd pushed aside, tried to eat, but simply couldn't force any down. 'I'm a bit unwell in the mornings.' That stopped them nagging her, though in truth the nausea had faded to a faint queasiness now, as if her body had accepted what was happening to it.

During the day more people arrived at the Home looking for maids. Matron insisted on meeting everyone who offered employment to check that they were respectable.

Reece was one of the first through the gate and Cassandra almost begged Matron to let her hide from him. Then she stiffened her spine. She'd never thought herself a coward before.

He looked solemn and his eyes had dark circles beneath them, as if he hadn't slept properly. Well, neither had she.

'I'm sorry,' he said simply.

'Oh? What for?'

'Reacting like that, treating you so badly.'

He tried to take hold of her hand but she wouldn't let him.

'It was the shock, you see. I had to go away and think it through. No use offering you false coin. I had to know what I wanted.'

'It doesn't matter. I wish you well, Reece, and since I'm not without money, you don't have to worry about me. I shall be perfectly all right.'

'That's not what I meant. Cassandra, I still want to marry you.'

'No.'

'I've grown used to the idea of the baby. I'll make it mine too. You'll see.'

She looked at him then, feeling desperately sad. He thought he could do it, but she didn't. His reaction yesterday proved it. 'I'd already decided that it would be too much to ask of any man.'

'It isn't. I still love you, want you.'

'Reece, a child created in that way . . . you'd be bound to wonder what its father was like, to treat it differently from . . . your own. And children know, believe me they know how people really feel about them.'

'Cassandra, I—'

She stood up. 'I've never been as certain of anything as I am of this. For the child's sake, I'm not marrying you and no one can make me!' She saw him stretch out a hand towards her, open his mouth to speak, and ran away before she could burst into tears again.

She knew she had made the right decision, but turning him down was the hardest thing she'd ever done in her whole life, and the most painful.

Matron intercepted the visitor as he tried to follow the fleeing woman into the Home. 'I told you yesterday that you're not allowed in there, sir.'

'I need to see her, persuade her . . .'

'Cassandra came to see me this morning and told me she doesn't want to marry you. Apparently you knew each other before she married Mr Lawson, but she's still grieving for her husband. Look, Mr Gregory, it's far too soon for her to think of remarrying. Especially with a child on the way.'

He looked at her, tempted to tell her the truth. But he'd already worked out that it'd hurt both Cassandra and the child to make the facts known. People could be merciless about bastards, so he said only, 'I'm not leaving it at that. She needs me.'

'Wait till she's had the child. She'll be thinking more clearly then, be over the loss of her husband. Believe me, I know what I'm talking about.'

She watched him go, as she watched all of those who stayed at the Home or visited it. That was her job, after all.

A clerk from the Governor's office brought the purse back two hours later. Matron summoned Cassandra and made her count the money in it before she signed the piece of paper to say she'd received it, then checked that she had somewhere safe to keep it.

'I've made a special belt for the coins, to wear under my clothing.'

'Good. Some of the people here are unfortunately the sort who are easily tempted into wrongdoing. I've been told what went on during the voyage.'

Later that day, the Barretts came in, looking for a maid. Mrs Barrett nudged her husband and pointed to Cassandra, but he scowled and shook his head vigorously.

Matron had heard the tale of him accusing their maid of theft and she wouldn't have advised Cassandra to go and work for them again. Anyway, it could only have been a temporary position, with the baby due, so she introduced them to some other young women, none of whom suited.

In the middle of the afternoon, Mrs Southerham came in to repeat her offer of a job for the youngest sister.

Knowing Pandora had already refused it, Matron took the girl into her office and gave her a good talking-to, but Pandora refused to change her mind.

Matron wanted to give her a good shaking. 'But Mrs Southerham is also offering to house your sister. The two of you will never get another chance like this, never.'

Pandora looked at them both unhappily. 'I know. And I'm sorry, really I am, Mrs Southerham, but it's Reece, you see. Cassandra doesn't want to be where he is, and who can blame her?'

Matron waited until the girl was out of earshot and turned to Mrs Southerham. 'If you can be patient for a day or two, I think I can persuade them to change their minds. I doubt they'll get another chance to be together.'

'You really think they'll change their minds?'

'I do.'

'Well, I've plenty of things I need to purchase, so I wouldn't mind staying on in Perth for a bit longer. And my husband wants to see about getting some convicts assigned to us. I'll come back in two days to see how they're feeling. But after that we'll have to leave.'

Matron sighed as she went to deal with another employer, finding for him a rather cheeky but cheerful young woman who was prepared to work in the country. Life there would come as a shock to her, because it wasn't like the country in England, but she'd probably find a husband quite quickly since she was pretty. Even the ugly ones usually found husbands with ten men to every woman in the colony.

By the end of the day, the Blake sisters had turned down several offers to employ them singly, and Matron was extremely angry with the lot of them.

20

The next day another employer presented himself at the Home. Conn Largan was someone Matron didn't know and when he revealed that he was an emancipist, she couldn't help regarding him less than favourably. He was Irish too, from his accent.

He leaned back in the chair, a slight twist to his lips, as if he could read her thoughts. 'My mother's not an emancipist, you know, and it's she who needs the help. She's crippled by arthritis, so we really need two maids, one to care for her and help around the house and the other to deal mainly with household matters.'

'I'm not sure—' she began then realised suddenly that this might be an opportunity for the Blake twins. 'I'd really prefer to meet your mother myself before deciding.'

'That's easy enough if you'd care to walk round to our lodgings, but she'd not be able to walk here, I'm afraid.'

She hesitated. Normally she'd not have put herself to such trouble for an emancipist, but as he said, his mother had committed no crime and if this provided jobs for those two girls, then the other sisters would surely look more favourably on Mrs Southerham's offer. 'Where do you live?'

'I've bought a property in the hills to the south of Perth.' He explained exactly where.

Even better, she thought. They'll not get anything closer to the Southerhams. 'I'll come with you now to meet your mother. You'll understand that I have to be very careful of the young women in my charge.'

'I'd like to meet them first. I too am careful and I won't have my mother served by a slut.'

She stared at him in annoyance then decided what he'd said was fair. 'Wait here.'

She went to the group of young women sitting sewing in the garden. 'Maia and Xanthe, I have a possible employer for you both. Put that sewing down and come with me.' She hesitated. 'There's just one thing: he's an emancipist.' She saw that they didn't understand the implications of this and added, 'That means he was transported here.' She saw the surprise on their faces. 'Probably a political prisoner, since he's Irish. His mother isn't well and needs help. One maid for her, one for the housework.'

'Let me do the talking,' Xanthe hissed to her twin as they followed her across the garden.

The man staring at them was tall, his hair a shade that was neither red nor brown, his expression guarded. He looked as if he'd been through some hard times and there was a scar along one edge of his chin. He nodded as they were introduced and continued to stare. 'You're not really alike,' he said at last, in a voice with only the faintest of Irish lilts.

'Most people think we are,' Xanthe said, surprised by this.

'No, your expressions are very different. I could never mistake one of you for the other.'

She listened carefully as he explained exactly what he needed them for.

'It must be hard for your mother,' Maia said.

'It is.'

'And you'll be within reach of your sisters if they take up Mrs Southerham's offer,' Matron added. 'It's the best chance you'll ever have of being near one another.'

'Oh. That sounds—' Maia began.

Xanthe dug an elbow into her ribs to shut her up. 'How much will you be paying us, Mr Largan, and will we have regular time off and a way to see our other sisters? We're a very close family, you see.'

'I'll pay ten shillings a week each and all found. And yes, you'll have time to visit your family. Far be it from me to come between sisters. Close families aren't common these days.'

She wasn't sure whether he was being sarcastic or whether she'd glimpsed a hint of sadness in his eyes. 'What does that mean?'

'If they're living within reach, I'll lend you horses to go and see them if you can ride, or a gig if you can drive.'

'I'm sure we can learn. No one's ever accused us of being stupid.' She put up her chin defiantly and saw a slight smile dawn on his face. It made him look younger, that smile did, and she couldn't help wondering why he'd been transported.

'I'll just come and meet your mother first, Mr Largan, to make sure everything is all right,' Matron said.

'Can we not come too? After all, if we're to be working

for Mrs Largan, we want to be sure we'll all get on.'
Xanthe heard Matron's breath hiss inwards as if she was
shocked by this, but she didn't care. She wasn't working
for a harridan, no matter what.

'Sure, and why not?' He stood up. 'No time like the
present. She's always better in the mornings.'

Xanthe found herself walking next to him and sneaked
a quick glance. He had a bitter twist to his mouth when
he wasn't speaking, as if life had treated him badly, as if
he'd been sorely hurt.

Mrs Largan was sitting on a chair. 'Please excuse me
if I don't stand up,' she said in a low, musical voice.

She looked young to be so twisted with arthritis. *I'd be
surprised if she's a harsh mistress*, Xanthe thought.

'You've got unusual names,' Mrs Largan said.

Tears filled Maia's eyes. 'Dad loved anything Greek,
was even trying to learn it. He called all four of us after
ancient Greeks.'

'It's hard to lose someone.' From the sadness on her
face, she too had lost someone close recently.

Xanthe looked at her sister for confirmation, though
she didn't really need to because they always knew
instinctively when they were in agreement. She turned
back to Mrs Largan. 'If you think we'd suit and if the
Southerhams live close enough, we'd be happy to take
employment with you.'

'Where exactly do they live?'

'I don't know exactly – south of Perth near the foothills.'

Matron hesitated, glancing at the clock. 'I must get
back. If I give you the address of the Southerhams' hotel,

perhaps the three of you can go and find out their exact location?'

'That sounds like a good idea, does it not, Conn?'

He nodded, his expression softening as he looked at his mother.

They found Mr and Mrs Southerham just setting out from the hotel to do some more shopping and when they introduced Mr Largan and explained what they needed to know, everyone went back inside again.

After some discussion, during which Mr Largan seemed a bit impatient with Mr Southerham, he said, 'I know where it is now. It's about an hour's drive away, close enough to visit from time to time, though not in bad weather, as the roads are only dirt tracks and they sometimes get flooded in winter.'

He turned to the twins. 'Well? Have I found the help my mother and I need?'

Xanthe answered. 'Yes, Mr Largan.'

'Then we'll set off tomorrow morning, if you're agreeable.'

'We still have to check that our sisters will take the job offered by Mrs Southerham. We're not being separated.'

He let out a little growl of annoyance. 'I've never had so much trouble finding help as I've had here in Australia. I'll come round to the Home in an hour's time to get my answer, then.'

'He seems angry about something,' Mrs Southerham said after he'd left. 'Are you sure you'll be all right working for him?'

'It's his mother we'll be working for,' Maia explained. 'And she's lovely.'

'You'll speak to your sisters? Get one of them to come and tell me if I have a maid or not?' Mrs Southerham said with a smile.

'Yes, of course. But I think you will have.'

As they walked back to the Home, Maia said thoughtfully, 'I wonder what Mr Largan did to get himself transported.'

'He doesn't look like a criminal.'

'No. But Mrs Southerham is right. He looks angry – deep down angry.' She threaded her arm in her sister's. 'Isn't it lovely to be out of that place on our own?'

'Yes, but we'd better hurry back and talk to the others.'

When Cassandra heard that the twins had provisionally accepted employment with the Largans because it was reasonably close to where the other two would be, she looked at them in dismay. 'But I told you: we're not going to work for the Southerhams.'

There was silence, then Pandora said, 'We might have to, love, if it's the only way we can be near one another.'

'No! No, I can't do it.' She couldn't bear the way they exchanged glances, was desperate for some time on her own, so walked outside, gesturing with one hand to stop them following. But there was little privacy to be had in the garden, either. Only in bed did she have time to think her own thoughts, and she was sleeping so badly she wasn't even thinking straight there.

She felt powerless, as if fate was still dragging her along in a direction she didn't want to go. She saw Pandora come outside to join her. 'I suppose they've sent you to persuade me to go to Mrs Southerham's!'

'Yes. But I don't need to persuade you. You know it's the only way we can stay together . . . don't you, love?'

'Does no one care how I feel about being near *him*?'

'Yes, of course we do. Though I think you're wrong not to marry him. But . . .'

'But there's no other choice.' Cassandra sighed and suddenly felt too weary to fight any longer. 'Arrange what you like. I'm going to lie down. I'm exhausted.'

She didn't expect to fall asleep but next thing she knew, Maia was waking her for the evening meal. By then it had all been arranged and they were to set off the following morning.

Although she'd slept for hours, she still felt tired and muddy-brained, unable to fight against what fate had done to her.

Reece! She'd be with him every day. How could she cope with that? Why couldn't she just stop loving him? Why was she still hankering after the impossible?

Pandora watched Cassandra as they repacked the few things they'd taken out of their trunks. She saw the bone-deep weariness and ached for her sister. She ached for herself, too. She'd dreamed of Outham last night, dreamed she'd been walking on the moors, been desolate when she woke up and realised where she was.

Would it never end, this homesickness? And how long would she be able to hide from the others that it was eating away at her?

A man with a cart arrived to pick up their trunks at

six o'clock in the morning. The vehicle was already piled with sacks and boxes. They hoisted themselves into the back, sitting on boxes, for lack of anywhere else, and were bumped through the streets to pick up the Southerhams – and Reece.

When the trio came out of the hotel, Reece stared at Cassandra and she at him, then they both looked away without a word.

Pandora felt so sorry for them, for the unhappiness and longing she saw in their eyes. She wasn't at all sure her sister was doing the right thing in rejecting him. Look at the way they pretended to be indifferent to each other, yet stole the occasional glance. Look at the love in their eyes. You couldn't mistake that emotion. She hoped one day she'd love again, as she'd loved Bill, dead two years now, poor fellow.

Her aunt had a lot to answer for and she hoped fate would deal as unkindly with the horrible woman as it had with the four of them.

You were supposed to forgive your enemies, but she would never forgive Aunt Isabel, she knew, not only for hurting her sister so badly, but for driving them away from Lancashire.

In Outham Mr Rainey received a polite note from the lawyer. He read it quickly. 'Featherworth wants to see me, my dear.'

His wife looked up. 'Did he say why? His letter about the inheritance can't have got to Australia yet. It'll be months before we hear from the girls.'

'No. He didn't say why, just that it was urgent. I'll walk round to his rooms now.'

'I'll be at the sewing class when you come back. It's going well now that we've got our people out of the Vicar's clutches, but everyone is longing for the war to end and cotton to start coming here again. I feel so sorry for those poor girls. They sit and sew but their hearts aren't in it. They always used to be so cheerful when we saw them in the street, didn't they?'

He walked into town and was shown into Featherworth's rooms.

'I heard from the place where they're caring for Mrs Blake. She's refusing to eat or drink and is going downhill rapidly. Spends her time talking to her husband. The owners want someone to go and see her, so that no one can accuse them of not treating her well. Will you come with me?'

'Shouldn't the doctor go?'

'He says he's not got time and anyway, he knows the fellow running that place, trusts him absolutely. Still . . . I do feel I should go, just this once.'

'Very well. I'll come with you.'

'I'll hire a carriage. It's a very isolated place. No railway station nearby. Amazing how quickly we've grown used to the convenience of trains, isn't it? Tomorrow all right?'

'I'll have to rearrange a few things, but yes. Let's get it over with. I'm not looking forward to seeing her again, I must admit. And though I'm a Christian, I can't forgive her for what she did.'

About eleven the following morning, they arrived at the big country house bearing a sign on the heavy wrought iron gates saying 'Rest Home for Gentlefolk'. A man came out to open up the huge iron gates and let them through, and shut it at once behind them. As the two horses clopped slowly up the drive, the two visitors stared round.

'The place is well cared for. They can't be short of money. Well, they charge enough, do they not? It's outrageously expensive.'

They were admitted to the house by another burly man, who took them to the office of the owner, who was a doctor.

'Please take a seat. Can I send for some tea?'

'Could we get the visit done with first?' the lawyer asked. 'I must admit I'm not looking forward to seeing Mrs Blake. She was very violent last time.'

'She's not violent now. We give such cases a calming potion every day. It's better for them, and makes them easier for us to deal with.'

He led the way upstairs and turned right. 'We keep the violent cases in this wing, the harmless ones have more freedom.'

A woman who looked as strong as the men they'd seen led them to a room and unlocked the door.

The woman inside looked up. Her hair was a tangled mass of grey hanging down her back, her face had been blank but at the sight of the lawyer, that changed to a look of hatred and she lunged at them.

The nurse and doctor stepped between them and as Mrs Blake began to scream another woman came running.

'Chains!' the doctor called.

She went away and came back with manacles. It took three of them to attach one to Isabel Blake's ankle and then to the iron foot of the bed frame.

She stopped screaming once they'd done that, but the way she glared at them was enough to make both men shiver and without a word they left the room. She hadn't said a word, but her expression had been horrifying, so full of hatred.

Downstairs they accepted refreshments and sat in silence.

'There's nothing we can do to help her,' the doctor said quietly. 'All we can do is keep her calm and clean – and as you can see, sometimes we can't even do that. We do try to do her hair, but she throws such a fit of hysterics if we try to touch it that we merely wash it every week or two. I don't know why she's obsessed by hair. She seems afraid we'll cut it all off. But with your permission, we shall cut it much shorter. It'll be easier to keep her clean.'

'Do whatever you think best. She looked very thin.'

'As I wrote to you, she won't eat.' He hesitated. 'We can force a little food into her, but not enough to maintain life in the long-term. I wanted you to see how she is. I pride myself on offering the most modern and humane treatment available to these poor creatures, but some of them . . . Well, medical science knows of no way to help people like her.'

On the way back, Featherworth said suddenly, 'It'll be a mercy if she dies.'

Gerald Rainey nodded. He felt the sight of Isabel with that madness in her eyes would stay with him for a long time. 'I'll pray for her soul. Let me know if you hear any news.'

As the carriage rolled through the countryside, the

lawyer said suddenly, 'What do you think of Harry Prebble, the fellow managing the shop?'

'I don't know him. He's not a member of my congregation.'

'There's something I don't quite like about him. I can't work out what, because he's always very civil, and he seems to be making a fair enough job of running the shop. Oh, I'm probably just imagining things. Think no more of it.'

But Gerald told his wife and she said the same thing.

'Mr Prebble is always very polite when he serves me, but . . . I agree with Mr Featherworth. I really cannot like him.'

'As long as he runs the shop properly, it's not necessary to like him.'

'Do you think the girls will come back?'

'Surely they will?'

Zachary watched Harry, who had been putting on airs since he'd been asked to manage the shop until the new owners could be found. It was very hard to put up with the other's officious ways.

When a message was delivered by one of the many lads hanging around in the streets these days, Harry read it then beckoned to Zachary. 'The lawyer wants a word with you.'

'Me? What about?'

'I don't know. But he wants to see you immediately, so you'd better put on your jacket and go.'

As if he needed telling that! Zachary hung up his long apron and left. What did Mr Featherworth want with him? Surely they weren't going to dismiss him? They needed extra help in the shop, not less, without Mr Blake. He sighed. He missed the kindly old man. He didn't miss Mrs Blake, though. She'd always been strange, even before she went mad, and had treated that poor maid shockingly. Zachary hated to see anyone bullied.

He was shown straight into the lawyer's office.

'Ah, Carr. Sit down, sit down.'

'Is something wrong, Mr Featherworth?'

'No, no. But I'm wondering if you could help me.' He explained the situation.

Zachary gaped at him. 'You want me to go to Australia?'

'Yes. I know it's a long journey, but I need someone who recognises Mr Blake's nieces and of course, they'll need a man to escort them on the journey back. All your expenses will be paid, of course, and—'

For a moment, Zachary considered it, then sighed and shook his head. 'I'd like to go, I really would, sir, but I'm the sole support of my mother and sister. What would happen to them without my wages?'

The lawyer frowned at him and Zachary held his breath. If a solution could be found – oh, he prayed it would – he'd go like a shot.

'Are they without work because of the Cotton Famine?'

'No, sir. They didn't work in the cotton mills. My mother looked after the house and my sister was too young to work. But my father died suddenly and though my sister's seventeen now, there's no regular work to be had for young women in the town, so I've been supporting them for a few years.'

'Very commendable. I'm sure we can arrange to pay your wages to them. If we do that, will you go? I much prefer to send someone I know and trust.'

'In that case, I'd be very happy to go.'

'Excellent! I know I can trust you.'

Zachary stopped outside the lawyer's rooms, his head spinning. He wanted to run, shout for joy, tell the world, but contented himself with clapping his hands several times. He saw an old woman stop to stare at him and grinned at her. 'I just had some good news.'

She smiled at him and walked on.

He set off, enjoying stretching his long legs. The sun peeped out from behind the clouds and though it was still cold, he felt warm with happiness.

He got back to the shop all too soon. There were no customers, so Harry beckoned him into the back room.

'Well? What did he want?'

Zachary told him and wasn't displeased to see Harry scowl. The two of them didn't get on, never had, but Harry was good at ingratiating himself with people, so had been made senior, even though they were roughly the same age. And of course, Harry was good-looking, which made life easier for him, while Zachary knew his face was too bony to be considered attractive. Well, he couldn't afford to court a young woman, not with his mother and sister to support, so that was of no importance.

'Why did Featherworth choose you? Why did he not ask me?'

'You're managing the shop. Would you want to miss that opportunity?'

Harry shrugged. 'I'd have been happy to help those poor young women.'

I'm sure you would, Zachary thought. You'll be ingratiating yourself with the new owners before they've even crossed the threshold, you will. Aloud he said only, 'He said he needed to send someone who would recognise Mr Blake's nieces.'

'You don't know them all that well.'

'I've seen them many a time. We live near their old house.'

'I still think Featherworth should have found someone else. How am I to manage if no one else knows how to do the work here?'

Zachary didn't let Harry's ill humour affect him. It had been a bleak few years since his father's death, the responsibility for his family sitting heavily on his shoulders. Now, he was to have an adventure, learn something about the world, and still know that his mother and sister were all right.

The thought of travelling to Australia excited him more than anything ever had in his life before.

The Southerhams and their servants set off at four o'clock in the morning, in order to make it to the farm in one day. During the journey Cassandra barely spoke a word. To Pandora's surprise, Mr Southerham maintained a cheerful conversation with his wife, discussing what they'd bought and the prices they'd paid, acting as if the three servants in the cart were not able to hear every word.

Mrs Southerham showed more consideration and brought them into the conversation several times, telling them about the farm and what she and her husband hoped to achieve there. They'd decided to call it Westview, because it looked in that direction. A name should mean something, should it not?

Sometimes they got out and walked, in order to lighten the load for the horses, and they stopped twice to make a quick meal of bread and cold meat. Each time Reece lit a fire and brewed tea with an ease that surprised Pandora. Each time Cassandra avoided even looking at him.

As the journey dragged on and they stopped yet again to rest the horses and stretch their legs, Mrs Southerham glanced at the sky. 'It's later than we'd hoped, so we won't get home till after dark. I did tell you you'd be sleeping in a tent, didn't I? Reece used to sleep there. It's perfectly comfortable.'

When Cassandra said nothing, Pandora turned to him. 'Will we be taking your bedroom, Reece?'

'No. I sleep at the neighbour's house now. He's old and needs help, and I'm leasing some land from him.'

'What sort of land?'

'Oh, just some pastures on which I can run a few sheep later on, when I've cleared the land. There's a shortage of timber here, so I can make a little money from selling the bigger trees I fell. It's in the lease how much I can take each year. Kevin doesn't want to lose the woods completely. Though he calls them "the bush".'

Cassandra still said nothing, but her sister knew she was listening intently.

When at long last they drew up at the farm, Pandora tried to hide her amazement that people like their employers could be living in such a tiny house. And although there seemed to be quite a lot of land, it was mostly uncleared bush and Westview was even more isolated than she'd expected. They hadn't passed another dwelling for a while, and then only the occasional farm, not a single proper village.

The long purplish shadows cast on the other side of the trees by the setting sun made everything seem unreal. She looked back in the direction they'd come to see the sun about to slide beneath the horizon. Even as she watched, it stopped looking like a sphere, seeming to be sucked down by the black horizon below it.

After that it went dark so quickly they had to finish unloading the food supplies by the light of two oil lanterns, which immediately attracted several large moths. Mrs Southerham showed them how to put the fresh food in a square box with mesh sides whose feet stood in cups of water to prevent ants getting into it.

'There's hardly any twilight at this latitude,' Reece explained when Pandora commented on the fast onset of darkness. 'I'll just start a fire to heat the water, then perhaps you could help me move some of the things in the store tent, Mr Southerham to make more sleeping space for Pandora and Cassandra? Those boxes are too heavy for the women.'

He spoke civilly to his employer, he always did, but it was his voice they heard giving directions from inside the tent. And it was he who had taken the lead after they got off the cart. Some words she'd read in a poem, *Who's master, who's man?* came into her mind and she wondered who had written them. Dean Swift, she remembered a moment or two later, pleased that she hadn't forgotten everything from the old life. How she missed books and poetry! How she missed – everything!

She realised her new mistress was speaking and tried to pay attention.

'We'll just have bread and ham tonight, I think,' Mrs Southerham said. 'And some fruit. We'll eat it out here at the table. I'm looking forward to a cup of tea.'

They stared in surprise at the huge tin mugs she was setting out and the enormous tin teapot.

She pulled a wry face. 'They aren't very elegant, but one gets so thirsty here that ordinary cups and teapots are useless.'

They helped her as best they could and were soon enjoying the simple meal.

Reece and Cassandra took seats at opposite ends of the table and addressed not a word to each other. Pandora could have shaken them!

Bed, the sisters found afterwards, was a blanket on canvas laid on the bare earth, with another to cover them and two more blankets stacked nearby.

'I don't have any other pillows,' Mrs Southerham said. 'I'm sorry. We must see if we can get some feathers from somewhere and make pillows. I've given you extra blankets because it gets quite cool here during the night.' She hesitated. 'Will you be all right? I've found you a candle and some safety matches, in case you have to get up in the night, but please take care if you have to make a light. If the bush catches fire, it can destroy everything in its path.'

'Yes, of course.'

When the two sisters were lying side by side in the darkness, looking at the shadows of branches cast by moonlight on the tent wall, Cassandra let out a long sigh.

'Are you tired?' Pandora asked.

'Yes. Very.' Silence then, 'It was worse than I'd expected, being with Reece.'

'You still love him, don't you?'

There was no answer. But Pandora didn't need one. It was clear to everyone how much those two cared for one another.

Reece walked slowly along in the moonlight to Kevin's house. He was tired and soul-sick. Cassandra had barely spoken to him during their journey and yet he'd been aware of her every movement, even when he was driving and had his back to her.

The connection between them was still there, always would be. He'd not felt this deep a love for his wife. But what would it take to change Cassandra's mind about marrying him? There was something so firm and obstinate about the way she held herself, the way she kept her lips pressed tightly together, the way she avoided him.

He saw a lantern shining on the veranda at Kevin's and found the old man sitting outside smoking a pipe and waiting for him.

'Saw the lights in the distance and knew you'd got back.'

'Yes.'

'How did it go in Perth?'

'I had a few shocks and—' His voice faltered and he suddenly found himself sitting on the rough bench, telling

Kevin the whole sorry story, as if the old man was a second father to him. Second father! He'd hardly had a first one, because his own had died when he was still a lad. And if his cheeks were wet when he'd finished, there was no one to see that except a wise old man who accepted everything calmly, even his own failing body.

'Give her time,' Kevin said in the end. 'It's a great healer. The poor lass must have been hurt badly, first by those brutes and then by you. You did wrong to walk away from her, but I don't need to tell you that, lad, do I? She'll be needing peace and quiet to find herself again before she can think about you.'

'Do you think I stand a chance?'

'Who knows? If it's meant to be, it'll happen. Fate has a way of twisting our lives as it wants, not as we'd prefer. I'd like to meet her, though.'

'I'll invite her and her sister to tea on Sunday.'

'No, I'll invite them. You just take the note I write. And give it to the sister, not her.'

They sat in companionable silence for a few minutes then a yawn caught Reece by surprise. 'It's late. I'd better be getting to bed.'

'I wonder if you'll do me a favour tomorrow? I'm asking you now because you'll be long gone when I wake up.'

'Of course.'

'Will you be giving the letter you'll find on the table to Mr Southerham first thing tomorrow morning? I've a small favour to ask of him.'

Reece hesitated.

'I know he'll not want anything to do with an ex-convict, but I don't think he'll refuse a dying man's wish.'

'*Dying?* You've some time left yet, surely?'

'I hope so, but I'm getting steadily weaker. I'm grateful to have your company at this time, lad. I didn't want to die on my own.'

Reece reached out to clasp his hand for a moment.

'You need to get yourself to bed. You've a hard day's work before you, I'm sure. That employer of yours is a fool. 'Tis you who're running things, from what you say.'

'Don't tell *him* that! If he takes charge nothing will get done properly.'

Kevin chuckled and Reece was still smiling as he sought his bed. Poor Francis. A nice fellow, but such a dreamer. He'd never make a success of the farm on his own, and Reece didn't intend to give up his own life to support the Southerhams. He was fretting already to finish his time as their servant.

21

The following morning Francis read the letter Reece had brought him from Kevin with some surprise, then showed it to his wife.

'We can't refuse a dying man's wish,' Livia said. 'Let's walk across there now, before it gets hot. It's ages since I've really stretched my legs. We can't see the house from here, but there's a path marked already where Reece walks to and fro. I'll just tell Cassandra where we're going.'

They're good workers, those girls, he thought, watching her speak to their new maids, who were conducting a washday under difficult circumstances. Every bucket of water had to be carried from the well. The tin washtub sat on an outdoor bench Reece had made and the two young women were rubbing away vigorously, chatting quietly as they worked.

Francis turned to study Reece, who was also watching the maids, or rather, watching Cassandra. He'd strung a line for the finished clothes and was now whittling rough pegs from narrow branches, using the dry, fallen wood. We didn't even remember such mundane articles when we packed for our great adventure, Francis thought with a wry smile at his own inadequacies.

'Leave the other tent till we get back,' he called to his servant. 'It'll be easier to erect with two of us.'

A nod was his only answer.

Together Francis and his wife followed the faint path across the gentle slope on which both properties stood. They stopped from time to time to look at something, a lizard sunning itself on a rock, some pink and grey galahs screeching in the trees, a line of ants busily carrying debris away.

He kicked a piece of dead wood as if it was a ball and splinters flew everywhere. 'It's very different here, isn't it? Not what I expected. It's not a fit way of life for a lady. I've been a poor husband to you.'

'We're here now. And we agreed before we left: no regrets. You're bound to get better in a warmer climate.'

'I hope so.'

Her voice faltered for a moment. 'And whatever happens, we shall make the best of it. It's an adventure, after all.'

Her voice was calm, but he heard how bitter his own voice was. Well, he felt bitter. 'Don't pretend. I tried to be practical about this, I really did. But I'm put to shame by my own manservant, who always knows a better way of doing something. Only he's planning for the time he can set up his own farm. What will you and I do then?'

'We'll find another servant.'

'We didn't even take the two convicts we were assigned because we didn't like the looks of them. We're not very practical. My love, you should have found yourself a better husband.'

'I've never wanted anyone but you, Francis.'

She put her arms round him and they stood for a minute or two, close together, taking comfort from one another.

He was right about their situation, she thought. Francis was a dreamer. Neither of them had expected things to be this difficult, though. Farms to her meant green fields dotted with sheep or cows, rows of green plants, not a landscape like this, coloured by the beiges, browns and faded greens of an Australian summer. She took hold of his hand. 'Well, let's start moving again.'

Their neighbour was waiting on the veranda. He stood up and thanked them for coming, offering them seats, waiting till Livia had sat down before taking his own place, easing himself down into his chair like a man whose joints were painful.

Then he explained what he wanted.

As they walked back, Francis said thoughtfully, 'Lynch was clearly a gentleman once.'

'He's a gentleman still, from his behaviour and speech.'

'He's an emancipist!' His tone was scornful.

She hated to hear people scorn one another. 'Are we to spurn half the population of this colony because of their past?'

'We needn't spurn them, exactly, but I don't care to have my wife meeting such people socially.'

This attitude irritated her, but she knew she'd never change him. His family were of quite a high social status, compared to hers and he'd been bred with an innate sense of his own superiority to common persons.

She could have been friends with Cassandra, whom Francis considered merely *a maidservant*. Yet that young woman had a fine brain and was more interesting to chat to than any of the *ladies* Livia had known back home. She'd hoped to find a freer society here, and it was in some ways, but men like her husband had brought their prejudices with them and were trying to recreate the same sort of society as the one they'd left. And ladies seemed as circumscribed in what they could do as ever. That never failed to irritate her.

She wondered if they'd succeed with the farm. Seeing Reece, so capable and clever, comparing him to Francis, who flitted from one job to another without finishing any of them properly, she didn't think they would, even if her husband's health improved. Well, his family wouldn't let them starve if the worst came to the worst.

They walked in silence for a few moments, stopping by mutual agreement when their own house came in sight again.

She'd been nerving herself to say something and what better time? 'We'll need to add another room or two before winter sets in, my love, or those boxes on the veranda will get wet. I know we agreed not to spend money unnecessarily, but . . .'

'We do need more space. I'll turn my mind to it. I think the horses will do well enough in the bark shelter during the colder months. They don't get frosts here, apparently. I'll have to bring someone down from Perth to build extra rooms, I suppose.'

'Did you notice that Mr Lynch's house had rooms added on? Maybe Reece can find out from him how it was done. There may be someone nearby whom we can employ more cheaply.'

'I suppose so.' Francis waved away a fly. 'Strange business, that. Must be awful to grow old alone, to have no family left – or at least none who will associate with you. Lynch looked very frail, didn't he?'

'Yes. I felt sorry for him. Couldn't we invite him to tea sometime? He must get very lonely. It's Christmas in four days. We must mark that.'

'Livia, we can't take on every lame dog we find. And he *is* an ex-convict, may I remind you. He's paying the price for committing a *crime*.'

She sighed.

'I'd take you up to Perth for the occasional trip, but we need to conserve what money we have, what with the building work. We already have one more mouth to feed than we'd planned, and when we do get our convicts – there must be some who do not look so villainous – there will be more still to feed.'

'I couldn't have left Cassandra on her own in a strange country. I just couldn't.'

'I know, and as long as those two can manage in the tent during the winter, it'll be all right. The woman's a worker and more than earns her daily bread, I'll give her that. We can't afford to build them a proper house, though, not this year. Perhaps Reece can make a bark shelter over the tent, something similar to what the horses have.'

She didn't argue. At least he'd agreed to extend their shack. She'd ask Reece's advice about the maids' quarters when Francis wasn't there. She didn't want them suffering from cold or a dripping tent during the winter.

★

As the sisters continued with the washing, Cassandra said quietly, 'You're still homesick, aren't you, Pandora?'

'How did you know? I've never said anything.'

'I know you better than most. You *are* homesick, aren't you?'

'A little. It'll pass. What choice do I have but to stay here?'

'You could go back to another part of England.'

'On my own? Are *you* prepared to go back with me?'

'I don't know yet. I really like the warm weather here and the space. I didn't think I would, but just look at it.' She made a sweeping gesture towards the bush behind the house. 'I like the unfamiliar trees and plants, the grey-green of the gum leaves, the fallen branches and leaves. It's beautiful.'

'Do you really think so? I don't. It gives me the shivers. No neighbours for miles, except an old man. And people talk about bush fires. What would we do if one came through here?'

Cassandra patted her arm with one wet hand and waited. If you gave her time, didn't question too hard, Pandora usually told you her thoughts.

'It's Lancashire I miss, not England. It's – home. But even if we wanted to go back, how could we afford the fares back for four of us?' She bit back further words and tried to speak calmly. 'There's no use dwelling on it, love. I'm sure I'll settle down now we've somewhere to live and work.'

'We'll be living in a tent. That will never feel like a home.' Cassandra looked towards the house. 'And their house isn't much better, is it? I'm amazed to see people of their class living in such a – a shed. Here, catch hold.'

They each took an end of a sheet and twisted it till they'd got as much of the water out as they could, then slung it over one of the ropes, using the new pegs to hold it in place.

Reece stood up. 'Would you like a cup of tea?'

'I'd love one.' Cassandra was annoyed with herself for answering so warmly. She'd vowed to speak coolly to him and had broken that vow within a couple of hours.

'Give me ten minutes.'

She turned back to the tub of rinsing water and dunked another sheet in it, not caring that she splashed her pinafore and skirt, since they dried almost instantly in hot weather like this. 'I don't see how we can starch anything.'

'I don't think we should even try. Anyway, Mrs Southerham didn't buy any starch. She forgot quite a few things.'

'She doesn't understand what's needed.'

'It'll have to be enough that the clothes and linen are clean.' Pandora giggled. 'There are rather a lot of underclothes to wash, aren't there? They can't have done any laundry for ages.'

'They're used to having servants to do that. And they have so many clothes that it wasn't urgent.'

Reece hung the kettle over the fire and came across to join them. 'Next time you've got some hot water, can I bring my own clothes across and give them a bit of a wash in the water that's left?'

She couldn't ignore that question. 'Why don't you put

them out with the other things? We're washing our own clothes as well as theirs, so we might as well wash yours. Your job at the moment is to make us a lot of pegs.'

His smile was so warm, she felt herself flushing and bent over the tub again. When she looked up, he was back at the cooking fire, which was set between neatly arranged stones. She watched him check the damper he'd mixed that morning and move the camp oven away from the hot embers. Taking the boiling kettle off its metal hook, he poured hot water into the big teapot, his movements so neat and precise, he was a pleasure to watch. He refilled the kettle and set it over the flames again.

Sighing, she pulled the final sheet out of the water and with Pandora's help got that rinsed. They put the next pile of dirty clothes to soak and went to join Reece at the table.

'We'll need some more hot water soon,' Pandora said.

'I've put some on to boil. I'll draw a fresh bucket of water after we've had our tea. We need more buckets and washing equipment.'

'Are we allowed to stop work like this?' Cassandra asked. 'At the mill there were always set hours of work.'

He smiled at her. 'We all work hard. They can't grudge us a cup of tea, and we know better than anyone when we need a rest. Anyway, it's so hard to find maids, they'll know to treat you both well. I think it's shameful not paying you any wages, Cassandra.'

Which showed, she thought, that he'd not missed anything. She shrugged. 'I'm just glad to have somewhere to stay until – afterwards.'

He was stirring his tea, round and round, avoiding her eyes as he asked, 'When exactly is the baby due?'

'May.'

'There isn't a doctor near here. They're very short of doctors in this colony. But if we can get to know the people who have farms nearby, maybe we'll find a woman who can help you with the birth.'

She stared at him in shock. He was talking as if he was involved in the situation.

'I'll ask around for you,' he said softly. 'I see more people than they do. There's a shop an hour's drive away that Kevin told me about. I did the shopping for them there once and found the owners very helpful. From the looks of it, I'll have to go there again soon. Mrs Southerham is more practical than her husband, but not a lot. The things she bought in Perth were mostly for herself, not household necessities.'

'Thank you.' Cassandra drained her cup quickly and got back to work. It was too easy to get intimate with Reece, far too easy. They'd always been able to chat to one another comfortably, right from their very first meeting.

And if Pandora said one word about the situation, hinted at anything . . . she'd . . . she didn't know what she'd do. But to her relief, her sister said nothing.

When their employers came back, Mrs Southerham praised what they'd done, then sighed. 'I'm not a very good cook, but I'm even worse at washing, so I'll make the meals today. We need another batch of damper and that I can manage, thanks to Reece's teaching. Francis kills a kangaroo whenever we need fresh meat.' She smiled across at the man sitting by the table, whittling. 'I think you're going to have to make a lot of pegs, Reece. There's so much washing.'

Cassandra watched Mr Southerham sit down at the table and take out his pocket knife.

'Perhaps I can help you with the pegs?'

But he proved useless at whittling and soon got tired of trying, so went off to kill another kangaroo.

The only things Mr Southerham seemed able to do, Cassandra thought, were care for the horses and shoot. She saw Reece watching his employer with a resigned expression on his face, then he turned, caught her watching him and winked.

She bent over the washing again, but soon her back began to ache. How was she going to manage such heavy work in the final month or two? The bump wasn't very big yet but the child had quickened, become a real person in her mind. She kept wondering whether it was a girl or a boy, what it would look like, if it would be clever – if it would be cruel like its father.

She stood up to stretch her back, pressing one hand to where it was aching from bending over the washtub. She was conscious of Reece watching her, conscious of him every single minute they were together. She'd known this would happen if they lived at such close quarters.

But when the child made her look ugly and clumsy, he'd feel differently, she was sure. He'd not be able to bear the sight of her then.

Xanthe and Maia took it in turns to ride next to Conn on the cart. He'd had to bring his mother with him to

Perth because there was no one to care for her back at his homestead. It must have been hard for a man to do the things Mrs Largan needed help with.

After an hour, he scowled at Xanthe and said, 'You two had better call me Conn. I'm not fond of being called Mr Largan.'

'We can't do that if you're our employer,' she protested.

'You can if I tell you to.'

'Why don't you like being called "Mr Largan"?'

'It sounds like my father and brother, and I'm not fond of either of them.'

Xanthe turned to exchange surprised glances with her sister at this strange comment and saw Mrs Largan looking at her son sadly, as if she understood exactly why he was saying that.

What had happened to break up the family? What had he done to get himself transported? Were his father and brother dead? They must be or his mother wouldn't be here in Australia with him.

They drove along gently, and she could see how Conn tried to choose the smoothest part of the track and kept to a slow pace so as not to give his mother pain. He was also thoughtful for the horses' comfort, not pushing them too hard, letting them rest.

When they stopped, she and Maia helped his mother. They also slept on the floor in her room at the rough and ready inn where they spent the night.

Xanthe was itching to discuss the situation with her twin, but they were never alone, not because they were under strict supervision, but because Mrs Largan needed their help in everything she did, poor woman.

'The journey to Perth exhausted her,' Conn said abruptly as he and Xanthe got the cart ready for his mother, spreading out the quilts on which she sat or sometimes lay down.

'Travelling isn't easy here, is it? It seems so strange and old-fashioned not to have railways.'

'The whole place seems strange to me,' he said, talking to himself as much as her. 'And yet there's something about it. Look how clear and sparkling the air is.' He gestured with one hand. 'Back home in Ireland, it'd be raining or misty.'

'It would in Lancashire, too. I like the sun.'

When he'd carried his mother out to the cart, Maia said, 'I think it'd be better if I travelled in the back. I'm better at looking after people than my sister is.'

He cocked one eyebrow at Xanthe. 'So you'll be the housemaid?'

She shrugged. 'Yes. I'll do my best. I know how to keep a small house clean, but I've never served the gentry before.'

'I wouldn't call myself *gentry* now.'

He sounded so bitter, she didn't even try to reply.

They drove along without speaking for about half an hour, then, as if he could stand the silence no longer, he asked abruptly, 'Why did you come here?'

She debated briefly then decided on the truth. She hated lying to people. 'Our aunt forced us to.'

'You don't seem like the sort of girls to be easily forced into things. You've both got an independent air to you.'

She smiled. 'Lancashire manners, someone said to me on the ship – only she didn't mean it as a compliment.'

'So how did your aunt force you?'

'She had our eldest sister kidnapped and threatened to harm her if we didn't leave.' When he said nothing, she added, 'It sounds strange, but that's the simple truth.'

'I've learned that relatives can be far more cruel than strangers,' he said abruptly. 'And anyway, I believe you. You've got a very expressive face. It'd betray you if you tried to tell lies.'

'Dad used to say that. Oh, I do miss him! He died just before we left. Is your father dead?'

'No.'

He looked so grim she didn't ask the next obvious question, which was why his mother was here if her husband was still alive.

In the late afternoon of the second day's travel, they turned off the main highway a short distance past a wooden shack which he said was a shop. They were now on little more than a track. Here, Conn slowed right down, but even so the jolting was painful for his mother and her face was chalky white.

The house was only a mile or so along this road. A big wooden sign said *Galway House*. She was surprised at how large the place was.

An elderly man came limping out to greet them and stroke the horses' heads, murmuring to the animals in Gaelic.

'These are Maia and Xanthe, who are going to look after my mother and the house,' Conn said. 'This is Sean, who looks after the stock. He does speak English, though he prefers not to.' He picked up his mother, carrying her as if she weighed nothing. As they exchanged fond glances, he said softly, 'Home to stay this time.'

She patted his cheek, just once, and the sight of their love brought tears to Xanthe's eyes.

'Someone open that door, please.'

Xanthe hurried ahead to do this while Maia gathered up Mrs Largan's quilts.

'Last door on the left. Turn down the bed,' he ordered as he entered the house.

Not taking time to look round, Xanthe ran ahead and found herself in a comfortable bedroom which looked out on to a veranda at the rear. She turned down the covers, finding a soft feather mattress below them.

As he laid his mother on the bed, she sighed in relief and lay back on the pillows.

'I think if I had to make that journey again, Conn darlin', it'd kill me.'

'I won't ask you to, Mother.' He looked at the two newcomers. 'Not unless our new helpers let us down.'

She smiled at the two maids. 'I'm sure they won't. I'm a lot better when I can lead a more peaceful life, so I won't always be as troublesome as this, girls. Welcome to Galway House. I hope you'll be happy here. Now, if you'll leave us in peace, Conn, I'll get these young women to help me undress.'

When Mrs Largan was in bed, with Maia still fussing over her, Xanthe went to look for the kitchen.

She found Conn there, heating water on a proper stove, which had a hot water tank to the right of the fire, an oven to the left of it and a hob above. 'I can take over now, if you like.'

He turned round and nodded. 'Just hunt through the cupboards for what you need. We still have some of the bread we bought in Perth, though it's stale. There's no milk today, but I'll arrange to buy some from our neighbours from tomorrow onwards.'

'You have neighbours? I thought yours was the only house on this lane.'

'They're about four hundred yards away in that direction.' He pointed. 'We buy milk and eggs from them until we can set up our own stock properly.'

'What about a meal for tonight? What should I make?'

'There's a ham hanging in the cellar. It's down there, and it's a lot cooler than up here.' He pointed to a door. 'The candles are on the shelf at the top of the cellar steps.'

Then he was gone and she was left in charge of a strange kitchen. Xanthe stood for a moment, looking round. This one room was as large as their whole house had been in Outham and seemed to be used as kitchen, dining room and sitting room, as if it was the living heart of the house. It needed a good clean, but she and Maia could do that.

For the first time since they'd landed in Australia she felt a sense of home.

Wasn't that strange? Perhaps it was because Mrs Largan was such a kind, friendly woman. Or because it was such a lovely house.

Humming, she went to find the ham and cut them some slices, using the fat to fry the stale bread, guessing she'd be feeding Sean as well and that he'd eat as heartily as his master.

*

Conn watched her from just beyond the doorway, noting that she didn't slack off when she thought no one was watching, enjoying the sound of her humming.

Xanthe had set a tray for his mother already, found a little lace-edged cloth to lay on it, and one of the pretty plates. His mother would appreciate that.

The smell of the frying bread made his stomach rumble so he went in to join her. 'That smells wonderful.'

Xanthe gasped and turned round, one hand to her breast.

'Sorry to give you a shock. That smells so good.'

'Are you hungry?'

She didn't say 'sir', didn't seem aware that she ought to, but what did that matter? She was doing what he'd brought her here for, looking after the house and his mother. Perhaps now he could start making plans for this strange property he'd bought, which had been built by a man with more money than sense, a man who'd built a huge rambling house before he'd cleared the bush and made fields for his stock. The fellow had moved to New South Wales now, but Conn doubted he'd do any better there. Some men seemed born to fail.

At least the property had come cheaply, because no one wanted to buy a place out here – no one but an emancipist who preferred his own company to the scorn of others, and intended to use what money he had to advantage.

Unlike the previous owner, he was grimly determined to succeed. He'd made careful plans, practical ones too, things a man could manage step by step. The first stage had been interrupted when his mother suddenly arrived to join him in Australia, having left home and family in outrage at what they'd done to him.

Now that he had the maids, he could go ahead with his plans. He wondered if the two sisters knew how desperately he needed them. He'd have to make sure they were happy here.

He smiled at the sight of a plate of simple but appetising food as he sat down at the kitchen table with Xanthe. It hadn't occurred to her to set the table in the dining room for her master, and he didn't intend to tell her. It would be easier if they all lived in this large room.

'Maia's helping your mother with her meal,' she said cheerfully as she picked up her knife and fork. 'I hope your food is all right.'

He cut a piece of ham and lifted it to his mouth. Strange how much more appetising it was when fried – and when you had company to eat it with.

He was tired but felt more hopeful than he had for a long time.

And his mother, his wonderful mother, had the care she deserved.

'He still loves you, you know,' Pandora said quietly as the two sisters finished washing the dishes from the evening meal, performing this duty at the outdoor table in a tin bowl.

Cassandra couldn't think what to say, was weary of protesting that she didn't want anything to do with Reece.

'You should give him a chance.'

'I have the baby to think of.'

'And will you make two people unhappy because of a baby, which need never even know how it was fathered?'

'Why are you going on about this?'

'Because Reece asked me to talk to you, plead with you to listen to him. And I was happy to do that. Oh, Cassandra love, do talk to him. You decided *for* him, not *with* him. Dad always said people ought to make their own decisions. He let us do that as much as he could, even when we were quite small. Can't you allow Reece the same privilege?'

'No. I just – can't. Daren't. For the baby's sake.'

Pandora opened her mouth as if to protest, then closed it again.

'I'm sure Reece would be kind to your child.'

'There are no guarantees.'

'You're not even giving Reece a chance!'

'I might have done if he hadn't reacted as he did when I told him. Now I daren't . . . I just daren't.'

The following evening, Cassandra walked across to throw the last of the day's rubbish into the pit. As she reached out for the shovel to scatter earth over the debris, someone caught hold of her arm. She looked round to see Reece by her side.

'Give me a chance,' he said quietly. 'At least listen to me.'

Her throat filled with anguish but she was afraid to do as he asked. As she swung round to walk back to the cooking area, he caught hold of her arm again and this time he wouldn't let go.

'I won't ever force you to do anything again, but you're being unfair, so I'm going to insist you listen to me properly.'

She tried to pull away, but his grip tightened and he was stronger than her after his months of hard physical work. She looked round, intending to call for help. The Southerhams were standing on their tiny veranda, staring across at them.

'Let's go for a walk. It's the only way we'll get any privacy.'

When Reece started dragging her away, she fought him, saw Mr Southerham take a step towards them as if he intended to stop this. But Pandora hurried across and began talking earnestly to them, then Mrs Southerham grabbed her husband's arm to stop him.

Mr Southerham threw up his hands, shook his head

as if not approving of what was happening, then went inside the house, followed by his wife.

Pandora moved back to the table and made flapping signs with one hand as if to urge Cassandra to go with Reece.

She gave up struggling but when he tried to pull her arm through his, she shook him off. 'I'll listen, but you won't persuade me.'

'This way.'

Without a word, she followed him along the little path he took every night.

He stopped by a huge fallen tree. 'Could we sit down?'

She hesitated but she was tired after another long day's work so she sat on the trunk, putting her arms round her knees, not looking at him. His voice was so close to her it seemed to wrap itself round her.

'We've had no real chance to talk since I behaved so unkindly to you at the Home in Perth.'

'Your reaction was no more than I'd expected.'

'My reaction was shock more than anything. I couldn't believe such a thing could have happened in Outham. Or to you.'

She continued to stare down the slope at a dark landscape crowned by a huge expanse of star-filled sky. Even such a short distance from the house, it felt as if they were the only people alive in the whole world. And that sense of space and peace soothed something inside her, gave her a feeling of freedom.

'I walked by the river that day in Perth,' he said, 'and it took me a while to understand and come to terms with it all. I was so furious at those men, at what they'd done to you, but I wasn't angry with you, never with you.'

'It still drove you away from me.'

'I needed to think and what I realised eventually when my anger subsided was . . . Don't you see, Cassandra? I've been given a second chance with this child of yours.'

'I don't understand.'

'I lost my wife and child. The baby was very small, white and limp but perfectly formed. He never breathed, poor little thing. They tried to hide his body from me, to carry it out like rubbish, but I insisted on seeing my son. And then –' his voice thickened with tears, '– Nan died a few hours afterwards, just . . . bled to death. They couldn't save her. So I lost them both. It wasn't till I met you that I started to feel happy again, as if my world had fallen into balance once more. And I stupidly left you. That damned Cotton Famine. It drove so many people away from Lancashire, parted families and lovers.'

He held up one hand. 'No, wait! Let me finish. It wasn't Lancashire I missed, not even Outham, but *you*.' He raised Cassandra's hand to his lips and kissed it very gently. 'Now I've been given the chance to love another child, one who needs a father more desperately than most. But that child doesn't need me half as much as I need you.'

She drew in a breath that was almost a sob and felt tears form in her eyes.

'You think I'll hate the baby, or at least resent it. But I won't. I promise you I won't. Because whoever the father is, *you* are the mother. And because I've never stopped regretting that my son died. Strangely enough, if it was a boy, I was going to call him Edwin. If yours is a boy, I'd like him to have the same name, for your father and for my dead son.'

One tear ran down her cheek but she didn't try to brush it away. There was no doubting Reece's sincerity. Could she, dare she believe him?

'Almost as soon as our ship left England, I knew I was the greatest fool on earth to have left you.' He reached into his pocket and pulled out an envelope. 'This is the letter I wrote to you, asking you to come out and join me here.' He pressed it into her hands. 'Read it. You'll see how much I need you.'

She looked down at the letter, surprised at how thick it was.

'I won't give up until I've persuaded you to marry me, so there's another thing you need to consider: where you want to live. I like it here, think I can make a good life for myself and my family. But if *you* want to go back to England, then I'll go with you. I'll do anything to make you happy – *anything!* – because having you as my wife is as necessary to me as breathing.'

Now the tears were flowing. 'Oh, Reece.' She looked down at the packet then sideways at him, seeing tears on his cheeks too, seeing the loving expression in his eyes, the anxious way he was watching her. Suddenly the doubts fell away. 'I don't need to read this. I never heard a more eloquent speech, no, nor read one either.'

His voice was rough. 'What does that mean?'

'It means I believe you and . . . that I'll marry you.'

With an inarticulate cry, he drew her to him and showered her face with kisses. She laughed through her tears as she kissed him back.

When he pulled her to her feet to embrace her properly, the envelope dropped to the ground unheeded.

It felt good to hold and be held, so good she didn't try to break the embrace, because his touch seemed to cleanse her, make her feel whole again.

Nor did he move for a while. Then he pulled back, breathing deeply. 'I promise you I'll make a good life for us. But we'll wait till we're married to love one another properly. I want more from you than your body; I want you as wife, friend, mother of my children, starting with this one.' He laid a hand gently on her belly.

'*We* will work together to make a good life,' she corrected. 'And I want all those things, too. I like it here already, only—'

'Only what? Tell me? There must be no more secrets, no more barriers between us.'

'It's Pandora. She's dreadfully homesick. You must have seen how unhappy she looks sometimes, how thin she's grown again. I'm really worried about her.'

'I'd guessed there was something wrong. I've seen her look sad and brush away a tear when she thinks no one's near. We'll find a way to help her settle – or we'll send her back.' He bent down to pick up the envelope, dusting off the sandy grit and pressing it into her hands. 'Read this anyway.'

She clasped it tightly, let him take her hand and they walked back to tell the others their news.

Mr Southerham was the only one who didn't seem pleased by it. But then he didn't seem pleased by anything these days. Something seemed to be worrying him.

Well, Cassandra wasn't going to let him spoil her happiness.

She waited until Reece had left for his friend's house and the others had gone to bed to read the letter, sitting at the table with an oil lamp in front of her in a world filled with stars and soft warm breezes. It took her a long time to read it, because she kept stopping to smile fondly at a page or to reread a paragraph.

None of the stories of love that she'd read, not a single one of them, matched her own now that she'd read the words Reece's heart had dictated. She was quite sure of that. She had found her soul-mate as well as her husband.

'It's Christmas in two days,' Livia said the next morning. 'We must do something to celebrate.'

'I could bake a cake,' Pandora offered. 'You have some raisins, flour and sugar, I know. I like cooking.' She smiled at her sister. 'And I think I'm better at it than Cassandra is. But without butter, it'll be a poor excuse for a cake.'

Francis's expression brightened. 'A cake of any sort would be a big treat. I really miss sweet things here.'

'And we could sing hymns and Christmas carols in the evening,' Reece said.

'Good idea.' Livia shot a glance at her husband. 'I think we should invite Mr Lynch to join us.'

Francis glared at her, but she continued to stare at him defiantly. When he didn't speak, she added, 'I don't like to think of anyone being alone at such a time.'

He stuffed his hands into his pockets. 'Oh, do what you want!'

Reece waited a moment or two, but when neither of

them added anything else, he said, 'If you're sure, I'll ask him tonight.'

'I'm very sure,' Livia insisted. 'Pandora and I will look through our stores and see what treats we can devise.'

Two days later, Reece drove Kevin the long way round to join the celebrations.

'I'm still surprised they invited me,' he said as the ugly mare clopped up the gentle slope to the farm.

'Mrs Southerham invited you. Mr Southerham usually does as she tells him.'

Kevin grinned. 'Well, I'm glad to have some company, I am indeed, not to mention a good meal. And if you and your young lady will speak to me from time to time, I'll be satisfied to sit quietly and try not to upset my host too much.'

When Reece helped him down, Kevin took the bottle of port wine he'd brought as a gift and presented it to his host with a small bow.

'Thank you,' Francis said stiffly.

'Just what we needed to crown our celebrations,' Livia said.

It was the strangest Christmas he'd ever had, Reece thought. A hot day, still too warm for coats or wraps even after the sun had gone down. They ate outside at the table, spread for the occasion with a white cloth. There were no church bells pealing, only the rustling of trees and the occasional call of a boobook owl, which sounded more like a cuckoo than an owl.

Reece joined in the hymn singing, his eyes meeting Cassandra's and their voices blending well together.

'It gladdens my heart to see those two,' Kevin murmured to Livia as the song finished. 'He's a good man, Reece is.'

'Yes. They're well matched, I think.'

As the two men drove back through a moonlit landscape, Kevin said quietly, 'I like your young lady.'

'So do I! I just hope I can make a good life for us here.'

'If hard work will do it, you'll succeed.'

'Sometimes fate won't let you succeed.'

'No.' Kevin fell silent, staring ahead, clearly lost in his own thoughts, and Reece could have kicked himself for making that remark.

'It's all right, lad.' Kevin patted Reece's hand. 'It's not what you said that's upsetting me. Christmas always brings back memories. It was the last meal I shared with my family, you see. I only saw them once afterwards, and that across a courtroom.'

Two weeks later Mrs Southerham produced a long list and handed it to Reece. 'We ladies have put our heads together and we need a lot of things if we're to live comfortably. I want you to go and see how much of this you can buy in the little shop on the highway.' She gave him a conspiratorial smile. 'And you'd better take Cassandra with you. There are some items better chosen by a woman. Oh, and you could ask them where you can get married. You may have to go all the way to Perth for that.'

'Thank you, Mrs Southerham,' Cassandra whispered to her as she got ready to leave.

'I'd like to help you two. I married the man I loved and for all his faults, I'm happy to be with him. While you're away, find out how near you are to your sisters so that you can go and tell them your good news the following week.'

'You're so kind, so very kind!'

'I like to see people happy.'

The 'shop' was another small wooden house, with the front room full of sacks and basic household necessities. Stock feed, farm materials and a few tools and nails were in a shed nearby, so Reece went out to see what he could find while Cassandra dealt with the other items on the list.

'Your husband looks happy today,' the woman who was serving her said, clearly wanting to gossip.

'We're not married yet, but we will be as soon as we can find someone to marry us. I was going to ask you how people round here get married.'

'There's a visiting clergyman who comes the first Sunday of each month. He holds a service in our barn. Most people attend, whatever their religion was back home. It's the same God we worship, after all. He'll marry you – and you won't have to wait for banns to be called, because he can only come once a month.'

'That's wonderful news! I'll tell Reece. We'll come in February. Um – do you know a place called Galway House? Is it close to here?'

'Ten minutes away by cart. He's a strange one, that Mr Largan, never smiles though he's civil enough, you have to give him that. Do you know him?'

'My sisters are working there as maids. I'm hoping to go and visit them.'

'Ah, I've met one of them. He brought her here shopping. She had a strange sort of name. Began with a Z, I think.'

Tears filled her eyes. 'Xanthe.'

Reece came in just then and the women stopped chatting as the final purchases were sorted out and payment made. Quite a few things had to be specially ordered from Perth, which would disappoint Mrs Southerham, and they had to pay half their cost now to make sure the shopkeeper wouldn't be left with them and lose money.

'Ready to leave?' Reece asked. 'I'll just load this on the cart.'

Outside he said, 'We'll go and visit your sisters now, if you like. I have the directions. It's not far. We can only stay for an hour or so, though.'

She flung her arms round him and hugged him, regardless of who saw them. 'I was going to ask you. Oh, I feel so much better to know they're within reach.'

When they were on their way, he said, 'We can get married—'

'On the first Sunday in February,' she finished for him with a smile.

'We can live at Kevin's afterwards. I've asked him. You can still work for the Southerhams for a while, but only if they pay you.'

'I don't think they can afford it.'

'Then I'll suggest they take it off the months of service I still owe them.' He beamed at her. 'In fact, I'd prefer that. There are so many things I want to do for myself. Oh, and Kevin wants you and Pandora to come to tea on Sunday. I hope you don't mind living with an ex-convict. I'm building us a new bedroom on the side of his house. He was transported to New South Wales for political reasons, but was given an absolute pardon once they'd got him out of Ireland.' He hesitated. 'I know respectable people don't associate with convicts, but I like him.'

'I do, too. And *I* don't look down my nose at people, as Mr Southerham does.'

Galway House was a huge place, though its roof looked slightly lopsided, some of the veranda posts were leaning a little, and many of the windows needed cleaning.

As the cart stopped in front of it and Reece helped Cassandra down, Conn Largan came round from the side of the house, but before he could say anything, there was a shriek and Xanthe flew out of the front door, flinging her arms round her sister.

It was the most joyous of reunions, and the twins were delighted that Cassandra was to marry Reece. When Conn was asked, he agreed to bring the two maids to the wedding, and his mother, if she was well enough. She'd certainly seemed better since Maia had started looking after her.

Surely an hour had never passed so quickly, Cassandra thought as Reece pulled out his watch and said they must leave. It seemed as if they'd only been there for a few minutes and she found it hard to tear herself away.

★

On the following Sunday Pandora walked across with the engaged couple to take tea with Kevin. She breathed a deep sigh once they were out of sight of the Southerhams. 'I'm so glad to be away from there! I don't think I was cut out to be a maid. The way Mr Southerham tosses orders at me makes me want to say something very sharp to him about manners.'

'Or remind him that we're not stupid,' Cassandra added.

'Anything but,' Reece said with a smile. 'He even treats his wife as if she's not very clever sometimes. I can't understand why she doesn't pull him up on that. He didn't seem as bad in England.'

'She loves him dearly and I think he needs to feel superior to someone, because he's not a very capable person, is he?'

Pandora walked along the top of the log where Reece had proposed to Cassandra, arms spread out for balance. 'Mrs Southerham is much nicer to deal with. In other circumstances, I think she could have been a friend.'

Reece grinned. 'He'd never countenance her making friends of *our class*, just as he hated having Kevin to tea on Christmas Day. I'm glad they agreed to witness Kevin's will. It seemed to set his mind at rest. He's says he's left me "a little bit of something" which was why I couldn't witness it. He's shown me where the will is kept and has asked me to deal with it when he dies. He's looking better, though, now I'm living with him and can see that he eats properly. I mean to keep him alive as long as I can. You don't easily lose a good friend.'

'Who has he left the main estate to? Will you lose your lease when he dies?'

'I don't know who he's left it to. His family, I suppose. But my lease is safe for five years. He made sure of that. By then I hope to have saved up enough to lease a bigger property.'

The tea party went just as well as the visit to the twins had done, with much laughter and an occasional piece of wise advice from Kevin. They inspected the house and the half-built room which would be their bedroom. Reece promised to build them a bed frame, and buy enough straw to stuff a mattress with. It wouldn't be a very good one, but it would be enough. Cassandra would make curtains out of one of the old sheets Kevin had offered them.

'We won't own much, I'm afraid,' Reece said as they walked back just before dusk.

'I don't mind. We'll have each other.'

Pandora had been more cheerful while away from the farm, distracted by helping plan her sister's first home as a married woman. However, she grew silent again as they approached Westview.

Cassandra glanced at Reece and saw that he too had noticed the sadness return to her sister's face.

Sometimes you could do nothing about a situation.

EPILOGUE

Cassandra wore her best skirt and bodice for the wedding, though she'd put on weight and had to alter them. They were a soft blue in colour and she'd found some creamy lace in Hilda's trunk, so was able to add that to the bodice. She got up as soon as it was light each day to put in an hour's sewing before her duties began, because she had the straw mattress ticking to sew as well, for their marital bed.

She smiled when Pandora made a fuss over her, insisting on helping her wash her hair in the washing tub the night before, and helping her dress in the morning before they left. It didn't really matter what she looked like. She was quite sure that Reece would have loved her just as much in sackcloth as in silk.

It filled her with warmth and a sense of wonder every time she thought of him, and she was excited about making a life together. In spite of the horrors she'd been subjected to, she was surprised to find that she wanted him to touch her and he'd promised her it'd be very different when you loved someone.

She'd lost most of her fear already, because Reece was so gentle, so concerned not to upset her that his kissing and caressing bore no resemblance whatsoever to the acts that still occasionally gave her nightmares. Making love, he said, was very different from animals rutting.

She beamed as they drove across to the barn in which monthly services were held, enjoying the hot weather and bright sunshine that left poor Pandora and Mr Southerham drooping with exhaustion.

Reece had insisted on Kevin joining them for the wedding, which made Francis Southerham pull a face but with Livia on their side, the old man's presence was accepted.

The journey passed very pleasantly, with the ladies using umbrellas as parasols, and the horses clopping along in an unhurried way, one cart under Mr Southerham's charge, the other under Reece's.

The four sisters hugged and kissed one another, moving to one side for a little private conversation.

'You can tell they're sisters, can't you?' Livia said to Reece. 'It must be nice to have sisters. Do you have any?'

'Just a brother. He's older than me, lives in Yorkshire. We're not close. I'm much closer to my cousins.'

The ceremony was brief, as theirs was one of three weddings to be conducted by the visiting clergyman that day.

Afterwards Cassandra walked out of the barn on Reece's arm, trying to feel married. But being with him now was no different from before. He was just – Reece, her love, the man with whom she hoped to spend the rest of her life.

After the ceremony, Conn Largan took everyone a short distance along the road to a clearing where logs provided seats and a picnic could be eaten in the dappled light under the trees.

'Happy, Mrs Gregory?' Reece whispered.

'Very happy, Mr Gregory,' Cassandra answered with a smile.

'I'll work my fingers to the bone for you and this child and any other children we're fortunate enough to have,' he said softly, raising his tin mug of tea as if it were the finest wine in a crystal glass.

'We'll work together. I'll—'

'Kiss the bride properly now, Reece!' Xanthe called. 'You only pecked her cheek after the ceremony.'

He stopped Cassandra protesting at this with a kiss and there was a round of applause from their friends and families.

Cassandra blushed but on a sudden impulse, she pulled him closer and kissed him again, wanting to show everyone that his loving was fully returned. They would make a good life together, she was quite certain of that.

ABOUT THE AUTHOR

Anna Jacobs grew up in Lancashire and emigrated to Australia, but she returns each year to the UK to see her family and do research, something she loves. She is addicted to writing and she figures she'll have to live to be 120 at least to tell all the stories that keep popping up in her imagination and nagging her to write them down. She's also addicted to her own hero, to whom she's been happily married for many years.

Read on for an extract of the dramatic sequel to
Farewell to Lancashire:

BEYOND THE SUNSET

Anna Jacobs

In the untamed outback of Western Australia,
the Blake sisters are together again despite what
seemed like insurmountable odds.

For Cassandra – reunited at last with the man she loves –
the Swan River Colony is a refuge that seems like a miracle
after her ordeals. And two of her sisters have fallen in love
with their new way of life. But then a messenger arrives
from faraway England, and it is the fourth sister, Pandora,
who jumps at the chance to make her way back to the
Lancashire moors she misses so badly.

The way home, though, will be even harder than the voyage
to Australia. The only ship that can take her and her new
protector back to England lies many days' journey away,
across country that would daunt even a hardened explorer.

And when she reaches Outham, a devious, dangerous
enemy will do anything to prevent her taking charge of her
family's inheritance . . .

Out now in hardback

HODDER &
STOUGHTON

PROLOGUE

Swan River Colony (Western Australia)
December 1863

Pandora Blake heard footsteps and tried to brush away the tears as she saw her eldest sister coming across the garden of the Migrants' Home towards her.

'Breakfast is ready.' Cassandra put an arm round her shoulders. 'Oh, dear! I don't like to see you so upset. You know we can't return to Lancashire. If we did, I'm quite sure our lives would be in danger.'

She nodded and tried to summon up a smile.

'Don't,' Cassandra said softly.

'Don't what?'

'Don't pretend with me. Isn't the homesickness getting any better at all?'

Pandora could only shake her head blindly and try to swallow the lump of grief that seemed permanently lodged in her throat. 'It was cruel of our aunt to force us to leave England. Why does she hate us so much?'

'Father always thought it was because *she* couldn't have children.'

'That's not our fault.'

Cassandra gave her a quick hug. 'I know.'

'You should have seen her that last time she came to visit us. She was terrifying, and strange too. She had that piece of your hair that they'd cut off, still tied with your ribbon, and we were certain if we didn't do as she asked and leave the country, she'd have you killed. We thought we'd never see you again. It was a miracle you escaped to join us on the ship.'

A bell rang from inside the building. 'Breakfast is ready,' Cassandra said again.

'I'll join you in a few minutes. I need to calm down.'

'All right.'

Pandora sighed as she looked round the garden, relishing a few moments on her own. The ship had been crowded with other single women brought out to the Swan River Colony as maids, some of them quarrelsome and noisy. All the Lancashire lasses had been thin at first after the long months without work because of the lack of raw cotton, but no one else seemed so badly affected by homesickness as she was. What was wrong with her?

She stared round. She'd thought she'd feel differently once they got here, but she didn't. It was so unlike the soft cool colours of her native Lancashire. Even at this early hour, the sun blazed down from a cloudless blue sky and she felt uncomfortably hot. Wiping her brow, she went to sit on a bench in the shade of a gum tree. It had pretty red flowers, but the leaves were sickle-shaped and leathery, of a dull green. Even the stray clumps of grass in the garden were more beige than green, burnt by the searing sun, while the ground was sandy, shifting beneath your feet as you walked. How anything grew in it, she couldn't think.

A pair of galahs flew across to perch in the tree, squawking harshly at one another. She'd called them 'parrots' when she first arrived but Matron had laughed and told her they were cockatoos, not parrots. Their calls were ugly, but they were pretty to look at, with pink throats and chests, pale grey wings, heads and crests.

One began to nip the flowers off the gum tree with its strong beak, not eating them but simply letting each one drop to the ground while it sought another blossom to pinch out. Was it doing this for sheer devilment or was there some purpose?

Even if she wanted to take the risk, how could she return to Lancashire? She didn't have the money for the fare and she didn't want to leave her sisters. No, somehow she'd have to come to terms with this terrible longing for home. She stood up, took a deep breath and went inside.

As usual the twins were sitting with their heads close together, talking animatedly. Pandora got herself a plate of food and didn't comment on the way Cassandra was staring at her plate, eating very little. Her eldest sister had her own problems, was now carrying the child of a man who'd raped her just before she left England.

Afterwards Pandora helped with the clearing up, trying to speak cheerfully to the other women.

She *would* get over this homesickness, she told herself firmly – or learn to hide it better. She'd never been a whiner, wasn't going to start now.

I

Lancashire: 1st January, 1864

Mr Featherworth leaned back in his chair and studied the young man sitting on the other side of his desk. Not good-looking, Zachary Carr, too tall and bony for that, but still, he had a reputation for honesty and common sense, and a steady gaze. The late Mr Blake had thought a lot of him, had said several times that you'd go a long way to find a more decent fellow. That was much more important to the lawyer than how a man looked.

The more he talked to the young man, the more he warmed to him. Carr had been the breadwinner for his mother and sister for several years, so was clearly a responsible person, and he seemed intelligent too. He might never have travelled overseas before, but he was young and strong, and at twenty-five, he'd grown beyond a young man's rashness. He even knew how to ride a horse, because his uncle had a farm. That was a big advantage, because Mr Featherworth had been told there were no railways in the Swan River Colony.

Most important of all, though: Zachary knew the four Blake sisters by sight.

Yes, Mr Featherworth was sure he'd chosen the right person to send on this mission.

'It's not taken as long as I expected to find a ship going to the Swan River Colony – or Western Australia as some call it now. I've booked you a passage on the *Clara*, which is due to leave London on January the 11th.'

Zachary's face lit up, then the date sank in and he looked startled. 'But that's only just over a week away! How will I ever get ready in time?'

Mr Featherworth held up one hand. 'Please let me finish.'

The younger man gave him an embarrassed smile. 'Sorry. I'm a bit excited about it all.'

The lawyer smiled back at him. 'It's not surprising. Few young men of your station in life are given an opportunity to travel to the other side of the world. But as you know, the Blake sisters had already left England when their uncle's will was read, so someone has to tell them they're the new owners of his grocery emporium, and escort them back from Australia.'

Zachary nodded. 'It was a sad business, that. I thought a lot of Mr Blake. He was a good employer and a kind man.'

'Yes indeed.'

They were both silent for a few minutes. Who would have thought the late Mrs Blake would go insane, murder her husband and force her nieces to leave the country in fear of their lives? The idea of all that still gave the lawyer nightmares.

'Now, as to the details of your voyage, I had at first intended to send you steerage, because one has to be careful when spending a client's money. But this is a vessel taking convicts to Western Australia, not a normal passenger vessel, and I've decided you'll be far safer as a cabin passenger. Not that the steerage passengers mingle with the convicts, certainly not, but still . . . I was fortunate enough to secure the last vacant bunk for you – though you'll have to share the cabin with another gentleman.'

'What exactly does "cabin passenger" mean?'

'It means you'll be travelling with the gentry, away from the convicts and in more comfort than the steerage passengers, both going out to Australia and when you bring the young women back. However, you'll not be in the first-class cabins, whose occupants eat at the Captain's table, but rather in the deck cabins, which have their own dining area and less generous accommodation. Your travelling companions will still be a better class of person than you would find in steerage, though.' He studied Zachary. 'You look worried.'

'I shan't know how to behave in such company. I've served the gentry in the store, but they live differently from us. I don't want to let you down – or embarrass myself.'

'I'm sure you'll do nothing to upset people, but if you're doubtful how to behave, watch others whom you respect and imitate them. You can also ask advice of the ship's doctor or one of the ship's officers, if need be. The main thing is not to pretend to know something you don't or be something you aren't. It'd not look good to be caught out in a lie.'

'Yes, sir. I'll try my best.'

'I'm sure you will or I'd not be sending you. Now,

you'll need better clothing than you have at present – no, don't be embarrassed. In your present position, your clothing is perfectly suitable. But for this journey you'll need other garments if you're to gain people's respect and assistance, not to mention extra changes of clothing for the three-month voyage. I've asked my tailor to make you some new clothes. He's prepared to work day and night to supply you with what you need. I shall myself escort you to London and we'll purchase anything else necessary from a ship's chandler near the docks.'

He paused and frowned, because this was a delicate matter, something his wife had pointed out. 'It might be a good idea for you to eat your evening meals at my house from now on, so that we can make sure your table manners are correct. There are niceties of eating, ways of using various pieces of cutlery . . . well, you understand, I'm sure.'

Zachary flushed but nodded.

'You'd better stop work in the shop immediately. Go and inform Prebble. Tell him we'll find a replacement till you return. Then come back and my clerk will take you to see the tailor. You'll also need to go to Hawsworth's to purchase underclothing and whatever else you're in need of. The clothing will, of course, be yours to keep afterwards.'

'Thank you, sir.'

'We'll discuss the arrangements you'll need to make for the journey home to Lancashire after our evening meal tonight. How surprised those young women will be to hear about their inheritance! They'll be so happy to be able to come home again.'

'And if they ask for details of their legacy, what am I to tell them?'

Mr Featherworth hesitated.

'I'm not asking out of curiosity, sir, but they're bound to want to know.'

'Broadly speaking, they own the shop, the building in which it's located, including comfortable living accommodation above it, as you know, plus several cottages and houses which are rented out and bring in extra income. There is also a tidy sum of money in the bank. This was to have been used to provide for Mrs Blake during her lifetime, but was not needed in view of her death so soon after her husband's – though that was a mercy, given her state of mind.'

He raised one finger in a cautioning gesture. 'Mind, you are not to tell anyone else, *anyone at all*, these details.'

Zachary nodded. No need to say that. He wasn't one to tattle about other people's affairs, let alone betray confidential information.

Excitement swelled within him. He was going to Australia, travelling the world! What wonders would he see on his journey?

Pandora walked back across the yard of the Migrants' Home to join the twins after speaking to a lady seeking a housemaid. It had been an effort to answer the questions. What did she care about finding a job when Cassandra was in such trouble? Before she left the ship, her sister had been accused of stealing money by her employers and was now confined to the Home. As if any of them would steal!

'The lady you were talking to looks very annoyed,' Maia said.

Pandora shrugged. 'I told her I couldn't take the job. She lives a long way from Perth, somewhere to the north. It takes five days to get there by cart. I don't care what Matron says, I'm not going that far away from you all.'

'I hadn't thought it'd be so hard to find work near one another.'

Maia linked arms with her twin, Xanthe, and the three of them moved to a quiet corner.

But people pursued them there, all seeking maids.

'Why did you come to Australia if you don't want a job?' one demanded.

'I shall complain to Matron about your attitude,' another said huffily.

Pandora didn't try to respond to that. Bad enough to be so far away from her home. Unthinkable to be separated from her sisters as well.

A little later that day a well-dressed lady came into the Migrants' Home, accompanied by a man who moved through the crowd ahead of her. With a shriek, Pandora ran across, so happy to see someone from home that she flung herself into his arms, laughing and crying at once. 'Reece! I can't believe it's you!'

He stared at her in blank astonishment. 'What the— Pandora, what on earth are you doing here?' He looked round. 'Is Cassandra with you?'

'Yes, but it's a long story. Not for public telling and—' she began, stopping as she realised who he was with.

'Mrs Southerham! Oh, I can't believe our luck! You're just the person we need to see.'

Livia smiled at her and the twins, who had come across to join them. 'Isn't Cassandra with you?'

'They told her she can't get a job yet. They think she stole some money. She says *you* gave it to her.'

'I did give her some.'

They all tried to talk at once, explaining what had happened.

Reece beamed at them. 'I can't believe it. Cassandra's here in Australia. I was going to send her a letter asking her to join me here.' To marry him.

Matron came over to see what was happening and speak to Mrs Southerham.

Reece listened for a moment or two, then asked who this Mrs Lawson was. Matron looked at him in puzzlement. 'Mrs Lawson is the sister of these young ladies.'

'Cassandra? Then she's the woman I want to marry.'

Silence, then, 'Is it a while since you saw her?'

'Yes.'

Pandora poked him in the ribs. 'We'll explain later.'

Matron finished talking to Mrs Southerham, who confirmed that she had indeed given Cassandra the money, then went to write a note to the Governor. She took Reece with her, because he was insisting on seeing Cassandra. 'You can speak to her at the other end of the garden. I'll send her out to you.'

Pandora waited anxiously. She found it hard to talk to Mrs Southerham about a job because she was hoping desperately that Reece would still love Cassandra and, in spite of what had happened, still want to marry her.

When she saw him stride round the corner of the Home with an agonised expression on his face and walk out into the street without even stopping to explain, her heart sank. She said a hasty farewell to Mrs Southerham and hurried back to their quarters to find her sister.

Cassandra was weeping.

'Oh, love, what's the matter?'

'He walked away when I told him about the baby.'

Pandora had expected better of Reece, who had been a friend of the whole family back in Outham, who had courted Cassandra, but hadn't been able to marry her because he was out of work since the mills had stopped for lack of cotton from America. 'Then he's not worth loving. You were raped. It wasn't your fault.'

'How do you stop loving someone? I told myself it wouldn't be right to expect him to marry me, not now, but I hoped. I couldn't help hoping.'

It was a while before Cassandra calmed down and took up her sewing again, but Pandora hated to see the bleak unhappiness on her face.

Things seemed to be getting worse since their arrival in Australia, not better.

Zachary walked slowly through the streets of Outham, his head spinning with information and excitement. As he entered Blake's Emporium, Harry Prebble, who made everyone all too aware that he was now the temporary manager, looked up with a sour expression on his face and gestured to him to come into the back.

'You've been away long enough, Carr.'

The two young men stared at one another, antagonism fairly humming between them. Harry might have been chosen to run the shop until the new owners could be brought back to Lancashire, but Zachary knew he was still jealous of the other being sent to Australia to fetch them home. And he'd always been resentful of Zachary's extra inches. He was over six foot tall while Harry stood a bare five foot six.

The doorbell tinkled and Harry took a quick peep into the shop. 'There's Mrs Warrish. You'd better start serving now, Carr, and—'

'Mr Featherworth says I'm to stop work immediately because I sail next week and there's a lot to be done. He says you can take on other help while I'm gone. I'll get my things and leave you to it.'

'I need help now. I must say it's very selfish of you. Didn't you remind him it's Friday, our busiest day?'

'He and I were talking about the journey, not the shop.'

'It's all right for some!'

'*You* have nothing to complain about. You've been appointed temporary manager, haven't you?' Zachary bit back further hot words, annoyed at himself for giving his feelings away. He'd have loved to run the shop, and after working there since the age of twelve, he was sure he'd do it just as well as Harry. Better, because Harry always fussed about details and ordered the same old goods, never looking at what was happening in the world, how people were changing and wanting to buy different things.

Railways had changed everything in the past twenty

years and it was now possible to get foodstuffs from all over the world as easily as they'd got them from Manchester in the old days. Mr Blake had often talked about this and Harry had listened with an intent expression on his face, but the implications never seemed to sink in.

'Well, don't forget that you'll be coming back to work under *me*.'

'*If* you get the appointment as permanent shop manager. That'll be up to the new owners.'

'Who else could they appoint? I know everything about how this shop is run. Haven't I worked here since I was twelve?'

'We both have!' And Zachary had been there for a year longer, actually.

'Well, I'll be able to *prove* my worth to Mr Featherworth while you're gallivanting round the world, so the job's as good as mine. Those nieces of Mr Blake's are only mill girls, however intelligent they're supposed to be. They'll know nothing about running a shop, so they're bound to turn to me for advice. I'll make sure the profits rise while I'm in charge. That's what will matter to them.' He jutted his chin challengingly.

It wasn't worth arguing, so Zachary went into the rear of the shop and took down his apron from the hook on the wall, retrieving his lunch box. You couldn't afford to waste good food in troubled times like these. So many people in the cotton towns were going hungry for lack of work, thanks to the war in America stopping raw cotton getting through to the mills.

A year and a half ago, in 1862, Mr Blake had started providing food for his staff at midday and broken biscuits with their cups of tea at other breaks, knowing those still in employment were going short to help their hungry relatives and friends. But Harry had discontinued that practice as soon as he took over, not even providing cups of tea on the pretext that he didn't dare be extravagant with someone else's money. You'd think what he saved was going into his own pocket.

When he got back from Australia, if Harry was put in charge, Zachary intended to seek employment elsewhere, even if he had to move to another town to find it.

He left the shop and looked back at it thoughtfully. A huge plate glass window that had caused a sensation in the town twenty years previously when first installed, because it was so different from the small panes that all the other shops had. Tins and boxes were displayed there in carefully arranged piles. The words BLAKE'S EMPORIUM stood out in foot-high golden letters on a maroon ground above the shop window.

It must be wonderful to own such a business.

He felt sad as he passed a group of men loitering on a street corner, their clothes ragged and their faces gaunt with the years of hunger. He'd be eating well at the Featherworths' that evening so on an impulse he shared the contents of his lunch box with them. Not much for each one, but something, and it broke his heart to see how carefully they divided the food, so that each would have the same amount.

Men like these were such a contrast to the more affluent customers who came into the shop. If only the war in America would end! People said the South was getting the worst of it now, but Zachary didn't care who won.

He just wanted the Americans to start sending cotton again. Without it, the mills of Lancashire stood silent, no smoke pouring from their chimneys, or only a trickle when they fired up the steam engines to keep them working properly. The clear sky still looked strange to him, because on fine days he was used to seeing smoke trails criss-crossing it.

Even the relief schemes that had been set up in the town couldn't feed so many families adequately and that showed in people's faces.

Zachary realised he'd stopped moving and clicked his tongue in exasperation at himself. Why was he loitering around daydreaming when he had a thousand things to organise for his adventure?

Although Reece came back to the Migrants' Home the following day to apologise to Cassandra for walking out on her, she steadfastly refused to marry him.

Pandora watched them both from the shade of the tree where she had again taken refuge from the heat. They loved one another, she could tell. But although her sister had wept when Reece walked away from her, she said it only proved she was right to decide not to marry him. She didn't want the child to be treated badly. Strange how protective Cassandra was to her unborn baby.

Maybe if I met someone I loved, I'd be able to settle down here more easily, Pandora thought. But she knew with a sick certainty that she wouldn't. This place was . . . wrong for her. It wasn't *home*. She found the heat particularly trying and her face felt raw with sweat. Even the nights were hot, though occasionally an afternoon sea breeze that locals called the 'Fremantle Doctor' brought a little relief for an hour or two.

She was getting better at hiding her misery, though, and was rather proud of that.

At the moment her best hope was to find a job near enough to her sisters to see them regularly. Reece's employers, the Southerhams, had offered her a position as a maid of all work, and they were kind enough to say Cassandra could go too. But they couldn't afford to pay two maids, so her sister would get only her keep.

It was a fair offer, probably as good as they were likely to get, given the circumstances, but Cassandra refused to accept it because Reece also worked for them.

Well, Pandora wasn't leaving her sister on her own, not in that condition, not if she had to defy the Governor of the colony himself.

Later that day a man called Conn Largan turned up at the Migrants' Home, offering jobs to the twins, caring for his invalid mother. They lived an hour's drive away from the Southerhams, which was quite close, it seemed, in Australian terms.

In the end Pandora confronted Cassandra. 'Working for the Southerhams is the only way we can all four stay together. You *have* to accept the job, whether Reece works there or not.'

And at last, because there truly was no other way to keep the family together, Cassandra gave in.

Pandora felt for her, they all did, but it was a relief to have their immediate future settled and to get away from the restrictions of the Migrants' Home.

★

The week following the interview with Mr Featherworth passed in a blur of activity for Zachary. The tailor finished his new clothes with amazing speed, finer garments than he'd ever worn in his whole life.

He was also supplied with an incredible number of other clothes. There were a dozen beautiful shirts, some in lightweight materials like gauze cotton, because the weather was much hotter in Australia. Each one had three matching collars and there was a whole box of studs for attaching them to the shirts. There were also a dozen travelling shirts of flannel, a dozen cravats of various colours, several sets of braces, cotton drawers at half a crown a pair, under-vests at four shillings and sixpence each, and nightshirts at ten shillings each.

He was speechless at how much this must add up to and tried to protest to the clerk that he could manage with less.

'Mr Featherworth has taken advice from those who've travelled overseas and this is the minimum number of garments you'll need on such a long voyage, young man.' Mr Dawson patted his shoulder. 'There are those who take twice as many clothes with them.'

Zachary could only shake his head in wonderment. He didn't tell anyone, but he was delighted to be so well turned out, for once. It was a struggle for him and his family to stay decently dressed on his wages alone. Normally his sister Hallie would have had a job too, at least until she got married, and her money would have been a big help in supporting their widowed mother. Because of the Cotton Famine, however, jobs were scarce and few families in Outham had more than one breadwinner.

But he remained concerned at how much this was costing the heirs. When Mr Dawson mentioned buying a trunk, Zachary felt comfortable enough with the lawyer's clerk to make a suggestion of his own. 'Why don't we check the attics above the shop and see if there are any trunks or other items of luggage? There are all sorts of bits and pieces stored there. I've seen them when I've carried things up for Mr Blake.'

'Very sensible idea, young man. We'll go there at once.'

Harry came out of the rear of the shop to see what they were doing when they entered the living quarters. 'Oh, it's you!'

He'd known perfectly well who they were, was just being nosey, Zachary thought, saying nothing.

'Carry on with your work, Prebble,' Mr Dawson said, in a sharp tone that said he didn't like Harry either. 'This is none of your business.'

When the clerk turned away, Harry glared at him, then saw Zachary looking and went back into the shop. But his expression had been so inimical that Zachary couldn't help worrying. Harry had a reputation for getting his own back on those who had upset him. He'd not be able to do much to a man like Mr Dawson, though, surely?

The attics were very dark and there was no gas lighting up here, so Zachary ran down to ask the maid for a lamp. 'How are things going, Dot?'

She smiled at him. 'It's been really peaceful. I'm so glad Mr Featherworth has let me stay on. There. This is a good bright lamp.'

'I'll see to lighting it.'

She lingered to chat. 'Mrs Rainey's cousin is coming

to live here soon. Miss Blair's been ill but she's a lot better now. She's been to visit and seems a really nice lady. I'll feel better to have some company.' She lowered her voice and glanced over her shoulder. 'Apart from *him*.'

'Harry?'

She nodded. 'He keeps coming in, saying he has to check that I'm doing my work properly. And he sits up in the sitting room sometimes after work. No one told me I'd have to answer to *him*.'

Amazed by what she'd told him, Zachary took the lamp up to the attic and with its help they soon found what they were seeking. 'There!' He pushed some boxes aside. 'A trunk. It's a little battered but I don't mind that.' He opened and shut it, finding all the hinges and locks in good working order. 'I shall be happy to use this one and save some money.'

The clerk nodded his approval and went back to searching, finding a large portmanteau of scuffed leather under an old rug.

Zachary hesitated, wondering whether to interfere, then decided the poor little maid needed protection. 'Dot was saying that Harry keeps coming in to check up on what she's doing, and . . . he sits in the owner's quarters after work sometimes.'

The clerk looked at him in surprise. 'What happens with the maid or in the living quarters is no concern of his, none whatsoever. I'll mention it to Mr Featherworth. No one need know you told me. You and Prebble will have to work together after you get back, so we don't want to stir up bad blood between you. The Methodist Minister's cousin is to move into the flat soon, partly because I don't trust Prebble. He's taken a few liberties since Mr Featherworth made him manager. Miss Blair will make sure everything is looked after properly and will do a complete inventory of the contents for us. It's asking for trouble to leave a place with so many valuable things in it empty, especially in hard times like these.'

Harry came out again to watch sourly as Zachary and the shop lad carried the trunk and portmanteau down the stairs and out to a handcart.

'Have you no work to get on with, young man?' Mr Dawson asked sharply. 'This is the second time I've seen you neglecting your duties today.'

'I thought you might need some help.'

'Well, we don't.'

Scowling, Harry went back into the shop.

'Sitting in the flat, indeed!' the clerk muttered as they walked back down the street. 'Well, that's going to stop.'

Zachary had wondered why they felt the need for someone to occupy the flat. Mr Featherworth was a kindly man, but his clerk seemed more astute. Zachary didn't think they'd have any worries about the financial side of things, though. Harry Prebble had never been anything but honest and industrious during the years they'd worked together.

But Zachary still didn't like him, he admitted to himself – hadn't when they were boys, and trusted him even less as a man. He'd never understood why.

The next day Zachary's mother was advised on how to pack his new possessions for a long journey by no less a person than Mrs Featherworth. Two extra sets of clothing and underclothing you needed, because it was not only hard to wash clothes in sea water, to do it for so many people was impossible. Trunks were brought up from the hold each month so that people could change their garments during the voyage, which would last approximately a hundred days. Just imagine that! What a great distance he'd be travelling.

Every evening he went to dinner at the lawyer's house, the first time so nervous he doubted he'd be able to eat a mouthful. But his hostess was a motherly woman, whom he'd sometimes served in the shop, and it was impossible to stay afraid of anyone with such a warm smile.

'You won't mind if I help you improve your table manners, Zachary dear?' she said gently, taking his arm as she led him into the dining room, with Mr Featherworth and his two daughters following.

'I'd appreciate any help you can give me, Mrs Featherworth.' He tried not to stare round but was awed that they had a big room like this purely for eating in.

As everyone took their places, she pointed to the cutlery in front of her and said in a low voice, 'The trick is to start from the outside pieces at each side of your plate.'

While Mr Featherworth said grace, Zachary stared down at the daunting array of cutlery. So many pieces for one meal alone. How much were they going to eat?

The minute grace ended, a maid carried in a soup tureen which she set in front of her mistress. Mrs Featherworth ladled its contents into bowls and the maid passed them round, then left. Everyone seemed to be waiting to eat and no one started until the mistress did.

Zachary took up the big round spoon on the right

when the others did and watched how they used it before starting on his own soup, a brown meaty concoction served with crusty rolls.

The food was delicious and for once he had more than enough to eat. He only wished he could take some of his share home for his mother and sister to try.

After the four courses were over, they went to sit in the drawing room. Mrs Featherworth patted the sofa next to her and Zachary sat down, already trusting her.

'There are other things my daughters and I can teach you, for instance, what subjects to discuss with ladies, how to offer your arm.'

The two young women sitting nearby nodded their heads and smiled at him. Nice lasses, they seemed, about the same age as his sister. He wished Hallie had a fine dress like those they were wearing, because she was just as pretty.

'Do you enjoy reading?' Mrs Featherworth asked.

'I love it. When I have time, that is.'

'Good. We've found some books for you to read on the journey to help pass the time. I do hope you'll enjoy them.'

The elder daughter got up and from behind her chair produced a pile of about a dozen books fastened together by a leather strap that even had a carrying handle on the top.

He stared at them in delight: *A Tale of Two Cities* by Dickens, *Westward Ho!* by Kingsley, a book of poetry. He'd had little time for reading in his busy life, because the shop stayed open until late. 'Thank you so much.'

'We got you a diary too,' the younger daughter said.

'Mama thought you'd want to remember your big adventure. You can write down what happens every day. I wish *I* were going to Australia. It sounds *so* exciting.'

Mr Featherworth said little, but let his womenfolk do most of the talking, sitting watching them with a fond smile.

The older daughter carried a fancy wooden box across from a side table and set it on the sofa between Zachary and his hostess.

'This is an old travelling writing desk, which used to belong to my uncle,' Mrs Featherworth said. 'It was lying around in the attic, not being used, so we thought you might like it. We've furnished it with letter paper and envelopes, plenty of nibs, and ink powder so that you can make up more ink as you need it.'

He opened the lid and the box became a writing slope, the interior covered in dark red leather with a pattern embossed in gold round the edges. There were compartments at the front for pens, ink and sand bottles, though of course people used blotting paper these days not sand to dry the ink. 'Thank you. I'll take great care of it for you.'

'Please keep it afterwards as a memento of your adventure.'

He swallowed hard and tried not to betray that this extra unnecessary generosity had moved him almost to tears. From being a man struggling to dress decently as well as provide for his mother and sister, he was suddenly being loaded with possessions. He would, he vowed mentally, not let the lawyer down whatever happened.

His hostess patted his hand in a motherly gesture. 'If

you have anything else to occupy yourself with, be sure to take it with you. The journey will go on for many weeks.'

Drawing materials, he thought. *I used to love drawing as a lad. I can afford some plain paper and pencils, surely? And a rubber, too.* He smiled at the memory of an elderly uncle, also fond of drawing, who'd always called rubbers 'lead eaters'.

Zachary walked home carrying the books and the writing desk, his mind humming with all the information. He was amazed at how pleasantly the evening had passed, considering how nervous he'd been. But the lawyer's daughters were nice lasses, for all their fine clothes, and you couldn't find a kinder lady than Mrs Featherworth, so he'd soon lost his fear of upsetting them.

It was cold and rainy and he couldn't help shivering after being in such a well-heated house. It was hard to believe that he was going to a country where in summer the weather was hotter than it ever became in Lancashire, and where it never snowed in winter. It was hard even to imagine how that would feel.

When he got back, he found his mother and sister waiting up for him, eager to hear how the evening had gone.

Hallie pounced on the books while his mother marvelled at the travelling writing desk, running her fingers over the gleaming wood and examining each bottle and compartment.

'Oh, you're so lucky!' Hallie sighed. 'What wouldn't I give to have all those books to read! I've read everything I want to from the public library.'

'Choose one and read it while I'm away. It'll remind you of me.'

'Are you sure?'

'Yes, of course.' He gave her a hug, surprised at how tall his little sister had grown lately.

She picked out Mary Barton, her fingers caressing the tooled leather binding of the novel. 'I'll take this one, then. Thank you so much, Zachary.'

He smiled indulgently. 'I know how you love your stories of romance and adventure.'

'It's nice to dream sometimes.' She gave him a quick kiss on the cheek. 'I'll dream for you now. Perhaps you'll fall in love while you're away, meet a wonderful girl on the ship or . . . No, better still, fall in love with one of the Blake sisters and then the shop will be partly yours. That'll solve all our problems.'

He didn't like this and drew back from her. 'Don't be silly! Mr Featherworth is trusting me to bring them back safely, not to prey on them.'

'Falling in love isn't preying, Zachary.'

'It would be in this case.'

She flounced one shoulder at him. 'Oh, you! Sometimes you're too noble for words! And once you get an idea fixed in your mind, there's no changing it. Why can you not dream and let things happen as they will?'

Because he'd never been free to dream, he thought bitterly, biting back an angry response. He'd had the responsibility for supporting them from a very early age. Not that he minded, of course he didn't. And though they disagreed sometimes, as brothers and sisters always do, he loved Hallie dearly and didn't want to quarrel with her just before he left.

'Now, calm down, you two,' his mother said, giving her daughter a quick kiss, then her son. She lingered next to Zachary to beg, 'Don't let all this go to your head, son. It's a great adventure, to be sure, but you'll still have to come back and work at Blake's.'

'If Harry Prebble stays in charge, I'll be looking for work elsewhere.' He wished he hadn't told her that when he saw the anxiety in her face. 'Don't worry. I shan't do anything rashly.'

'No. You never do. I wish you did sometimes. We've stopped you being a young man, haven't we?' She began to light their candles ready to go up to bed, shaking her head sadly. 'As for Harry, you two didn't get on at school, were always fighting one another till you grew so much bigger than him, and it doesn't seem to have got much better. It's not good to make enemies, Zachary love.'

'Sometimes enemies make themselves, Mum, whether we want it or not.'

'Well, see that *you* don't behave ungenerously, whatever *he* does. A man should do nothing he's not proud of, whether he's poor or rich. And the same when you're out in the world. Always make me proud of you, son.'

'I will.' He went to check that the front and back doors were locked, extinguished the paraffin lamp in the kitchen and made his way up to bed by the wavering light of his candle.

Zachary knew that whatever he said or did, Harry Prebble would always be suspicious of his motives and would continue to act in a mean-spirited way if left in charge. You had to stand up to a bully, or he'd get worse. Zachary had learned that lesson as a lad and it held true for grown men, too. But sometimes it was an unfair world and bullies had more power than you, so you couldn't challenge them, could only walk away.

No, he'd definitely look for other work. And surely, if he performed this task well, Mr Featherworth would give him a good reference?

CONTACT ANNA

Anna Jacobs is always delighted to hear from readers and can be contacted:

BY MAIL

PO Box 628
Mandurah
Western Australia 6210

If you'd like a reply, please enclose a self-addressed, business size envelope, stamped (from inside Australia) or an international reply coupon (from outside Australia).

VIA THE INTERNET

Anna has her own web domain, with details of her books, latest news and excerpts to read.
Come and visit her site at
HTTP://WWW.ANNAJACOBS.COM

Anna can be contacted by email at
ANNA@ANNAJACOBS.COM

If you'd like to receive an email newsletter about Anna and her books every month or two, you are cordially invited to join her announcements list. Just email her and ask to be added to the list, or follow the link from her web page.

READERS' DISCUSSION LIST

A reader has created a web site where readers can meet and discuss Anna's novels. Anna is not involved in the discussions at all, nor is she a member of that list – she's too busy writing new stories. If you're interested in joining, it's at HTTP://GROUPS.MSN.COM/ANNAJACOBSFANCLUB